THE CARD~~ ~~~~~

The Diary of a Woman Racing Driver

William James Timothy

TIMOTHY
CHIPPENHAM   WILTSHIRE

ISBN 978-1-5262-0728-9
Printed in Great Britain by
Arthur H. Stockwell Ltd
Torrs Park   Ilfracombe
Devon EX34 8BA

2010

19 FEBRUARY 2010: Something happened to me today. No, I haven't menstruated, I have not bled my way to womanhood. That pleasure has yet to come my way. At school somebody picked on me, so I fought back, beating the shit out of them. I defended my honour. I stuck up for myself. I want the world to know all about it. It gave me a terrific feeling, from now on I want more of it.

What went on today in the school playground got me into deep trouble. But what the heck, I can handle myself. After today nobody will dare mess with me again. It has given me some kind of mystical power over the other children, who didn't expect my reaction. It caught them off guard, so to speak. Yet the day started so well, so normal. My dad took me to school, walked me to the gate, kissing me on the forehead as he did so. Then said goodbye. It was eight fifty in the morning. As a bright orange sun rose high in the blue sky. It commanded us to look upon it, on Mother Nature's instruction.

This evening my dad planned to take me for a drive, over to the family garage business in Llandaff. I always look forward to these visits. But today was a bit special for me. I could not wait for school to finish. My best friend, Cristobel, met me by the school gate. Turning round I waved to Dad one last time. He returned the wave, like he always did. As the school lollipop lady Mrs Bates ushered some children across the road. Her lollipop banner held like a knight's shield in her right hand. As she stood proudly in the middle of the road, dressed in her white coat. Mrs Bates has been doing the same thing each morning, plus afternoon, for at least thirty years. We all know her, she is part of the school, like the front door or the playground. I don't think she'll ever leave, or go away. We all say good morning to her as we walk by – a school ritual.

We are the same age – indeed, we started school on the same day. I regard her as my sister I know her that well. So when she turned up to school sporting blonde highlights streaked all over her black hair I could not help myself, I was in the mood to dish out some sarcasm. So Cristobel got a large dose of it. It woke me up in an instant, the adrenalin pumping in my body.

"What've you done to your hair?" I said, giggling.

"Nothing wrong with it, is there? Looks cool."

"You look like a fucking zebra, love."

"My mum likes it, so do I. Up the teachers."

She then gave a two-fingered salute towards the school door.

Then, along with a dozen or more other children, we both climbed the thirteen steps that led us into the school, then down the main corridor. It is the walk to hell. But together we pushed, we shoved our way to the classroom. I would not mind so much, but it was the only pleasant thing to happen to me all day long. After this things got deadly serious. Right now it is not a laughing matter. My dad went berserk when he arrived home this evening. I am in deep trouble. The doghouse, no less, as they say. All I did at the end of the day was stick up for myself. It may have been over a trivial thing to others, but to me it was a matter of pride. I must state that today, Diary, was a rarity. I am by nature not a fighter. Only throughout life you must defend yourself sometimes. I mean life can force it upon you when you least expect it. As it did at school today for me.

The first two lessons went off without a hitch, with dreaded English the third. It was heavy going from the start. Our teacher Mrs Bell is nearly always good to us. But today she was the pits. For some godforsaken reason she desired the whole class to write an essay all about what we want to do once we leave school. Personally, I think it is far too early to be walking down that road. The road that takes you out of the protection of the schoolyard, then out into the uncertain, dangerous adult world beyond. A world in which no prisoners are taken, only the brave survive. Yet despite this I actually do know where I wish to travel in life. My goal, my route, has already been mapped out for me. It is in my blood. I cannot escape my destiny, or blind myself to its charms. I may be only ten years old, yet I know that I live in a world full of mad insane people, doing mad insane things to each other. Turning the world upside down. Diary, from this day forwards, you must know, as a friend-cum-lover, I am not one of them. Why, even now, I live, I breathe cars in all their glory. The faster the better. The environment in which I live has ensured this. So with that in mind this essay was a breeze for me. I put in my best effort. It was one of my better performances at school. I know the subject that well. I knew for a fact that Mrs Bell would not be disappointed, or the rest of the class. The real cheese about that boast, about all this.

I could not have been more wrong if I'd practised. Oh boy, I sat there in the silent classroom labouring away like some boffin from Oxford or Cambridge with only academic glory in mind. But enjoying myself like never before. Indeed, I had great difficulty stopping. Allowing my vivid imagination to run riot. I left out nothing, it got me all fired up, living out the rest of my life on paper. Treating this essay like a rare manuscript worth millions. Only trouble loomed ahead for me.

The classroom was full with nobody absent. A pupil at every seat, with a mind ready to blow. Two children sitting at each desk. Cristobel sat next to me, chewing gum all the time. After about two long hours Mrs Bell rose up from her desk at the front of the classroom, underneath the blackboard. She had the air of a matron about her, the eye of the bully in her. We all looked at her as she told us to stop.

"Stop what you are doing, place your work on the desk now," she said, and we blindly obeyed her instruction.

After a few minutes she began to walk by each desk, glancing at each one of us as she passed. It was then that she called out for a volunteer. I tried to attract her attention. But she pointed to somebody else. Alice Crowthorn, the little bitch. This girl gleamed with pride as Mrs Bell pointed to her, asking Alice to read out her essay. It came as no surprise to me, or anybody else in that classroom. According to Alice she wanted to be a nurse when leaving school. We all sat there looking like we were interested in what she had to say. It was all right, I guess, but ordinary all the same. Personally, I couldn't have cared a shit about her bloody life. It bored me to hear it. Even if it is a noble profession, one that does nothing but good to the human race. When she'd finished her eulogy, Mrs Bell picked on somebody else. Hands went up; I kept mine down this time. I tried to appear almost invisible to the teacher. It worked a treat, as another brat called Maxwell Braithwaite was called upon to get top marks, set the world alight. Be a shine on the rest of humanity.

There's one in every classroom, in every school throughout the land. We all hate them. They make me sick to the stomach. This little arse was no exception to this educational rule.

Maxwell is indeed the class creep. A right little clever dick if ever there was one. Short blonde hair, decked out with heavily rimmed glasses. He always wears the school uniform. Neat black trousers, a blazer with the school badge displayed on the top right-hand side. The immaculate white shirt, school tie. Yes, he has all the credentials of academic genius written all over him.

He looked like he knew everything anyone needs to know. Top marks all the time, never lower than a straight A. Leading later on to who knows what – a PhD, or a BA! Hell, there's no limit to what people with a brain like that can achieve. Only Maxwell is a wimp. I gazed at him across the classroom as his hand shot up high into the air. Mrs Bell saw his pleading little face as he shouted to gain her attention.

"Miss, oh Miss," he cried out. Then he cried out again, almost wetting himself in the process.

I found it pathetic to watch, nauseating to hear. His father's an officer in the RAF. Somehow that made him special, or so he thought. A boy to carry on his father's tradition. He couldn't be a plumber, a technician, a stockbroker, or something like that in the city. A job, a trade, to suit his intellect. No, Maxwell had to go one better than just the good old RAF, like his dad. Carry on the family line in the armed services.

"I want to be an astronaut. Go to the moon, travel the cosmos."

The whole class erupted with laughter, me included. I pointed at him as I roared with glee. Maxwell just looked blank, then annoyed. It was all I could do just to stop laughing at him. He looked, he sounded silly. Perhaps it was the way he said it, or the way he looked. Sitting there at his desk, then stretching his arm high into the air as he put it up for the teacher to see. Maybe it was the way this boy shouted, pleading to be picked out by Mrs Bell. He was showing off to the rest of the class, like many times before. He knew he had the best essay, so he should, by natural selection, read it out. Again top marks assured. As I watched him perform, I just wanted to punch his lights out. A right-hander to make him bleed.

He began by describing how his father had been in the RAF for twenty long years. Had won some medals for his flying ability. He loved flying, just like his father. An inherited wonder. Neil Armstrong his hero. But I just sat there boiling over with anger. Wanting this brat to stop, only he wouldn't. In fact, it took him five long minutes to finish. Then just as long for Mrs Bell to compound my agony by praising him for his effort. Mrs Bell apparently could not wait to read, then mark his essay. When it was finally over, this little bastard sat down with a clever, arrogant smile painted across his face. At that moment murder took over. My mind wasn't right.

All throughout that lesson I had rehearsed the reading of my essay. Then suddenly Mrs Bell called out my name. My knees turned to jelly. I tried to stand up at my desk, then face the rest of the class. But I couldn't find the courage. My stomach turned, I was consumed by fear. Only she called out my name again.

"Ann Marie, stand, girl, read out your essay. Try for once to please us all."

I stood to attention, got a grip on myself.

She then said, "First tell the class what you want to be when you grow up."

I faced the class, then said, "A racing driver like Tia Madrid. Beat all at speed. Show them what I'm made of behind the wheel."

There seemed to be an eternal pause. I was frozen in time, caught in a time bubble. The rest of the class just looked at me.

I became an island of fear in a sea of children's faces. Then, like Maxwell before, I appeared as a class clown. I retaliated, defending my honour again. Then Mrs Bell saved me, as she told them all to be quiet. Only a single voice was heard above the childish din. It was the voice from hell – Maxwell Braithwaite, the shit.

"Girls don't drive racing cars," he declared.

We looked at each other eyeball to eyeball across the classroom.

"Yes they do," I stated.

Then Mrs Bell brought order from out of the chaos. We obeyed her, but Maxwell had to have the last say.

"Girls can't drive racing cars," he shouted at the top of his voice. Then he delivered the ultimate insult: "What a thick brick you are. An idiot." He then started laughing all over again, and others followed.

Mrs Bell, a saint for the day now, told him to shut up. Then silence took over – you could've heard a pin drop. All the attention turned towards me. I was allowed to read out my essay. My ambitions in life regarding sport laid out for the world to hear, then judge.

"I want to be a racing driver like my hero, Tia Madrid," I said proudly.

Then Mrs Bell used her wisdom again: "Max, how do you think I got to school today? I drove my car, believe it or not. Just like a man, your dad perhaps."

He then tried to justify his remarks aimed at me: "I know women can drive cars. I never said they couldn't. Only motor racing's a man's game. Women don't have the guts, aren't brave enough. Or they'd have done so before now. There's no woman out there to prove their point."

At this statement I fumed as never before. This little shit now challenged me head on. For a moment we just stared at each other, as before, across the classroom. Hate now figured for the rest of the day. It did too. But that said, after all those bloody interruptions I finished reading my essay. The rest of the class seemed to like it, something a little different, out of the ordinary. If being ordinary is to be like Maxwell stinking Braithwaite then I'd rather be unordinary, abnormal perhaps. A much better way to live, I fear. Certainly Mrs Bell was well pleased. For once at school I hoped for a good mark. As I sat down again, I winked to Cristobel the way friends will do. The torture was over.

The time was high noon, lunchtime for all. The playground was full of activity. It looked for all the world like some Olympic training ground before the contest. To my left a couple of girls skipped. Another read a book leaning against a wall. A group played tig-tag running all over the place. I saw kiss-catch. A boy ran after a girl, caught then kissed her bang on the lips. It made me smile. But it was the football match in the centre of the playground that caught my eye. Along with Cristobel I watched from the side. Coats acted out the role of goalposts. The white football was kicked all over the concrete pitch. From one end to the other. I chewed gum – it gave me added confidence. Plans had been made in the toilets long before. As I observed the football match, suddenly there he was in all his arrogant glory.

I walked up to meet him, saying, "Now we'll see who's got the guts, who's brave enough."

Slowly along with Cristobel I walked towards Maxwell. We walked deliberately, menacingly. Soon we were on the pitch with the football game being played all about us. Sweaty boys ran, tackled, or kicked the ball. A boy headed the ball. There was excitement, a goal had been scored. The boy who scored hailed a hero by others. The cheering loud, the praise well earned. We both continued to walk midst this sporting mayhem.

A few minutes drifted by, nobody noticed us, they were consumed by the game. All we could hear above the intense cheering was comments like "Great goal, Mickey" or perhaps "What a score!" But then, as in the classroom before, he stared right back at me. Our eyes met, not as lovers' might, but two enemies. He seemed startled, caught unawares. The game stopped as the white football bounced in front of me. I blew some gum. The pink bubble grew in my lips, much like a New Year's Eve balloon at midnight. Then it burst.

"What are you looking at?" he said timidly.

I caught the bouncing ball.

"You!" It was said with a long lingering breath. I repeated myself twice more.

He started to walk away from me, but I followed the little creep. Other boys shielded him from my anger. It did no good for him though. I continued to harass him. Cristobel winked at me again. Yes, Diary, I had him just where I wanted him. In my power, on this bright sunny day. I needed to teach him a lesson in manners.

"So I'm not brave enough. No guts, no eye for speed. Well, Maxwell, do you have what I don't?"

He seemed scared, rolling his sleeve down, wiping his glasses dry, saying, "Go away, Amo, we are playing football."

"He's afraid. Yellow as a ripe banana."

Cristobel laughed; so did I.

"Thick as shit too. All you do is talk," I said mockingly.

8

"Amo only wants to kick the balls off you, Max darling."

As she said this a lone voice screamed from the playground, "A fight, a fight." At that moment we were face-to-face, silent, aggressive. I pushed him backwards, he nearly lost his balance.

"Go away, both of you."

He did nothing save just stare back at me. Now children were all round us. I must say, Diary, it felt great, as I was the centre of attention. A large crowd gathered to watch the combat. They encouraged us to fight, egging us on to blows. I caught him by the scruff of the neck. I could've happily strangled him right there. But settled for second best, grabbing him by the tie, holding tightly, squeezing all the while.

As I fought, I insulted him, spitting in his face: "Don't you ever talk to me like that again, you silly little bastard."

I pulled him towards me, children cheering, roaring with delight. Maxwell, like a beaten prizefighter, started to give in to my power. By this time though I was in full flight, now screaming like some mediaeval town crier. He looked back at me fear in his contorted face as fists swung in all directions. I drew blood; so did he. Fists, arms, then feet lashed out to all the points of the compass as I attacked him with every ounce of strength God had placed in my fragile female frame. Other children called for more. So I gave it to them as I wrestled Maxwell down to the floor.

Then, just as suddenly as it had started, the cheering stopped. Silence ruled. Just as I was about to get on top of Maxwell in order to finish him off a hand gripped my shoulder, a man's voice boomed all over the playground. It was Mr Thomas.

"Well, what have we here? You again, Osborne. Stop this now, the pair of you."

He was very strong, lifting me clear off the ground. Then he separated us both. A bead of hot sweat trickled down my forehead, running down my warm cheek. A satisfied smile embraced my face. I was now a heroine to the other children.

This engaged me to do some more damage, inflict more pain, while my time was good. Soon it would not be. I turned, moved closer, then spat in his face again. He stood there trembling with fear. I half expected him to burst into tears. Victory, revenge, was all mine. It felt glorious, but I knew only too well what was now coming my way.

Mr Thomas marched us both across the crowded playground. Indeed, half the school seemed to be watching. It was truly wonderful to be the centre of all that fuss. All wanted to know me, be my friend. My strength returned as some other girls wished me well. A few other boys admired me as I passed them by. Like a model, or actress. Soon we arrived inside the main school hall. I felt like a prisoner being taken for punishment, execution perhaps. Maxwell walked by my side, saying nothing. I hoped he felt shame at being whopped by a girl. The only indication of failure, humiliation, was a face red with both fear and embarrassment.

Standing to one side, the other children then fell silent. Within minutes I found myself sitting at a desk in an otherwise empty classroom. Mr Thomas screamed at us both for fighting in school. I got it worse for being a girl. Double for starting the fight in the first place. He lectured us on the morals of sound school behaviour. I was not listening, hearing not a single word of his counsel. Deaf to the sound of his voice. Just wishing for this ordeal to end. Soon the welcoming sound of Cristobel would cheer me up, send me back to the real world, where laughter ruled OK. Then the door of the classroom opened and the headmaster walked in, mad as hell. Now I was for it.

In for it, you bet, Diary. My appearance did not help, looking a right mess. This didn't help my cause. I did not look very ladylike. School values, which the headmaster kept like the Ten Commandments from the Bible, were missing from me today. Maxwell too, I hasten to add. I had smeared blood over my face, under my nose. My knees were scratched. My hair matted, alive with dirt. I had fought well, like a Roman. My honour saved, intact. Even the soles of my shoes had been scuffed. Now home would be the problem to confront next. Father's anger the next test of my resolve. We looked at each other, but silence was now the order of the day. The deeds had been done. As we sat there Mr Thomas beckoned the headmaster. They joined forces, held a conference about us. Deciding what fate awaited us. At that moment, like an accused woman in the dock at the Old Bailey, a knot tied up inside my stomach. I was becoming nervous about what might happen to me.

Our headmaster, Mr Fitzgibbon, has all the presence of a military gentleman about him. Diary, he is a man with an army background for sure. A major or general in the Guards. Hell, the only thing missing is a row of medals displayed proudly on his chest. Letting the world know how brave he had been both for Queen and for country. He is a man to be feared. I tell you now, right there I feared him. What would he do to me? He is about sixty, sixty-five. Close to retirement. He has been headmaster of this school for at least twenty years – a long time in charge. We don't mess with this man. He comes from the old school. He is intimidating. When we walk into his room we are quiet. Equally, if he walks into a noisy room, it descends into silence

10

at once. His head is covered with a wave of jet-black hair, grey has yet to take over. His cheeks rugged, rosy red. Under his nose a dark well-groomed handlebar moustache decorates his face.

He is indeed good-looking, regal perhaps, even majestic. Always well turned out, his suit never changes at all. English tweed, three-piece, with a silver watch chain hanging loosely on his waistcoat. White shirt, black tie. This completes his fashion statement of command, authority. But it is his shoes that give him that air of fear. Brown brogues, well polished with steel toecaps, heels as well. If he walks down a corridor, his footsteps echo as if on a parade ground marching in time to the music. You hear him coming long before you see him.

"Osborne!"

"Sir!" I replied sharply.

"This is the second time we cross swords. I've better things to do than waste time on a lout like you. You're being sent home. Your mother's coming to pick you up. I'll deal with you tomorrow. Get out of my sight."

With that he left the room, slamming the door behind him.

Watched over by a prefect, I waited for Mum. Now I feared home. Only never mind. Thanks for listening, Diary. I have to write this all down, have somebody else to confide in.

Goodnight. See you tomorrow.

20 FEBRUARY 2010: Yesterday was hell. I have never seen my dad so unstrung, angry. He shouted at me so loudly, he scared me. He is normally so calm; yesterday he lost it. Yet I really don't blame him.

It is one of the great mysteries of being a parent. The contradictions of adulthood. It confuses everyone, especially us children. One minute they're telling you to stick up for yourself. Then when you do, like I did yesterday, they roar at you for it. That was Dad – swine. Lots of different advice from all sides. Leaving us confused all around. Yet, I adore my dad. He's my hero; Mum's the heroine.

From nothing my dad built up a mini empire. We aren't rich, but we are not poor either. I want for nothing. We even live in the same council house, on the same estate, right here in Cardiff. Dad didn't want to lose his roots. The house itself has been done up a shade. It stands out from all the other houses. The flowers, the rockery, hedge, fish pond. A lush green lawn. The back garden is decorated by a large chicken coop, plus allotment. We grow our own fruit, vegetables, herbs, spices. This is the only statement of wealth. Why, we don't even have a swimming pool. Wish we did

– I'd never be out of it in summer or fall. But Dad says it would be far too grand. So the chickens together with the vegetables win.

That said, I am proud of my dad's rise to power. It has become legendary around here. In this part of Wales, he commands nothing but respect. One hundred years ago hats would've been doffed. Out of nothing he built something. It has to be admired for sure.

Osborne Motors is one of the major businesses around this part of Cardiff. What started out as a one-man show now dominates. My dad has always loved cars. From a very young age he was always tinkering with them. He couldn't leave them alone. Learning to drive before he was fifteen. Legend says he got a speeding ticket the very same week he passed his test. A proud boast for him to make. Speed is a way of life – he still says so. A natural contender for the lure of motor racing. The speed, sweat, danger, death. My dad loves it, driving him onwards in life. He finds inspiration from it. It defines him. His own enthusiasm is infectious to us all.

Based on the Llandaff road, Osborne Motors has a large white forecourt, packed with row upon row of second-hand cars. The odd new model breaks up the pattern. The showroom itself has an immense glass front to it. A vast array of different-coloured bunting gives the forecourt a promenade look to it. Dancing with the breeze. All over the showroom an assortment of stickers advertising this car, that car. At this price or that. Plus financial advice for those who need it. It appears as brightly coloured wallpaper decorating a child's bedroom, my own perhaps.

At the far end is Dad's office. The nerve centre of operations. All over the place people busy themselves with work. Telephones ring, fingers play on the keyboard of a word processor, like a piano. A family photograph adorns my dad's desk.

At the back is housed the garage complex. A place I love to visit. Always a beehive of activity from eight-thirty until five. It is like this six days a week. Its smell, powerful aroma, a rich scent of sweat, grease, petrol, paint. All this exchanged with the bustle of men shouting, singing, swearing. The downing of tools on the floor. Engines starting. The glorious sound of cussing mechanics. How I adore this environment. It is a blessing. Yet today I was denied this pleasure. Part of my punishment for my awful behaviour at school.

When he came home Mum told him what had happened. The fight, disgrace. I would have to face the glum truth. She told him all the glorious details, leaving out nothing. But failed to mention the torment together with the awful ridicule I endured in class. As I lay in bed I could hear them arguing in the kitchen. My name repeated over, over, then over again. I was made out to be a rebellious wayward daughter who has gone astray once too often this time. My dad could not understand what had got into me at school. Mum tried to say something in my defence for all that. But it cut no ice with Dad, who just flipped his lid. They even swore at each other as the truth came out. The telephone call from the headmaster. Collecting me from school under the cloud of suspension, red-faced with guilt. The fighting daughter, a girl who feared nothing. Then, all of a sudden, silence. Followed by the menacing sound of my dad's footsteps as he climbed the stairs, advancing towards my bedroom door. My nerves were on edge. What on earth might he say or do? Slowly, the door opened; I lay on my bed hugging my pillow watching the door open. Out of the corner of my eye I saw the huge silhouette of my dad. Anger etched across his face.

"What the hell have you been doing, my girl?" He stared at me.

At first I was speechless, saying nothing for a moment. Then I muttered something: "Dad! I was just protecting myself." I sat up straight.

He walked up to the side of my bed, then sat down on it.

"Sent home for fighting in the playground. A girl of mine fighting. I couldn't believe my ears when your mum told me." With that he shook his head in disgust. "So what are we to do?"

He didn't look like he would give me a clip around the ears, so I butted in: "I don't know, Dad, but he got what he deserved. He really did."

"I want you to tell me just what happened. The truth, mind."

Then I went for the jugular, bursting into tears. Dad then cuddled me in his arms. I wasted no time at all. I dived in head first, searching for the sympathy vote. Luckily, promptly finding it. He did not let me down: he gave in to me, but only just.

"All right, Ann Marie, calm down, calm down." This time in a very soft voice that was easy to tame. Now he was not shouting, or losing control.

We just talked all about what had taken place at school. Despite his apparent concern about my welfare, he was really angry at what I had done. It was more of a pep talk than harsh discipline for his only child. He never said it, but something in the way he dealt with me told me he was proud of the stance I had taken. At the mercy of a mere boy. He even told me to buck up then come downstairs.

"We have to talk about how we'll deal with the headmaster tomorrow. Now come on, Ann Marie, dry your eyes. I think you need to cuddle Tippy. That dog's going crazy – poor thing doesn't know what to do. Animals can sense when their mistresses aren't happy."

I smiled back, dried my eyes, composed myself.

Diary, what a day this has been! All emotions felt, even at my age. Oh! When will it all end? Perhaps tomorrow in the headmaster's office. I dread the morning, but at least I'm still alive. Cuddling my little dog helped a lot. This dog of mine knows how I feel all the time. Thank God for animals. Sometimes they are better company than humankind. Glad today is over.

21 FEBRUARY 2010: The dog woke me up this morning, at 5 a.m. Boy, was I mad! I didn't need it, licks to the cheek, paws all over the place. A couple of hours of precious daydreaming lost forever. He just jumped upon the bed, licking my face all over. Leaving me wet through, angry. I pushed him off the bed down to the floor, where he belongs at that hour of the morning. He tried to climb back, only I wouldn't let him. Sorry, dog. I was in no mood to fuss over you this morning. Because this was judgement day, when all would be revealed.

I hold a secret behind the school gates. It is something my parents aren't aware of, do not know, or suspect. Yes, their sweet little blonde-haired goody-goody is, in fact, a bully, a thug. At school nobody fucks with me, or Cristobel. We rule the roost, call the shots. I am feared. We are loathed by the other children, even the teachers. After yesterday even more so. They will fear us both. I fought, won the day. In our class alone we are a couple of hard cases. I even smoke, have drunk beer from a can. I am in no doubt that today all will be revealed to the rest of the world. The headmaster will take care of that – love it as he does so. One thing I know, when faced with this prospect – in front of the headmaster with my parents listening – I will now need all my courage to survive, pull through, stay intact. That boy, Maxwell Braithwaite, will be going through the same ordeal. For a different reason altogether. He will feel some shame, just like me. We will both be punished in some way. I hate school, cannot wait to leave the hole. But expulsion? Never! My parents would be devastated if that happens today. My fingers were crossed this morning, long before breakfast.

In a way Dad has already made me suffer, by depriving me of the one thing he knows I enjoy more than anything else on this earth. That being driving a car. Last night he did not give me a chance to get behind the wheel. Most nights when work is over he takes me to the large car park behind the garage.

14

Then gives me a driving lesson of sorts. Even at my tender age, he knows how much I adore driving. It sends me forward, gives me strength. Indeed, it is in my blood by the pint. Our family genes transmit this wonder down the line. It is all my dad's fault – he gave me the passion. Perhaps this is why I'm so good at it. I must say, Diary, I may not be allowed on the road just yet, but I can still hold my own. Behind the wheel I find power, it thrills me like no other. Better than a boy's kiss. Turn, reverse, stop, start, even parking the car. I can do it all. With my dad by my side to guide me, teach me. This is my real education. I was denied this as part of my punishment for fighting. Being told not to do this hurt like hell. I found myself watching television, daydreaming, when I should have been sitting behind the wheel of a car, driving. Before we even set off for school this morning, Diary, the penny started to drop, the lesson already learnt. Being a thug, a bully, hurting others, bringing pain through making people fear you is all wrong. I do not need the headmaster to tell me this for the one millionth time.

Breakfast was a sombre affair. Nobody said much – I certainly did not, deciding silence was indeed golden. It did the trick, I think. The car journey to school was not as bad as it might have been. I felt like a prisoner being taken for trial all over again. It was Mum who broke the ice. I sat on the back seat, out of sight, but not out of mind.

"Well, I never thought I'd ever be doing this," she said softly almost to herself.

"Calm down, dear. It might not be that bad. Let's see how things go." Dad tried to cheer her up.

"Glad you see it that way. I don't."

At that moment we stopped at a red light. I began to feel guilty, wishing, for the first time, the incident had never happened. A green light followed, the car moved on as school got ever closer.

"The shame of my daughter fighting." Mum was now almost in tears.

I had to jump in, say something: "I'm sorry, Mum, I really am."

Both Mum and Dad just seemed to sigh with despair. Suddenly, we turned into Hollow Street, with the high iron school gates dead ahead. My stomach was all tied up in knots. Boy, was I nervous as Dad parked the car!

School has an aroma all of its own. I noticed it today much more than usual. It hits your nose as soon as you open the school doors. A smell of soap, disinfectant, bound with that of polish.

There to cleanse the mind along with the body. To prepare us for the dangerous adult world outside the safety of the school gates. From the cloistered setting of education, no prisoners would be taken alive. God help those who fail the system.

I dutifully followed my parents as they walked up to the reception desk, where Mrs Deeds greeted them. The appointment was confirmed. In the background a typewriter rhythmically clattered away as another letter was typed out for the school. We then entered a sort of doctor's waiting room. A tiny little table covered with magazines stood in the middle. Over in the far corner a large lamp stood. Leather chairs neatly arranged by the wall. We all sat down, then waited for the appointed hour. It was not long in coming. In front of me a window was slightly open. The school playing field stood ahead of me, like a large green fitted carpet. To one side some girls played netball, dressed in dark-blue knickers along with white shirts. A teacher refereeing blew a whistle, the girls cheered. As they played on, time grew longer for me. I drifted into a dream. The sound of a recorder being played brought me back to the real world. Suddenly, the door opened, the headmaster beckoned to us.

"Please enter. Mr Osborne, Mrs Osborne, glad you could come."

As he said this false greeting, I smiled to myself, looking the other way. Then he said my name too, looking at me sternly. He didn't smile.

"Please sit down. Some tea?"

As the headmaster said this I could not help but giggle, as he tried to turn this court martial into some polite fucking tea party. He just stared back at me sternly as he heard the chuckle come from my dainty little lips. Then we all settled down.

The inquest began as the headmaster sat down behind his oak desk. Then my interrogation, my private trial, began in earnest.

"This is indeed a sad day, young lady." The headmaster was in a tyrannical mood.

"Let's get on with it, please. The grim facts," demanded my dad.

"I've been a headmaster for a long time, Mr Osborne. This is a first. You want the grim facts then I'll give them to you. It does not make a good read."

The headmaster was chilling. These words of his sent a shudder down my spine. What the hell would he say now? As he said this, Dad looked at me in despair. The headmaster opened a notebook, reading from it. He smugly sat back in his chair, loving it. Right there I was powerless to stop him from taking me apart, piece by piece. God knows, now what? I was made out to be the school bully, the thug. A dress-wearing pugnacious little bastard. The one the teachers hated. The rest of the school feared as no other. Along with her sidekick Cristobel, an easily led, gullible friend, who would do anything I asked. No matter how cruel or unwise it might be.

"The fight that took place here at school yesterday, started by Ann Marie, was not the first, Mr Osborne."

Dad looked agitated. This piece of news clearly upset him very much, disturbed him greatly. He glanced back at me in alarm. My poor mum hid her face with embarrassment, perhaps shame. The headmaster just carried on damning me. Yet it was only the beginning. He seemed to revel in my horror.

He carried on: "I have a record of discipline here that's more suitable for a wayward boy than a girl."

He looked across at me, assessing my reaction. I gave nothing away.

Dad followed, likewise saying, "Ann Marie, what have you done?"

But the horrible headmaster continued with his angry diatribe against me: "What Ann Marie has done is a serious infraction of the rules. Be sure I will deal with it so. I will not tolerate such behaviour from anybody, especially a girl pupil. We have standards here all must comply with."

Mother had always thought of me as a good girl. Her pride, her joy. So the next revelation shot her in the butt. All previous preconceptions about her daughter's ladylike behaviour were ended there.

The headmaster fumbled about in his chair, then gave my parents the truth about me: "Your daughter's nothing but a bully, scum. The school is sick of the sight of her. Ann Marie does not listen to authority. She has developed a gang-like culture that has no place in this school or, dare I say it, society. If she does not change, prison awaits her with open cell doors. I will not mince my words, or water this down. This sad day has been coming for a long time."

Dad jumped in, stopping him from speaking further. Why had he not been told of this before, if things were that bad?

The headmaster carried on, in love with his job: "A few months ago Ann Marie was caught red-handed picking on two other pupils. Along with her sidekick, Cristobel. They bullied without mercy. Just because these girls were quiet, yet clever. What do you say about that, Mr Osborne?"

There was a long pregnant pause, nobody said anything.

Then the headmaster continued: "I mean it is incredible, Mr Osborne. For no sound reason, save cruelty, your daughter pulled their hair, pushed, shoved, slapped faces, then called names. A name can be as awful as any punch. This is pupil harassment on a grand scale."

Dad enquired boldly, almost coming to my aid. He wanted to know why he hadn't been told about it earlier. The headmaster told Dad about the wasteful times spent trying to get me on the straight path to righteousness, all to no avail. He was told all about the detention, and the punch. Saying sorry now would be difficult for me.

It took over one long tedious hour for this hell to stop, normality to return to my world. But eventually it did stop. I looked at all three adults pondering my fate. Would Maxwell get the same?

Astonishingly, I was given another chance. I have my dad to thank for that. It was all most embarrassing to hear him beg for sympathy from the school. I have received detention again. If I digress once more, psychological counselling is an option for the school. Me in the nuthouse? Never, Diary! I'm not that bad. This crap all starts tomorrow.

Well, Diary, my trusted friend, I am glad today's over with. School in the morning. Dog to cuddle.

22 FEBRUARY 2010: Good evening, Diary. How are you today? After yesterday today has been a blessing. At least I was able to smile, have a laugh with Cristobel. We did that in style.

The drive home was another sombre one. Nobody said much until we passed the garage on the High Street. Lots of bunting moved with the breeze. Until it looked like something at a fairground. It caused my dad to make comments about the future of the business. As he delivered his brave optimistic vision of the future years ahead. On the forecourt a valet hosed a car down that he'd been cleaning with pride. A dealer politely invited a client to browse over a nice-looking second-hand car that was value for money. An Osborne Motors 'DEAL OF THE WEEK'. Over in Dad's office Mavis typed with a smile. The unseen mechanics worked to perform miracles at the sacred temple of the family garage. I could even hear somebody swear at the top of his voice. Even recall the chattering sound of Mavis's typing, as we drove by.

Dad did not even look at the garage. He, as my father, had preoccupations to ponder over in his mind. He was deeply hurt by my actions at school. He decided to take the rest of the day off to concentrate on the education of his only daughter. He instructed me, as he drove along the High Street, to take my punishment. I was to yield myself to detention, homework. From now on there would be no more driving lessons until I proved myself worthy.

I smiled warmly, told him how much I loved him, when he dangled the carrot in front of me. Just the incentive to do better. If I knuckled down to it, the offer to race in a junior go-kart race would be given to me. I jumped at the chance, the idea of racing a car. It would be at The Arena in Bristol. I readily accepted. Just the thought made me feel good about life, something to aim for. I thanked Dad, saying I would do much better, never letting them down again ever. It was said from the heart with girlish enthusiasm.

Dinner at home last night was deadly serious. Over roast duck, business was discussed at length. Dad and Mum, along with Leyth Swain, his foreman, talked with great relish about the recent investment in the garage by Mr Murray Proctor-Hale.

Dad said to us all, "If this financial deal with Proctor-Hale goes through" – he sipped wine as he spoke – "it will enable us to venture into our ultimate goal, Formula One. A dream come true after all these years of waiting. A team with bite. We will be a force to be reckoned with. All Wales will rejoice. The secret of our empire is the fuel we possess – X7. The Welsh trump card here."

"I agree, boss. I can't wait to get started. He provides the money, we supply the brains along with the hard work."

With that sentiment Dad got all emotional, weepy for the future. He stood up, then proposed a toast: "To Wales, the power of the Welsh dragon. To my own pride, my joy, my own little baby X7. Liquid gold in your petrol tank."

Then we all cheered. Right there, this evening, the future seemed as bright as the farthest star. To be honest, Diary, I must say that I was glad of this distraction. For a moment, it took the heat off what had been a frustrating day at school.

School started with history, then dreaded mathematics. I was cheesed off by them both. Today most of the teachers became my enemy, people to be hated. It felt like they were watching my every move, waiting for me to step out of line. Then they could march me in to punish me. Only I held back from trouble for the sake of my family, remembering the promise made to Dad, which I was now bound to keep. The very thought of go-karting was my best form of discipline at school. The carrot on a stick. Dad has promised this treat before, but not delivered. It is up to me to make sure he does this time. 'Sweet are the uses of adversity,' as Shakespeare once said.

For February the weather has been very warm, almost springlike, very pleasant. So lunchtime was a real gas, fun. Along with Cristobel I walked down to the chip shop, 'The Smiling Cod', on the corner of Cheap Street. We gorged ourselves on pie, peas and chips, drowned in salt, vinegar and sauce. Above us stretched yet another deep-blue sky, not a cloud in sight. It was warm, balmy even. We reaped the benefits of global warming. July in February. The chips stank of vinegar; the pie, tomato sauce. A wonderful school dinner for us both. When indulged, we sat down on a brick wall, then watched the world drift by, forgetting school. Covered in sauce, with bloated bellies, we enjoyed an after-dinner smoke to aid our digestion. I guess we had been sitting on the brick wall for about fifteen minutes. At least two buses had stopped, then drove onwards to Cardiff. A number 8 via Canton, the library. A man came out of a bookmaker's across the street, smiling with a handful of money – his winnings, no doubt. A police car raced by, its lights flashing, a call to duty. But as I took another swig of my drink, a very old man caught my attention. As he got closer to where we sat, Cristobel lifted her leg, then let off an almighty vinegar-smothered belch, backed up by a tomato sauce fart that echoed down the street. The old man nearly fell over. Laugh, I nearly cried it was so funny.

"Not very ladylike," he said. "Why aren't you at school?"

"Mind your own fucking business." I shouted it twice.

He stopped walking for a moment. Then he just stared back at us as we teased him even more. He then began a four- or five-minute monologue about schoolgirl morality. Like we would listen to the old bat! He then threatened to report us to the headmaster. I told him to go right ahead as we didn't care. The old man then turned away in disgust at our outrageous behaviour. We watched him slowly walk away from us, giving him some abuse with our two fingers. Heading back to school one hour late.

Nobody seemed to notice our absence. We missed one lesson, religious study. Then Cristobel, along with myself, casually walked into geography. It was a totally boring sixty minutes of crap. A discussion about Central Africa. I was more interested in the upcoming go-kart race over in Bristol, hoping my dad meant it for sure this time. There was also a boy sitting over on the other side of the classroom. I must say he is new to me, just started here. His name is James. He is a dish. At first glance the best-looking boy in the whole school to date. As I kept staring at him, a date is just what I had in mind. He is my age, dark-haired, well muscled, with hands to hold, lips to kiss. This boy is bright too. The only one to answer a question correctly about The Gambia coast. All I need now is a green light from him to set the fire alight. I haven't been out with a boy for a good snog for far too long. Times must change, or I'll forget I'm a girl at all.

I kept my eye on young James all afternoon, until the bell sounded for the welcome end of the school day. As we all trooped out of the classroom, I decided to wait by the main gate, just to see if I could catch this boy's attention. I saw him walking all by himself across the playground. He seemed lost in his own world. The telltale sign of a thinker. His hair all ruffled up, untidy. School tie loose, shirt unbuttoned at the neck. Carrying his briefcase. He looked like he had just finished at the office in London, or New York. Perhaps earned yet another million, making himself even richer. Yes, this is a boy I could swoon for.

As he walked right by me, I called out his name. He gazed back at me. Then we walked down the road together, side by side. I saw Cristobel, but she kept her distance, knowing I was on the pull. It was polite conversation – talk about home, where he'd come from (his family came from Watford), along with his dad's job (in furniture, no less). The pavement was crowded with other children, but we walked alone. At the bus stop we parted, but I'm going out with him on Friday night. Hellfire, I can't wait, the fever is coming on, yet again. A tingling sensation all over my body.

Goodnight, Diary. Will I be the same on Friday?

26 FEBRUARY 2010: Hurrah! Hurrah! Hurrah! Let the whole world know, let the bells ring out in exultation at the glorious news. Yes, Diary, tonight I bled my way to womankind. The mad world of adults has been entered by me, with Mother Nature's blessing, thank you very much. What a bastard! Apparently, I'm old enough to have babies, but not old enough to drive a car. Now where's the sense in all this craziness? In some places scattered about the world this transition would be celebrated – not here though. My white bloodstained sheets were hastily removed. Then a box of pads handed out by Mum as she told me to get on with it, combined with words of how to watch myself when out with boys. Some hope, me with a date soon too. Poor James, he can look, but not touch. While all this commotion was going on Dad remained silent. This had been women's talk, no men allowed. Will the day get any better? I thought to myself, 'Roll on six o'clock.'

Tonight while getting ready for this date I must remember to pack some lipstick, cotton buds, gum, pads, a mirror. I tell you, Diary, this menstruation lark is already a drag. This once a month until I'm fifty. I wish I was a boy with all the right tackle. Women, huh!

I met James, my dream guy, at five thirty outside the library. He arrived fifteen minutes late. But oh my God, what a sight greeted me! A sight to make any girl melt. His lush dark hair neatly combed. Blue denim suit, shiny shoes, he looked like a film star or footballer to fall for. Tonight he was all mine. I didn't do too badly either, wearing my light-blue top, white miniskirt, tights, along with matching knee-high boots. I looked for all the world like eighteen, felt like it as well. With my handbag casually slung over my shoulder, we kissed each other on the cheek as we waited for the bus. A number 21 to Cardiff Central. James paid for the tickets – that was so sweet of him. We had decided to go into town to watch a movie, *Hail the Hero*, starring American heart-throb Cliff Wain. But to be honest, Diary, I was not interested in the bloody film. I had other things on my mind. Wicked kissing was all that counted from James tonight. Question: could he, would he, watch me instead of the film? All I could do was hope.

It said, 'NO SMOKING'. I lit up anyway, needed a drag. James made me laugh a lot tonight. Lots of people got on the bus, which seemed to stop every five or six minutes. At every stop it came to people got on, few getting off. Soon the bus was crowded with people making their way home from work. I promised Dad I'd be home by ten; Mum I'd behave myself. Some hope they'd got tonight. I needed my well-earned freedom. Sought on the back row, if you know what I mean.

Before we went to the cinema, James took me for a burger, washed down with some shandy. Personally, I wanted something a little stronger than weak beer. But I'm too young to take the risk of ordering alcohol here in Cardiff. I'd never get away with it. One day though – a night out on the piss cannot be far away. Look out, lads, I'm coming. At six forty we held hands as lovers might in the queue, for that's what it felt like. Does this always happen to young hearts captured by love's embrace? You must behave ten years your senior? Look adult, even though you're most definitely not? I guess we all go through this phase. Tonight it was my turn.

We sat right at the back, just where we wanted to sit. The room became dimmed as the lights went out in the crowded cinema. The film began as the roar of the theme music echoed all over the auditorium. I fumbled at my popcorn basket, spilling some on the floor as James pretended to watch the blessed film. I went all aquiver, on row ten, seats eight to nine.

Who cared about the film? I didn't. But we embraced again at the bus stop, before the journey home. Oh yes, another date was set long before the town hall. James was a gentleman, too good for me. Intelligent, witty, always with an enquiring mind. But tonight the only thing he wanted was me. Going on a picnic over at St Gwynno Forest. Perhaps on Sunday afternoon, if the weather's nice – let's hope so. Arrived back home all right, on time as well. James saw me to the door of our house. We walked hand in hand right through the estate. People watching too. He kissed me goodnight, a peck on the lips – it felt great. As the front curtain moved, it was Mum checking my safe arrival home.

Parents can be so suspicious. Mum questioned me about what had happened on my date. Was I or wasn't I still pure? She never actually said it, but that's what she meant. Cow!

20 MARCH 2010: Well, Diary, today was payback time for being such a good little girl at school. It was worth the wait, for today has been one hell of an adventure for me. Giving me a taste for danger, a thirst for winning, the lure of fame, sporting glory. I want more of it. The hunger is here. Once is simply not going to be enough.

It can be said that women look best when inside a posh dress. But not this wombat, not this girl, certainly not today. Dirty jeans, along with gallons of sweat, were the order of the day. To show everybody in the world just exactly what I'm made of. Four o'clock could not come quickly enough for me, even at breakfast this morning. I write up today's historic day, Diary, my breath alive with living, my body alive with excitement, thinking of the good things to come. The promise has been delivered to me. Out of that, I can surmise, people can be trusted after all.

Dad paid the entry fee for me to race in a junior go-karting event over at Bristol, against children my age. He told me at dinner a few nights ago. I threw myself at him, giving him a big kiss, then an even bigger hug. I was overcome with joy, childish excitement at the wonderful news. He had kept his promise. We would celebrate with a glorious day out for the family. Sport will never be the same again. Not after Bristol.

So this morning we set out across the River Severn towards Bristol. Everyone was there, even my grandparents. Cristobel came too for moral support. As I do not have any brothers or sisters, my friend Cristobel, somebody my own age, was necessary. The race was not until late in the afternoon. So the morning was spent shopping. My mum with Dad went on a shopping spree. We spent four long hours traipsing from shop to store. It seemed endless, while all the time I got more nervous. The adrenalin pumping through my body at twice the speed of sound. It took my mind off the shopping. But do all sports people experience this phenomenon before a contest? In one store they ordered some new furniture and bought a brand-new dinner service with matching glasses. Some flowered wallpaper was inspected by Mum, then rejected. Blue curtains sampled to blend in with the rest of the decor. Then more walking along the pavements of the city. But it did not in any way dampen my spirits, as we experienced a sudden downpour, walking through the city of Bristol. Soon we sought refuge in the dry warmth of a coffee shop down by the river. Hot onion soup was ordered.

Cristobel spoke first: "What time do we have to be there, Mr Osborne?"

"Oh, about three," he replied. Dad then looked at me as I dipped bread in my soup. "Well, love, are you nervous?"

I tried to look brave-faced about it, hide my true feelings from him. Today I had to be the fearless sportswoman. "Why no, Dad, not in the least. Can't wait to get started, race away."

He smiled along with Mum at my confidence, saying, "That's my girl. You'll be fine. Go out there, enjoy yourself."

Mum reassured me with similar comfort, while Grandma just nodded in agreement. I then muttered something about not letting them down, doing my best for the Osborne clan, making sure of a good show come what may. I mean, Diary, so much has happened in the last couple of months it's hard to keep up with events as they unfold. The fight at school, the awful punishment that followed. The humiliation for my parents. Sometimes, Diary, I can take responsibility, act like an adult. I feel I owe it to my family.

When we had finished Dad paid the bill. We left the coffee shop, surrounded by people in damp, wet clothing. A man coughed, a woman shook her umbrella dry as we headed out back to the car. I sat next to Cristobel on the back seat. The drive was slow, the city of Bristol crowded with cars, shoppers, busy pedestrian traffic. Rovers played City – this didn't help matters. It was bumper to bumper. This afternoon, though, only one sporting event would make its mark. That was my go-kart race with little old me at the wheel.

As we approached The Arena, my heart began to beat like an Indian drum out West. It took my breath away. Once inside, to my horror there seemed hordes of people watching. Did I really expect an empty arena, no spectators? A bleak track lined with hundreds of used tyres introduced itself to me in the centre of the stadium. Every so often bales of straw acted as crash barriers, especially at each bend on the track. As I looked, I thought, 'Will I need their services?' I hoped not. All the dreams of the last couple of days suddenly appeared difficult. As I observed the heady scene, I was truly gripped with fear. I did not wish to lose, almost wishing I was back home in safety.

The race was at four thirty. Two go-kart races came before mine. I tried to watch. Take it all in. Perhaps learn something. I found that I could not concentrate enough. As the go-karts sped by me in the grandstand, the crowd cheering then yelling the children on grew louder all the time. The stadium was full of enthusiastic parents, much like mine, encouraging equally energetic children. These would be my first rivals, to be taken on, to be beaten. To one side a man waved a chequered flag as a race ended.

Celebrations for some lucky people began. For myself, a light tap on the shoulder brought me back to the real world. It was Dad offering me some advice on race tactics. Then I was ushered away to get changed, emerging later wearing a white jumpsuit that was just a shade too big for me. A crash helmet to match. Go-kart 9 was the one I was bound to race in.

The go-karts were flimsy, fragile motor cars. An engine wrapped in a steel frame low to the ground. The four wheels seemed enormous and the steering wheel appeared small. I found the brake, along with the accelerator. The driving lessons Dad had given me would now prove their worth here. They should give me the edge over the other children. Slowly, I drove the go-kart on a couple of practice laps, much the same as a Grand Prix driver might, searching for pole position. As I passed Mum she waved to me. I ignored her. Concentrating on the job ahead. Then the race was called to start.

I shot away in an instant. The go-kart raced away, getting third place at the first bend in the race. I bumped a few karts out of the way as I drove on. The other drivers seemed to move over to one side, letting me through. Suddenly, I found myself out in front with only four laps left to go. The black tyres flashed by me, the bales of straw missed. Faster, as even more speed was called for. The track whizzed by at twice the speed of sound, as I asked for one more effort. Soon I found myself speeding down the track, taking the flag. I had won in grand style too. The others were nowhere to be seen. It gave me a fabulous feeling inside.

The adulation by other people, aimed at me, is I think a taste of things to come. Today, I experienced winning for the first time in my life at sport. Before, kicking some poor sod gave me a buzz, but this is much better. Putting in my best effort for maximum gain. This is life in the fast lane. But, after all that care, I took my eye off the ball, hitting a straw bale, coming to an abrupt halt. Sad to say, Diary, I even screamed. Officials, plus my dad, came to my rescue. Hugs, kisses, plus praise followed, soothing my wounded pride.

Once out of the go-kart I walked towards the crowd. As I was applauded off the track, I waved to them, returning their good wishes at being the victor. This afternoon I felt like one million dollars. A girl on top of the world. I was duly awarded a certificate, letting the rest of the human race know I had won a motor race. It was presented to me by the race official, Mr Savage, shaking my hand as he did so. I soaked up all the applause like some actress on a first-night call. Diary, the certificate is now framed, hanging on my bedroom wall: 'Ann Marie Osborne', winner of a junior go-kart race in good old Bristol, written across it. I am proud of myself. Dad says he'll let me race again soon. What a day this has been!

2011

30 MAY 2011: Dear Diary, can you believe it, matey? On the hallowed, sacred turf of Wembley, Swansea City played themselves into the Premier League. Manchester City along with United, Chelsea, Spurs, Liverpool, Arsenal, even faithful Wolves, will all travel there, hopefully in fear to Wales. Hell, what an achievement! What next indeed? Europe? The veneration of Swansea City.

Good ole footy! Where would we be without it? Lost!

15 JUNE 2011: This is turning into a difficult summer. A couple of days ago my mum bought me my first bra. A small cotton thing, designed for girls my age. I wore it for the first time today, at school. It made me feel good, like a woman for the very first time in my life. This afternoon we had games. I went for a run with some other girls – just a couple of miles across country, close to the school. It was such a lovely summer day that I took five minutes out, sitting on a farm gate. I had a quick drag as I admired the view. On a health bender. My body is filling out now – I'm growing up fast. Diary, I noticed it more today as I took a shower after the run.

I must state right here that I like what I see very much. I need a bra now, no escaping that simple fact of life. Question: do boys go through this too? They must, just differently. The hair, sweat, voice change. Then the first dreaded erection. I am not alone in the way I feel – all the other girls at school feel the same way about this change in their being. Seeing this change in myself is the good part of summer.

Now for the bad. The boy I've been seeing for a year now, James, is leaving Wales. His dad has been transferred in his job, all the way to bloody New Zealand. They are emigrating to the other side of the world. My heart is broken, I may never see him again. It is awful. They leave at the end of the week. A party, a farewell barbecue for the family, has been planned. I saw him today – we went for a bicycle ride. I said goodbye to many things, James along with something else.

Today was a private affair between the two of us. Before the chicken wings with salad, we said our farewell in a special way. I made sure this was a treat he wouldn't forget in a hurry. It was one o'clock this afternoon when we arrived at Wood River Park. Holding hands we sat down in the long grass, while he told me about his dad's new job. His dad believed it was an opportunity not to be missed. Only I wasn't listening to a word he said. Indeed, I dabbed away a few tears, upset at him leaving. They weren't crocodile tears either – I meant it. I now admit to you alone, Diary, it is the first time I've cried over a boy before. A new experience for me, I tell you. We have been together for a whole year, had lots of fun times. James even spent some of Christmas Day with me at home. As I write this instalment in this diary tears stain the page. Sorry about that, but that's love for you. My first broken heart.

The bicycle ride had been planned by us both, one week before. It was our own private farewell. I knew exactly what going-away present I would give James. What a surprise he was in for! We both promised to write, keep in touch. Later on, visit perhaps. I must say, Diary, the idea of a school holiday spent on the other side of the world is appearing a whiz. Don't worry, Diary, you'll be coming too.

The weather this afternoon was fine. We sat together in the long grass, hidden from view as the sun set over Cardiff. A view to die for, I fear. The park was empty of any other people. As if the rest of humanity knew we wanted to be alone. Say goodbye the way lovers do. You bet we did, Diary, you bet we did. Even at our tender age when puppy love rules the heart, as they say. The slight breeze blew in my hair, making it cascade across my face. James commented on how nice I looked.

But the bicycle ride back home was a silent one. I had nothing to say to James. He rode his bicycle in front of me. I watched him pedal away, perhaps twenty yards ahead, arriving home at just gone eight, kissing goodnight by the garden gate of our house. Cannot wait to tell Cristobel about it in the morning.

Question: Diary, am I a woman at last?

20 JUNE 2011: Today was a very sad one for me. I said farewell, then waved goodbye to my first love. Yes, James has finally gone. My heart is in shreds, torn to pieces. I lost my virginity to him – far too early, but I simply had to do it. Now he's vanished, never to be seen again. I doubt whether I'll ever see him again. Not with all that distance between us. New

Zealand! He may as well have gone to live on the moon.

Yesterday at the barbecue was a night I'll never forget in a hurry. We had a great time, along with all the neighbours in our street. The Bronwells have not been here that long, but, that said, they were well liked. I really thought they'd be here for ever. A right old Welsh send-off was had by all. Yet another Welsh family has deserted our shores. Like the Irish, we are all over the globe – the rest of humanity can't get enough of us.

The jamboree started at eight o'clock, in the garden of number 4. It looked like something out of a church fête on May Day. A white tent decked out with lots of bunting greeted us. As we arrived the deep welcoming aroma of roast pork, apples, and roast beef with onions warmed our noses. It made us hungry at once. Already people were dancing, as rock music echoed in the night air. A large poster proclaimed to the rest of the world 'MAY GOD BLESS THE BRONWELL FAMILY IN THEIR NEW LIFE. WE WILL MISS THEM DEARLY.' They were treated like royalty for the night. It seemed to me, at least, that every family in our street attended. None of them absent.

I drank orange juice in front of Dad, along with Mum. I felt so good – in the mood, as they say. But I wanted something much stronger. Only one person could I rely on to do the job: my friend Cristobel. She arrived on the scene armed with orange laced with vodka. The dare was great, the thrill wonderful. We both arranged it beforehand. She stole a bottle from a store that evening, lacing the orange juice with it. Only thing missing was ice. Right in front of everybody else we drank vodka laced with orange, slowly getting light-headed. We stood to one side, eating burgers, drinking vodka. Soon James came over to join us. It must've been the drink that made us feel so good. But my parents left us alone. They trusted me like an angel. Sometimes, Diary, I must let myself go. Getting kicks is very important, part of life, growing up. Having an illicit drink was the last thing my parents would suspect, or wish for. I was safe.

The deception carried on all night. As friends, neighbours, acquaintances alike swapped stories of times gone by, of a wonderful life past, a life ahead, people danced on. Mr Bronwell was hugged for the hundredth time. I danced close up with James as Cristobel got pissed up in a dark corner on her own. Dad danced with Mrs Bronwell, Mum with Mr Bronwell. The smell of freshly mown grass blended with the night air. I could smell it as midnight struck, a kiss wished for.

It was one as the party drew to a close. The kiss wished for was in fact a full-blown snogging session. Dad bought them a Welsh blanket, hand-knitted, from Neath. Plus – a rare sight indeed – a family portrait of the Osborne clan in colour, taken in the back garden of our house. Smiling at the camera, one big happy family.

A tearful goodbye. I hugged him very tightly, he waved, then he was gone. By the morning the house will be empty.

See you, Diary. This has been a sad day – hard to write it all down.

27 JUNE 2011: Had a restful day, Diary, spent in the good company of Uncle Vernon. He lives alone in the remote village of Holliswell Trenon. His wife, Aunty Mead, died last year. I miss her dreadfully. She was so much fun to be with. But poor old Uncle Vernon's now a shadow of his former self. He used to be such fun too, just like her. All he wants now is to silently let each day pass by, morbidly wanting to die, then be with Aunty Mead forever. People who've been married for over forty long blissful years end their lives that way, I guess. Sad, yet wonderful.

It wasn't the uneventful day that dragged by, but what happened on the drive to his house. Dad drove us there at nine. The day would consist of small talk, tea, more small talk. The same small talk as the last visit. Uncle Vernon played rugby for Holliswell years ago when in his prime. Scored his fair share of tries. It was the normal thing that young rugby players get up to on a Saturday. Hero at three, legless by nine. But he never learnt to drive a car, ever. He made his manly statement on the rugby pitch. Not like now – here's the point, Diary.

While driving on the Swansea Road a car driven by a young man raced past us. My dad swore back at him for being so bloody careless, dangerous. I joined in the abuse. This car raced past us, almost clipping the side of our car in a forty-miles-per-hour limit. This young idiot must have been doing eighty plus. I mean he roared away, leaving us way behind. But miles further down the road we came across this car again, police attending, ambulance on the way. He lost control of the car, hitting a tree trunk head on. Dad was simply glad no other car was involved. Showing off? Booze? Who knows why. But the driver could only have been a teenager, not much older than myself really. He deserved all he got from the law. Personally, I have only one thing to say to describe male drivers like him, who shouldn't be on the road. Do you want to know what that is, Diary? Well, I'll tell you. They are just duck-bonking, horn-honking, throttle-thumping, fear-giving, death-delivering little idiots once they get behind the wheel of a car. They just don't care. That bastard this morning will get points on his licence, maybe a ban for a few months. The law's an arse. Male drivers like that should lose their licence for the rest of their lives. Have it taken away from them. No second chances at all. Let's clear the roads of these unworthy people – female also.

Goodnight, Diary. Let's hope there's no flowers by the roadside tomorrow.

15 JULY 2011: Nearly one month has gone by since James left me for foreign climes. On Monday evening Mr Bronwell telephoned us from their new home in New Zealand, telling us all about how they were all settling down to their life away on the other side of the world. I was out, Dad giving me a driving lesson. So Mum took the call. James asked how I was keeping. He misses me already. I now have a website to visit. Maybe I'll use it, after all, to keep in touch with him.

The driving lesson went rather well. In the car park Dad put me through my paces, doing most things. Parking the car in a tight space brought praise aplenty from him.

"Parked like a veteran, Ann Marie. Well done indeed, my girl," he said, smiling.

It was after the lesson that life got all serious for us both – yes, me included too. Dad went into his office, emerging later with some papers tucked under his arm. I asked what they were, why he needed them so much. So he told me, as if I was his trusted secretary, Mavis. The garage was empty – everybody had long since gone home. Half-fixed cars lay to one side in neat little rows. Some tyres were strewn around the garage, untidy-like. Oil stained the dirty floor. Toolboxes seemed everywhere, some locked, others open. A mechanic had left a girlie magazine open at the middle page. A pretty young lady lay naked, displaying her body for all to see. For the rest of mankind to gloat over. What manner of woman would do such a thing? It was the sound of Dad's voice that woke me from my dream, telling me to hurry on up. The picture seemed so wicked. I would never stoop so low.

Dad walked towards me, some papers tucked under his arm, and we then walked out to the car for the drive home, dinner, television, then bed for the sane. I asked him why the papers were so hell important for him. Could they not wait until the morning? I asked. The answer was most definitely no. He drove onwards towards home, talking all the while to me. There's to be a very important meeting with Mr Proctor-Hale, Dad's financial backer, the money man for us, to be held at the St David Hotel in Cardiff. Here the future business would be discussed in depth. Soon the Welsh Dragon racing team will make its first all-changing step towards Formula One racing. The top of the mountain for all concerned. Dad's putting all his faith into the next twelve months – it's all or nothing for us. I dread to think what will happen if he fails, we fail – the country can't. Dad goes all broody, moody, sulking, when things don't go right. Thinking deeply, silently, about how to solve the problem, make it work. At this meeting all the components of this brand-new wonder car will come together. My dad says the Welsh Dragon will show the way for the rest of the world. After what he told me tonight this car seems almost too good to be true. But he's convinced about the future. It is his baby, his invention, Proctor-Hale's money. Without his money the project's dead in the water. Ideas in the head, dreams in the mind.

As we drove back home Dad opened up his heart to me. His hopes, his fears, his dreams of glory for Wales – they all came flooding out. At one point, as we drove past the city hall, I thought he might break down, cry like a baby. He seemed quite unstrung. This sporting quest means all to him. He had found the right man to back him, finance this venture, share in the glory, so to speak. Now all he needed to do was discover the right driver. Another human being to drive himself along with Wales to everlasting sporting glory. A glory without end.

Mum has argued with Dad many times over the last six months or more. But to her credit she is right behind him, backing him to the hilt. She wants motor-racing success just as much, with a passion to boot. The commitment must be total from the whole family, me as well. Financially, all could be gained, or lost. It will make or break us. There seems to be no in between here, or halfway house. He carried on, and I listened like a dutiful daughter would.

"This meeting with Proctor-Hale will secure the green light for us, or halt our very progress in sport. Ann Marie, my dear, I fear for our future – indeed my own sanity depends upon it. One word from him will make me smile or frown for the rest of my life. Never have I wanted to hear the word yes so much as right now. All the hopes, the dreams, along with years of hard work, condensing as one unit. Oh, Ann Marie, the work I must do now so we can turn this racing car of ours into a world-beater! The Swansea fine tyres, X7 fuel, forty-five high-roller engine, cooled by a full air-cushion system. It will advance the Welsh Dragon car to move like the wind."

As he spoke about the technical side of this racing car, I tried to comfort him, steady his nerves. I said the only thing that made any sense to me at the time: "Of course you will, Dad. Mum, with the rest of the family and the team, we are all rooting for you."

He smiled back again, saying, "Yes, my darling, with that kind of strength we can't fail, only succeed."

With that sentiment he drove the car into our street. Suddenly we had arrived home.

Diary, what a day this has been to write up about! I swear all human feeling has been felt. For one awful moment tonight I really thought I would see Dad cry like a baby. Perhaps he did, out of sight. Tonight I saw the real man: brave, fearless, determined not to fail.

20 JULY 2011: Who knows what makes people tick? Diary, I seek the answer to this curious human enigma. When it comes to the religion of sport, we seem to lose all reason. I read it in a newspaper today. I watched it broadcast to the world on the late-night news, with disbelief, a numbness of the soul. I still can't believe, or understand it. Skagway Jackson is dead, killed trying to honour the great god of sport by winning. It cost him his life. Burned alive in his racing car during the Spanish Grand Prix, at Cataluña, aged just twenty-two years. Yet another American wonder boy has been taken from us years before his time. What a waste of a life it seems to be. To dance with such danger is to waltz to the grave.

My own bedroom is filled with photographs of such men. Human beings who diced with death each day of their lives. It singled them out from the rest of us mere mortals. For these brave men it gave them the edge over us, in the way they conducted their lives. On my bedroom walls are hung picture after picture of my sporting heroes. Men I admire with a kind of godly worship, reverence. They gaze down on me as if from the safety of a sporting heaven above. They watch over me, guiding me along life's way.

These photographs are dedicated to motor racing. The Grand Prix races, circuits, drivers, lifestyle. Each one committed to leaving their mark on history. If there is nothing on television, I would rather come here to my bedroom to gaze at my pictures in a land of dreams. Just like I'm doing now.

The list of racing drivers is endless to behold. Alberto Ascari, world champion in the early 1950s, killed in a car crash, 1955. Sitting next to him is a picture of Juan Fangio, the Latin hero who drove to his own immortality in 1950, 1951, 1954, 1955, 1956 and 1957. He was a man who could not be beaten in a racing car. Displayed next to him is a photograph of Graham Hill. I go all gooey when I look at his picture on the wall. He above all was a sporting great, winner in 1969 of the Monaco Grand Prix. But Hill was more than just a great racing driver; he was a sporting gentleman. Killed in a plane crash in the early 1970s, Graham

Hill is still missed by all. At the time it was a great loss to sport, the nation, perhaps the world. He died years before his time. Men such as Graham Hill should live forever in the minds of us all. Below Hill hangs a photograph of Brazilian daredevil Ayrton Senna. A god of the last century in motor racing, perhaps sport itself. All of them look down on me, like a divine light from above. Ayrton Senna, more than most from beyond the grave, is encouraging me to go for glory.

Oh, to be that good, to sow the seeds of greatness! I mourn for that dear, darling, departed Brazilian baby, savagely killed during the San Marino Grand Prix in 1994 towards the close of the last century, driving like a hero should, only to be taken from us, sent to his Maker before his time, at the Tamburello Kink. In his beautiful mid thirties, my Brazilian baby should have lived to see his children's children. Died an old contented man. But he watches over me, a face in a photograph, to spur me on in life. To make me feel like I can conquer the world. It says something about life itself when the living seek solace through the dead.

Next to the photograph of Ayrton Senna hangs my current hero of the hour. A man very much in the present tense. A great Spaniard, a Latino winner who cannot lose a race. The Costa Brava lover Tia Madrid. A man I've been in love with for years, ever since I first watched him drive to victory at Istanbul a couple of years ago. Went all weak at the knees when I listened to him speak. Quivered as he smiled to the rest of the world, when winning.

His life has not always been one of glamour or grace, accompanied by wealth beyond good measure. Indeed, he was born to great poverty in a family who had nothing to offer save hope for a better future. A firm belief in the Almighty, he had to fight his way to the top the hard way. Nothing was easy for this man, Diary, I tell you now. His parents slaved as hotel workers for little money. In the summer they had plenty, in winter nothing. After school, with no qualifications to speak of, Tia Madrid went to night school to study, then obtained several good grades, enough to get him through university. Yes, my man has got brains as well as brawn. All the qualities I desire in a man. His brains got him to study civil engineering at Madrid University. But brawn won the day. As his passion for motor racing took over, his rise to power ten years ago was truly meteoric.

As an amateur racing driver Tia raced under his own banner – 'The Spanish Bull' – with great success all over Europe. He attracted attention from America. He was signed up, and the rest, as they say, is history. Every time he won a Grand Prix he was paid a huge bonus. Bolstered by his Spanish good looks, with a charm to match, no hot-blooded woman could resist. I mean, Diary, he can be my lover anytime he wants me. Shout to me, I'll come running – it's that easy. After knocking on the door for a couple of years, he took the first of his world titles a few years ago. Since then nobody can catch him. Unchallenged by his rivals all over the globe. This year will be no different. I'll be cheering him on to victory, kissing his photograph each night before bed, wishing he was mine for real.

There is a problem: he is currently dating a movie star from Hollywood, Peach Diamond. A right slag-bag as far as I'm concerned. He is too good for her by far. The newspapers are full of pictures of them, watched wherever they go. Can't fart without the rest of us having to be told about it. A few days ago, for instance, they attended the premiere in New York of her latest blockbuster, *Say Goodbye to the Wind*. It stars Chuck Winters, alongside little Miss Diamond herself. They say she's great in it, acting the pants off leading man Chuck. Now, that I believe – probably had his pants off for real. Getting paid a fortune into the bargain.

Hollywood has never seen such a devoted couple. Not since Miller loved Monroe, or Silver kissed Hanson-gate, or Merry had Rudolf's love child. They are the talk of the town, and love blossoms on the world's stage yet again. Nobody can deny that simple fact of life. But, Diary, I can dream on, can't I? Will we ever meet, or kiss?

The latest pictures to adorn my walls are those of dashing Lewis Hamilton beside brave, patient Jenson Button. These two men carry on the tradition of these shores, breeding racing drivers. Look at Button. It took him ages to get to the top – head down, don't give up, keep going, world champion. A fine example to us all. That aside, when it comes to Tia such unrequited love must pass for the moment, staying at the fore of my vivid imagination. On Sunday I will sit down glued to the television, cheering him on to victory in the Portuguese Grand Prix. Even if that bitch is at his side, kissing him, holding his hand, smiling to the rest of the world's press. I will still applaud his effort, watch his every move. Only before that comes along this week, I have to endure the return of the family Sunday lunch. A meal I dread. Uncle Iestyn is coming with Aunty Mildred. I must be there to do my bit for the family. If I'm really unlucky they will whisk me off to chapel first thing in the morning.

I had been dreaming of my Spanish hero, when suddenly Dad popped his head around the bedroom door.

"Hi there, apple blossom. Your mum's got the dinner ready.

34

Think you'd better come downstairs." He then walked into my bedroom, sitting on the end of my bed. "Good God, Ann Marie, don't you ever think of anything else?"

I smiled, saying, "No, I guess not, Dad."

With that he looked at some of my pictures, stopping at Tia Madrid's.

"Pity he won't be driving for us next year. I wish."

Then I giggled. "Me too. I can't think of anything else this time of the year. Not much else to do."

He carried on, casual for once: "Guess you don't at that."

There was a kind of puzzling frown about me right then. "But who will drive for us next summer?"

Dad paused for a moment, then answered, "The boss, along with myself, has decided to use a young chap. Met him last fall. He drove to victory in a saloon-car competition during the season. Not the champion, but good sound driving material."

I beamed with delight as I realized just who Dad was talking about. An English dish, a piece of Cornish muscle named Wilson McCain. This man has been good news. I have seen him once, when he came to the office a few months ago for a business conference with the boss. I can't wait to meet him.

Dad got up from my bed, then looked at my pictures hanging on the walls. He gave me a running commentary on all the racing drivers. Some he recalled, others not so much. He told me all about Les Hawksbill, Guy Right, also the lamented James Hunt. Racing drivers who made one shed a tear, like many others, all killed or died long before their time. Risk was all part of their job, part of the game. No risk, no sport. He stopped at the picture of Tia Madrid, inspecting the picture at close quarters. The background, the event, the honour, the man himself.

"Dad," I asked, "will you be going to watch the British Grand Prix at Silverstone, like you said?" I smiled back, hoping for a yes.

"Well, I don't really know for sure, darling." He scratched his head for a moment. "The boss wants to go as a matter of business. I ought to go as well. I mean, I haven't watched the race for a couple of years now, what with one thing or the other."

This time I looked back at him like a pleading dog might. Then, Diary, he gave me the good news.

"Under the circumstances, it would make a fine day out."

As he said those words I jumped in with enthusiastic menace: "I need to see Tia in the flesh, watch him perform, win a Grand Prix."

Then as Dad walked out through the door he turned back to me, saying, "If we don't take you now, we'll never hear the last of it. I guess you've earned a crack at that ruddy man. Tia bloody Madrid indeed. Come now, your mother's calling yet again."

Well, Diary, it's now, fingers crossed, Silverstone here I come.

25 JULY 2011: Well, Diary, what a day this has been! A day full of contradictions. You've guessed it, we all went to chapel today. It was as if all my family had gathered, along with friends, to attend chapel at St David's in the tiny little village of Brontally, high up in the Black Mountains. Most of my family were born there, died there as well, buried underneath the ground forever. I was baptised there. This Sunday we all joined each other in worship. Like many a Welsh chapel, we raised the roof in song, glorifying the Lord the only way we know how. Even the boss, Proctor-Hale, came along with his wife in tow.

It has been a beautiful Midsummer Day. This month has been so hot, it's as if Wales has been moved to the tropics. Today in chapel the heavy wooden doors were left open to let in some fresh air, and above the July heat the wonderful sound of many people singing echoed all over the valley. The melodies of many hymns must've drowned out the sound of sheep bleating, or cows lowing at pasture. This Sunday we were all there, the whole family, the Osborne household, three generations of us, singing our hearts out. Proctor-Hale even got in on the act, singing under his breath for all that. I didn't even know he was religious, didn't realise they needed God too. It surprised me greatly, but they have reason to pray. Perhaps the real reason they attended chapel is that they have something to pray for. I mean I've never known them to go to chapel before, or even church in England. My dad's always believed – now of course more than ever – he needs divine guidance. Like most folk who wish for something out of life, we pray to gods higher than ourselves.

My own thoughts drift in that direction, even at my tender age. I do believe in the Almighty. But my religion goes much deeper than a simple belief in a Greater Power. I celebrated my own gods this afternoon. In the shape of the religion of sport. Motor racing was worshipped, along with Tia Madrid. I speak, Diary, as a little girl, a devout servant, disciple, follower. Lots of other people across the globe will do the same. Pay homage to their heroes. I couldn't wait to sit in my own private chapel, the temple of my bedroom. Cristobel at my side. Sipping red fizzy, or something like it, glued to the television. Watching the Portuguese Grand Prix, cheering Tia Madrid on to certain victory, much like Christ being cheered as He delivered the Sermon on the Mount.

I tried to get Cristobel to come and join us in chapel, but she wouldn't. Dad even invited her, but she does not believe – not that type of girl. She missed a great service. One day she'll go to chapel with me, I told her so on Friday.

"One day, Cristobel, you'll feel the need to be at my side."

But she just laughed it off. Not really her style. That said, the singing, prayers, sermon alike, Father Ponsonby entertained like never before. He preached about the gift of life, the sheer joy of living, of Mother Nature's charm. A true gift from the Almighty Himself.

A packed chapel listened intently to his magical rhetoric. When the service ended, Ponsonby stood by the chapel's wooden door, his white cassock blowing with the then welcome breeze. It blew in time with his white hair as he shook hands with each member of the congregation. Polite exchanges were made as he greeted them. Along with cordial banter about local gossip. Soon a long line of people made their way towards him. A few older members were helped on their way down the front steps of the chapel. It looked like something from Victorian England, another age altogether. But this is the magic of rural Wales for you. I adore it very much. As I stood in line, waiting for my turn, it was as if time had stood still for 100 years plus. I couldn't see any cars. They were parked behind the chapel, out of sight. The only thing missing was a carriage with horses.

Back home the ritual of Sunday lunch was observed in fine detail. From the soup to the beef, the sweet course to the cheese, fruit, tea or coffee. Aunty Mildred was in excellent form; so was Uncle Iestyn. The family history was laid bare regarding Sunday lunch.

"The family was always together for Sunday lunch. Nobody was allowed to miss it. I hanker for the old days. People eat in separate rooms nowadays – they don't talk any more. When I was a little girl Sunday was special, but not any more – very sad."

Aunty Mildred's outburst was nothing new. She said the same thing almost every week after chapel. As we ate our lunch we expected it; so did the dog, I swear.

When it was over, the family made their way to the patio as it was such a lovely day. Sitting outside we enjoyed with relish the beauty of a Welsh Sunday afternoon. Council estate it might be, but the view from our back garden is stunning, something any castle or palace would envy. To one side the city of Cardiff, to the other the green mountains of South Wales stretch way across the horizon, seemingly without end.

As the afternoon wore on, they played some poker, talked

about many things, some important, others trivial. At two I went into the kitchen to help Mum do the washing-up. She was glad of my help – even more so as I volunteered to do it. I wasn't asked by her. I used my savvy, knowing she would leave me alone to watch television. I tell you, Diary, I'm not stupid. I know the score. As I dried the dishes I kept my eye longingly on the wall clock hung up on the far wall. It ticked by ever so slowly, like waiting for eternity. Mum was fair pleased with my efforts. There are times when I've got that woman right under my thumb. But then it struck two on the dot, a sound from heaven above. Then a carafe of red wine was taken outside, plus a flagon of ale. Placed on a wooden table for all to consume. With the heat of the afternoon, the cards, the poker, they were well pissed by the time the lights went on for the race to begin.

The Grand Prix could not come quickly enough for me. At just after two the doorbell sounded. It was Cristobel. In jeans, a dirty sweater, dirty shoes, along with bubblegum, plus a bottle with something in it. I don't mean tea either. Exchanging pleasantries we went to my bedroom.

The race was just about to begin when I turned on the television set. This is indeed my temple, a time to worship gods, heroes, losers alike. It made no difference to me at all. Tia Madrid may be the flavour of the month, but, to me at least, all racing drivers are brave, fearless men, heroes all. Nobody would see my wrath today, no matter what they did or where they finished in the race. They all deserved praise of the finest. Cristobel cheered them on with me, from the start to the finish. The dog followed us up to the bedroom, then lay down on the bed, and we both sat next to him. Soon we sat down on the floor, relaxed at ease. The small bedroom window was left slightly open, enough to allow us to hear the chatter of the people below in the garden.

"That's it – I fold," shouted Dad.

"I'll raise you ten!" exclaimed Aunty Mildred with glee. She was obviously holding a winning hand.

Cristobel opened her backpack, producing a bottle of lemonade. My heart missed a beat.

"It's the usual, girl," she said.

Like I would not know this! It was vodka laced with lemonade. Hidden neatly inside a plain bottle, with no label on it. Why, it could've been any damn thing. All I needed was for my dad to walk in, then catch us right in the act of taking a swig of the stuff.

"Wow, Cristobel, it's a little strong today."

I shuddered as it hit the back of my throat. But television makes the insane sane. The Portuguese Grand Prix was about to start. The lights changed, the cars raced away down the circuit. The race was on.

Just before the race started Tia Madrid had been interviewed on television. A part of the pre-race build-up. Standing there before the rest of the world, me included. He spoke; I melted. My heart pounded against my chest. My new bra almost broke free from my body. I could have given myself to him, girl to hero. As Tia spoke he gently ran his fingers through his black Spanish hair. My God, don't do that. Stop it. But that's pin-ups for you, Diary. A fantasy lover – somebody to admire.

It was lap three and Tia was in second place as Cristobel tried to light her first cigarette. I had to shout at her, quietly of course. I mean two schoolgirls getting drunk, smoking their heads off was not on. One sin too many. Having the odd sip of booze, then hiding it with mints to camouflage the breath afterwards – we could get away with it no problem. After all, we'd done it many times before. But smoking? Piles of ash-filled cups are not on at all. I have told her about it before, but it just won't sink in. Cristobel's my best friend in the world, but she can be a bad influence sometimes. Having said all that, I'm no saint, for sure. This afternoon, though, common sense prevailed. She put the cigarettes away. We just sipped drink as the race unfolded.

Tia Madrid overtook Hitchcroft on a tight bend. After lap two he drove like a man possessed, full throttle all the way. Cristobel screamed his name along with me, lap after lap. We cheered him on to victory.

"Ann, what's going on up there?"

I responded by hanging my head out of the bedroom window. "Tia's gonna win, Dad. They'll never catch him now."

This afternoon Tia Madrid won the Portuguese Grand Prix in fine style. My dad joined us in my bedroom to watch the last couple of laps. Indeed, he cheered louder than us two, all the way to the chequered flag. This means that Tia's moved ten points clear of his nearest rival, Marvin Burger from the USA. Again I implored Dad to take me to the British Grand Prix so I might see my hero in the flesh. Seeing him perform on the television and drooling over his pictures on the bedroom walls just isn't the same. I know he's going with the boss, so they could take me too – in fact, a trip for the family, Mum as well. It could easily be arranged.

Well, Diary, once again fingers crossed.

31 JULY 2011: It happened, Diary, just like I dreamed it would. I will never wash my face again, so long as I live. Today has been a day I will treasure until the sun freezes over. I felt like a devout Catholic attending the Vatican for the first time to pay homage to the Pope, God's ambassador on earth. Ever since Tuesday morning, when Dad told me the good news, I have had a trembling sensation inside my stomach, all aquiver. Unable to eat or sleep, or stand still. Drooling over my pictures on the walls for hour upon hour. Ah yes, like a Catholic off to meet the pontiff, or a Christian off to Canterbury Cathedral, or a rock fan off to a gig. I have been to the sacred place of worship. Dad made good his promise today. The whole family's attended the British Grand Prix at Silverstone. I went to the temple; I saw my god, who did not let me down. I am more devout than ever, a follower to the grave. Today I saw, met, conversed with, then kissed Tia Madrid. Life can be so good sometimes. This has been a wonderful day to be alive.

Right from the start the day has been perfect. One that will live in the memory forever. To make matters even better, I have some photographs to help prove my point in the future. My own children will one day know all about the glory of today. Personally though, I see here inspiration for the future. Watching Tia has given me a huge boost of self-confidence. I want to drive more than ever. I am addicted to speed. The faster the better. Indeed, on the journey back home I found myself racing in my dreams, right up until the brakes locked on our front driveway.

"Come on, smarty pants, it's time to get out of that pit. We'll leave without you. Dog's up." Dad then Mum yelled at the top of their voices in a desperate bid to get me up, out of bed.

But they needn't have worried. I had been wide awake for hours. Sleep had been impossible for me, the excitement of the impending day just too much for me to handle. Truth be told, I had been lying on my bed since three, dreaming of the day ahead. The whole week has been spent with my head up in the clouds. The anticipation of meeting my sporting hero, Tia Madrid, keeping me alive for the night. I kept clock-watching. This made the night tick by even slower. A contrast to the entire day, which has flown by too quickly. But isn't that the way of the world? When you enjoy life it simply races by – you don't even notice it. Time drags when you don't.

Tippy, my faithful old dog, was the first living thing to greet me with any kind of affection. I made a fuss of him, and he returned that affection with licks to the face, the way dogs do. It made me feel good, smile, then leap out of bed to face this wonderful day. My clothes had been laid out the night before.

A denim suit, coupled with black knee-high boots. Cristobel said she would dress the same way. She arrived here to join me at eight, then the day really did begin.

I arrived downstairs for breakfast, washed, perfumed, ready for action on the sporting front.

But I found my nerves so bad I couldn't eat a thing, despite Mum's protest. Only the welcome arrival of Cristobel made me settle down. We both went to the lounge, then pored over the sports pages of the national press. Tia was everywhere to be seen, spread all over the back pages. He was gloriously photographed driving his car, saluting victory on the podium, lying on a beach, then just smiling at the camera. I kissed his face on the newspaper. Held him close to my breast, like a mother with a baby. Soon I would see him in the flesh, so to speak. A delightful prospect.

I guess we had been dreaming, swooning over those pictures for perhaps one whole hour when the cry came volleying up the stairs from Mum: "Come on, you two. Mr Proctor-Hale's arrived."

I looked out of my bedroom window, numbed by what I saw. A jet-black Bentley had been parked outside our front gate. At the end of our driveway stood a liveried chauffeur. He stood by the open door of the car. I have never, Diary, seen anything like it before in my life. Along with the chauffeur it appeared out of place here. It belonged up the West End, or Mayfair perhaps. The entire estate seemed to be there. They watched, talked, joked, pointed to the car itself. Men, women, children, even their dogs became enraptured by the strange, overpowering event taking place down our street. It was as if the whole estate had come to bid us a fond farewell, wishing us a good day out. Mr Proctor-Hale had come to collect us. Then drive us all the way to Northamptonshire – to Silverstone – making sure we travelled in style. We'd be coming home the same way. Ah yes! I could tell this would be a day to remember.

As we reached the shiny black car, a woman's voice caught my attention: "Gone up in the bloody world, haven't we?" It was old Mrs Pritchard from across the street. Her deep gruff Welsh voice boomed all over the drive as she inspected the car. Then roamed her eye over the handsome young chauffeur. I could tell she quite fancied him, as I did too. Even Cristobel told me the same. One of the trappings of success, your very own chauffeur. As for my dad, this was a busman's holiday to treasure. For the ultra-rich Proctor-Hale, money was no object, no expense spared. Everything had been laid on for our own comfort. Picnic hampers, along with chilled champagne, had been included. It was unreal, Diary, I can tell you. An old-fashioned day out in the country.

As we all climbed into the Bentley it might have been the royal family leaving Windsor Castle, or arriving for a state occasion someplace, never mind our street.

I even found myself waving to onlookers, like the Queen herself. I mean, as if she'd visit our dirty old street!

'Tia, my darling,' I thought, 'I'm on my way.'

The journey to Silverstone was uneventful for all that. Dad talked business with Proctor-Hale, as if we weren't even in the same car. Mum read, then engaged in small talk with Mrs Proctor-Hale. As for me, I just sat there daydreaming about the day ahead, while Cristobel slept. The chauffeur just drove the Bentley in silence, mile after mile. Indeed, the man hardly said a word all day. Only speaking when commanded to do so. I did not blame him. I mean, he looked so neat, tidy-like, just doing his job. A job he did do well.

We arrived at Silverstone at lunchtime. A picnic was had by us all. I ate, then drank myself silly. Dad even allowed me to taste some wine; so did Cristobel. The excitement at finally being there was too much. The atmosphere electric, like a disease. Silverstone was alive with people. A sporting carnival prevailed. I saw people singing, dancing, drinking, eating. We passed a man Bible-thumping. This young man of God stood upon a soapbox overcome with the spirit of the Lord in his soul. He told all who would listen to him about the evil of the motor car. That Jesus Christ Himself only needed a donkey. How we should walk for God. A crowd gathered to hear him out. Nobody laughed, except me. Yes, it seemed as if the entire human race had converged upon this hallowed ground. A busker sang close to where we stood. She played a guitar, then sang a beautiful song about peace, love and drugs. I threw some change into a battered old straw hat laid by her feet. Why, Diary, I think it must have been the same thousands of years ago, as the Greeks descended on the site of Olympia for the sacred games. I have never been to such a sporting event before today. Most sport is watched on television, which is simply not the same. Crazy television commentators take away the magic with their overexcited rantings, fast speech, unwise words. I mean, like the general public cannot work it out for themselves!

When the feasting was over, it was off to the grandstand to watch the race. Dad, along with the boss, spent most of the time debating the pros about their own motor-racing future. Occasionally well-dressed men in dark suits stood or sat next to them. They shook hands, laughed, joked or appeared wrapped in thought. Something very important must've been discussed. But when the time came, Dad accompanied us to our seats. We had prime positions, right opposite the starting grid. The chequered flag would be waved right next to us. I had a seat at the end of a row, so I had an unhindered view of the race. As I sat down next to Cristobel, sipping Coke, munching crisps, I was overcome with joy. Across on the grid a long line of brightly coloured racing cars stood regally, waiting for the off. Then suddenly there he was, standing right in front of me. He was in pole position, wearing a light-blue jumpsuit, surrounded by the press. It was Tia Madrid himself. I nearly choked on the barbecue sauce. It was wonderful to behold.

He must have been stood there for at least five long minutes, interviewed for Spanish television. I don't think I blinked once. I just stared back at him. My lap was a carpet of crisps – I kept missing my mouth. Cristobel was in the selfsame trance. When the interview finished, he turned, then waved to his adoring fans, me included. Instantly, I returned the wave to him, blowing a kiss as I did so. Then he got into his racing car.

Cristobel turned, then looked at me. "Well, Amo, what do you think of him now?"

For at least one second I was lost for words – I swooned in my seat, Diary.

"I'm gonna hug him, then float away up in the clouds," I replied, almost in tears. Then excitement took over. A loud chorus of screaming took over. "Slam 'em, baby." I must've repeated myself twice over, hoping he'd hear me.

As I sang out, Silverstone came alive. The lights changed and the cars roared off the grid, down the circuit. The British Grand Prix commenced in earnest.

Travelling at extreme speed around the circuit, the cars raced past us for lap after lap. My hero Tia was overtaken just once during the race, after his second pit stop, by unknown Lance Willis from New Zealand. At lap thirty-four, by Woodcote, Tia regained the lead. He stayed there in first place, unchallenged, until the finish. Each time he drove by the grandstand, both Cristobel and myself broke into wild fanatical cheering. As if we were devoted fans on the terraces on a Saturday at a home match. The afternoon wore on, and in no time at all it was the final lap. Glory approached.

There was a buzz amongst the spectators. All heads turned to the final bend as the two lead cars approached. We could hear, but not see them coming. My heart pounded, I felt nervous, I held my breath.

Dad placed his hands on my shoulders, as if to steady me, then whispered softly, "Here he comes, Ann Marie, just for you."

Then in the far distance two black shapes came into view. The heat of the July day shimmered in a haze above the circuit as the two cars raced towards the chequered flag. They seemed locked together, engine to engine. Then as the two black shapes got closer, ever closer, it became apparent that Tia Madrid was going to win. I jumped up from my seat, cheering my hero home to victory. The flag dropped, I went berserk – we all did. I hugged Cristobel. It felt great.

With the lap of honour completed, Tia Madrid held aloft his trophy for all it was worth. He basked in his glory before the sporting press. It was what happened afterwards that took my breath away. It was unexpected – a bonus for my girlish pride. Tia opened the traditional bottle of champagne, spraying all who stood in front of him. Then he walked towards his adoring fans in the grandstand. Oh yes, yes! Diary, you've guessed it: Tia Madrid, champion of the world, walked directly towards little old me. I stood there rooted to the spot as this dish of a man came to celebrate yet another motor-racing victory. The fans cheered wildly, his jet-black hair, light-blue jumpsuit then wrapped itself against me as I hugged him. He felt warm, smelt divine. He thanked me as he kissed me full on the right cheek. Dad took a photograph; Mum followed me in this adoration of a sporting hero. We could not help ourselves – why should we?

It has been the greatest summer day of my life to date. Twenty-four wonderful hours to savour.

We drove back from Silverstone in the Bentley, arriving home in Cardiff at one in the morning. The whole family was tired, yet in good spirits. Also, Diary, I will tell you a secret: I have not washed my face tonight. I can still feel Tia's tender Spanish lips against my cheeks. I may never wash my face again.

16 AUGUST 2011: Well, Diary, I scored a few points for myself today. It poured with rain all day long, and sad to say I spent most of the day watching television. All hell's broken loose all over Britain – civil unrest creeps about like an unwanted visitor. Parts of London, Manchester, Birmingham, Bristol, plus a few other cities burn. Huge crowds have gone on the rampage, looting, mugging, causing havoc, fear. A sense of hopelessness prevails. Some of the things I witnessed appear out of place here – they should be happening somewhere else, not here in Britain. It made me think – my mum agrees with me on that at least. As a result ordinary hard-working folk have had their lives turned upside down. Politicians tell us the nation's broken. I say they are wrong, millions of miles off course. Wrote a poem about it after dinner, read it to Tippy. When school returns I'll show it to Mrs Bell.

In Praise of Glorious Britain

A nation at five in the morning, waking to the rising sun.
Half the world wants to live here, the other speak our tongue.
Yet we keep talking ourselves down,
Telling the world about our plight.
We are a sparkling jewel in the world's crown,
So we must be doing something right.
In this precious land the good must always beat the bad.
The happy triumph over the sad.
Pass this message down the years,
Then there'll be no room for people's tears.
A land lived in by the good.
From now on until the world ends, just like it should.
Indeed, the rest of the world is smitten,
In love with glorious Britain.

Not Shakespeare, but I like it.

24 DECEMBER 2011: Christmas Eve arrived again in style, as befits her. What a wonderful year this has been for me. In school, not so good; outside her gates, aceamundo-fabulosa-brilliantini. Oh yes, Diary, a fitting description of a mixed-up year of contradictions. Perhaps one for the record books. My school suffered, as my wild streak took over in full. The tomboy image, which I confess I love, rose up to rebel, as never before. But, privately, I believe I triumphed.

It must be said that my schoolwork and the reports last summer were appalling, but in two subjects, at least, I excelled. With some pride I must state I became top of the class in both religion and history. This much to the surprise of both my parents. Dad was over the moon, Mum dumbfounded.

Dad said, "My girl, I'm right proud of you."

This remark made me sit up, then smile all day long. Indeed, from Dad a compliment to treasure. It made me feel so good. At school an achievement that was rare. Rare, because I'm not academically minded. It was so unexpected of me. But it didn't do me any good at all. I ask a question that needs answering right now, today, tonight even: just how do you measure somebody's intelligence? How can we judge a fellow human being? Like me, so young, naïve, with all my life ahead of me. I fell into this trap, hook, line, sinker.

Over the last twelve months I have been called everything, by all people – a genius, a smart female, bright, intelligent, as well as lazy, stupid, boring, tough, sweet, sour, smelly, a bully, an animal, a thick bastard with no future and a child with all to live for. For heaven's sake I am just eleven years old. How can I be called all these things? Where am I going? It is so confusing for me. Who must I listen to? Myself? Spend the rest of my life talking to myself in the bedroom mirror? Maybe.

Maths has always been a weakness for me. A subject I find hard to absorb. I don't have a head for figures. Besides, the teacher's constantly bugging me, picking on my very soul. He knows I can't add up. He scares me. I have never seen such an evil, bigoted man on this earth. He has a size-nine boot displayed on his desk – woe betide the child who does not answer correctly. That would always put the fear of death inside me. I would simply clam up, go all silly, silent, brooding. Whenever he asked me a mathematical problem, I would always feel he was picking on me, knowing I could not answer, getting it wrong in front of the entire class. Why, Diary, over the last year how many times has that dreadful man called me stupid? Far too many, I feel. But just who is he to judge? During the past year at school he's said it so many times that sometimes I've found myself believing him. At times to my own detriment. Leaving the classroom a quivering wreck. But on the same day, perhaps within the hour, I might find another teacher – Mrs Beck, say, who teaches religious study – praising me for being so intelligent. She might pull me out in front of the class to read from the Bible. Then she'll let the rest of the world know what a fine sage of intellect I've turned out to be. I find this see-sawing of emotion tiresome in the extreme. Throughout the entire year that is how life has been for me.

Putting school aside, life has been nothing short of ecstatic. A personal truth about myself has been told, even at my young age. It puts that maths teacher firmly in his place. Sure I've got brains and bravery along with beauty. During last summer I made sure the world saw it in full. Dad allowed me to compete in four go-kart races, here in Cardiff, at Bristol, and also, for something different, a fresh challenge, Swindon. I lost in Cardiff – could only finish sixth, driving poorly. I lacked the dash of old. But across in Bristol I hammered the English boys, destroying them again in Swindon. I have the photograph of me on the front page of the *Herald*, looking good, holding the trophy aloft. The headline reads 'A CLASS ACT FROM WALES'. It is now framed, hanging on my bedroom wall, over my bed. I join my racing heroes at last. The picture will inspire me from now on, drive me on to greater glory. Who needs teachers now? Not me, for sure. Ah yes, as a young racing driver, on the up, I held my own behind the wheel. I want, demand, more next year of just the same. The thing is, Diary, nobody from school, not a fellow pupil, not a single teacher, not the headmaster, or that fucking maths teacher, knows anything about it. Only my friend Cristobel bothered to help out, be with me, care. God knows what I'd have done without her. A true mate, for sure. My dog was always there as well, to cuddle, kiss, walk with, no matter what

As usual the whole family attended Midnight Mass tonight. It did not disappoint. The candlelight service was wonderful to be part of. For days before, I tried in vain to coax Cristobel to come and join me. Being a non-believer, she tactfully declined the offer. She missed a heart-moving service.

She told me frankly, "I don't need God, Jesus, or heaven on any day of the year."

Even Dad failed to convince her to change her mind. Getting the normal response from her. I worried about her, where she was, what she might be doing. I guess she hung about the streets, stole a bottle of something. Yes, even tonight at her age pissed on Christmas Eve. But she will still give me a present, wish me a happy Christmas for all that.

By the way, Diary, *Nadolig Llawin*.

2012

14 FEBRUARY 2012: Changes come, changes go, but I keep rolling on. This is my twelfth birthday, yet my body appears as twice that age. So does my attitude. Not a patch of puppy fat to be seen anywhere. Long blonde locks complement the rest of me. Oh yes, I'm ready for action – can't wait to be twenty.

This morning I told the dog; now I'm telling you, Diary. I swear there are times when I seem like a woman on the move, growing up fast. A girl going places in a blind hurry, but where? But the events of tonight simply speed, enhance, that forthcoming day by a couple of years. Let me explain. The deceit, the naughtiness, added to the pleasure. I arranged it all, along with Cristobel weeks beforehand. She has nerves of steel, stealing two bottles of cider from Mrs Grant's store this afternoon. We then proceeded to meet up with some friends from school, down by the river. This for sure was a school piss-up like no other. There must've been at least six of us – three boys, three girls, just the right mix. The other kids brought stolen bottles with them as well. The night was young, the lies old, well rehearsed. Spending the evening with Cristobel at her house. My dad even kissed me goodbye.

"Have a good night, my petal."

Well, I did for sure. For once I did not care about whether I hurt them or let them down. I needed to explode. This has been a night for living life in the fast lane. The weather might have been rainy, inclement, but I was hot for adventure. I behaved like the local wench, a weasel. A slag, as they say. Since my victories on the go-kart circuit, I have become famous. Most of the boys at school fancy me a lot. They will do anything to date me. Every time a good-looking boy makes a pass at me, I take full advantage – even at my tender age, I know the score. Cristobel arranges it for me, like a minder. This was the purpose of tonight's gathering.

Meeting down by the river in a disused workman's hut. The weather might have been foul – cold, windy, the remnants of a bad storm passed by – but inside the wooden hut we were warm, lively, bursting with energy. My clothes became the centre of attention. Grass could not take his eyes off me. My fame, power, intimidating all around me. I tell you now, Diary, my friend, when I dress right I breathe sexuality. If I can do this now, what the hell's it going to be like when I'm eighteen? I could pull anybody from Neath to Holyhead. Grass was scared stiff of me. I love this power. It is marvellous. Tomorrow I'll be the most talked-about girl in school, when word of this gets out. Ah, the price of fame.

24 MARCH 2012: I looked out of my window this morning with some alarm. It was pissing it down – cats, dogs, monkeys, the lot. Why, it seemed as if the Welsh monsoon season was upon us. Indeed, it was the loud crackling of rain against the windowpane that woke me up. Along with the dog asleep next to me on the bed.

The day looked like being a complete washout. Yet that was far from the truth. Today has in fact been wonderful, fun to be a part of it. Another driving lesson, given by Dad, followed by daydreams aplenty, backed up by love. This afternoon I saw a dish, a dream guy indeed. I couldn't take my eyes off him. His name is Wilson McCain. Today he started work for Dad, as a driver-cum-mechanic. So I'll be seeing much more of him. Why, I do believe Cupid's arrow struck me clean through my heart.

Wilson McCain is eight years older than myself. A rare talent behind the wheel of a racing car. He has been signed up by Dad, with the backing of the boss, to drive for their team, the Welsh

Dragon. A build-up to their goal: Formula One. He arrived at the garage this afternoon, dressed as if off to the office in the city. A dark pinstripe suit with matching shirt, tie, shoes. His shoes had shiny brass buckles on them. With his neatly combed hair, and a white handkerchief worn in his top pocket, he cut a fine handsome figure – a man any woman, or girl, would swoon for, be bowled over at a chance to be with him. I know that I felt that way.

McCain himself has a very impressive background in motor racing, as a junior champion then family-saloon winner. He has won sixteen of his twenty-three starts in all forms of competition. Now, according to my dad, he will be groomed to be the first Welsh motor-racing World Champion. Tough words from a man with unbending commitment to the future. A belief that will not change.

As my dad told the press, "He will put Wales firmly on the sporting map."

Yes, there is much talk about this boy. No denial of his fine young talent behind the wheel of a racing car. Dad, along with the rest of the team, is right behind him. Proctor-Hale has invested well over £10 million of his own fortune to be the best in the world. Much faith is now placed on their brand-new racing car, along with the ability of their driver, to deliver the goods. The question being asked now is will he cut the mustard? In my own humble opinion – I want to date him already – this boy has great lips that need to be kissed, with a body that yearns to be hugged. I am just the lady to oblige.

There are times when my dad can be both the best and also the worst driving instructor ever put on this earth. All in the space of just one eternal hour. For that was what happened this afternoon.

One minute he'd be singing my praises behind the wheel. Then screaming blue murder at me the next. At times he could be quite monstrous towards me. He almost made me get out of the car, break down then cry. But I will not let this shit bully me. I will stand up to anything he delivers with his big mouth. This evening at just after five I did just that. I think he felt a little lost, unsure at the retaliation. For a spilt second he had no answer to my outburst. I don't need to listen to his bully-boy tactics – just tell me how to drive the blessed car, I'm not deaf.

After school, Diary, as usual I took a walk down to the garage to meet him. All the employees had already gone home, save one guy, Wilson McCain himself. It was love at first sight, I swear. A meeting had been held that afternoon in my dad's office, where the future of Welsh motor racing had been discussed. The plans for the Welsh Dragon's next twelve months had been talked about at great length. Where it should go, together with the financial package offered. Proctor-Hale chaired the meeting himself, but he'd gone by the time I'd arrived. Only Dad with Leyth Swain remained, Wilson standing aloof. As I walked into the office, all three greeted me, including Wilson. I do believe our eyes met for the first time, across the table strewn with all manner of papers, notes, pens and used coffee cups by the score. Surprisingly, Wilson McCain, this great big hunk of a man, who has all the signs of a Hollywood star about him, reached for a packet, then lit up, inhaling deeply, forcing me to fall in love with him right away. Two empty beer cans could be seen.

"Come, Ann Marie. This is my daughter." Dad gestured towards the end of the table, beckoning me.

I walked towards him. He cuddled me proudly.

I went all shy, embarrassed, just managing to whisper, "Hi, Daddy," in a barely audible voice. Then it all happened, as never before. Wilson came a shade closer to me, then kissed the back of my hand. This act of gallantry made me blush, then giggle. For the first time in many days, I was lost for words.

"Wilson's going to drive for us over the next five years. We signed him up today, my dear – a time for celebration. All we need now is a glorious summer."

Wilson held my hand a little after he'd kissed it, saying, "That's right, young lady. The Welsh Dragon's now well on the way to winning." He then winked, looking at me out of the corner of his eye.

Dad's an eternal dreamer – I guess when you dream this big you have to be. Sport does not listen to wimps, or the fickle. It takes no prisoners. Only the brave survive, to win at their pleasure. Who knows where the dream will end up, or where the Welsh Dragon will go. In that office, at least, everyone was full of hope.

"I'm taking this girl of mine for a driving lesson over at Sea View Heights," said my dad.

Wilson smiled, saying, "Why, we have something in common, young lady. Perhaps I'll be able to give you a lesson myself one day?"

Dad laughed, then nodded in agreement. Wow, a driving lesson by my dream guy. It seemed a surreal fantasy at that moment. A dream I look forward to very much though.

The driving lesson that followed was something like a pleasant drive in the countryside on a Sunday afternoon. It started out so well. As we drove, it gave me strength, making me feel good. For Sea View Heights is the name of a remote farm, way up in the hills overlooking Cardiff Bay. Dad drove towards Castell Coch, arriving at the long farm track just after six, at which time we changed places. This put me firmly in the driving seat, where I belong. The grassy track then winds its way for at least two or three miles, along the borders of a sheep farm. The grassy track hugs the edge of two huge fields, all of them filled with lush green grass, with perhaps hundreds, maybe thousands, of sheep. Most of them were peacefully grazing on the lush green grass carpeting each of the fields. Then I arrived, destroying this peaceful setting of rural Wales at her very best.

I drove slowly at first along the pathway. Sheep to the left scattered in all directions, bleating in protest at having been disturbed. Soon it will be lambing time, when these fields will be filled with young lambs. A time for living, not dying. More than once as I drove along the track a pregnant ewe refused to move out of the way, forcing me to slow down to avoid hitting her, using the car's horn to send her on her way. It was at about this point I changed gear, thrusting the car to hit a steady forty. Dad went ape – abuse followed – but I smiled, putting my foot down hard to the floor. Showing off, I guess! The car skidded to a halt, sending him into a rage, yelling at me louder than ever. I didn't know so many four letter words existed. He accused me of being careless behind the wheel. Yet, after putting me through the same lecture several times on the virtues of careful speed, he allowed me to drive back to the farm gate, by the main road. He even let me do a magical twenty miles per hour. This, Diary, was great. My imagination told me I was at Brands Hatch, Silverstone or Monaco, winning a Grand Prix, fans going wild for my victory.

Dad drove us home in peace, thank God. He's a good old sod really. Another lesson next week, Diary. I'll try to be careful next time, I promise.

19 JUNE 2012: Dear Diary, I had this weird dream that I was stuck in a lift with Her Majesty the Queen. One of us farted. I knew it wasn't me; she knew it wasn't me. We both knew it was her. I took full responsibility, received a birthday honour, became Dame of the British Empire for services to the crown, appeared on the front pages and was interviewed on the television. Does this mean anything?

Dame Ann Marie Osborne!

15 JULY 2012: Oh, Diary, my friend, this has been a bad day. I will be glad when it's tomorrow. School reports came out today. It didn't make good reading at all. I did not come out of it at all well. In fact Dad went bazooka when he read what school said about me. All his aspirations were shot to pieces. My intellect has fallen well short of the intended target. To be perfectly honest, Diary, I couldn't give a monkey's foreskin.

Right now school does not mix well with me at any time of the day. This morning my parents both studied my school report with horror. Dad was most displeased with my whole approach. I failed in all subjects: stone bottom in mathematics, rock bottom in all others. The only subject I had shown any interest in had been history. Indeed, two essays submitted during the past year had scored high marks, getting A or B grades. So there was some light at the end of the tunnel. These essays had been about the history of sport around these shores. Motor racing goes without saying, but football, rugby and athletics all got a mention too. We don't do all that bad really – champions aplenty. It brought out the best in me, allowing my imagination and intellect, backed up by a desire to do well, to shine like never before. Only this morning even this achievement was overlooked.

Dad called me lazy, undisciplined, without order. "You've let me down again. I don't know how you dare bring this muck home. It's nonsense, all of it, girl. Fancy allowing me to even read it. I can't think why you didn't throw it away in the nearest bin, where it belongs." With that he threw it back in my face, leaving the room.

Only the dog seemed to understand, or care.

"I've done my best – what more do you want from me?"

Dad poked his head from behind the door, saying, "A lot more, Ann Marie. A lot more."

He slammed the door shut, making me feel useless, a failure. To be told this sort of thing at my age can't be right, or just. But one day I'll show them all, you'll see, Diary. Just stick around.

19 AUGUST 2012: Well, Diary, like you I have earned a holiday. Soon you will be glad to know we will both be off to the South of France for our annual vacation. Up to no good all over again, just the two of us. As the Olympic Games thunders on in London, we have more important things to dwell upon. The German Grand Prix comes up soon – Dad can't think of anything else. Wilson's silent, brooding, no time for me at all. For the next couple of weeks he can get stuffed. Cristobel's just as excited as myself about the coming holiday ahead. Time away from sport, but one thing must be mentioned, Diary: good news from London. Otis Carlyle stormed to victory in the steeplechase, a fine performance by him to win gold.

But the only gold that matters to me is that when I return

home to Cardiff a golden brown will be the colour of my skin, after weeks of loyal sunbathing.

You bet, Diary.

21 AUGUST 2012: This week the summer holiday kicks into full swing. We are staying at the plush home of the boss, at the coastal resort of Vallon on the Côte d'Azur, in the South of France. It is a wonderful place, like nothing else on earth. A white marble palace set against the impressive blue backdrop of the Mediterranean Sea. I love the place, always engulfed with hundreds of flowers, alongside green foliage. A sweet scent hangs in the air, the aroma spellbinding. Whenever our family stay here, it feels as if we are the guests of royalty. We visit here at least once a year. Beats Port Talbot any day.

We arrived here last Thursday – two more weeks to go, a time to savour. But this year is different. The family is taking the vacation in the middle of the motor-racing season. In fact, Dad has been away for most of the time, like a politician dealing with affairs of state. Tonight he attended a private dinner dance at the house, hosted by the Proctor-Hales. All their family was there tonight, as ordered by the boss. But I enjoyed it all the same. We all got dressed up – it was truly a fine, sumptuous evening. It went on well into the night. I loved it all. In the morning Dad will leave again for the German Grand Prix, along with the rest of the team. Only things aren't going at all well for the Welsh Dragon. All that bullshit at the beginning of the year, all that investment, the promise of greater things to come! To date, after ten races, all have been lost. What is more, we've been well beaten to boot. Not even getting on the podium.

Faces may be glum, pride hurt on the circuit, yet here in this paradise on earth I count my blessings. All I have to look forward to is lazy days down by the pool, drinks on the beach, eyeing the local boys, keeping my tan nicely brown and listening to rock music all afternoon. Cristobel has joined me. I could have gone to Germany – I was invited, declining the offer. There is a time and a place for all that stuff; not now, Diary. I may be still just twelve years old, but my body grows daily into adulthood. Two young women on the loose – those poor French boys don't know what's coming their way.

Before I go into what happened at dinner tonight, I must tell you, Diary, about Cristobel – what she did this afternoon down on the beach. It was decadent, indecent. The kind of thing frowned upon back home in Wales. Not here in France. Yes, she went nude; so did I, following her every move. We joined perhaps a couple of hundred other people lying on the sand all afternoon, like a couple of wealthy aristocratic young ladies. It was great, paying homage to the sun.

At six o'clock this evening we found ourselves back at the big white house, getting ready for this posh dinner. The guests arrived at about eight, sitting down for dinner at nine. Dinner was taken outside on the patio, under a star-studded night sky, sickle moon almost above us. The food was posh too, in accord with the mood of the evening. There was serious sporting talk over dinner, where a rescue stratagem for the Welsh Dragon was put forward. Several people of importance were there, including Wilson, Proctor-Hale with his good wife, and Swain, along with the boys. A working dinner, you might say. My parents sat together, opposite Wilson, leaving Cristobel with me, as good as unnoticed by everyone else, to get on with our dinner.

The food was so good that motor racing was not on my mind. I know for a fact, Diary, the panic button has been pressed. Proctor-Hale is in turmoil over the millions of his own money that he's ploughed into this venture. Right now that all seems like a bad investment. A poor risk indeed to have made. The best place achieved to date is tenth, coming at a rain-sodden Swedish Grand Prix, held at Malmö. I went along to watch, cheer them on. It was awful to behold. The racing car with all its supposed technical advances simply didn't perform. Wilson McCain is doing his level best, but he can only do what the car allows him. He has taken some flak over his performances as the number-one driver. I feel sorry for him; my heart pours out for his soul. Tonight the bare bones were laid out at the dinner table.

As they ate, then talked, Cristobel along with myself tucked into this dinner, served by a butler. I wore a white summer frock, Cristobel a red one. The food consisted of the following menu: clear onion soup, followed by lamb Napoleon and raspberry soufflé washed down with Challon champagne or Rhône wine – the local brew. It was great fare indeed. I crammed two plates of the stuff into my hungry gob, empty belly. The trouble came as I daintily shoved another mouthful down my throat, when Dad almost broke down, weeping like a baby.

To my surprise Wilson hardly said a word all night. The occasional mumble was all we could get out of him. He ignored me altogether. Proctor-Hale did most of the talking, worried more about the money than anything else. I guess you can't blame him for that. The car's performance was then taken apart piece by piece, with no answers offered save that the Welsh Dragon must soldier on regardless. Perhaps next year would be better – hope raised eternal. It was just then that my dad's nerve faltered, as a man about to break down. Another mouthful tickled my palate, the crisp pastry mingled with the lamb, herbs, mint. I sipped another glass of champagne as a lady might at Windsor. Then the evening was brought to a standstill by Dad.

It made me feel awkward in the room – I don't know how Mum felt. But the gruff Welsh voice, speaking with such passion, emotion, made all listen to his every word.

"I can't believe how badly things have gone. All the hope, the dreams, the vision – where have they gone? If Germany doesn't work out, it's back to the drawing board for us. Oh, God in heaven, are You listening to me? Where shall we go for our Welsh sporting salvation? Give me the answer?" With that he looked up to heaven as if searching for the clue to solve the problem.

I have no answer either, Diary. I hate seeing my dad in such a state, such turmoil. He has put so much effort into this venture. I guess tomorrow is another day. Somewhere, out there in sporting dreamland, lies the answer.

24 AUGUST 2012: They've all gone to Germany for the Grand Prix at Holenberg, so we have the run of the place. They trust us to behave like a couple of angels. What folly! What fools they are! I have spent most of the day with some guy called Andrean. We met on the beach. I lied about my age, told him I was, in fact, eighteen. The silly arse believed me. We are meeting for dinner tonight at his place – this is all the encouragement I need. I have him just where I want him. What a great couple of days lie ahead. You know what they say back home when parents trust children: "When the Welsh cat's away, the Welsh mice will play."

Only one thing spoilt my day. Before leaving his cottage, we watched the early morning news on television. All I was interested in was the sport, in particular the result of the German Grand Prix. As I feared, we lost again, badly beaten. An outsider, Fredericko Gonzales from Chile, stormed to victory. Bryman second, Hakkiki third. We came nowhere. Daddy will not be pleased. God in heaven, how will our luck change? Diary, I need to know right now.

19 NOVEMBER 2012: Dear Diary, I watched television with Tippy on my lap. I'm in cuckoo land – in love at school I may be – but it made disturbing viewing all the same. The Middle East explodes before my very eyes, supposedly for my pleasure. Yet all I saw was the blind madness, the utter fucking lunacy of the human race. So I penned a short poem about it. It makes sense to me if no one else.

The Question Verse

From the dewy fields of Agincourt,
To the majestic slopes of Jerusalem's hills.
Over the ages so many peoples all deceased.
When will we hail the immortal peace?

Kissed the dog goodnight all the same.

2013

1 JANUARY 2013: Last night we celebrated the arrival of yet another New Year. Who knows what the coming twelve months will bring to our family? All I know is that we welcomed its arrival singing, dancing, then kissing the old one out in grand style.

At The Halfmoon Hotel over in Penarth, anybody who was anybody was there. The Proctor-Hales, Gowers, McCains, Swains and even the Tattons were there in force. I seemed to dance the night away with everybody, on the dance floor all night long. It was a wonderful fun way to bring in the New Year. Wilson was supposed to be my beau for the night, but there are times when he can behave so timidly, shy, bashful. A real paradox to his persona: a brave, fearless racing driver. I saw that last night in all its rawness. He came across as clumsy, awkward, unsure of himself, even in conversation. He had two left feet, with a similar tongue, tripping over them both all night long. I mean on the dance floor he was hopeless, even when we came close together, almost as if he didn't want to be near me. In the end I gave up, looking elsewhere for company. The boys from the pits adore me, even if he doesn't.

Dinner of course was the dreaded haggis. Cheese crisps would have been more edible, for me at least. Dad let me toast in 2013 with a glass of champagne. I had three actually – don't tell him though. On the stroke of midnight 1,000 balloons fell from the ceiling. I popped many balloons, lunging at anybody for a kiss. I enjoyed a kiss from all the boys, all victims of my uncontrolled excitement. But Wilson, to my pleasure, gave me his first real kiss. I loved it. Yes, I love him for all his faults, even now.

I look forward to the 10th – off to London. Ah, the West End! The day, the night, will be just as good, better perhaps, than last night.

Goodnight, Diary. Happy New Year to you as well.

10 JANUARY 2013: Spent the day at the garage before heading off to dear old London. The day has been marred by disaster. A customer complaint that got out of hand brought nothing but chaos, despair and fear. I tell you, Diary, my dad found it hard to take in.

We arrived at the garage just after eight thirty, and it was already a hive of intense activity. I went along just for the hell of it, but, once there, I helped out in the office, hoovering the carpet for Dad. But this was more than simply helping out at the family business. He needs all the encouragement he can get. The garage has been suffering badly, business slack. After what happened there today, even slacker. Dad had a very angry confrontation with a distraught customer, complaining about the condition of a second-hand car he'd been sold.

I suppose I had been diligently hoovering away for about half an hour as Dad went over the accounts with his secretary, Mavis. Between them both, they dissected the finances of the garage – every penny, every pound, had to be accounted for. But the peace of this busy office was broken by the rantings of a man's angry voice. It seemed brutal, out of control.

"Where's Mr Osborne? Get the bastard out here now!" he demanded.

The man's voice boomed out all over the garage forecourt. It forced my dad to stop what he was doing, looking sharply up from his desk. Mavis followed suit. Two or three minutes passed before he did something about it. Getting up from his chair, leaving some papers on the desk, he looked out of the office window.

"What the hell's going on out there? What's all the fuss?"

By this time, almost talking to himself, out on the forecourt a scruffy man was being restrained by a mechanic, Bryn, as Melvin Jones tried to calm the irate customer down, stopping him from walking any further. But the scruffy man flew into a rage. Words rang out all over the place, every word audible, swearing as clear as day. They stood inches apart, and for one horrible moment it looked like a fight might break out. A schoolyard fight, a barroom brawl on our garage forecourt. I switched off the Hoover, and its whirl slowly wound down to silence. I watched Dad bravely walk out of the office to confront the man.

I recall every word in my mind – at three in the morning, it makes me smile.

"Ah, there you are, you cheat. See what you've done to me. That's a wreck."

The man pointed to a car parked by the main entrance. It was a Blue Raven 08. The car itself looked in immaculate condition, as if brand-new, like the day it rolled off the production line. But it was not – far from it. As I observed the scene from the office window, I thought the man might burst into tears on the spot. Dad approached the disgruntled man as a gunfighter might in a Western street, outside the saloon. For a brief moment both men faced each other, as if a duel was about to be fought. For an instant Dad looked scared, frightened. Both men froze, then faced each other eyeball to eyeball, nose to nose.

The man spoke first: "You are a cheat, a liar."

My dad tried to calm him down: "Calm down, my friend. What's wrong?"

The man pointed to the car. "That's what's wrong, very wrong. That car you sold me last week has already broken down. Why? The battery's dead."

Then the man delivered the verbal body blow, just as Dad turned to walk away towards the stationary car. It made my dad unable to respond. He just stood there open-mouthed, his pride wounded.

The man continued the attack: "Mr Osborne, you are the most amazing piece of shit. You can't win a Grand Prix; you can't sell a car either. You just sell yourself with lies, lies, more lies."

Dad then pulled himself together. "I'm sure we can sort this problem out. Now, let's go to my office, then talk this thing through."

As I looked out of the window, some of the mechanics came to my dad's aid. Lance, Joe, Ben and Dai stood round my dad in a circle, protecting him. But the man carried on with his diatribe. Things seemed like they might get out of hand, violent even. A punch or kick at any moment.

"You sold me that car with a dud battery. No power. I've broken down twice in just one rotten week. I want things put right. A bloody disgrace. You are just a no-good second-hand-car salesman, nothing else. No wonder you can't win a Grand Prix – none of your cars bloody well work, that's why."

The man waved his fist in Dad's direction, almost catching him on the chin. But young Dai saved the day. He pushed the two men apart, escorting the man away, doing everything possible to calm down the situation.

I watched Dad adjust his tie, saying, "Now, don't worry, I promise we'll put this right. Should never have happened in the first place. Most irregular. I pride myself on my fine reputation. A dud battery is a rare fault with our cars, sir, believe me."

But the man shouted back: "Irregular, my arse."

This remark made me burst into laughter as I packed the Hoover away.

Soon footsteps could be heard coming along the corridor towards the office. Luckily, I vacated it just in time as they approached the door. Clumsily, I walked away from the office, almost falling over the Hoover, one eye on where I was going, the other on Dad escorting this customer up to his office. He demanded satisfaction – a new battery, car, or money back. But the angry voices of a few minutes before were calmed down a shade, civilised, reasoned, and a solution was arranged.

"I can only apologise, Mr Conrad. I will personally make sure this mistake is put right with haste. This garage will uphold the warranty that goes with our cars sold here. A 100-point survey of the vehicle's roadworthiness and a year's MOT is what we are noted for."

Dad appeared to have regained his pride, the fear gone.

The man had wanted to travel up to Bangor to help out at his brother's farm. Well, Diary, he hadn't gone ten miles when the car just stopped. He had to get a tow back home – cost him hundreds of pounds too. Now he wanted his money back, plus some more. He finished his accusations with a legal threat against my dad: he'd sue if redress was not sought right away. It sent my dad into a spin, a panic perhaps, to pacify this gentleman quickly. Leaving me to ask, 'Will the day get better?' Like it would do anything else! I knew what was coming; so did everyone else.

Wembley is heaven – it has become the cathedral of sport to the nation. The great English place of worship, where football reigns supreme. This is where we watch and cheer our footballing heroes. The current apostles of the game, Jarvis, Smith and Hartback, along with the powerful left foot of Cranberry, conduct their service whenever they are called to honour their country.

7 JULY 2013: Dear sweet Diary, so the great Scot Andy Murray has at long last won the Wimbledon singles final in fine style. The man will receive a knighthood, sainthood, then be offered the role King of all Scotland. King Murray the First. A fitting title for a man who's clearly on the up. The other players of tennis merit that have beaten him in the past all lost this year. Thus paving the way for his everlasting glory. Now immortal, he can win Wimbledon as many times as he likes. Let's hope he does. He is still Scottish – nothing wrong with that, but not English. The only question remaining to be answered is where were the English, the modern-day Fred Perrys, in his pursuit? Answer: of course nowhere. Yet again they go begging. I guess it's the old tale that will never go away. It will take a heavenly being to retake that title, always lost each year. But when?

Tell me something new?

7 AUGUST 2013: How many times have I heard my mum say with relish, belief, "Have a good day at school," then kiss me on the cheek? Far too many, I fear. School's out soon for the summer break, but today hooky was the order of the day – far too nice for a day spent at bleeding school. I told Mum what sort of a day I'd have at school, the lie well practised, repeated a million times over. Then I ran amuck for the rest of the day. Then returned at four, nobody the wiser. The last twelve months have been full of it. The great deceiver! All that said, we had a great day down by the river.

Shopping with Cristobel in the big city soon. I need some new swimwear for the beach.

Who cares what they think anyway? I don't; neither does the dog.

24 SEPTEMBER 2013: Just back from attending the Belgian Grand Prix. For the first time we have a good result. Wilson drove like a champ and we managed a place on the podium. At last, points on the board! Now let the press slag us off. This afternoon, hope springs eternal. Dad along with Proctor-Hale smiled all the way home, as well he might. Perhaps we can challenge for glory after all.

As usual when something good in sport happens, after the race the press swarmed around my dad, pestered him as never before. They wanted, demanded, comments about the car's performance. They took Wilson's driving apart bit by bit. Like driving instructors before the test. Analysing the car's wonderful Grand Prix with question after question. Every one of those shysters had nothing but praise about this unexpected result. All had a cool buzz about them, milking the moment for all it was worth. But the gutter press will wash us down the drain, into the sewer, without thinking about it if in two weeks time we don't repeat this in China. Newspapers, in collusion with television will once again write us off as a weak team, not up to the job. So let's savour the day, Diary, grab it by the balls for all it's worth. Right now China seems a lifetime away, another world.

5 NOVEMBER 2013: Attended a bonfire party with the rest of the family. Cristobel tagged along. I was glad of that tonight. In the right mood she's great company, can be such fun, a laugh a minute. Tonight we all needed cheering up, in the fullest sense of the word. Work-wise this has been an awful year for the family. I feel sorry for them all, dog included. Despite some good fortune, it has ended in sporting failure yet again. Humiliation on the sporting battlefield. All of them from Cardiff to Bangor and the sunny shores of Llandudno castigated my dad along with the boss for being a failure. From today the press are the sworn enemy. I saw it coming months ago, as the season drew to a close. According to the press we gave Wales hope where none was available. Spending millions without reason. They wanted us not to just do well at rugby or golf, or even horse racing; but motor racing was a dream too much. Fly's buttocks to them all! Just wait till it clicks, Diary – then you'll see what we can do. All Dad needs is Lady Luck – she's out there someplace, I know she is.

Tonight has been wonderful. I declare it's been the best Bommy Night ever. Better than last year, by far. The party was held in the large back garden of the Proctor-Hales' mansion, just outside Cardiff. There must have been 100 people attending, enjoying the festive atmosphere. Money is no object for them. I am told that £50,000 worth of fireworks went up in smoke tonight, just for our enjoyment.

Most of the guests at this party were strangers to me. A few of the team came along from work, bringing their families with them. But I hitched along with Cristobel, holding on to the coat-tails of Wilson for most of the night. He acted out the role of beau protector. He was lovely, a gentleman.

The bonfire itself was huge, magnificent. It stood out like a giant wooden mountain, slap bang in the middle of the garden. Branches of trees, limbs, boughs, were decorated everywhere, along with what seemed like one million planks of wood of every shape, every size. On top of this enormous black mass stood a large effigy of Guy Fawkes himself, dressed in traditional costume, right down to his hat. It must have taken somebody a long time to create such a large guy. I think it was Proctor-Hale's grandchildren. I wish they'd asked me for help

61

– I haven't built a bonfire on Guy Fawkes Night for a long time. Come to think of it, children these days don't ever stand on street corners shouting at the top of their voices, "Penny for the guy, penny for the guy!" then watch a sweet tin fill up as people give the odd coin or two. Rushing off to buy bangers by the ton. Have the youth of today lost their childhood? Like me, they probably have. In this day, this age of PC by the score, we aren't allowed to enjoy ourselves any more. To be perfectly honest, Diary, I've never held a firework, ever.

At eight thirty on the dot the fireworks were let off, the bonfire lit accompanied by rockets shooting up in the night sky. Gold mixed with red, silver, even green, covered the night sky in multicoloured streaks. The odd loud bang made even me jump. Fireworks of all descriptions exploded above us. A firework raced upwards like a Saturn rocket, then there was a tremendous bang like something out of the Blitz from the Second World War during the last century. I gripped Wilson's hand tightly for comfort – his smile made me feel much better. More fireworks were let off, and hot soup served with warm bread followed as the guy burned fiercely on the bonfire.

Standing there with my friends, we watched the bonfire burn as we waved sparklers at each other. A giant Catherine wheel, nailed to a post at the far end of the garden, suddenly went off. It spun round very fast, leaving a yellow trail in the night sky. It was spectacular to watch. Everybody applauded wildly as another went off next to it. As we watched the fireworks, tucking into some flapjack, then ginger cake, Dad along with Mum came to join us. Mum offered me half a baked potato that was smothered in butter, and the whole thing melted in my mouth. I can still taste it now, all this time later. I washed it down with a mug of hot chocolate. All the while I could not take my eyes off Wilson's unshaven smile. Yes, this has been a night free of motor racing – motor anything. A cold night, tailor-made for a warm heart.

My dad seemed aloof though, standing at times away from the rest of us. At one stage he stood by the bonfire all alone, solitary, head bowed, deep in thought. It looked as if he carried the whole weight of the world on his shoulders, as Atlas might. I have observed him in such a state before, during the summer, only not with such intensity. When Dad has a problem he clams up, keeping the worry to his silent self. His moods will fluctuate from good to bad, happy to sad in just one hour of the day. But complicated men have brilliance in their making. As I watched my dad tonight, bathed in the glow of that bonfire, I prayed for this to be so, for the Almighty to give him the answer to his sporting dream. After all, the Welsh Dragon only managed a third place this year – in Belgium, of all places. Piss in the street, boyo!

2014

14 FEBRUARY 2014: Glorious St Valentine's Day arrived yet again – my birthday. Well, boohoo. But this year the celebrations have been, to say the least, subdued. Just my damn luck to have my birthday fall on a Sunday. Ah yes, the only day of the week when the family all get together, to attend chapel, over at Brontally, like we always do. I must confess that I did not want to go. I had plans to join Cristobel for some downtown fun. Alas, I had no choice but to do as I was told. Chapel it was, then, at eleven this morning. How can anybody with bounce celebrate their birthday in chapel?

Dressed as if going to a wedding, in a posh frock with matching overcoat, I sat in the pew next to Aunty Mildred, attempting to join in, singing, praying, listening to the sermon delivered by Father Ponsonby. There has been a heavy snowfall right across South Wales. The roads may be clear, but the countryside – the fields, the mountains – lie covered in white. He talked about how the community spirit should abound in this freezing weather. How we must help the elderly to stay warm, whether they are our relatives or not. As he spoke these words, I winked at Aunty Mildred, then held her hand. She loved it. A warm moment on this very cold day. When the good Lord speaks from the pulpit you do as you are told.

There was a birthday tea this evening, which I found nice. Dad, along with the rest of the family, put on a show for me. My special birthday present, given to me by my parents, consists of a shopping voucher to the tune of £100 to spend how I like. I've already called Cristobel, so, next weekend, Cardiff here we come!

Goodnight, Diary. By the way, you've been such a loyal friend that I intend to reward you as well: another brand-new pen. One day a quill for you!

20 FEBRUARY 2014: Today I was let loose on to the good people of Cardiff, as never before. It was time to spend my birthday present – £100. To do my patriotic bit to improve the economy of Wales. Being a traitor would never do, would it, Diary? Today £100 will not go very far, but I managed to buy some new clothes. That will make a difference. So this morning, with Cristobel in tow, we both hit the fashion stores of downtown Cardiff.

Griffith Owen was the first store we raided, opposite the stadium. I had a new skirt in mind, with matching knee-high boots. My favourite gear at the moment. Cristobel fancied jeans, nothing else. She told me she had been given the money by her mum, but I have my doubts. I did not enquire any further. I leave that to honesty itself. In her purse she had more money than I did. Boy, were we loaded!

One day I'm going to shop in New York, Paris and Rome. I can feel it in my bones. There will be champagne dinners, chauffeur-driven cars, photographs galore, money accompanied by men. But for now, at least, it was more down to earth. Lunch today was a double cheeseburger washed down with strawberry shakes. Cristobel pigged out with me. Then we hit the stores in town with an open purse. I must've tried on several outfits before deciding on the one that will wow the boys best of all. Flesh-coloured tights showed off my legs from the knee upwards. Yes, this afternoon has been great fun, a rehearsal for the future.

But I said something today, as we queued at the till – it just came out. I could not stop myself from saying it – a comment said with relish. "One day, when I'm world champion, we will celebrate by shopping till we drop in glorious Alice Springs."

"Alice Springs!" came the surprised response.

I don't think Cristobel knows where it is, Diary. At times she can be a silly ignorant cow.

7 MAY 2014: Well, Diary, half-term at last! No school for one fantabulous week. I spent this afternoon down by the river with Cristobel. It has been a red-hot day. Temperatures way up in the nineties, no clouds at all. Even old Tippy found it uncomfortable, panting, struggling to find any shade. I wore my red swimming costume, Cristobel a pair of cut-off jeans. She took a pair of scissors to them, just above the knee, all frayed at the edges, stains on the arse. She looked great in them, her long jet-black hair complementing the white T-shirt. All I can say is that I wish I'd done the same.

What a lazy day this has been, listening to Gillam Diss, lounging on the riverbank. When the mood took us we went swimming in the cool river. Sometimes we would talk, then laugh about nothing at all. The way friends do. Today, at least, the rest of the world with all her problems was someplace else.

I invited Wilson to come with us, but he wasn't allowed to.

The Grand Prix season has kicked into action. Dad's all fired up for the challenge. Life has become serious again, when laughter should've taken over. But, that said, we sipped red wine stolen from a shop the night before. Cristobel can steal any damn thing, from anywhere. I love her to bits. In between the wine, the smiles, the laughter, I cast my mind forward to the end of the month. We will be doing the same, but in the South of France.

29 MAY 2014: Another weekend spent in Monaco. What a poor little bastard I am! How many other children have a dad in such a profession? A teacher, doctor, miner or shopkeeper? This is bliss for all time – one permanent holiday.

This afternoon the Welsh Dragon raced in the Monaco Grand Prix. Wilson drove wonderfully well. He did his level best in the face of much better competition. I was very proud of him. All the same, the fact remains we finished tenth. At least it wasn't last place – thank God for that. Long before the race there had been talk of improved gas performance, fuel saving, more powerful acceleration, better handling on the circuit. As I watched the race unfold, by Mum's side in the pits, this plainly did not happen. A washout – that's how the press will report it – another poor Welsh performance, a let-down. We fly home in the morning – another silent flight.

No Grand Prix next week, but I'm sure to find some way to enjoy myself. I wonder how?

5 AUGUST 2014: Had driving lesson this afternoon. All went well, save for one awful thing. Today politics came in the way of my future. The country has gone to the polls. Yes, a general election has been called. So, as a result, Dad only gave me instructions behind the wheel for one hour at the back of the garage. All the same, I did rather well.

What else?

We didn't do that much – just routine stuff. Turns, reverse parking, a drive in a straight line at a steady ten with a promise that a mock driving test will follow soon, just after Japan. That pleased me no end. In just two years' time I'll be able to take the real thing, for now you can take the test at just sixteen. This is something I look forward to with eager anticipation, for I have made a promise to myself to pass first time. In saying that, I still haven't read the Highway Code – not one sentence of that motorist's bible. I tried to study it tonight, but found myself sitting next to Dad as Mum knitted. We watched the election results come in. I became distracted by a speech made by the newly elected MP for the Isle of Wight, Nicholas Rachael, twenty-five, handsome as hell. A young MP with film-star looks, a voice you want to hear, a smile to die for. He certainly gets my vote. What a dish!

24 OCTOBER 2014: The Lark Hotel, Watkins Glen, New York.

Attended the US Grand Prix this afternoon. This motor race recently returned here after a lengthy absence. I must say, Diary, this is the prettiest Grand Prix circuit I've visited yet. Very impressed. Upstate New York is divine to the core. Today even more so, because – you'll never guess what? – well, we got a result. A good solid sporting miracle took place here – something not experienced in sixty-odd years of motor racing. A sporting first if ever there was one. My dad is over the moon; the whole team walks in a dream, a trance. The Welsh triumphed here in the good old USA. An unexpected win in a Grand Prix. Overjoyed? Tell me about it! We're elated with victory. This day will silence the critics back home in Cardiff – come to think of it, across the globe. Even the North Pole.

Today, in the heat of New England, I saw how the power of winning can heal the pain of losing. There has been far too much misery, racked with endless heartache, dour reflection, guilt. Especially by my dad. So let's hope that has all come to a welcome end.

Wilson drove like a god this afternoon, as if he owned the circuit. For the first time in years I watched my love, my true love, use all his skills behind the wheel to good effect. He blew the opposition away. All those hours my dad spent fine-tuning the car to perfection paid off in full. I could see that for myself. The car handled well, its acceleration wonderful to observe. Starting the Grand Prix from grid three, Wilson simply raced away past the rest of the field in just half a lap. By the time he drove by the grandstand on lap two, he was in front. I could not believe it. I cheered for all I was worth, like a silly arse.

Each time the car raced, whizzed, past me, I yelled out his name as if it was part of the engine itself, helping him to stay in front with each turn of the wheel. The racing car seemed to eat up the Tarmac. My infectious cheering encouraging all to follow suit, like an inspired football chant as we all watched the white racing car take the final bend, its red Welsh dragon displayed for the rest of the world to see, to advertise our nation. It hugged the final bend, cutting the grass, shooting away to the chequered flag. I heard 'Land of My Fathers' echo across the Atlantic Ocean.

This has been a memorable victory. An outsider has beaten the favourite without question. Never before in the noble glorious history of motor racing has the Welsh national anthem been played to honour the winning driver as he stood on the podium, breaking open the champagne, smiling to the press, making the world sit up then take notice. Today he's a true sporting hero.

We fly back home to Wales on Monday night. On Tuesday it's school again for me – normal life resumes its monotony. It will be my dad and Wilson who'll face the press, tell them how wonderful they are, explain the workings of this incredible racing car they've developed. That will tame the sporting world. The result that will appear in the world's sporting press tomorrow will read as follows.

The US Grand Prix, 2014

1. Wilson McCain	Welsh Dragon	Wales
2. F. G. Lofty	Ramsome	New Zealand
3. Lin Chou	Changzhou	China

The celebrated American driver Big Joe Long Grass, a Crow Indian, tipped to win the race, could only manage fourth.

Yes, Diary, this truly has been a wow day for all. I am glad for my dad – in fact for the whole team. All that hard work over the years has been rewarded at last by winning this Grand Prix. Let's hope this trend continues.

27 OCTOBER 2014: Question: What does a girl like me give as a reward to her fancy man? Guess, Diary? Well, I gave it to Wilson tonight, in style. As a perk for winning the US Grand Prix, I gave myself to him. Well, to be honest, Diary, I asked him to give me this long-awaited driving lesson. He agreed, so at six this evening he drove me out to the remote spot called Jebbs Point. There amongst the coastal lanes, with sand dunes on both sides, Wilson let me drive his brand-new London Blue 12 sports car – a low-slung, sleek, fast speed merchant. He let me drive at speed, foot down, voice screaming. But what's the point of building a car designed for the open road (where the speed limit is maybe thirty, fifty, sixty or seventy) to be able to reach speeds of 200 or 150 on the speed dial? There is none.

That said, we had a great time, joking, laughing, talking, listening to music. Dad would have thrown a wobbly if he'd known. Another lesson next week, after Bali.

7 JANUARY 2015: The weather today has been foul – rain, rain, sleet. It's been like it for three days now. Will it ever stop? No snow this year in the valleys. Even the mountaintops aren't white. That alpine picture that sometimes paints itself in Wales isn't there at all. A dull greyness greeted the New Year; Christmas was no different. Then, to cap it all, I watched my dad make a fool of himself on local television. He was interviewed on the news, and I listened to him making predictions about the coming motor-racing season, looming up. He sounded as if we'd won the world title before it even started. God knows what got into him tonight. What I heard came across to me as confident stupidity. Sports people are always doing it: going to the media, telling them what they are going to do, how they'll do it, how wonderful they are, how they'll win in style, before the contest even starts, then losing with excuses. They seem to revel in it. It seems to be part of the game these days.

I was so angry at him. My dad looked and sounded like a right plonker. I walked the dog in the pouring rain. I took off my hat and coat and got soaked. Who cares?

16 FEBRUARY 2015: Well, Diary, my best mate, I've had a good day. Got myself in my mum's good books by helping her do the housework. She nearly dropped her knickers when I volunteered to shampoo the lounge carpet this afternoon. Well, to be honest, I am going to a football match soon so I need some more pocket money; also, much more important than mere football, there is a wonderful book that's just been published about the history of motor racing, so I'm saving up for it – Sir James Arsk's *How the Brave Die*. A bit gruesome, but a good read, with some great photographs in it. A few more pounds nearer the purchase were earned today. To be shamefully blunt, Diary, the dog crapped on the carpet yesterday, so I really had to. I did not bother to measure out the shampoo, just poured it out into the machine. Soapsuds all over the place – lots of sham to pick up the poo. But the carpet looks great again, smelling like a flower in springtime, unlike my armpits tonight. That was hard work, for sure. Who would be a housewife? Not me.

Come on, Murray! Up the lads!

19 FEBRUARY 2015: Sport has always been the great leveller – that is what makes it so special. Unlike politics or religion, it unites the peoples of the world as no other power on earth can.

The outsider can beat the favourite and the great can be humbled. Sometimes those who shouldn't *do*. I say, long may it stay that way. Sport must never die. If sport dies, so does the human race. Tonight I saw this in all its glory. This has been a special day in sport. Tonight I saw a legend born. I feel honoured to have watched it.

On this cold winter's night I saw a killing take place – a murder with no equal. A football slaying, a giant-killing as no other. I watched it. I saw it with my own eyes. I didn't believe it at first, but it happened. Murray Athletic beat Manchester United in the FA Cup at Old Trafford. The noble score was 2–3, a well-earned away victory for the Wiltshire side. So in go Murray, out go Manchester. A guy named Tompkins has suddenly become the best footballer in the country. Yes, a plumber is king.

What I saw tonight was sport at its very best. Not even the most fervent Manchester fan could've objected about the football match played tonight – the game itself, the atmosphere, the result. Sport soared to dizzy heights in Manchester. As for Murray Athletic, they have invented an exceptional brand of football, called by their manager 'The Whack-It Policy' – to whack the ball into the back of the net. Such blind confidence has not been seen in football for a long, long time. We listened to the car's radio on the long journey back to Cardiff. Murray Athletic have gone football crazy. The fans can't believe, or understand – they just celebrate in style. It sounded to me as if they had actually won the FA Cup. The whole place has gone insane. There will be many a hangover tonight for sure. The victorious team will be given an open-top bus ride through the city centre in triumph. I guess you cannot blame them. I mean, knocking out the mighty Manchester United has been their own FA Cup Final victory! Boy, did they do it in breathtaking fashion.

Cristobel's dad is a lifelong United fan, a supporters' club member all his life, so he got three tickets for the match. I was invited last week, and gladly accepted. I'm not a great football fan myself, but I'm proud to have witnessed this spectacle. The sporting press slammed the game, from the very start, as one-sided. They expected Manchester United to run away with the match. A dangerous thing to do. A cricket score was on the cards, so they said. But from the kick-off such unsung heroes as Alfie Spree, Joe Tompkins and Nobby Weston had other ideas. The whole team played well right from the start. They were out for a result – an upset. They got it, Diary – my God, they got it. After all, that's why they won. Those three though stood out from the rest.

We arrived at Old Trafford two hours before kick-off. As we

approached the stadium, we could see this huge white, luminous light ahead of us. It stood out against the black night sky. The white light was so bright it looked as if a spaceship had landed from Mars. All about us thousands of people streamed towards Old Trafford, where the gladiatorial contest would take place.

Once inside the football ground, a lush green pitch greeted us along with the roar of thousands of people shouting from all corners. A chant went out as the teams came on to the field. The red of Manchester, the black stripes of Murray. My nerves made me tremble, or perhaps it was the cold night air. I wanted Murray to win so much. But how could they defeat this superior enemy?

From the kick-off Murray Athletic went on the defensive. As Manchester United piled on the pressure, with attack after attack, shot after shot was aimed at the goalmouth. Keeper Alfie Spree proved his worth: the vet used his mighty hands to gather in the ball safely on every occasion. As I munched on my flame-grilled burger and sipped my Coke, Alfie Spree rose like a giant, tipping the ball over the crossbar with the ends of his fingers. The crowd roared with approval as the Italian striker Scilarno blasted a thunderous shot at goal. It was a magical moment in the game. Dozens of other shots were given the same treatment. But United had their confidence shattered after twenty minutes. With the United keeper off his line, Murray winger Joe Tompkins kicked a shot at goal from outside the box. I watched the football launch itself high in the cold night air and drop like a mighty time bomb into the back of the net. The net shook and so did the team, along with a stunned crowd. Murray took the lead. Now what?

The rest of the football match had me sitting on the edge of my seat. It was riveting stuff – I didn't want to miss anything. Suddenly Manchester United had a corner. Lance Tack took the corner, forcing Alfie Spree to rise up high above everybody else, catching the ball. But after thirty minutes the pace of the game changed as United broke away, catching Murray unawares. A breathtaking sprint from almost the halfway line, by Elsie, resulted in a shot to the back of the net. Alfie Spree had no chance. All was level. The half-time whistle could not come quickly enough. For the next forty-five minutes I watched men perform miracles on the football pitch. Just after the start of the second half – twenty-six seconds, to be exact – Crown took a wild shot at goal from what seemed an impossible angle. It caught Alfie Spree off guard. Murray were now behind – all to do, you might say. From then on Manchester United took the small fry on with relentless attacking football. At one time Murray had all eleven players inside their box. Each time there was an attempt at goal, a wall of Murray's players stood like a brick wall in an effort to stop a further goal from being scored, thus ending the match, killing the hope. United had a free kick; Wallace took it, aiming his thunderous shot to the safe hands of Alfie Spree. He then threw the ball out to Nobby Weston. As Murray launched a counter-attack, I crushed a handful of crisps in the palm of my hand, hand held tight.

I looked on in utter disbelief at what happened next. The world seemed to stand still next to me as Nobby Weston hit the ball, firm, hard, solid, past the United keeper, leaving him stranded in front of the goal. The ball seemed to roll over the line in slow motion. Murray had equalised – it was 2–2. How would this game travel? Murray had everything to play for now – this could be their night. I thought the impossible, as the clock ticked to the final whistle.

The night air got colder and I shivered in my seat. It was like the Arctic, or Alaska in the deep of winter. Who said this team could not be beaten? The United supporters had been hushed into silence. The cheering of before had stopped as Murray Athletic pushed forward with venom. Once again Alfie Spree threw the ball to the feet of Halstead, who passed the ball to Cuthbert. Nobby Weston was unmarked. United fell back, the defence ruffled, as Jones cut down Weston. The referee gave a foul, then a yellow card – a free kick awarded. Murray Athletic grasped the moment. Nobby Weston took the free kick quickly. Tompkins just forced 'The Whack-It Policy' to its finest. The ball hit the back of the net like a missile in flight. The whole stadium erupted as the last minute of the game ticked by. Then Manchester United's players fell to the ground in despair as the final whistle was blown. I punched the air in victory. Murray Athletic had destroyed Manchester United. A home tie with Forest looms. Yes, Diary, I have borne witness to sporting excellence tonight.

So the mighty have been humbled. But to be fair to Manchester's supporters, they gave Murray's players a standing ovation as they took a well-earned lap of honour. Thunderous applause rang out across the football ground. But the long drive home back to Cardiff was a sombre affair. Cristobel's dad, while acknowledging a fine win, drove the car in brooding silence as the fallen, the vanquished, will.

Personally, I'm proud to have watched the encounter, glad I went along. An epic encounter indeed – one for the history books of football and sport in general. I pray for yet another slaughter on the sporting battlefield on behalf of little Murray Athletic Football Club, Wiltshire's finest. On the front pages of the press in the morning, a plumber, a shopkeeper and a vet will become heroes of the nation, for one day at least. When the favourite gets beaten by a rank outsider, the world's a better place to live in. Just like it has been tonight.

20 AUGUST 2015: My darling little Diary, I won another go-kart race at Newport's Hell Pit Circuit. A glorious triumph gained. I have discovered the eternal secret of winning – make the difficult look easy. I am in love with myself tonight for sure. Amo the Great!

2016

16 MARCH 2016: Mum's brother Daffyd died on Friday. He was just fifty – the black sheep of the family. A kind of loveable rogue, as they say. Always in trouble. He spent time in the nick – he did two years for theft. I do recall him vaguely many years ago, drunk at a church service, being a smiling, laughing, naughty guy. Never had any money, always broke. I even loaned him my pocket money once. I cut the grass for two quid, then he promptly asked me for it. Like a joke I gave him the money – never saw it again. As far as I know he's spent the last couple of years drawing social. I've been spared the ordeal of going to the funeral, missing nothing. Uncle Daffyd was a lazy, lying, untrustworthy, drunken, silly little twat.

5 JUNE 2016: Soon the day will force its hand upon me. She will ask me the big question. My problem is can I answer her? Will destiny be satisfied with my actions? For at the end of the month I leave school. The big ugly world with all its dangers beckons me to her bosom. My performances at school are a legendary failure – nothing to boast about there. I take exams at the end of term, but nobody, including me, holds out much hope. So for the last couple of months all hell has been let loose in preparation for my driving test. All agree this is where my own destiny lies. A lot is at stake. I must prove myself here. Failure is not an option any more.

Why should I care? But I do – I don't want to let anybody down over this. A life on the road lures me, like a mermaid lures a sailor on board a ship heading for the rocks. The big questions now are these: Will a life behind the wheel of a car be the making of me? Will I discover my true purpose in life? I say yes to both of these questions. So do others – parents and boss alike. They have already discussed my future in great depth, all agreeing that my value as a human being can, or will, be found right there. If I pass my driving test first time, I have been offered a job working for Dad as a delivery driver for the garage. Everything to play for now, I fear. It will not be easy, but I'll give it my best shot. I mean, the driving test has been made much harder – now many people fail. I will not be one of them.

My dad is away with the rest of the team in South Africa, for the Grand Prix. Last year's victory has long been forgotten. Things aren't going well at all. I banned myself from going with them. For this morning I learnt that my driving test will now take place on 7 July, next month. So I'm studying very hard. No nights out with Cristobel or the boys. Time to live like a nun.

Roll on the 7th.

7 JULY 2016: The day I have been waiting for has come at last. It lived up to all expectations. The fear, the hell, the excitement of it! Yes, Diary, my old mate, this has been a wonderful day indeed – twenty-four hours to savour. I want the world to know I passed my driving test in all its glory. Let the proclamation go out to the known world, like some decree from Rome herself. I, Ann Marie Osborne, now walk this earth. What is more, I will not go away. Man will know of my existence.

From the moment I got up this morning, with fear tucked inside my heart, I could feel it in my bones. This would be the day that changed my life forever – yes, the dust of infinity has blown in my face. Stardust scattered from above, by who knows what!

Right away as I walked out of the house, receiving a fatherly embrace, with encouraging advice, I seemed to exude self-confidence. I knew with every bone in my body I would pass without effort. The driving part of the test was easy, the theory slightly harder, the practical mechanics hell, but I managed to bluff my way through. So at exactly one this afternoon it was confirmed that I had passed my driving test with flying colours. The world is now my oyster.

So as this exciting day draws to a close I find myself sitting by the bedroom window. It has just gone midnight after yet another sweltering summer day. I gaze up at the night sky sparkling with a billion twinkling stars. A full moon stands regally to one side. All appears calm, but the heavens are busy. It's as if the gods are calling, blessing me with their power, confirming my destiny to do their work on this earth. A divine light shines from above.

The dog licks me on the cheek, making me smile yet again. All is well with my life tonight.

8 JULY 2016: There is a time for work, a time for play, a time to kiss the boys, as they say. A time to hug, a time to squeeze, a time to do nothing else but please.

I had a date with one of the mechanics at work from the garage. Diary, the box ticks are as follows. His name, Mark; age, eighteen; looks, ordinary, but not ugly; manners, silent. This guy has had a crush on me for some time, so I granted his wish. Since the glory of yesterday, I have basked in my own private arrogance, like some graduate from Oxford or Cambridge with one eye fixed firmly on the PhD or BA. It is a pity my real education didn't get the same kind of treatment, or attention, or perhaps I'd be on my way to sample the delights of those historic places of learning for myself. My chance to shine, proving to all concerned that I have a brain, will come soon. Just not at those places.

Tonight, at least, I gave in to the pleasures of life. An evening down the pub has been something to look forward to all week. Jeans and sweatshirt made me look good, Diary, pass for a woman of age. My make-up bag took care of my good looks, including a pack of six crammed by the side of my lipstick. I don't mean beer either. After all, when I'm on the loose I'm unwrapped. I mean, let's face it, life is short enough – even I must grab love when it comes. What happened tonight was not love, but, Diary, you know what I mean. Without shame, I think it's great that yet again an employee has had the chance to shag the boss's daughter. The lads compete for the honour. Let's say I'm doing Dad a big favour, keeping the workforce happy.

26 AUGUST 2016: The Lakeside Hotel, room 420, Zurich, Switzerland.

It is now one in the morning, and the last twenty-four hours has been an experience to treasure for all time. I now have the urgent need to jot it all down on paper. Diary, you are the only other person I dare confess this to. Right now I'm naked, in bed with the man of my dreams. I saw him in all his manly splendour tonight. His skin shone, his muscles became taut against me, his touch drove me wild for more. Most of all, this brave, fearless sportsman showed me tenderness. His soft baby talk, spoken in shy whispered tones against my ears, sent me all aquiver. The man I lie with here in the small hours of another morning has treated me like no other in the past – like a lady. Then again, he's a gentleman.

I know for a fact that most women in this country would give anything to be in this position. Yes, Diary, Wilson McCain has given himself to me tonight – a man to drive Wales to motor-racing glory. The first in a sport of many. We exchanged vows together. No other man on this planet has spoken to me the way he did just a few short hours ago. Up until now I have been a lump of shag meat; from now on no more of that. I must grow up, be a lady. This has been something else for one so young. Diary, I really have fallen in love for the first time. I love this man. I've known it since the very first time our eyes met, in my dad's office of all places. Even I can't avoid the arrow when it's fired. I can't recall just when, but it happened tonight. Perhaps I've always loved him. Just twelve hours ago he drove to victory in the Swiss Grand Prix, here in Zurich. This Welsh sporting hero thundered past the chequered flag in glorious style for our second win this year. Was it then that I fell head over heels for this man? Or was it the moment when he held me tightly underneath him that Cupid's arrow pierced my heart? Either way, life will never be the same again.

From now on I vow never to love another.

24 SEPTEMBER 2016: Received my first pay packet from Dad. It stinks, Diary. It reeks poverty. No favours there for the boss's daughter. So I've made up my mind, something must be done. I must help myself, it seems. After all, nobody else will. I must now pay my own way in this cruel world. One thing you can be sure of, Diary, this kid will not go through life poor as a church mouse – no, sir. I can now compete in saloon-car races, but that will be next spring. So what the fuck am I to do till then? The prize money for these petty car races amounts to nothing, not a hill of beans. Compared to Formula One, top flight, it's not the juice of the whisky. This job with Dad will not solve my immediate cash-flow problem. So what must I do? Perhaps rob a bank, hold up a post office – just don't get caught. My friend Cristobel's got a job behind the counter at Crabapple Marks, but that's not for me – slave wages, I think. The way that girl talks she'll end up a tart, or something worse. Despite this I will not be a kept woman; I shall pay my own way, for sure.

Today, with all my complaints about wages, it has been a fine day. I love driving the van. On a good day I'll drive perhaps a couple of hundred miles, lost in a fantasy world of my own. Just like this afternoon. I made two deliveries: one to Mountain Ash, the other all the way to Reading. Almost 300 miles of pure bliss.

I had to deliver a brand-new front bumper to a private address over in the small market town of Mountain Ash. Mr Atkins always buys his car at Dad's garage. He even comes all the way from his home to have his car serviced. Now, that's loyalty for you indeed. My dad has dozens of other such customers. He has such a good reputation – a fine record for all that. The car is a 2015 red Escort Tracker, with 30,000 miles on the clock to boot. He is a travelling salesman, driving a car for a living, just like me. The other call was to a garage just outside Reading, Berkshire, to collect some wheels – a special type for Dad. A distance of over 300 miles. I could do with a trip like it once a week at least. Blow the cobwebs from me, let me think straight. What is more, to make matters even better, the weather was fine all day long. So with the window wound down, the CD blaring, doing a steady seventy all the way there, I felt good about life in general. With such heady dreams inside my head, all I could do was plan ahead. I mean, what else does a girl do when behind the wheel. You think of cars, money and sex, in that order.

It is amazing just how well the new low road anti-roll suspension acts at speed on the open road. Especially a motorway like the M4. This van Dad's just bought, the Dorset Heavy, acts like a ballet dancer – it drives so light, handles so well. I adore it. Today it was a pleasure to drive.

As Dad told me on my first day, "The road's your office from now on."

If the road is really my office, then it stands to reason I must be comfortable in the workplace. Well, this van's comfort in heaven.

I spent all morning driving across to Reading. Staying in the left-hand lane, I cruised along, making just one stop on the way, at the motorway service station near the village of Leigh Delamere in Wiltshire, named romantically Buzzard's Roost. The usual ladies' call was followed by Coke, crisps, pie and chocolate bars by the score, bought in a greedy flurry. I browsed for at least thirty minutes or more. The headlines of the day caught my eye – they made grim reading for some, glory for others. Political unrest all over the world. A sporting scandal involving a call girl having a one-night stand with an England player who should've known better. His career was now threatened. But it was *Jam Tarts* that caused me to dream the unthinkable, allowing my imagination to run riot. Row upon row of daily newspapers told the same story on the front page. The press are quick to recognise a hero when they see one, only to damn them when things go wrong, the pen acting like some inky weapon to bring them down. Poetic hatred flows when called to do so. There was a picture of a Chinese farmer standing by the side of a very large cactus-like plant, and the headline read, 'CHINA TO SAVE MANKIND'. Elsewhere, war, starvation and empty suffering were bringing chaos along with despair mixed with hopeless turmoil to the human race. Just another day in the life of Mother Earth.

It had gone twelve as I found myself driving away from Reading, making my way back home to the safety of Wales – the warm embrace of the valleys – the back of my van loaded with the wheels. But with all that good news pouring out of the media, tempered with the bad, I smiled all the way home. Yes, *Jam Tarts* will be my financial salvation.

Diary, my old friend, I trust you not to tell my parents. They must never be told of my daringly brave plan.

7 OCTOBER 2016: Celebrated the Indian summer in style, down on the Pembrokeshire coastline. I have spent the day at Nan Carrs Cove, a tiny, remote beach close to nowhere at all. Cristobel joined me with her current boyfriend – Grass, of all people. As for myself, Wilson tagged along for good measure in all his finery. He told me he needed to make the most of this unseasonable heatwave. A chance to relax before the last Grand Prix of the year, to be held on the other side of the world, down in New Zealand. Sadly, I will not be joining him. As Dad reminded me yesterday, I must work six months before being entitled to time off. So I will stay here, working, instead of being with him, by his side. It would have been an honour to watch him drive to another victory, score his fourth win in a Grand Prix, placing him as one of the top drivers. A vast change from a few years past!

But, for today at least, I had him to myself. To look at, to touch, to talk with. A few hours to treasure before he flies off to compete. It was an old-fashioned beach picnic: a rug spread out on the sand, lazy people enjoying the heat of the afternoon. Cristobel was very quiet, saying little; Grass was no different. They listened to music while smoking some weed and sipping beer, dressed in scruffy clothes – something pulled out of the ragbag. They hadn't a care in the world to speak of. At about six they started eating some strawberry smash.

As Wilson told me, "It's all the rage in clubland at the moment. Try some, Amo – you'll love it."

So I took his advice. It is nothing more than strawberry cake laced with marijuana, only very strong, but I had three slices of the stuff. It made me feel awake one moment, sleepy the next. Wilson seemed to know what he was doing, familiar with the substance. He did not need Cristobel's advice on how much to eat. Wilson cut slice after slice, like at a birthday party or something, washing it down with beer. I followed him in dismay. Sitting cross-legged on the sand, my mouth filled itself with the cake. Soon the taste of warm strawberries filled my mouth, like drinking a liqueur. My head felt light, my mind wandering slightly. I recall heavy rock music in the background, a ship on the horizon, the day unreal, overflowing with happiness. Then I must've passed out, or something.

I have important questions to ask. Firstly, if this is what trendy people are eating in clubs, discotheques or late-night pubs, how come I've never heard of it or had any? Secondly, more importantly, does my dad know about Wilson's habit? The boss would chuck a wobbly if he found out. The press would have a field day. Oh, God, is my true love a junky, dicing with death each time he gets behind the wheel of a racing car?

Diary, should I say something?

24 OCTOBER 2016: As I was watching television tonight, all alone save for the dog, who is too old to enjoy himself any more, I received a glorious telephone call from Mum, all the way from New Zealand. She informed me that we had won yet another Grand Prix. The Welsh Dragon had triumphed down under. Wilson had driven like a demon, and the car performed like a miracle on the circuit. Everything about today has been nothing but good. Dad, the boss and the entire team are feeling over the moon. The call went on for over one hour. She told me about the whole day, minute by minute, from the second they woke up to face the day's sport. The press swamped the racing car. Wilson was interviewed until he could talk no more, Dad the same, the boss filled with pride. Now his investment in Welsh motor racing will start to pay great dividends.

The Grand Prix was not screened on television – I don't know why – so I must wait until the morning to study the papers, find out the details of this victory. All I know is there will be a nymphomaniac welcome to greet Wilson on his return.

Have we discovered the secret of success at last?

25 NOVEMBER 2016: Something happened at home. It has been coming for a long time. I discovered to my horror that Wilson takes heavy drugs. I have always known about Cristobel – her natural wild disposition gave that away. She will never change her ways. I guess I would not want her to. Cristobel would be such a dull friend to have, in that sense. The way she behaves, she's always fun to be with. The perfect cure for a bad day. When I'm in her presence I always feel good, want to smile.

My God, him of all people! He has a lot to lose. Why, only the other day he was headline news, not just here in Wales but all over the world. The sporting press are hailing him as a world champion in the making. He had his photograph on all the back pages. There was also a picture of him driving to victory down in Auckland, the Welsh Dragon racing car speeding past the flag, Wilson's arm raised in salutation to the cheering crowd. Is he barmy, or what?

Out in the garden, he left me for a moment or two. I followed him to a spot out of sight of the other guests. What I witnessed shocked me. I saw him, bold as brass, inject himself in the right thigh, then brace himself like a drunken man trying to be sober. I said nothing for the rest of the night. It was all I could do to stop him from falling over. He kept leaning on my shoulder. We must've seemed like two people hopelessly in love with each other, hanging on to each other for dear life, as inseparable as Romeo and Juliet.

This has been one hell of a night. Wilson's selfishness has placed me in a terrible dilemma. Should I tell Dad or Proctor-Hale? First the strawberry smash, now this caper! What the hell did he inject himself with? All I know is he isn't a diabetic. Another bloody party tomorrow.

2017

14 MARCH 2017: I remember the shop well – the trip to Llandudno in July 2007. Well, today I revisited it. A kind of childhood memory that needed rekindling. On the way up to North Wales we stopped for a rest at the glorious town of Builth Wells. How it all comes flooding back!

Glasfynydd's bakery shop on the High Street, established in 1857 – ah yes, I recall the wonderful aroma of freshly baked bread. As you opened the front door of the shop, a bell rang out letting Mr Glasfynydd know he had customers that needed his personal attention. Most of the local people called him by his first name, Bryn. The service seemed one of care for everybody in the town – a rare thing these days.

The day that I ventured into that abode, the talk was of a new baby, the dialect broad Welsh. My ears heard the chat, and my nose smelt a million things all at once coming from the bakery's kitchen. Cakes, buns, bread, cream, fruit. I could smell or even taste their warmth, they were that fresh. The sight combined with all that colour made me hungry indeed. A long glass counter was laid out in front of me. Four sections divided everything up. I could see cakes in one, buns in another, loaves of bread next to that. Then at the very far end were fancy home-made tarts of all shapes, sizes and fillings. It hit my nose with the force of a heavyweight fighter. I loved the punch of it – it stayed with me for the rest of the day. This included jam tarts – the very thing I did not want.

The journey up to this gastronomic paradise was uneventful. As a new servant of the road, I was obeying her every rule to the letter, my dog sitting still on the passenger seat, not moving at all. I made just one stop for coffee, thinking deep thoughts. My mind was made up – nobody would change it now.

Whenever I have a problem, the best way to solve it is to get behind the wheel of a car, any car, then just drive the crap out of it for mile after mile. I find it soothing. It makes me think deep thoughts, feeling the better for it with some music in the background. No quack, or psychiatrist, could offer such a cure for the troubled mind. Men could learn from us women drivers – certainly drivers like me.

My problem is of course that money, or lack of it, stops me from improving my lot in life. But no more poverty for me! All it takes is a letter – one that I'll post first thing in the morning. I know for a fact Proctor-Hale is to plough £10 million of his fortune into the business. The Welsh Dragon motor-racing team will become much stronger as a result of this investment.

The engine refined, X7 more efficient, the tyres designed for all weathers, the braking system stronger. Yet despite all this cash being thrown about like confetti at a wedding, none of it is coming my way. Wilson's getting a mighty pay rise for his efforts on the race circuits of the world. Perhaps I should stop taking the pill, get pregnant, marry the man. Why not? But carrying his seed does not appeal to me at all. Having babies will have to wait its turn in life. I have too much to do. Babies are all wind, pee, poo and vomit. Please, Diary, not just yet. No, the only way to get out of this cash problem is to sell myself to *Jam Tarts*.

After visiting Glasfynydd's today, I made the homeward drive constantly munching on cakes. I shared some with the dog. From today, Diary, I'm a self-helping free-wheeling dude, an independent woman of this earth. I have only one thing to say, Diary: I'm seventeen, able to drive faster at more miles per hour down the road, men to lust. My knickers are coming off.

10 APRIL 2017: Well, the day of days arrived at last, thank heaven. I am London-bound, with a handbag and purse, plus a great deal of courage. Cristobel came with me for support, the way a good friend would. She gave me much needed strength of purpose. My parents think we are going on a shopping trip. Believe me, Diary, this was no shopping trip. That was just my cover story, to fool them. I went up to London yesterday to do some artwork for a magazine called *Jam Tarts*. Well, to be honest, it was nude work, posing for a men's glossy. They paid me two years' salary in a lump sum. Just what the doctor ordered. If I've anything to do with it, this will be only the start.

Diary, my friend, I shall leave out none of the gory details about what happened in good old London town. Yesterday was for sure an historic day in my life, even if I live to be 100 plus a day. Yesterday, on 9 April in the year of our Lord 2017 I became financially independent. I suppose my own boss. This cheeky piece of labour has served a great function. I intend to reap the benefits of this cash-rich harvest for all it's worth. You can be sure there will be more than one crop gathered from the field.

Before we ventured out into the unknown, I gazed at myself in my bedroom mirror, giving myself a sly little wink out of the corner of my eye, saying, "It's now or never, baby face." I felt so naughty.

The journey to London was uneventful. At 7.45 from platform 2 the train pulled out of Cardiff Central, heading eastward to London. What Brunel would think of the reasons for my journey I can only surmise. Poor old Isambard would throw a Victorian wobbly, be horrified about my awful morals – a woman of the street! The only things missing from this artistic epic are a bottle of gin and a dose of the pox.

As the countryside hurtled by, Cristobel slept like a baby opposite me in the carriage. This belied the truth. Her black hair fell about her face, shoulders and back. It covered her closed eyes as she dozed. But what on earth was she dreaming about? The night before perhaps? The booze? The love? She'd partied with Grass until five. They had been to The Hell House to watch local group Rats in the Kitchen. The only reason I didn't join them was because I needed a clear head. But at Temple Meads the carriage filled up with commuters – travellers of every kind. A well-dressed man sat next to me, studying *The Times*. At Bath Spa he attempted the crossword in silence. Soon after that the train flew down the track at 1 million miles per hour. The stiff, rigid, phallus-like train then entered with passion the vaginal hole of the Box Tunnel. When the consenting travellers move along this particular section of railway line, they make love with rail travel, like no other. The journey on board a train becomes something special. At least that's how I saw things in my dreamy mind as I gazed out of the train's window. I watched the Wiltshire countryside flash past me. First Chippenham, then Swindon raced by me. I didn't even notice them.

My nerves only came alive when, sitting a few seats away from me, some dotty woman began a very annoying conversation on her mobile. She talked so loud we could hear every word – showing off, I think. She claimed to be talking to some arse in New York.

"Tell Mr Ball I'll accept half a million up front. Give my love to Gerry."

When the conversation ended, this arrogant, boastful businesswoman made sure we all noticed her. I tell you, Diary, it was ten minutes of infuriating waffle. What has gone wrong with the world of business? Do they have to conduct it on a train, or the number 7 bus? What's so awful about the good old office? That's where it belongs.

As we approached Reading, the M4 could be seen running parallel with the railway line. Suddenly, I wished I was on it, doing seventy in the left-hand lane, overtaking on the right. Living life in the fast lane. Coffee was taken as my baby slept, then slept again. Slough, then the patriotic sight of Windsor Castle caught my eye, the Royal Standard flying, telling me that the monarch was indeed home for the day. Soon after, the train pulled into Paddington, but for a rotten moment I could not wake Cristobel. I even thought to myself she'd overdosed. She was dead to the world. I know she'd taken something the night before. But after about five long minutes I brought her back to the land of the living. Sometimes we both live far too dangerously for comfort.

A Tube ride underneath London took us to the Soho office-cum-studio that settled the reason for the visit. Boy was I nervous – a female bag of trouble. But once inside I was greeted by Mr Jason Rathe himself, who turned out to be a perfect gentleman. Not the dirty old man I had envisaged. I have to say this, Diary: he came across as extremely effeminate. Gay perhaps? If the answer to that question was yes, then at least I'd be safe while nude. I would not be set upon, or approached for sexual favours. In this man's presence all seemed well.

Cristobel followed me into a tiny little room. It had a table, chair, dresser, and tea and coffee facilities if I needed a brew. I put on a white dressing gown, which fitted me perfectly. Underneath I was as naked as the day I was born. Then I waited for the call, like some actress on a film set. Then came the knock on the door. I stubbed out a cigarette, then ventured into the unknown.

The session took place in a large white-painted room, filled with both cameras and lights. Only Mr Rathe was there with us, as agreed. I didn't fancy the idea of being naked in a room full of leering men, gay or not. I guess that's the contradiction of all time, since all kinds of lusty, dirty, horny men, will spend time gazing at me, drivelling, foaming at the mouth. But that's for another time. Yesterday, at that time, all I could think of was the money I was being paid. So on his command I lay down on a red rug, then posed in all sorts of positions. The session took just twenty minutes before I found myself changed, with a fat cheque tucked away inside my purse. I have told Mr Rathe I'm available for more work. He's impressed.

We lunched at The Raven Arms on Regent Street, then secured the lie by shopping at Guild Smith Farrow at Knightsbridge, buying stuff I didn't need, or want. It was important to arrive back home in Cardiff with bags of shopping underneath our arms. If Dad, who was to meet us at the station, had to help us carry the stuff, the lie would be sound. So it turned out. We both arrived back home in Cardiff at one in the morning, catching the last train from Paddington. Dad asked how the day had gone, and more lies flowed from my imaginative mind as he assisted us in carrying our bags of shopping to the car like some elderly porter.

Banked the money this morning. It feels great.

22 APRIL 2017: I am a girl in pursuit of many things. Will I succeed or fail? Pity those talented, gifted people who fall foul of the deadly disease that's killed many a fine human being-cum-scholar, driven them to suicide. The illness of being star-crossed, a cancer of the soul. May God forbid this terrible fate to me. After today I'm just a poor little Welsh girl in love with winning.

Diary, I've far too much to do.

15 MAY 2017: The world has gone potty-Adam, along with my poor old dad. The Chinese have done it again. Will they ever stop? Dad has just taken on a new project that might enhance future travel. The boss, Proctor-Hale, is at the moment in China, making a business trip to a small village called Chowne, a company named Chowne Battery. Let me explain, Diary. The motoring industry is about to move into the space age. A slow snail-like change is taking place right under our very noses, and my dad must be a part of it, or so he says. So today I played my part in the future of mankind's travel into the mists of time, across this dear planet of ours. I had to drive all the way down to wonderful Penzance in Cornwall. The car I drove was, to say the least, strange, but delightful in its own way. Dad has taken on a small contract to sell a new type of vehicle: a battery-operated car, made in China. It is called the Graceful Swan, a small family saloon, powered by a tiny battery. Yes, folks, a battery – no petrol tank, no exhaust, thus no emissions. The cleanest car on the planet, or so the Chinese claim. Who am I to doubt them? I actually enjoyed driving it down the M5. I got a huge kick out of being the only person on that motorway driving such a car.

Yes, Diary, no pollution given out by little old me today. I must say it made me feel good about driving. Things must get better from now on. Just one massive drawback to all this hoo-ha: I had to take four batteries with me, then every 140 miles change the damn thing. Laddered my bloody tights right up to my dainty little arse. Sod that for a game of soldiers! Plus the fact that a top speed of just fifty miles per hour is just too slow for me. Great for a family in no hurry, but not for me. I am a girl in a hurry, eager to move on. I want fast cars, fast men, slow sex, in any order. But a price tag of just £10,000 brand-new might do the trick, selling it to the general public. My dad has agreed to sell just three of them this summer. A kind of trial, you might say. If all goes well more will be ordered. I believe that's what Proctor-Hale's gone to talk to them about. But I won't be buying one just yet, Diary.

I guess it's like changing from horses to the railway. So today I did my bit for the rest of the human race. Let us hope they see the light ahead. 'Chinese to Save Mankind!'

Hell, a new pair of fucking tights tomorrow. The sacrifices I make!

21 JULY 2017: Today has been a mixed bag. Good news from Cape Town, great news from the newsagent Mr Green, excellent news from Abbots Vale. Let me run through them for you.

First of all, in blazing South African heat we've struck another victory, winning the South African Grand Prix at Cape Town's Cheetah Run. Wilson telephoned me straight afterwards, telling me of the win. The press will want their pound of flesh when he returns; so will I. More bloody interviews. This marks the Welsh Dragon's second win of the season so far. The second piece of good fortune came in the shape of my acceptance for my first family-saloon-car race, over at Abbots Vale, next week. I can't get behind the wheel of my yellow baby quickly enough. The third lump of good fortune, of pride, has come in the form of my photo shoot. I saw a copy of *Jam Tarts* on the top shelf of Mr Green's shop, hidden away, out of reach. On pages four, five and six of that publication my colourful naked body can be seen by all. Yet still nobody knows my secret. Let's hope it stays that way.

Roll on Abbots Vale!

22 JULY 2017: Arrived at work just after eight thirty. The garage was alive with activity, only I didn't have time to mess about with the lads. It's been a routine day at work – nothing more to report on that score, Diary. Nothing special about today, I'm sad to say. Everybody's far too excited about our fine victory in Cape Town. Most of the newspapers are full of it, carrying the headline 'GREAT DAY FOR THE DRAGON', then a picture of Wilson toasting the win with champagne. Dolly girls dressed in skimpy outfits surround him on all sides. No, I'm not jealous – goes with the job, I guess. I mean, in a few days' time he'll be mine again. Underneath that another headline: 'WILSON McCAIN A WORLD CHAMPION IN THE MAKING'. I read the headline more than once, and it filled me with unending pride. The future seems rose-tinted, secure.

The rest of the day became very mellow, tame even. A huge drop back into the real world. I drove around the city of Cardiff. Engine parts, oil, brake pads, wires and even a window were delivered to homes, shops and garages galore. At Canton I had a fish-shop lunch, eaten in the van, washed down with a can of red fizzy. The CD was never off. Dick Fat Gut Blue's new hit single, 'Hit Me with Love', was played until I was sick of it. Got home at five, had a good soak in the bath, listened to the radio. The MP for the Isle of Wight has been promoted to the shadow cabinet as Foreign Affairs Spokesman. Wow!

27 JULY 2017: Well, kiss a duck's arse, Saturday finally arrived. It lived up to all expectations – it did not let me down. But more to the point, I did not let the side down. Last week my true love was a hero; this week it is my turn to bask in the glory. Today I drove for myself, for my family, for Wilson, and for Wales.

On Friday I gave the Flying Banana – that's what I've named my racing car because of its bright-yellow colour – a good sound drive, all the way to Pembroke. Throughout the journey all I could think of was this race I'm taking part in. A maze of race tactics was walked through in my mind. What to do, when to do it. I faced ten rivals of both sexes and all abilities. I became lost in the haze as I worked out a way forward. Planning ahead seemed the right way to secure a victory. This has proved the key to success, for this has been a wonderful day and an even better week.

This afternoon at Abbots Vale there was a record crowd of people. Thousands turned up to watch the motor racing on this warm sunny day. We arrived at just after noon. I tell you, the sight of all those people, in summer dress, milling about this quaint, picturesque Welsh village fairly scared the pants off me. The steep incline of Abbots Vale Hill appeared as a human motorway, with people walking up one side while on the other they walked down. Children played by the stream; families took a picnic on the village green. Outside the white-painted inn some men drank beer, then talked about the cricket match in the afternoon – Abbots Vale played Lancombe Hall. By the village square a young man rested his bicycle, glad for the cool drink he sipped. As we turned the car into the car park, a young girl eating an ice cream ran after her mother. They held hands, then walked away. But all the time people headed out to the motor-racing circuit. Soon they would be watching – hopefully, cheering me on to victory.

Lunch was taken at The Monastery Hotel. There's a private golf course with it – members only on Sunday. Way ahead a man stood on the first tee, rooted to the spot, waiting to take that first vital shot to the green. Pirouetting on his feet, he swung the club to hit the golf ball, sending it on its way. There was a loud crack as the ball was sent flying into the air. The well-dressed man twisted in motion, but he never moved from the spot as he followed through with the shot. He appeared to have the grace of a ballet dancer, making him seem as a golfing prima donna. I tried to watch the ball as it took flight towards the flag in hole number one, but I lost it in mid-flight.

Golf aside, this was a day for motor racing. I was honoured this afternoon by the encouraging presence of the boss. Proctor-Hale came along to support me in this race. Over lunch of pheasant pie, lemon ice and champagne, plans were made for my future. As they spoke, ate, drank, then ate again, my stomach turned over, fear grabbed me, nerves took over. I began to clock-watch. Soon three chimed on the grandfather clock by the pot plant near the log fire. Right there I was a sportswoman on the make for sure.

Proctor-Hale gave me some instructions about the race; Dad mentioned fuel saving. Their advice became lost in the abyss of my mind. For all their good intent, the details went in one ear and out the other. Wilson was quiet, saying little, but he held my hand all the time, right up to the time when I climbed into the car, waiting for the race to start. Yes, Diary, you've guessed it: once in the driving seat, I became overwhelmed with self-confidence, a feeling that I could not lose, that defeat was impossible. The Flying Banana zoomed away from the start of the race, with command and elegance, and with little old me at the wheel. My concentration increased ten-fold. I put my foot down hard on the accelerator, passing two cars as I did so. Soon I found myself in second place, a blue car ahead of me, but only just, as I waited for the chance to pounce in front of him, taking the lead. The thrill of the race for me came as I turned up the straight for the sprint to the chequered flag. I saw it to the right of me – the crowd in the grandstand at Abbots Vale cheered me on to victory. I might not have done it without their help. The first female driver to gain a place on the rostrum in many years! I tell you, Diary, the feeling of triumph today must've been a message from the gods themselves. At just seventeen, I cannot find the words to define just how I felt this afternoon as I passed the winning flag three seconds ahead of my nearest rival, a professional driver named Joe Backbone. He kissed me twice, asking for a date. I said no.

It is now four in the morning. I can't sleep. Diary, my old mate in words, my inky pal for life, today will be infectious until the day I die. I have read the headlines in today's evening paper, the *Welsh Night*, over one million times, or is it two million? It makes me tingle all over with pride.

I'll write it out for you, Diary, because I know you'll understand.

'She was marvellous, driving faster than a speeding train. Motor racing star Ann Marie Osborne, the Cardiff Flyer, slams rivals at Abbots Vale. She drove like a veteran, beating all before her. The big question now is where will our Welsh baby go from here?'

There's a party at Wilson's place at the weekend. The Hammer Heads are playing live in the back garden. Some gig that'll be! Well, goodnight, Diary, or is it morning?

3 AUGUST 2017: The victory party thrown tonight at Wilson's place has been a wonderful disaster, a mixed-up shindig, a horrifying glimpse into the future. Perhaps I should have been more vigilant. I mean, the signs were all there for me to see, but I chose to ignore them. To be honest, Diary, to make matters worse, I joined in. A willing participant with the man I love.

The rock band, the Hammer Heads, played well. A stage had been set up in the back garden, illuminated with bright lights. I would say at least 100 people turned up for the gig, with many hangers-on, creeps, weird people of all types. The band was very loud, with lots of rhythm backed up by bawdy lyrics. But soon booze, dancing, food, kissing, shouting and screaming took over, like a pack of wolves on the prowl. By nine the party was in full swing, Wilson playing the perfect host. For a man in his position he was soon surrounded by pretty girls – whether they were single, married, fat, thin, drunk, sober or horny, he acknowledged their presence. At midnight, though, he held my hand, kissed my lips and held my waist as we danced. The danger signs flashed before my eyes, yet I did nothing to stop them – put them out, so to speak. Joe Hallam, lead singer with the band, joined us in Wilson's bedroom, of all places.

Then he uttered the fatal words to me: "I'll strum this baby of mine while we all get high."

These words should have been a warning for me, but they weren't. Hallam appeared cocky as hell as he walked to the bedroom. Once inside, what I saw startled me. The room had been set up for one purpose only: drugs, sex and music, I believe in that order. What on earth was my true love doing tonight? I wondered. Looking back on the night's events, it was madness of the first order. Had he done this before many times over? Yet I stood there a willing partner in crime, as guilty as everybody else in that room.

The master bedroom has a four-poster bed set in the middle of the room. Huge china pots decorated with flowers of every kind added colour, along with scent. What a shame that the man I love, adore, hides a dark secret like this. This appears to be the price of his love for me. Question, Diary: is this price too high? As I recall events, it was two in the morning when the real trouble started. A thousand pin marks on my lover's arm should have given away a million secrets. Why had I not seen them before? Had love blinded me? But I joined in, a fellow junky with a past needing to hide herself. A human being mixing with the wrong kind, and doing nothing to escape. After last night this must be the case. All I can say in my defence is that I was too weak-willed to try stopping my true love from injecting himself, watching open-mouthed as he prepared for the first hit of the night.

Soft music played in the background, the lights dimmed. Out came two syringes, along with some heroin. What happened next shocked me to the core. Wilson wrapped a leather strap around his arm, then tightened it until a vein showed, carefully injecting the heroin into his bare arm. He smiled at me as his face contorted, his eyes rolled back, then he slumped on to some cushions.

"Come join me, angel face. Amo, let's travel to another place tonight."

I rolled up my sleeve, offering myself.

Wilson whispered to Hallam, "Fix my baby up, Joe, my boy. Give her a ticket."

With that sentiment, Joe Hallam helped inject me. I fell backwards, landing in Wilson's lap. By now though, he'd gone, looking like a sleeping baby.

'This has been done many times before,' I thought. 'A well-rehearsed act. The actions of a city junky, not a sporting hero of the future.'

Diary, I need help – I'm scared. So does Wilson.

18 OCTOBER 2017: Dear Diary, nothing happened. Ate a bad curry, farted the national anthem.

20 OCTOBER 2017: Sweden equals the 'Four S System' of life as it should be lived. These are sun, snow, sex and saunas, not necessarily in that order of merit. But today Welsh voices sang out from Stockholm all the way up to the North Pole. Wilson drove to a fine victory in the Swedish Grand Prix. The whole team are ecstatic. Indeed, this puts a smile on the face of a good year. The Welsh Dragon has finished sixth on the leader board. Wilson McCain sees his own name climb up to fifth on the drivers table. The victory ranks as the best one yet. The improved fuel consumption, lighter chassis and better steering compound all played their part in this Grand Prix win. Celebrations will last for a long time to come. Perhaps next year will be even better for us all. My true love is fast becoming a sporting icon amongst the young. Not just here in Wales, but right across Britain. With this media jazz comes responsibilities aplenty. After this weekend, I must question that tag.

Nobody can deny Wilson's ability behind the wheel of a racing car. The press hype of 'a future world champion' may well be more than some sporting dream that comes true. But his off-track antics are now a cause for concern, even by me. Hailed as Sportsman of the Year, he now openly brags about how heroin makes him relax, how strawberry smash feeds the hunger. Cristobel smokes cannabis like filter tips. Drink flows like a tidal wave day after day. Money seems to be everywhere, even on the floor of his house, like he's leaving it for the mice to spend. I make this confession to you now, Diary, asking for your wisdom. Yes, I have pin marks on my arm now. I am surrounded by drunks, junkies and layabouts whom I call friends. One I even call lover.

Help me, please.

2018

7 JANUARY 2018: Today has been a mixture of pride followed by anxiety. A trip to the newsagent's and a test run in the Flying Banana. Well, let me tell you, Diary, they could not have been more different. But my secret remains safe – for the moment, at any rate. On my way to work, though, it came perilously close to being discovered. It made my heart skip a beat.

Like some successful businesswoman from the city, my whole day had been planned well ahead. The morning started in the usual manner: delivering car parts for Dad. So with that in mind we travelled to work together. At the precinct we stopped at the newsagent's. My dad bought *The Times* for himself, plus a few odd things he needed. I bought a copy of *Engine Fast*. As we both walked through the shop to be greeted by Mr Green, smiling, wonderful, I went numb with fear. Nestling amid the magazines about world affairs, sport, music and even politics stood the adult publications on the top shelf, away from everything else. Just beside the other sleazy titles stood that week's copy of *Jam Tarts*, the edition I was in, pages six to seven. Thank God I was not on the front cover! In fact my photographs showed me spreadeagled on the floor in glorious colour, my body parts exposed for the world to see, gloat over. But as I walked nervously through the shop, Dad next to me, he remained in blissful ignorance. I glanced up to the top shelf. *Jam Tarts* was there all right. On the front cover there was a picture of some blonde, her breasts hidden by her hands, a cat strategically placed in front of her. The caption read, 'PLEASE TAKE CARE OF MY PET PUSSY'. According to the magazine it was Be Kind to Animals Week. Oh, my God, soon that will be me. I have been invited to pose for them yet again. I have taken up their offer. More money on the cards. What a secret to have!

Having survived this ordeal – as if my dad would buy such artistic rubbish! – the day behind the wheel simply got better. A great day at work in fact. At three, we loaded up the Flying Banana on to the truck, heading out to Abbots Vale. The purpose behind the trip was a practice run at the race circuit to boost my confidence for the season ahead. Like I needed it for sure! I was cocky as hell, but I did as I was told by Dad. I mean, who was I to argue with him?

Where was my true love, Wilson? Diary, I don't know and don't care. Probably recovering from a hangover or something. Right now I couldn't give a damn about that drug-taking little shit.

Today I was King of the Track, not him. I took Dad's advice to heart: brake hard at the bends and accelerate away into the straight, hugging the side of the circuit.

As he told me, "Cut the grass, my little apple blossom."

I drove to his command. The track record for Abbots Vale is 59 dead, set by Wayne Clifford in 2009. He drove a Formula Three car and clocked 175. Well, today, Diary, I knocked off one second from that record – unofficially, of course. But the point is I did it in style. Abbots Vale became my Olympia.

Goodnight, Diary, my friend. Tonight I sleep in peace. The world of sport can only get better.

10 MARCH 2018: Two weeks to go before the start of the coming motor-racing season. I am on holiday with Wilson, here to relax for a couple of sun-packed days. We are supposed to unwind, because next week the first Grand Prix takes place at Flower Garden down in Bali, on the other side of the world. Sent a few postcards and made some telephone calls home. All seems well, save for one fact: Wilson appears rather ponderous, not in his usual holiday mood. God only knows why! Perhaps it's the nerves setting in, or maybe the drugs. We shared some strawberry smash as we sunbathed this afternoon. Right now I wish we hadn't.

After tonight things might buck up a shade. Then this Spanish love-in might take off. Attended a Spanish guitar concert given by Don Raul Sebastian. I love his music. That's why we are here – to see him perform. I adore the setting – outside in the amphitheatre. Starting at nine this evening, he performed to a full house. Not an empty seat anywhere. It has been a lovely evening for me, but Wilson was very quiet, hardly saying a word all evening long. As I write this entry, Diary, the prospect of my true love proposing to me seems impossible. I wish he would. I am eighteen, with a strong maternal instinct at the moment. A baby would be nice, marriage a delight. But in this hotel room in San Carlos my true love sleeps like a baby. He sleeps so soundly he might even be dead. I hope he's at least dreaming of me.

See you, Diary. I'll be glad to go home.

7 JUNE 2018: It is all doom again on the home front. The sporting press are having a field day at our expense. The Welsh Dragon team appear to be a laughing stock. I guess we have become a victim yet again to the see-sawing nature of sporting good fortune. Since the first Grand Prix this summer, it has all gone wrong – gaga, as they say. We lost in Bali, Australia, Monaco, Canada and Germany. Then yesterday, in Italy, we didn't even finish the race. A mess? Tell me about it!

My poor dad was interviewed on television. Believe me it did not make for good viewing – looked bad, sounded worse. He appeared on the current-affairs programme *London Today*. The presenter, Harvey Chambers, was all smiles as he chatted to Lord Tufnell about his horse The Hayloft, which won the Derby on Saturday. When my dad came on the set Chambers went on the attack. He became aggressive. Chambers, like all television presenters, is arrogant beyond reason, a right bastard for sure. The parasites of the press hail one minute, and it's damnation the next. Chambers set about my dad without mercy.

"Tell me, Mr Osborne: we've heard it all before, why should we believe you now? Your motor racing team's just not up to the job, is it?"

Then Dad rose up to defend his Welsh honour.

"My dear fellow, we have won six Grand Prix races; more will come in the years to come. Like a fine wine, we'll improve with age."

It cut no ice with Chambers, who then tried to damn Wilson as a moderate driver, not up to the job also. For at least six more awful minutes of this programme Dad gave what he got. Then right at the very end of the interview Dad came up with an answer that stumped Chambers.

"Life is a game of cards. A jack or queen high, we all hope for a winning hand. Some, like us, need more than one hand to deal a victory."

With that, in front of millions of viewers, my dad just got up from his seat, handing the microphone to Chambers. Then he left the studio, leaving Chambers alone.

That Chambers got what was coming to him. It took my dad to deliver it. Serves the prig right.

14 JUNE 2018: Midnight, The Boating Hotel, Cowes, Isle of Wight.

Diary, I feel great. This has been a wonderful day. Sporting glory, followed by lots of love. I competed in a family-saloon-car rally, the Isle of Wight Classic, driving the Flying Banana. This afternoon I won the race in fine style a full ten seconds ahead of my nearest rival, James Fence, a veteran rally driver. I am very proud of the way I drove my car, performing miracles behind the wheel of my baby.

The rally consists of one complete circuit of the island. You follow the main coastal road all the way around the island, at times racing through the villages, towns and farmers' fields to test your driving skills to the limit. Behind the wheel, I had to be on top of my game. You drive through all the main towns and villages, reaching the end of the rally on The Esplanade at Cowes. It was certainly tough going, but by the time I arrived at Cowes my yellow car was covered in mud, grass and shit of all kinds. Despite this I felt cold sweat drip down my spine when the flag was waved for my honour. Victory!

Wilson, along with the rest of my family, was there to watch, cheer me on. Even Proctor-Hale appeared, overjoyed with me.

He told me, "Ann Marie, dear, you are the best female racing driver I've ever seen. You have a gift as no other. I wonder where it will all end." With that he kissed me on the cheek.

The local press interviewed me and took my picture. I told the reporter, "I hope to win more races like this. I adore the car."

I waved to the crowd, who numbered perhaps 1,000 people or more. This was no time for being shy. I milked it for all it was worth, loving every minute of it. The trophy that went with the victory was presented to me by the local MP, Nicholas Rachael, a dish of a young man. He even kissed me on the cheek, then I cheekily placed one back, right on his lush lips. I must tell you, Diary, because I know you can be trusted, our eyes met for that brief moment that tells of love and mutual respect.

Just a passing thought: what a cracker of a man! A dish, intelligent and rich too. Mr Rachael has just been promoted to the Foreign Office. According to *The Times* his pet subject is the Middle East. On Friday he's off to Jerusalem for important meetings. By the way, before I go to bed, Nick Rachael is single. Wowee.

Goodnight. I love politics.

12 JULY 2018: Managed to gain some vital industrial information today. Don't tell Whitehall though. Dad got pissed, cuddled me, then blurted out the name of the cactus-like plant that X7 comes from. The wonder-fuel that will change the world, then take our Welsh motor-racing team to everlasting glory, so he says. Grown in China, it is called – wait for it, Diary, my little pussycat, my trusted little friend – *Hybridcactipalmius lombaski*. Beat that, Grandma.

Whatever next, I wonder?

25 SEPTEMBER 2018: As of late, Wilson's depressed after yet another poor season behind the wheel. I guess the last thing he wants is my body. What a jerk that boy of mine has become. He will have his heroin, but not me. A needle in the arm, not prick in the puss.

Things have gone from bad to worse in motor racing. A poor driving error caused us to pull out of the Irish Grand Prix in Dublin for the second time this season. I mean, the same thing happened in Iceland. Wilson's taking all the blame, but it was much more personal after Dublin. He took it very badly – it clearly hurt him very much. The ridicule has caused some mechanics to quit. Morale has never been lower here in Cardiff. We won't even be attending the Moscow event as the car is now laid up. To my shame, there is now talk of packing in the game – too much money for too little return. Proctor-Hale's patience seems to be running out. My dad's down like all the rest of the team, only he won't hear of quitting the game. He loves it too much anyway.

As he told me over dinner tonight, beaming with eternal optimism, "Somewhere out there, my little apple blossom, Lady Luck is waiting to shake our hand, kiss our lips, bless us with her power. We must hold on."

I do admire his wild positive outlook on sport. Diary, I hope he's right.

26 SEPTEMBER 2018: Diary, I have not been disappointed, that I promise you. But let me tell you more, my dear friend. This afternoon I got all I desired. For once my true love was outgoing, giving, kind, a friend, just like you are. He offered himself to me all the way. At noon we got into his car, then went fishing together for the Black Mountain trout. At this time of the year down at Grwyne Fechan they are in profusion. It was one of those days –unexpected, welcomed by me. Hand in hand, arm in arm, lip to lip, we walked along the riverbank, where Wilson set up his fishing gear – something he hasn't usually got the time for these days. But today he found the time, and this pleased me no end. Sipping a cool beer, I watched him fish up then down the river. The clear mountain water crashed over the rocks in midstream. It has been a day well shot of motor racing.

Sex did not take place, I promise you that – didn't need it. We did not catch any fish either. But I caught something better than any trout or salmon you can name. I caught my man, hook, line and sinker. Wilson proposed to me – we are getting married soon, very soon, Diary. He became all passionate, kind, tender. Not the kind of man who has lost some bloody motor race, then takes it out on the nearest person next to him. Always of course that's been me. But today, down by that river, I forgave him. I am sure things will improve between us. I never thought I'd say it, but yes, I'm ready for marriage, babies, domestic bliss for the next fifty years or more. I guess I've fallen into the trap all women fall into sooner or later. So what? Count my blessings, hey!

Diary, I must get you a girlfriend now.

14 DECEMBER 2018: Dear Diary, I'm eighteen, drunk and in need of a piddle, so together let's celebrate the Jimmy Riddle. One last tinkle then it's homeward-bound. Oh, how I love to hear the sound of my own wee-wee as it hits the loo. It's a perfectly natural thing to do. It makes me feel better just like I oughta – what a relief to be passing water. I'm a casualty of getting blind drunk, so no more bleedin' elephant's trunk, at least until

Saturday night's sorrow. Sadly, I feel that's tomorrow.

God help my liver, then my brain! I will sleep it off all the same.

2019

17 JANUARY 2019: Guess what I did in bed last night, Diary? Go on, guess? I haven't done it in ages, but it was so much fun. The memory lingers clear in my mind – a pleasant sensation all over my body makes me tingle still, all these hours later. I slid under the bedcovers armed with a torch and ate six bags of steak crisps washed down with a couple of bottles of Miners Milk Bitter, pinched from the local shop. I then spent the rest of the night listening to a cricket match on the radio.

England played the West Indies off the park in Barbados. A gobsmacking 1,340 runs scored in their first innings, with just four wickets falling. The score card reads as follows.

England First Innings

Cartwright	not out		450
Linden	bowled	Mint	250
Beer	bowled	Hull	150
Essex	lbw	Nutts	300
Hardy	bowled	Mint	190
		Total:	1,340

Then the captain, Kent Essex, declared.

But it was a fast bowler called Sidney Grimshaw from Sheepsbottom-on-the-Willow, Lancashire, who stole the show. The mighty West Indies were bowled out for less than 200 runs in their first innings. Young Grimshaw made the ball bounce twice down the wicket – almost unplayable bowling. He took 9 for 150, including 21 maidens. Each tumbling wicket made me choke on my milk and spill crisps all over the sheets. For all that, it must be said, Diary, when any British side in any sport you care to name performs like they did it is good for the nation as a whole. Everybody feels good about it. The newspapers are full of it this morning. Tonight I will watch some of it on the television, then make for the bedcovers again. I bet even W. G. Grace himself never played in a side this good. All in all, I think it's fab-o. But one last comment, Diary, must be made by little old me: a rugby player's balls are much bigger than a cricketer's. Yes, much more my size. In passing, let's hear it for the English cricket team. They deserve it. I love the middle wicket. Thank God for cricket.

2 APRIL 2019: We're all searching for that lucky break in life. If you're not, then you should be. There was a very important meeting at headquarters today. Dreams have been planned, along with some much needed reality. The financial jigsaw has been put in place for the next two years. The Welsh Dragon may be down, but, like some boxer in trouble during the fifth, we are not out. Last season was a total shambles – no victories – but I flew the flag here at home. I scored three wins to my credit. So, Diary, as a result I have been promoted at work. Let me explain to you so you'll understand. After a total of six rally wins in all, this summer I am to be allowed to race in Formula Three at least once, just to see how I get on. It will be at Hawk's Bridge near Winchester. Dad told me last night. I'm absolutely thrilled; so's my dog.

I celebrated tonight with no inhibitions – lots of food, drink, love, laughter and Japanese Splendour. Wilson got engaged to me officially last fall. Now like some happily married couple we share our lives with each other. I moved in with him just before Christmas. I cook his food, put out his clean clothes, do the ironing, dusting and hoovering. On Friday I open my legs for him, the dutiful wife-to-be.

A date for our wedding has been fixed. Wilson will marry me on 10 December, as soon as the motor-racing season ends. Let's hope it ends with glory for all in our life to come. A honeymoon in Hawaii and a baby soon – more than one, I feel. Wilson earns more than £5 million – not bad for a supposed loser. No worries about housekeeping there. On Saturday I'm planning a cosy night in with my husband-to-be, just the two of us. Roast beef, cake, orange ice, fruit mix and a French 95 to complement the meal. Love will follow.

Diary, what have I done to deserve this kind of a life?

12 APRIL 2019: Like a devoted wife I kissed Wilson goodbye as he left for work this morning. He might well have been off to the city, but he wasn't. He will be driving in the Spanish Grand Prix next week. So today he tested the Welsh Dragon car again, putting it through its paces at Abbots Vale, searching for answers, hoping for improvement. Dad, along with the boss, attended. As for myself, I had to spend the day driving all the way to Tenby. I clocked off at five sharp. My love has been very down of late. I try my best to buck him up, to no avail. My turn to test my nerve in Formula Three will come soon enough. The race at Hawk's

Bridge can't come quickly enough for me. This is my big chance to shine. Ah yes, 10 July. The adrenalin pumps through my body as a mighty river.

When Wilson returned home this evening, I could tell by his expression that the day had not gone well.

Indeed, he told me frankly, "That car of your dad's is a lump of shite. Summer's over already. Where's my beer?"

I told him to "Go get the fucking beer yourself. I am not your servant." I meant it, pointing to the fridge.

He looked at me with an evil glance in his eye. It made me shiver. I had never seen this in him before. I backed off as he got up off his arse, making his way to the fridge. As the dinner cooked, as the wine chilled, tempers began to boil over. This has been a night I will not forget in a blind hurry.

The so-called cosy night in, where romance took over, love ruled, has turned into a nightmare all because of his bloody-mindedness. It hurts more because I made the effort, took so much care over it to get it right. He didn't. The table looked a picture with its patterned cloth, tall candles, shiny cutlery and crystal glasses. The soup was eaten in an uneasy silence. When the roast was served, it provoked a response from him: he took a mouthful, spitting it out, making a vile comment about my cooking. My excuse cut no ice. I ran from the room, knocking over a wine glass. Amazingly, Wilson threw the joint of roast beef straight at me, missing by inches. I screamed. He followed, catching me up, hitting me about the face, punching me in the stomach. I hit the deck, blood pouring from my face, bending in pain.

Diary, what am I to do? Who do I turn to?

I don't know what to do. My face is in agony – a swelling has formed on the right jaw. My nose bled and my make-up has run down my face. I look a mess. The red cocktail dress is now torn, bloodstained, ruined. Perhaps he's angry, or maybe just jealous. Something he said under his breath makes me think that way: "You little motor-racing whore, Daddy's little girl wonder." He then took a few bottles of wine to bed with him. Right now he's out for the count, having taken some Japanese Splendour. When he had gone upstairs, I telephoned Cristobel, who came at once to help out, like a faithful dog. She hugged, then kissed me. At the moment, as I write up my day, she stands guard at the door, my bodyguard, a protecting angel. She is staying the night. If he ventures this way, she'll smash his face in.

Diary, what do I tell Mum? How do I explain the bruises to Dad?

8 JUNE 2019: Well, well, well, the day has finally come when at last I got to drive a real racing car, experience speed behind the wheel, see life fly by at twice the speed of sound. I did not want the day to end. Everybody was chuffed to dickymint at the way I performed. Dad, Proctor-Hale and all the boys in the pits raved at the way I handled the car. Baby, it felt as natural as breathing as I pushed out the throttle and roared up the straight at Abbots Vale. Even the rabbits cheered me on. I swear a fox applauded me home, then winked at me as I flashed by him. It has been that sort of day. Only one thing has ruined everything I have worked for: the attitude of Wilson. He is now a drugged-up, pissed-up, shabby excuse for a man – a man who has developed a massive chip on his right shoulder. Then, to make matters worse, it's all my fault, to boot. Last night, as I prepared for this big day, there was nothing but bitterness from him. No encouragement, no good-luck message.

As he sniffed weed for lunch, all he could say was, "Daddy's little Goody Two Shoes off to the show tomorrow. You'll never amount to a thing. Only your dad's put you where you are today. That car won't run for me; it won't run for you. Get out of my sight." With that he stuck his two fingers up at me.

So I got out of the house like a bullet from a smoking gun. Even Dad has run out of patience with him. Changes will be made soon, that I do know.

Wilson lost in Spain, but finished. The press said nice things about him. Baines, from the *Cardiff Herald*, actually praised his performance. But he doesn't appear to care any more. The Welsh Dragon needs a Grand Prix victory as never before. I pray for one soon – Canada perhaps. My face has healed – the cuts, the bruises, the pain. I wish Wilson well, for I still love him, even with the violence.

Cristobel sleeps with me now.

10 JULY 2019: I finished sixth today in my first motor race. I drove well, only nervously. But, for the first time this summer, attention was not on me; Wilson gained all the applause. Ah yes, I saw, not for the first time, the squalid enigma of the sporting press, witnessed at their most gruesome. One man's poisonous words can bring the most talented sportsman (or woman) tumbling off his pedestal to in the end achieve nothing, where something just might have been possible.

Not that long ago the season for us looked over, lost in the fog of defeat. The gutter press took us apart, but two fine victories in Holland then Canada seem to have repaired the damage, filled in the gaps. My true love has been put back as one, tipped yet again, by the same press as before, to be a future world champion, someone all Wales can be proud of. Ronald Trethowan of the *Gazette*, who once called for Wilson's head, now sings his praises in print. They took photographs of him winning in fine style. My dad's beaming with pride about the rest of the season, saying all sorts of way-out things. And, most important of all, these unexpected wins have brought Wilson back to the world of the living. He kissed me this evening.

Of my motor race itself, read on. Diary, Hawk's Bridge is a lovely motor-racing circuit set outside the ancient city of Winchester, once the seat of kings, the house of governance. Today it became the arena of sport. The roar of the racing car filled the air. Yes, this was a race to cherish. I started the race from grid ten, way down the order of merit. Despite this poor handicap I made the best use of my disadvantage. By lap two I had passed three other cars, storming down the straight, taking them on the inside. This position did not change during the race until in the penultimate lap the car in front crashed out. So I held my own until the end of the race. Car nine tried to cut me down, but I squeezed him out each time. Serves the bastard right! I lost a few pounds in sweat and drank far too much water. All I wanted after the race was a good pee. As a young woman who desires more of the same, I only have one thing to say: where will this end?

Diary, today life is worth living.

14 SEPTEMBER 2019: It has been just another mundane day at work. I arrived back home at just after five thirty. Took the dog along – he was great company. Delivered car parts for Dad all over South Wales. Unbelievable as it may seem, I clocked up 300 miles altogether. Tomorrow will probably be the same. Got a call to make at Llanfairpwllgwyngyll – a new 1084 engine to a private address. Fancy, a day trip to Anglesey! The engine's all ready loaded up in the van. I leave at dawn. Another great day ahead – the road's my office again. Wow!

Gave my photograph of Stirling Moss winning the Monaco Grand Prix a million years ago a great big soppy kiss. Motor racing's favourite grandfather.

20 SEPTEMBER 2019: One thing about today sticks out like a sore thumb. It has been anything but mundane. Arranged months ago, this afternoon I attended, yet again, another photo shoot for *Jam Tarts* magazine. The owner, Mr Rathe, called me on Monday to confirm the appointment. The man was so impressed by my first, second, then third sessions. He asked me what I wanted.

As he said to me, "You call the play, Ann Marie. Whatever you want."

Since my first appearance, the magazine has soared in popularity, selling many more copies than usual. My body has fans – no doubting that. Men love, adore me. So call it I have. He met me, along with a team of photographers, in secret, at Swansea Station. Then by car we drove to a remote but wonderful spot called Fairy Spell Falls. Halfway up a mountain, a stream called the Glamorgan Well disappears into the mountain itself. Then way downstream it tumbles out of a sheer rock face, like Mother Nature's hosepipe, forming a lake at the bottom. I have always admired this natural creation. So I chose this place for my photo shoot. They took many photographs of me naked under the waterfall, as if taking a shower at home. I have asked Mr Rathe to name the sequence of photographs 'Mother Nature's Shower'. He thinks it's a wonderful idea. If the magazine continues to sell well, go past the 50,000-copies-per-week mark, he has promised me a fat bonus.

But, as he tastefully said to me, "The rest of the world must see your incredible body, the warmth of your skin."

I agree with all that. Just one thing bothers me about all this: I will be on the front cover.

The actual photographs will appear in the middle section of the magazine. I can't wait to see it. What's done is done, but I just pray my parents do not see it. They will both die of shame. I earn no more money for driving racing cars – that's still a dream. I shall say sorry to nobody about what I am doing, not even the Almighty Himself. Even He rewards those who help themselves. What else am I doing?

The six best photographs consist of the following. I tell you, Diary, because I know I can trust your integrity. I stood there this afternoon with the Welsh wind causing shivers, goosebumps and weak knees, naked as the day I was born, yet determined and bloody-minded as ever. Let us hope it stays between just you, me and the bank.

The first photograph shows me standing on the grey rocks with the waterfall behind me – a side shot, then full-frontal. The next captures my smile, amongst other things, exposed to the world. After this angelic piece of wonder, Mr Rathe suggested an even better picture worthy of merit. I lay down in some shallow white water, near some rocks, and a torrent of water foamed itself over my body. I closed my eyes as if being caressed by a lover. The best three shots came next. I stood beneath the waterfall, as if taking a shower, soaping myself all over. The sensation thrilled me, turning me on as never before. I hope all those men looking at me appreciate the effort I've made to keep them happy, make their day.

Hot soup, along with a shot of whisky, helped me keep warm. I will say this, Mr Rathe handled it all very well. In fact, I look forward to the next shoot, at some mansion down in Kent.

Goodnight, Diary. I am so naughty, so clever.

21 NOVEMBER 2019: Tonight was a celebration of all that has happened over the summer, which has turned out to be much better than expected. Five Grand Prix wins in all for the Welsh Dragon, with my true love voted Sportsman of the Year. It must be said that Wilson proved us all wrong. It has been a summer of drugs, booze and sex mixed up with bravery, plus a dash of sporting glory. He finished second in the drivers table. As for the racing car itself, it performed wonders on the motor-racing circuits of the world. My dad's mechanical brain made sure the car got better as the season rolled on.

The entire motor-racing team assembled at Botherald Castle, just outside Cwmbran. They came with their families, friends, mates and lovers. It was a formal black-tie affair, with good food, fine wine, laughter and dancing, until dawn arrived to spoil it all. Proctor-Hale was there with his good wife, who bought a new green jewel-encrusted evening dress from Giovanni Hali of Rome. Personally, I purchased a full-length pink gown from Betty's of Tonypandy, the fashion centre of Wales. Wilson looked good too – made the effort – but he was very quiet tonight. I expected much more from him. I know for a fact it was the drugs he'd taken for tea, not nerves, that made him behave that way. With that said and out of the way, tonight it was a pleasure to see all the mechanics dressed up like penguins, in smart suits, clean for once, their dirty overalls left back home or at the garage. I gave them all an individual kiss and a welcoming embrace. It was a great evening – we deserved it. After dinner, then speeches, back patting and wild speculation about the years ahead, we danced the night away until the sun rose over the mountains. Wilson got blind drunk, smoking his head off. I left him alone – he didn't dance with me once, or mix with the team. He was aloof, distant. James, then Bryn, took care of me for the rest of the night. James told me I needed a better man than Wilson to love.

All in all this has been a fab night. I need more of them. One thing spoilt it: Cristobel could not come. She stayed at home as her mum's ill. I will visit her in the morning – take some flowers or something to cheer her up.

22 NOVEMBER 2019: "I'm sorry, darling. Don't know what got into me last night." Wilson actually apologised for his boring behaviour at Botherald Castle.

At the family lunch this afternoon, he was sober, talkative, lively, a pleasure to be with. He was a perfect gentleman – a role he plays very well. Aunty Mildred, with Uncle Iestyn, attended this lunch – a family get-together. It was the usual mixture of good food with talk of Jesus.

"I've never heard such a monstrous sermon in all my life." Aunty Mildred repeated herself, she was that angry, as we waited for Sunday lunch to be served.

Uncle Iestyn nodded in agreement, saying, "The preacher must've taken leave of his senses."

Roast lamb is the only meat worth serving on a Sunday, and today was no exception. Dad carved at the table while we all watched in silence. The point of this, Diary, is the following. This has been the first Sunday lunch I've attended in many months. It's over a year, or two, I think. A sad reflection on my life at the moment. A family ritual on the wane. The last two Sunday lunches have consisted of nothing more than beer, whisky and chips, aided by strawberry smash for dessert and heroin to assist digestion – not a Sunday lunch to be proud of. Dad would have done his nut; Mum the same. As for Aunty Mildred and Uncle Iestyn, it would be a foreign language. But today Wilson's addiction, along with mine, is a guarded secret. I mean, last weekend the only things washed up were some dirty needles, along with our drugged-up selves.

The lunch was eaten in monastic silence. Only the sound of cutlery on porcelain, accompanied by the clinking of wine glasses being used, could be heard. But as we waited for the ice cream Aunty Mildred broke the stillness by asking the only question she cared for – one she wanted answering.

"Well, Wilson, Ann Marie, when will you be having children once you've settled down?"

She smiled at us across the table. Wilson went red with embarrassment next to me.

Then I responded: "Aunty, we are both far too busy motor racing at the moment. All the talk is of winning the title next year. A baby might get in the way. But we'll see – no promises, Aunty."

Dad supported me: "This is no time to be broody, Ann Marie, my love. Aunty, stop putting ideas into that girl's head. This is not the time or place to be starting a family. Plenty of time for all that. We want to give birth to a new chapter in Welsh sport, prove that the Welsh can do more than play rugby and sing."

But Aunty was as defiant as ever: "Nonsense. I've powdered many a baby's bottom. Yours, along with yours."

She pointed to me, and it made us smile.

The lunch lasted for about two hours – the usual time allowed at home.

Dad made a toast right at the end. He raised his wine glass, then proposed a toast to 2020: "To the continued success of my little baby, the Welsh Dragon motor-racing team. Most of all to my pride, my joy, Wilson McCain. May he drive us all to further glory in the coming sporting year, 2020. The world will sit up and take notice, singing his praises all the way to Bridgend. I swear nothing can stop us now – I can feel it in my bones. Life is that good."

I then stood up at the dinner table, spilling champagne over the white cloth, proposing my own toast to Wilson: "I promise all in this room, including Aunty Mildred, this time next year I will be married to the next world champion, Wilson McCain, and pregnant to boot."

The whole room filled with laughter, overflowed with happiness. The dog could not stop barking. Ah yes, the atmosphere was suddenly terrific. We were glad to be alive, glad to be Welsh.

For the remainder of the afternoon I sat with Wilson on the sofa, watching the new film by Limp Wizz, *Devil Takes the Lead*. At ten we said our goodnights, arriving home at eleven. By midnight we'd retired to bed. Despite his failings, I love him deeply, want him to succeed.

Tomorrow will be a long day.

23 NOVEMBER 2019: For a Monday this has been a hectic day. Up at six helping to get Wilson ready for his trip to London. I wanted to go with him, but Dad, the wanker, wouldn't give me any time off work. Hell, I could've gone up west with Cristobel. What a day out it might have been. Ah, shucks, instead I watched it on the television along with the rest of the family.

At seven he came downstairs to the kitchen: God, what a transformation! He might have been a company executive, a director of finance going up to the city for some important meeting. It was an incredible change. Gone were all the traces of drugs, booze and smoke. He wore a crisp three-piece, matched with a brightly coloured tie pinned to a white shirt. His black shoes shone like a mirror. I had to look twice before I accepted that it was indeed him. I whisked the eggs, then poured his first cup of the day. He was in bellicose mood, up for the fight. All he wanted was to put over the glory of things to come: how one day he would be world champion, the best driver on the planet.

As he stated, "I'll tell that arrogant silly arse."

I backed him up without doubt. I kissed Wilson on the cheek, lips and forehead, one after the other. As he climbed into his car then drove away down the gravel driveway, I waved back and the car's horn echoed in the distance.

I arrived at my parents' house just after eight. At nine we all sat in front of the television to watch Wilson perform on the Terry Basil show. Like before, he told the rest of the world, along with its next-door neighbour, just how good he is, and will be in the future. I indulged in another cream cake as Wilson smiled back at the camera, oozing with pride. Terry Basil has a fierce reputation as a television interviewer. His savage technique of asking potent questions has brought down many a tough politician, caught out many celebrities, humiliated many overnight stars with nothing else to offer the world but themselves. Wilson held his own. He was fab-o.

The night ended on a contented note of optimism by all. Wilson telephoned me on his mobile within minutes of the show. We exchanged vows, made promises, kissed down the line.

It is now three in the morning. I left Dad's house at midnight, after Mum retired. He still has not phoned, like he said. The dog sleeps on my bed, the light flickers in the hallway, I pace the floor. His car is nowhere. What on earth has happened? Where can he be? I left a message on his mobile, but he hasn't returned it.

24 NOVEMBER 2019: My hands are fine, my fingers too, but it's hard to write when your heart is broken. Oh, God, why? This has been the end of the world for me. A black cloud hangs over this house – a black mark, a curse, a cross. A voice of damnation has called out from the depths. My love, my true love, is dead. He is no more – dead, dead like the dodo. I weep on to this diary and tears blot the paper as they cascade down my face like a mighty waterfall, smudging the ink as they tumble. A great love has been torn apart. My heart aches like never before.

Like Virinia mourned for Spartacus, as Hamilton grieved for Nelson or Mary wept for Jesus, I weep for Wilson McCain. My husband who will never be. A man who will not father my children – our children. All that has gone. Another life just thrown away like a used tin of beans. People with something to offer the human race, who make this world a better place to live in, are too often taken years before their time. Just like Wilson, who did not get the chance to shine like a beacon across the globe. A man like so many others before him who saw his life, his talent, robbed from him. If there is a God up there watching over us, He's got it all wrong, the bastard. He must have or Wilson would still be here with me, by my side. He would have all to live for. Now all I can do is cry, sob, pine for that boy of mine.

25 NOVEMBER 2019: I have never had to face death before, but I do now. This morning I went to the mortuary, at my insistence, to identify his body. It was a very unpleasant task indeed. Wilson's parents were there, like my own. Proctor-Hale took us along in his car. The world seemed to move in slow motion this morning. My stomach turned inside out as we all walked into a white-painted room. At the far end of the room, lying on a trolley, lay a body covered in a white sheet. A policeman, along with a doctor, stood at the head of the trolley. They beckoned us closer. Wilson's parents were the first to identify the body, confirming who it was. Then his mother gave way to her grief, sobbing without shame. Then one by one we filed past. As I took a long loving look at his face, I also let go with my feelings, crying as never before on to a tissue. He looked so peaceful – closed eyes, a face asleep forever. Even his hair had been combed neatly. This betrayed the grim truth surrounding his awful death. It appears Wilson was involved in a head-on car crash on the Severn Bridge coming back home from London.

Press reports covering his death make poor reading for all concerned – especially myself. He died at midnight, losing control of his high-powered car, crashing over the central reservation, right into the path of an oncoming lorry, travelling eastwards. He was killed instantly – no chance at all. The car was crushed beyond all recognition. His body badly mutilated, he ended up underneath the lorry. At five in the morning police descended upon this house to relay the tragedy. Telephone calls followed. People made the effort, so early in the morning, to offer condolences and ask why? Already fans pay tribute – flowers line the country lane outside the house. Tears are shed all over Wales as the nation shares the loss.

Diary, I need you now. Even the dog weeps.

27 NOVEMBER 2019: Since the death of Wilson a few days ago, I've hardly eaten a thing, or slept. I feel so empty inside. Can this loss ever be filled? Right now I doubt it very much. Hell, Diary, food is the last thing on my mind at the moment. As for sleep, I could stay awake forever. The funeral details are being arranged by Wilson's family; my dad's helping out. They have demanded a low-key affair at St Edward's, Newport. The press bloodhounds are now baying for his flesh, as in most newspapers, television as well, they are going nuts about the autopsy report, published today. It makes dark reading: they've found a walking chemist shop on two legs. A range of drugs have been found, along with a high level of alcohol. I have been over it a million times in my head. I can't find the answer at all. What on earth had my true love been up to? Where had he gone after he telephoned me? I really need to know, to find closure.

Oh, shit, the day's headlines are abysmal. Gone, the sporting hero; in, the sporting fraudster. I've run down some of the headlines.

The *London Times*: 'Wilson McCain Died a Drugged-Up Alcoholic'.
The *Englander*: 'Motor Racing Star Died a Shamed Hero'.
The *Cardiff Life*: 'Welshman a Drink-Cum-Drugs Junky. Why?'
The *Sports Report*: 'McCain Killed by Heroin'.
The *Motor News*: 'Wilson McCain Dead. What a Waste!'
The *Sun Rise*: 'Lost Champion: McCain Dead'.

In honour of my true love, I vow from now on never to indulge in drugs or booze ever again. I vow to live life to the full, to achieve what he did not.

Goodnight, Diary, for tomorrow we bury my true love.

29 NOVEMBER 2019: The day I never expected or wanted arrived. I buried my true love. Like so many other sporting men before, he was years ahead of his time. My true love should have lived for greater things to come. We should have spent the next sixty years in married bliss. I should've borne him many children, with grandchildren to follow. But today, alas, the lovers' dream has been shattered to a nightmare.

To date this has been my darkest ever day, when all hope seems lost. Death is hard to celebrate. How can you sum up a life cut so short, where so much promise has been betrayed by death itself? I do not believe you can. Dressed in black, a veil about my head, looking like a dowager in mourning on the family estate, I felt very uncomfortable about the whole thing – out of place perhaps. On Friday I had everything to live for; now, as I recollect the day's events, I seem to have lost everything in just forty-eight short hours. Now what?

St Edward's Church was jam-packed with people. For a quiet family funeral it was a farce. Outside the church, the press didn't give a snail's fuck about privacy. The press camped outside the church; they made their home along the country lane by the side of the cemetery. By the front door, flowers had been left by the many sporting fans of Wilson. Oh yes, my true love had an army of Welsh admirers – in fact from all over the world. They all wanted him to be world champion. I studied some of the heartfelt messages that had been sent. It was very moving to read some of them. They were sent by strangers he had never met, but that did not matter to them. Their human side came out, touching us all with their words of sympathy. A fellow human being has been taken from us, and any talent he had will now rot in the grave with him, decaying with his body. It now represents yet another waste of a human life. Few of us mortals receive such an honour – to be mourned by complete strangers, to see an entire nation openly joining the family in their grief.

As the coffin left the house, draped in the Welsh flag, with a mountain of red flowers, along with some white, decorating the lid of Wilson's coffin, it seemed to me almost pretty to observe. Along the route to the church I saw people make the sign of the cross and take off their hats in respect. Young ladies watched the procession move slowly along the street. As we approached the church, the press made their ugly move, to record this awful moment – the burial of a fallen hero. They were not burying a potential motor-racing champion, but a junky, a heroin addict, a drunk. My atheist friend Cristobel refused to attend – it hurt, but I expected it. She could've made the effort and placed her disbelief to the back of her mind just once in her life. In the event she might have found herself on the front pages of the press in the morning. God knows what they'll read like. I dread to think. I hate the bastards – they turned today into a pantomime, a circus.

Despite that ordeal, I cried buckets of tears for Wilson. I wept as never before, without shame. There are times when only tears will do. I have a feeling my picture, deep in grief, will appear on the front pages in the morning, across the country. The strength I gained from hearing Dad and Proctor-Hale sing the praises of his life gave me hope on this dismal day.

"The cruel, senseless death of Wilson McCain has robbed this country of a great talent, a fine human being, a man going places in a hurry. I feel as if I have lost a son," said the boss.

All my dad said was this: "How shall we replace him? But we must for his sake, as for our own. We must find another. Life must go on as before or perhaps better."

I cannot sing for toffee, only I let go in church today. When we sang 'Nearer My God to Thee' I almost shouted those words. It was inspiring. Why do we have to die?

2020

14 FEBRUARY 2020: There is a huge difference about today. For the first time in my life, I'm alone. Even at school there were boyfriends galore. Boys to be kissed, squeezed, held. Boys who often told me how much they fancied me in the playground – a cunning ploy I soon became weary of early on that boys would use just to get my knickers off. Today the awful emptiness hit me hard. It has been four long months since the death of Wilson. I miss him so much. A void has been created that cannot be filled. I need him to love: with or without drugs, booze and violence he was my man – somebody with a future that was worth living for. This morning there were no flowers, no handwritten card with a lover's message penned on it. All I felt this morning was the most appalling loneliness inside. My whole heart ached as never before.

I rose at six, armed with a bunch of flowers, then made my way to the cemetery. Then for at least one hour I sat by the side of Wilson's grave, weeping, thinking, loving the man I'd lost. All I know is this: if I'm to get on with the rest of my life, I must stop behaving this way. It is a pointless, depressing way to live, going nowhere at all. I need to get behind the wheel of a racing car, then drive the shit out of it. After sixteen weeks of being dormant, perhaps the best way to mourn the dead is to honour them with life itself.

I talked to Dad about it this morning over breakfast. He is in agreement with me. The team has pulled out of this year's season, unable to find a replacement driver worthy of the task ahead.

The boss is talking to a couple of drivers. I just hope he doesn't sign that Russian guy Igor Kovski. I couldn't believe what Dad was advocating. A Welsh motor-racing team with a Russian driver at the wheel! It is an insult to Wilson.

4 JUNE 2020: Loved ones may die, but life goes on. The wheel of time will never stop turning for those of us left alive. It has been six months since Wilson's death. I have not been up to his graveside for many weeks. The whole process was making me depressed, unhappy. For far too long all I've done is live in the past, when it is the future that matters. But after talking to the dog just after Christmas, I decided to stop going. I made a pact with myself: no more tears, grief, wallowing in self-pity. Time to move on and find a new beginning – a bit like the country's doing right now. Tomorrow, to be precise, a general election has been called, and the leader of the opposition is Nicholas Rachael, the young intelligent MP for the Isle of Wight. The same man I noticed before with film-star looks and a dash in the eye. All this combined with Churchillian wisdom. I for one, along with millions of other women across the nation, intend to vote for him. Knickers, not underpants, will put him in Number Ten.

After a year of triumph combined with tragedy in my life there looms a ray of hope from out of the darkness. On the 14th of this month, we race for the first time since Wilson's death. I will defend the Isle of Wight Classic. What is more, Diary, it will be held just after the House sits for the first time after the election. This appears more than a coincidence to me. Will we meet again? It is generally reported in the press that Nicholas Rachael will heavily defeat the current incumbent, Travistock, and by a wide margin at that. It will be the old versus the new, the future defeating the past.

Two days ago my dad, together with some of the lads from the garage, accompanied me to Abbots Vale for a couple of important laps. I drove the Flying Banana. It was a great afternoon, which made me feel good. It put me on top of my game. My morale took a much needed boost. The car performed well. As for myself, the old spark's back, still there. Wonderful! I feel as arrogant as ever. I took that yellow car of mine to full throttle from corner to corner, over 100 when pressed. Each lap made me feel happier than ever before. I drove hell for leather up the stretch. I can't wait for this Isle of Wight race. I need to win again, beat other people in a racing car, be a goddess on the circuit. I want to take command over all else.

Tomorrow I shall park my arse in front of the television. God knows why, but I need to watch the general-election results appear before my very eyes. I have the day off, so I will vote early. I have only one thing to say, Diary: Rachael for prime minister. Cristobel may pop over for a few beers – hell, it'll be like old times.

5 JUNE 2020: It is almost midnight and the result is not in question; it just has to be made official. Most of the polls predicted a landslide by Nicholas Rachael, ousting Joe Travistock from Number Ten by over sixty per cent, the widest majority in many years. I may not understand politics, but like all sane women in this country I am as chuffed as a randy dog on a street corner. A decent piece of arse is to live in Downing Street. Let us hope he has the balls to do the job in question. Spunk is what this country needs, and spunk is what it will get.

The late-night news showed Rachael standing with his staff at his campaign headquarters, waving to his supporters gathered there. What seemed like hundreds of people mobbed him by the front door. They shouted words of encouragement, of victory at hand. As I watched the future leader of this country give a simple wave from an upstairs window, there was not a woman in sight – just several well-dressed men, his staff. I was shocked, saddened even. Oh dear, what a waste of an intelligent man.

In the press yesterday there was a long detailed article about the private life of the next prime minister. It mentioned the fact that the last time this nation was ruled from the Isle of Wight, Queen Victoria was on the throne, joined by Prince Albert. I must have read that article by Dune in the *Fleet Street Gazette* several times. It compared him to Joe Travistock – two very different men, from two different worlds. For instance, old Joe Travistock is sixty-four years old, a grandfather, married to the same woman for forty long, happy years. The man's a political giant, you could say, at the helm from the very start. Re-elected twice – a popular choice with the voting public. The article showed him surrounded by his large family. He will soon become a great-grandfather – Venice will soon give birth again. This man's a great achiever – a fine prime minister, who brought dignity and honour back to this proud office – something his predecessor, Halifax, did not, bringing scandal with dishonour to Number Ten. It is now time to bring a youthful zest to Westminster, let the young breathe. It's time to allow fresh thinking to make this country, and indeed the world, a better place to live in. Rachael's the man.

It is now two in the morning as yet another cup of cocoa nestles in my lap. The dog sleeps; Cristobel cuddles a cushion, lost in a dream. But I watch on. This is compulsive viewing for me – I must watch to the end. Warwick falls to the English Democrats, and Rachael moves a shade closer to that sacred address. They take Sudbury, Oxford, Salisbury, Manchester South and Plymouth. Like battles in the Civil War, these towns, plus more, fall to the opposition. Travistock can't seem to hang on to his seats of government. They all tumble, falling like dice being thrown.

The television anchorman Davis makes an announcement: "The result looks settled already. I hear that the Prime Minister may make a statement soon to the nation." He then gets all excited, delivering the hammer blow – the bombshell that puts the result of the election beyond doubt: "I hear from Hastings. Yes, it's now confirmed – the Chancellor of the Exchequer, Sir

Arran Baffler, has lost his seat, beaten by Hillary Dent. That is it for Travistock – the game's up."

Other experts make comments about the results coming in. A new man in Number Ten is now confirmed.

With sleep in my eyes, all the attention has turned to the English Democratic Party headquarters at Fiztroy Square. It could well have been New Year's Eve – a party mood had taken over on the office floor. When the news of Chancellor Baffler's defeat came through, cheers of approval echoed all over the office. Young people smiled and sang out for the great victory of the night. They appeared eager to take up office and run the country. I sipped cocoa, then smiled as my hero appeared on television. A happy, elated man, with a grin that had no end to it, waved to cheering crowds, chanting supporters. Union Jacks flew; bunting danced above as the newly elected prime minister spoke to the nation. He asked Travistock to do the honourable thing: concede.

Nicholas Rachael loosened his tie, removing his jacket. He beamed with pride, saying, "This has been a wonderful day. Not just for me, but for the whole nation. We must work together as one unit. We must bring new life to this high office, fresh wisdom to the world, for tomorrow will be ours for keeps."

Loud cheering followed.

I am glad he's won, but it's time for bed. It's 5 a.m. I have to be at work by eight.

6 JUNE 2020: I guess yesterday was the day I came of age, so to speak. I did what many young people my age managed to do: I voted for the first time. My cross on that voting sheet meant I contributed to the well-being of this nation. What is more, like many women from Boston to Tenby, and from Eastbourne way up to the windy shores of John o'Groats, my reasons for voting were not simply political – more a case of voting for the flesh of the man than for his intellect. On a personal note, as far as I'm concerned, Nicholas Rachael can be as cold as an iceberg and twice as thick. He can talk as much gobbledygook as he wants. When the door of Number Ten closes, he can play with himself all day long, perhaps watch *Children's Hour* and be a fan of Snuggles the Squirrel. I for one do not mind a hoot. What that man does in his private life will be no concern of mine. At long last we have a good-looking guy in charge, a man to drool over at PMQs, a dish with a brain. From the economy to foreign policy, and from local issues to sport, I'm sure he won't disappoint.

If what's to come over the next four to eight years is nothing but good, then yesterday was a sure arrow fired at the future. I voted at dawn at the local infant school, Edwin Treot's. I went into the voting booth before breakfast; Cristobel came with me. Like me, she voted for Nicholas Rachael without question. I drew a fine artistic cross in his honour – a love letter to him, sent from the heart to the heart. But, even outside the school, what appeared like hundreds of young people (not just girls, or women like myself, but blokes as well) queued up in line. They waited for their turn to put that man in power. If the sight that greeted us outside the main school door was anything to go by (even at that hour of the day, a snake-like line of the youth of today was repeated across the country), then it is no wonder that Rachael won the election by such a large majority. He could not lose. It takes a special kind of human being to connect with the young as he has done. All I can say is, Diary, watch this space.

Cristobel's coming with me tomorrow.

7 JUNE 2020: Travistock has moved out; Rachael's moved in. That's how quickly power changes hands in this country. Unlike the Americans, we don't arse about when the government changes hands. We move with the speed of light. A picture of the newly elected prime minister adorns every newspaper, waving to the crowds from the steps of 10 Downing Street. The customary meeting at Buckingham Palace took place first thing this morning. That made it official, I suppose.

I learnt all this while I took lunch with Cristobel. We both listened to the radio, Channel 8, heavy rock. As we pulled into a lay-by on the A3, just south of Petersfield, yet another blistering afternoon could not be abused by such sacrilege as work. We had to collect a sample of Dad's fuel, X7, from a scientific laboratory in Portsmouth, of all places, then bring it safely back home. Trials would begin soon at Abbots Vale. But a picnic lunch was called for. First of all ham sandwiches, washed down with cold beer. For the sweet course, cannabis. Then we listened to political developments unfolding in London. The afternoon became mellow, like our souls on this wonderful summer's day.

Abbots Vale here I come!

14 JUNE 2020: At last the great day's arrived. I have something to defend, a crown to wear again on my tatty Welsh head, to be worn with pride. I want to regain the Isle of Wight Classic – a race worth winning for the second time. As a woman driver I must stamp my presence on this sporting event, leave this island in triumph, make sure that all the people of this English isle know my name, can spell it, then say it, and understand what drives me forward.

The whole family has gathered here to support me. Even Aunty Mildred's here to cheer me on. This afternoon at two that victory will leave its intended mark, or not a blemish or trace will follow me home to Wales. I feel good about myself. I can win this race again. Unlike last year, there are some serious opponents to conquer. Most of Europe's major rally drivers are here this year. Their names represent cause for concern. To win this rally I will have to be at the top of my game. Concentration will have to be 1,000 per cent, or more, behind the wheel. There is another reason to be cool today. The prime minister elect, the Right Honourable Nicholas Rachael, will start the race from the High Street in Cowes, then drop the flag on the victor. Will that be me? Will love drive me on to win? My hero will be there. I will see and meet him; so will many others. For, unlike last year, thousands upon thousands of young people have gathered here to watch this sporting event unfold. They couldn't care less about the rally. They just want to see, cheer and mob the film star from Number Ten. The piece of arse that runs the country. If I have anything to do with it, I will not be just another face in the crowd.

There are three hours to go. Nerves have taken hold of me. Writing notes in this diary may prove impossible, but I will do my best, Diary, I promise you that. I will keep you posted on my progress during this day. To be honest, Diary, seeing the Prime Minister may prove the more difficult task. When you see Nicholas Rachael in the flesh, you must stare. Few politicians possess such a rare gift. This man does in abundance.

Lunch was taken at The Shot Duck Inn, just off Graveyard Alley, a quaint market-town inn with good food and fine ale that can be taken at dark secluded tables, housed within ornately carved wood panelling. Some craftsman over 200 years ago carved hunting scenes. He must have taken many long hours to perform this skill. The creation can still be loved to this day. I adore this inn – wish I could eat or drink here all day long. Today The Shot Duck was used to discuss the fine details of Welsh sport. How can I keep my crown? Where will I go from here?

The car's ready for the challenge, waiting to go. So am I, Diary – you bet I am. I want to make the Isle of Wight mine all over again.

Mr Proctor-Hale sat next to me, dressed in his accustomed pinstriped suit, pocket handkerchief neatly folded into a triangle. He looked very dapper. In fact for a man close to his sixty-third birthday he is a very handsome fellow. As he sipped his gin, then ordered food for us all, I really fancied him. As the smell of spiced curry wafted about our table, he made me feel very randy indeed. After all, Diary, isn't it normal for the girl to bed the boss

– the monied man in charge? Oh yes, as a tactical move, sleeping with the boss could be the answer to my dreams. But I do not have to stoop so low as that, I promise you that much.

Dad led the business conversation with a silly question: "Well, Ann Marie, my dear, are you nervous about this afternoon?"

He took a mouthful of beer, swigging it down his throat, as he washed down another mouthful of curry.

I just nodded back to him. I reassured him about myself, the car and the outcome.

Proctor-Hale spoke: "We trust you, Ann Marie. If things go well here today, your father, along with me, has a proposition to put to you regarding the future. But today, my dear, you must drive like the wind. Use your brains with every turn of the wheel and touch of the accelerator."

I took another forkful of curry, stuffing it into my mouth, wondering what the hell these two men had been doing – scheming behind my back. Diary, my old mate, what happened next caught me off guard. The gods must be smiling on me.

The boss then looked at me, as a lover might, right into my eyes, saying, "Ann Marie, my dear, you are well aware of the fuel testing about to take place this summer?"

I nodded to him.

He continued: "We have X7 just where we want it – the magic ingredient, the key to our success on the motor-racing circuits next year. If you perform well this summer, prove yourself capable – that you have the skills at the wheel to do it justice – on August the 10th we will test this new programme with you at the wheel. You may test-drive the Formula One car for us at Abbots Vale."

I choked on my curry and farted with delight at this revelation – this offer of the world at my feet.

I then tripped over my own tongue: "I have the balls, boss, don't worry about that. X7 is safe in my hands; so's the car. I've more balls than a Spanish bull loose in the paddock."

The curry then did its job in my tummy. Everybody heard. The boss looked dumbfounded, but nobody laughed – not even Aunty Mildred. Diary, I did though – couldn't stop for five minutes. This was what I wanted to hear today.

With that statement I toasted the memory of Wilson: "To Wilson – his memory. May I do him justice today and forever."

As the lunch ended, it suddenly dawned on me what they had just said – offered. Before the summer would close, to be taken over by the shades of autumn, I would sit behind the wheel of a Formula One racing car – a dream come true indeed! I would sit where Wilson once sat and did the deed for Wales. Soon that distinction would be mine. I could feel it in my bones. It may be just a test drive at Abbots Vale, but my own judgement would be placed on the line. This would be a momentous undertaking. In sport one must not let the moment go. You must reach for the opportunity to shine, to show your true value when it comes along. That time, that place, may not present itself to you again. Just fade into unwelcome oblivion. Indeed, today, then 10 August, could be that day for me. A day that must be perfect, where all goes right, nothing wrong. Diary, the rally calls me to duty. Let battle commence on this island.

With that thought, the boss paid the bill, upon which we all walked out into the street. The noble town of Cowes awaited us.

A carnival atmosphere enshrined the town. Crammed with what appeared thousands of people, bunting, buskers, booze and high spirits brought the town alive. A place normally associated with sailing now paid homage to the motor car. In the middle of the town's High Street-cum-square, twenty brightly coloured cars stood in line. Our car took third position. It had all the hallmarks of a summer festival of sport. As soon as I clapped eyes upon it, my adrenalin took over, shooting through my female body at twice the speed of sound. From that moment onwards, all I wanted to do was get behind the wheel of that car of mine, then drive the shit out of it.

All three of us walked in step, as if on a parade ground. Dad led the way, while I took my place next to the boss. Coming out of Graveyard Alley, then along Keel Street, we came into the Market Square. We passed a music shop, a flower seller, a baker, a coffee shop, then the post office dead ahead. I observed all about me. Suddenly there he stood, the Prime Minister, Nicholas Rachael. He looked magnificent – magical to me – as television cameras from all over the world recorded the event. A brigade of police protected him from the public, who stood there in front of him, straining just to get a glimpse of their man. A leader they believed, like Moses, would lead them to the Promised Land. He even signed autographs, like a rock star might. I have never seen a prime minister do that before. But, after all, they put him in Number Ten – why not? When he stood on the podium I almost expected him to suddenly pick up a guitar then burst into song – dance even. A heavy-metal tune to break the decibels, sending fans wild with frenzy. I glanced back to him – this will be a man of the people, for the people.

Four car mechanics greeted us as we arrived at the start – Dave, Joe, Ted and Bryn were there to administer their wholesome skills to guide the car through its paces during the race. If things travelled my way, of course, they'd not be needed. They were there with my dad's blessing. Each one of them welcomed me with a hug, a kiss, then a good-luck embrace. This in itself made me feel like a winner even before the race started. Yes, this could be nothing save fair fortune this afternoon. All these thoughts engaged my mind and enthusiasm took over – good karma. All the things a sportswoman needs before a contest. I just wanted to burn up the country lanes of this island.

The boys all performed a vital function. They looked after the engine, the chassis, fuel and wheels. Long before that car of mine set off, their call to duty made sure it did not break down en route to victory – something that could not happen or failure would only follow. I know them all by name. At times they've appeared as brothers, sometimes lovers. I needed them today, this afternoon, as both rolled into one. So it was Ted who opened the car door for me, like a perfect gentleman opening the door for a lady about to climb into a limousine. My family stood by the side of the car. My mother bade me farewell – one could be forgiven for thinking I was in fact going away for a long time, never to see her again for years on end, not just going on a sporting jaunt on the Isle of Wight. The Prime Minister took his place, and an official stood next to him giving advice. He sent off each car, one at a time, then called them in at the end. Starting this car rally around this island was a very important task in his own constituency. First he would start the race here, then throughout the rest of the country.

At one fifty I sat in the cockpit of the Flying Banana, revving the engine. I was the third car away. My crash helmet felt far too tight, but sweet Bryn, a heavily built Welshman from Merthyr Tydfil, heeded my plea for help. Normally a quiet, shy man, he spoke volumes to me about how my crash helmet should always fit properly.

He adjusted the chinstrap, then winked at me, wishing me good fortune for the umpteenth time. "Go get 'em, Amo, my lovely."

I smiled nervously back, waiting for the off.

Dad, along with the boss, gave me instructions, then wished me well. As they did so the first car, a red Vixen Pixie, sped away. The crowd roared with approval. Then it was my turn. Nerves were high as I gripped the steering wheel with gloved hands, car in gear. The Prime Minister stepped forward. I revved again, gazing into his pretty face. He raised the white flag and dropped it, giving me the thumbs-up sign. In a instant I was gone, racing away.

I heard him whisper softly, "Good luck."

Then he was out of sight – the race was on.

The beauty of this English isle was seen in its entirety from

116

the driving seat of my racing car. This became almost a holiday tour of the island. The first thing to catch my eye was an antique shop nestling on the corner of Willow Street. Old chairs, a hatstand and an oak table were displayed outside. By the main front window a rack of what seemed hundreds of gold, silver and pewter items were neatly arranged in a glass case. There were watches, wine goblets, rings, chains, fine jewellery and carvings of every description. Also outside the shop, to please the tourists, the Union Jack flew beside the French, American, Canadian, Irish and German flags. It caught my eye as I raced away down a street, then out into the countryside. Spectators lined the pavement as I weaved my way through the suburbs of Cowes. Having studied the map well, I was well aware that a couple of miles outside of town I would be directed through Parkhurst Forest. This would be my first test. I should point out, Diary, before I go any further, that in this particular car rally I was literally on my own. I had to be the driver-cum-navigator all rolled into one neat little package. Travelling at breakneck speed along the forest tracks, the mud, water and tight bends would really test me – see me at my very best. There would be no time to consult the map here. I had done my homework very well, Diary. My nerves made me shiver as I approached a race official standing on the left-hand side of the road. As I drove closer to him, he directed me to the left, into Parkhurst Forest. I slowed down a gear, turning sharply left, accelerating along a dirt track.

On each side of this brown, dirty, muddy track, the majestic forest reigned supreme. Tall pines and oaks, plus other trees, waved with the movement of the breeze. The forest seemed dark, forbidding, choked by foliage of all kinds. To my right a carpet of blue flowers gave summer colour to this dense green jungle mass. Suddenly, I sent the gears down, then accelerated away, speeding up to a mound in the forest track. It seemed like a humpback bridge. I flew at it without fear. The car of mine almost took off in flight. I swear all four tyres left the ground as I took it head on. We landed with a bump, skidding as we did so. Taking control of the car immediately, I raced down the twisting track, the windscreen wipers working feverishly to keep the window clean, giving me an unhindered view of the road ahead. Mud, water, grime and millions of dead flies splattered across the windscreen. An arch of filth surrounded a clean window every other second.

After what seemed four or five long hard miles of forest track, the road just twisted from left to right and from right to left. The car was difficult to control. More than once I braced myself in the car's seat as I tried to stop myself from being thrown about all over the place, the seatbelt anchoring me down. I changed gear twice as the road straightened out. Then a large puddle straddled the muddy track ahead of me. I found myself saying out loud, talking to myself, shouting to nobody save little old me, "Out of my way, buster. I'm coming for you." Then, acting in a state of female madness, I pushed the car up a gear, full throttle ahead. It hit this wall of water at eighty plus. The car parted the water on both sides, like a giant tidal wave, soaking all those spectators daft enough to stand too close. Several people ran for their lives when they saw me coming straight at them. I pushed my foot hard to the floor, and my yellow darling responded, racing away with me laughing like some madwoman. Curses followed, but I didn't care about them. I had no time to. The Flying Banana sped along the dirt track, racing through the forest for at least another two miles.

The country lanes had been closed to all other traffic – a driver's dream come true. For the next dozen or so miles I drove through pretty villages. In front the coastal town of Yarmouth faced me. Then Norton, Norton Green and Totland. In the distance The Needles rose like a white sea monster from out of the ocean depths. A sight to behold.

I passed Freshwater Bay. Surfers rode the waves to my right as I raced down the coastal road. All I could muster was "Lucky bastards!" I was jealous of them. It seemed to me, Diary, the right thing to be doing on this summer afternoon. If it wasn't for this race, I might have stopped the car, got out then joined them. Surfing is something I've always wanted to do, a pastime I feel sure I'd shine at. They bobbed up then down, seeming like black dots in the far distance as they rolled over the waves or, like contented seals, drifted with the water. One day my dream will come true: a surfing holiday with Cristobel, here on the Isle of Wight or in some other exotic location. Hawaii, Miami, Tahiti . . . the list is endless.

Last year I drove through Brighstone village. This year I did the same, taking a different route. I drove along a road that meandered past a thatched cottage I recognised from last year. It hadn't changed at all: a white-painted cottage with heavy thatching for the roof. A large chimney pot towered above. I noticed a weathervane that pointed southwards, sitting next to the chimney itself. Lattice windows were dotted all over the cottage's walls. A lush green garden had been carefully manicured by somebody who cared a great deal. I found myself driving with one eye on the cottage, the other on the flowers. I swerved to avoid hitting an open gate as I drove too close to the privet hedge. As I did, an elderly lady came out of the front door, a watering can held in her right hand, doubtless to give water to the hundreds of different-coloured flowers that dotted the garden – roses of all colours and honeysuckle, to name just a few.

After the hypnotic wonders of that cottage, a retirement haven, I put my foot down yet again. This time the route took me through more pretty villages, with cottages just like the other one, but I had no time to admire the riches of an English garden. Time for me was at a premium. The clock was ticking. If I was to retain my crown, keep the Isle of Wight Classic my own, chances would have to be taken. At that time the most difficult part of the course had yet to come.

My spirits were lifted when just after The Ship Inn near the town of Chale, I drove past the lead car. The driver, Stanley Duke, stood by the side of his car, which had broken down. The engine smoked a little; water or oil poured out from underneath. He waved to me, and I acknowledged him back but drove on with added relish. This is an event where you don't get out to help a motorist in trouble. It made me smile for the first time during the rally, and an urge to win took over.

The road narrowed in front of me as I drove past a tea shop with a school playground to my left. The school played host to some children, along with their parents, who cheered me onwards. This little gesture from local folk spurred me on to drive faster, making me feel even better. They probably did the same to all the other rally drivers when their turn came along. I must've been only the second car they'd seen flash by the school gate. At the end of the road, I turned sharply right again, driving past the ruins of Chale Priory, the ivy-clad walls telling tales of religious glory, then the hell of persecution. Having survived the Reformation, the priory was sacked during the Civil War by Roundheads, angry at supporters of the King still hiding on the island. As the King was imprisoned at Carisbrooke, the priory was burned along with the poor bastards inside it. But enough of the intrigues of English history – I had a rally to win this afternoon. The main part of this rally was to take me almost all the way along the coast road, taking in the towns of Ventnor, Shanklin and Sandown, plus a few more villages dotted in between. Only just before Ventnor, perhaps the most testing part of the rally was to come. I was directed away from the main road once again. This time the cars would have to negotiate ten miles of open farmland. Sure enough, I slowed down, driving off the main road into a farmer's field. All I had to do was follow the open farm gates, which would take me by the villages of Whitwell, Roud, Sandford, then Stenbury Down, arriving back at this same gate to continue the rally on the open road.

I knew for sure my little car would have its suspension tested to the limit. The ground would be rough and uncertain – much rougher than before. My own courage would come into play. A time check was taken. I drove across an open field of deep uncut wet grass. The ground made the car bounce all over the place, at one stage nearly ending up on its side. My female caution took over – 'Drive well, drive safe, finish the rally,' I thought to myself. 'This will be a bit of "dewdrop winking", if ever there was one.'

Every so often a race official would direct me to the next gate. Some guy almost sent me the wrong way. He waved the flag at me, hinting to go left.

I did so, then he shouted back at me like a foghorn: "No, love, straight on – follow the hedge."

I slowed the car down to a crawl. This manoeuvre cost me valuable seconds that could've cost me the race. Given a bit more time, I could have got out of the car then socked him on the jaw for being a silly arse.

Spectators stood inside roped-off enclosures. A white catering truck served hot dogs, tea, coffee, tomato soup and chips. At one gate a bunch of people waved me on. They cheered loudly, but a sudden midsummer downpour forced them to put up their multicoloured umbrellas. I pressed on. The yellow car of mine, my pride, my joy, became almost childlike, doing as it was told, responding positively. I raced the car across the middle of a field, yesterday home to a herd of grazing cows, today empty of such beasts. The tyres of my car squelched over the farmland for at least six miles or more. Standing by a gate some woman, cuddling a poodle, instructed me to drive left. The old bat directed me back on to the open coastal road. From then on it was Tarmac all the way to the finish. All I wanted to do was drive faster than the wind could take me. People clapped, as if in a theatre, wanting more. So I gave it to them as I headed out to Ventnor.

This town's one of the main resorts, at this time of the year crowded with thousands, perhaps millions, of holidaymakers. The Isle of Wight can rightly be called the 'English Hawaii'. People come here from all over the country for their two weeks with full board. I am told the Americans love, adore, the place. "Hell, it's swell," as they say from New York to LA. Whether that's true or not I can't say. No matter, I love it here. This island was created by God Almighty for rallying, never mind sunbathing, walking, swimming, building sandcastles or just having a family picnic on a warm summer day. Queen Victoria along with Prince Albert loved the place. Well, if they could, so can I. Two sporting events now dominate this island: Cowes

Week for sailing and the Isle of Wight Classic for rallying. Question, Diary: would I become the first driver to win it twice? You bet Prince Albert's arse I would.

The Flying Banana was by now a mess. The bright-yellow chassis was covered in brown mud and slime, stained with green grass from one end to the other of the car. As I pushed forward along the coastal road towards Ventnor, washing this car of mine was the last thing on my mind. The white lines of the road seemed to disappear underneath the car like flashes of lightning: one minute there, the next gone. I just looked ahead of me. The road was my office, for sure, this afternoon. But this was no time to be clocking out. In front, the road was flat, yet straight. Once again I put my foot down. The dashboard was difficult to keep a check on. I was supposed to do everything in the car this afternoon. I did for sure, Diary, but navigating and driving, combined with making sure the car performs well, not to break down, seems to be an art form in itself. I looked in my rear mirror – no cars behind me. Then slowly the speedometer crept up the dial: 50, 60, 70, 80, 90, then 100 hit the clock. I pushed for 110. Police cars, plus cops on bikes patrolling the rally, cast their presence everywhere along the road, for the public's safety. But I was a driver in a rally – this was legal, so the bastards couldn't give me a ticket even if they wanted to.

So I found myself yelling at the top of my voice, "Go for it Amo. Go for it, girl. All they can do is stand then stare at my speeding car that's oh so rare."

A policeman riding a fancy bike cruised just behind me as I slowed the car down to negotiate a troublesome bend in the road. Only once through it, I shot away like a bat out of hell, leaving the bike-riding copper in the distance. He just had no answer for the acceleration of my four-wheeled dream.

As I drove towards the outskirts of Ventnor the pavement became a mass of people. A long line of them stood by the kerb. It seemed to me awfully dangerous. Just a few police kept watch over them. Now as I drove along the promenade the weather changed. The sun came out, along with the attire of the holidaying public. People saw me drive along, this time a shade slower. They were wearing swimwear, carrying buckets and spades. Little children walked hand in hand with their parents to the beach or to the car park. Others just looked on in amazement, wondering what all the fuss was about – after all, television cameras were now filming the event. Once again I was forced to slow down when I really didn't want to at all. But halfway along the promenade, with the pier to my right, I had another time check. The Ferris wheel at the end of the pier began to turn.

As I drove away people cheered, with one leg of the rally to go.

The next stop would be the finish. But before that the road took me through the towns of Shanklin, Sandown and Ryde. I found the same Isle of Wight welcome from everybody along the route. All desired me to win. Well, the gods smiled upon me just outside the town of Ryde. On the normally busy main road, just after Quarr Hill, the road became straight for what seemed miles. I observed the lead car ahead of me, then, Diary, I became hot with a fever – the fever of wanting to win at any cost. The car in front was driven by an experienced rally-driving champion. Angel Harp, there waiting to be taken by me, sent into second place, oblivion. I raced towards him, trailing him for the next couple of miles, trying to put Angel Harp off his guard. The Vixen Pixie he was driving appeared slow, as if driven by an old-age pensioner at rush hour in the city, driving an old-fashioned Serial A. I gave him a two-fingered salute, shouting at him to move over and let me pass. I passed a sign indicating both Whippingham and Cowes. Victory was in sight. I cursed him again, in disbelief, then, fearing nobody, nothing, I took him. I swept past him like a professional. He had no answer to me at all. Yes, Diary, the devil took hold of me, speaking to me inside my scatty head, telling me to drive faster, go for everlasting glory. He whispered to me as a lover, in soft tones. A guide, a mentor, protecting me for the future. I drove on hell for leather. Angel Harp was gone from sight.

My heroine Queen Victoria's home Osborne House was advertised on a giant signpost to my right, then left. 'Sorry, Vicky, no time for sightseeing today,' I thought. The delights of that lady's house would have to sampled another time, in another era. I had a car rally to win.

After Osborne House, I could see in the distance the never-ending water of the Solent, the entry to Portsmouth Harbour. It bade a fond farewell to Nelson; would it greet me in the same fashion, the same way? I drove along without looking back. East Cowes approached – houses, flats, gardens, the suburbs. They were dotted with the odd industrial estate that belonged in working Birmingham, or glorious Newcastle perhaps. Soon I crossed the Medina river, the winning line in sight. Down below I saw a large expensive yacht with a huge white sail unfurled. It gently sailed downriver to the open sea, completely unimpressed by what was happening on dry land. The call of the ocean was greater for the sailor.

It's safe to say, Diary, winning this rally this afternoon gave out a statement to the rest of the sporting world. It's a new chapter, if you like – a brand-new beginning. This victory rubber-stamped my ability as a woman driver. This will make men quake in their boots at the mention of my name.

I drove along Medina Road, then there it was – the finishing line. The winning flag was dropped by the Prime Minister, Nicholas Rachael, with grace, style, dignity and a smile that had no end to it.

The police formed a barrier between myself, the public and the press. What seemed like thousands of fans, the backbone of the sport, crammed around the car after I came to a halt. They wanted to touch me, congratulate me, offer a victory kiss, wish me well for the future. Just to the right stood the mayor, next to the Prime Minister. The Flying Banana stopped. I got out, waving to the crowd. I had beaten the bastards right down to their underpants. The sheer magnitude of what I had done for the second time began to set in. But the sight of my family, who broke through the crowd, made me smile as never before. Dad was jubilant, his joy infectious. He heaped praise on my driving – could not stop. I sucked it all up, then all hell broke loose as I became buried underneath a mountain of pressmen, eager for a story. I hugged the human race this afternoon on the Isle of Wight.

The victory ceremony was something else, Diary, as good as the race itself. I stood below the podium, awaiting the announcement, which was made by the Prime Minister himself. I stood there like some dumbstruck teenager looking at a rock star. I simply watched his every move. Soon this man would have to kiss me.

For what seemed like an endless amount of time, as if caught in a bubble, as if waiting for the last grain of sand to tumble from an hourglass, the mayor made a speech. He talked about the merits of sport – the true value of competing. He then backed up this statement with the blessing of this island kingdom. He spoke about the competition that Monte Carlo, Dakar and Gumball had in their sights. The Isle of Wight Classic was here to stay. Ann Marie Osborne was the sporting heroine of the hour. The crowd applauded him, then even louder clapping followed as Nicholas Rachael spoke to the crowd and mentioned my name.

"The winning driver, Ann Marie Osborne, the Cardiff Flyer – Miss Osborne." He then beckoned to me.

I responded, joining him on the podium to receive my trophy. I was lost in a trance. Was the warmth I felt in my cheeks the faint embers of a tough day behind the wheel, or the first glow of love on my face? Beaming with joy I received my trophy. I leant forward; so did he. Then, Diary, it happened. We gazed at each other, froze for a second, then kissed. First on the cheeks, then a bout of madness took over as I placed a kiss on his political lips, embracing him as I did so. The crowd loved it, wanted more. Another kiss was stolen.

The trophy looks something like a football cup: tall, silver and engraved on all sides. A miniature car sits on its lid. The event, date and soon my own name would adorn its body. It is also heavy. As I lifted it in glorious triumph above my head, the town's brass band struck up a lively gay tune. This has been a wonderful day, Diary.

The Prime Minister's a dish – I love him.

15 JUNE 2020: I arrived home a little after six this evening from driving to glory in the Isle of Wight Classic. It was a day in my short life that will live forever in my memory. I say short – by that I mean life has really begun for me. This was a team effort. All the family helped out, plus the mechanics, who did a great job – so good in fact that I did not have any problems during the race. My mum even made the sandwiches.

I have made the front pages of almost all the daily newspapers across the country. All have nothing but praise for the way I drove to victory yesterday. The feeling it has given me is indescribable – no words in the English or Welsh languages can convey the way I feel inside. My soul is content this evening.

We caught the early ferry that sailed from Yarmouth to Lymington. A pleasant drive through the New Forest followed, with the early morning sunshine casting long, dark shadows in abundance over the countryside. It was wonderful to behold, appearing as if it had stepped off the giant canvas of a Constable oil painting, then suddenly come to life. Dad drove the truck that carried my dirty car homewards. From time to time I glanced backwards to watch it, sitting there strapped down with ropes, cables and even chains like a recaptured prisoner. I am immensely proud of my own little racing car – a car-rallying queen. As she rocked with the truck's suspension, the Flying Banana seemed to understand what she had done, kind of human-like. The pride of all Wales.

The Gazette has a photograph on the front page of me kissing the Prime Minister – on the lips as well! Somebody was observant for all that.

Diary, this weekend Cristobel will come with me up to London – another shopping spree.

18 JUNE 2020: I have a major problem: *Jam Tarts* magazine has contacted me yet again. I don't know whether they have recognised me from last weekend, but it bothers me a little. In no uncertain terms, after last week my clothes will stay on, especially my knickers. No more porn for money. There will be no need to strip off any more – none whatsoever. That said, I turned them down for more work. I am not interested. I wrote back to them, politely saying no. That bloody magazine has served its function; now it must go, scram, get stuffed. It does not have a hold on me – never will. Driving, combined with living life to the full, is all that counts from this day forwards.

Going up to London for a good time – need it too.

20 JUNE 2020: Diary, it is now two in the afternoon. Cristobel sleeps like a baby in the next bed. She sleeps off the booze and perhaps weed. She smoked something at the nightclub we attended just off Berkeley Square – a posh expensive joint for all that. I spent a couple of grand at that club, but we both enjoyed ourselves. All I know is that Cristobel didn't smoke any cigarettes. Her eyes, like mine, are a haze of red.

We arrived in London late – too late. We checked into our hotel, The Jezebel in Knightsbridge, then went straight to Mayfair. The name itself depicts wealth, implies class. If I lived in London this would be my home, my abode. But we were both excited about the pending night ahead – two young Welsh girls on the loose, dressed in almost nothing at all, on a hot, steamy, sticky summer's night.

Clubland has moved on with the times. There are no longer gay clubs – just nightclubs where the young, the old even, have a good time, love each other, dancing, drinking, smoking and eating. This particular club, The Live Pussy, has promoted this for ten years. It's always packed – they must make a fortune out of it. That is what people want these days. But before I go into all that, Diary, let me tell you what we were wearing (or not wearing, as the case may be). We dressed alike: a tiny pink summer frock, gee-string, no tights, black sandals. On nights like these a girl's silly to wear anything else – comfort first, stay cool, dance hot.

Venturing into this club, we saw men dancing with men, girls dancing with girls. Lovers aplenty doing the same, having fun, being loved. There were scores of straight couples who could not keep their hands off each other. A great scene to watch. The club has become so popular that we had to queue for well over one hour. In front of the club is a giant neon sign in bright colours. It shows a pussycat sliding down a pole, like a pole dancer might. The cat smiles, then winks at you. I adore this place – will come again, for sure. Outside the club, by some railings, stood some burly bouncers, keeping guard, making it safe for all the revellers there. As I stood with Cristobel, with everybody else, waiting to be let in, I found myself just another face in the crowd, a contrast to the week before. Arrogance has its place in the world, plays its part in the evolution of the successful on this earth, but not last night. I had to climb down off my high horse before I took a serious fall. Fame behind the wheel will take care of itself. It was time to stand still, shut up and cool off.

The first thing that caught my eye was the sight of two men kissing each other. Women kissed as well, close by them, but the music played on. The booze followed. We ventured towards the bar, discreetly, unannounced. I bought the first drinks – two chilled beers. We drank them out of the bottle as we watched everybody dancing. It seemed like the human race wanted to party until time ran out and the world ended. A party to celebrate being alive, human. An eternal bash to be proud of. A male pole dancer held our attention, sliding down a pole on a stage near to us. I could not take my eyes off him. He was all muscle, funky, randy, sweaty, gorgeous – the hallmarks of a man. He was tanned in all the right places, if you know what I mean, Diary. He kept on dancing.

I felt sorry for the young man, who must've been my age. It must be very hard to dance about a stage, to jump, jig, roll on the floor, climb up then slide down a giant pole in all sorts of positions in front of hundreds of turned-on young people without getting turned on yourself. But I watched this dancer slide down the pole three or four times, urged on by those around him. Soon a couple of girls joined him. People watching cheered and blew kisses. Clearly they were having a good time, but that was the reason for being there in the first place. At midnight a bright blue then red searchlight that looked like something from out of the Second World War cast its beam over all the dancers on the disco floor. There seemed to be almost no room to dance at all as they were so tightly packed together, body against body, hand against hand, lip against lip.

After a couple more beers and a smoke I retired with Cristobel to the ladies' room.

Inside the ladies' room there was a queue forming, but legs crossed, knickers taut, we stood in line like everybody else. It is a true test of friendship when you both share the bog together. Such was the night in Mayfair. I went first; Cristobel followed. While she got on with nature, I fiddled with my cosmetic mirror, attending to my lipstick, making sure my lips were lush, full of kissability. I wanted to make sure all the male animals could smell my sexual heat, like some lioness in the mating season in Kenya. We were both on the pull.

Back on the dance floor, we gave in, joining all before

dancing the night away. But, it must be said, there is nothing worse for a girl than to be approached by a young bloke who has a lousy chat-up line. Diary, it was laughable.

This dude started talking to me and his words were, "Well, my little hen, this cock wants to give you an egg to lay. Let's make out to the henhouse."

'My God!' I thought to myself.

Cristobel moved in to protect me from him, but he repeated himself two or three times.

My own response was just as funny: "I'm no hen; I'm a fully fledged chicken – one you aren't stuffing."

With that Cristobel blew some gum and threatened him. Then he walked away, head down. All those around us asked for some more, pleased at the man's humiliation.

Suffice to say, Diary, the night got better. I danced with several decent guys, letting them paw me all over. Cristobel did the same. I can still be such a slut when needed, choosing to do so. The night's joy came to an end at five. I got off with some guy named Bruce Digby-Smith – very posh. I pulled him earlier on, and we stuck with each other for the rest of the night. After inviting him back to the hotel room, 910, we went to bed; he performed well. Cristobel watched from the side – a turn-on indeed. A fine end to a great night out. He left after breakfast with a grateful kiss.

Only one thing to say, Diary, about this trip up to London: like Julius Caesar, I came, I saw, I conquered.

22 JUNE 2020: We were both due to catch the last train back to Cardiff, like the last time we visited London. Cristobel wanted to stay in bed till noon, but I persuaded her to join me sightseeing – a thing we had never done before. We had spent so much money at that nightclub that we decided to dispense with the shopping. The only store visited was Haledon Roe in Oxford Street, just to browse, preparing for the next time.

The weather was still very hot this morning. Summer clothes not an option, but the order of the day. Good old London teemed with people. The entire human race seemed to have gathered there, with all her relatives in tow. Along with them we watched the Changing of the Guard at Buckingham Palace – wonderful. Red-coated guards with black bearskin hats marched in time to the regimental band. We should have come the weekend before and watched the Trooping of the Colour. At twelve we lunched at the café by the Serpentine – salad washed down with white wine.

After lunch we walked together up to Westminster, through

Hyde Park, then Green Park and up Pall Mall to Trafalgar Square. As Cristobel stared up at Nelson's Column, I passed glances up Whitehall, then tugging the sleeve of her blouse I walked up towards Parliament. At Horse Guards she took a photograph of me standing next to one of the mounted soldiers, his shiny breastplate glistening in the sunshine, the horse standing like a statue. Big Ben struck two as we walked past Downing Street. A policeman stopped us on the kerb as a black Bentley drove slowly by. My eyes popped out of my head and I beamed with delight. There he was on the back seat – the Prime Minister on his way to the Commons. Seeing him in action, I relived our sporting kiss of the weekend before. It made me feel warm inside, glad to be there. Yes, Diary, this has been a wonderful day out. I don't want to go home.

London can be as pretty as any Welsh valley.

10 AUGUST 2020: I woke early, nervous as hell. I did not sing like the birds in the garden – I had no verse in me at six. Breakfast was bypassed, my stomach simply not up to the job. This has been one of those epoch-making days – a day that you can't mess up on any account. As I bring you up to date, Diary, midnight chimes. The dog sleeps soundly. I take another well-earned swig of whisky and the ice chinks against the shot glass. Tonight the world has thrown herself at my feet. The chance has come to shine, to be a beacon on this earth. With my parents' blessing and the backing of the boss I drove a Formula One racing car at Abbots Vale. We tested X7 and the car, not forgetting myself. The sporting news of the day: we all passed with flying colours. Who knows what will happen now? Where will this madness end?

This has been a day for sporting dreams to come true. A press conference has been called by the boss at Cardiff City Hall. The mayor will be in attendance. I need to pray, I fear, but the gods seem to be on my side after all. Take heed, Diary, this has been a day of hidden secrets. The sporting press of the day have been judge, jury and executioner all rolled into one. If all goes well they will not be given their chance for damnation, but they will have to wait until Friday. They must be kept away from the truth – they will be told just enough to whet their appetite. After this incredible performance, we have something special in Wales.

Abbots Vale itself was deserted. I found this scenario bewildering and strange. It's midsummer, glorious weather, yet no people, no animals. Even a farmer's field was completely empty of cows, sheep or pigs. As I beheld this scene, I thought, 'Has the bomb been dropped or has the message got out to the rest of the human race that the Welsh are coming? They have a secret you are not allowed to know, so get out, stay out and mind your own business. The good folk of Abbots Vale will return when we have gone home, when the tests have been completed, the secret still safe. It felt as if we were guarding a national treasure only the Welsh should know about.

I approached the car with all the presence of an astronaut as he walks towards a rocket about to take off on an Apollo flight to the moon. The white racing car was 'tattooed' with the emblem of Wales, a red dragon, on the engine, sides and rear. It stood there aloof, silent, proud, the four giant wheels going nowhere. Bryn appeared to dust the chassis, Dave fiddled with the steering column and Joe sipped water from a bottle, while Ted wrote some notes down on an official pad. It was all systems go. As the clock ticked closer towards the hour, my nerves came under control, the resolve stronger than ever to succeed this afternoon, not to let the side down. Dad was dressed in a dark suit, his shirt undone at the collar, tie loose, shoes scuffed. He walked by my side, talking all the time, like a racehorse trainer giving orders to a jockey in the paddock before a race, all the time gesticulating with his arms, unable to keep still for a moment. As for me, I baked in my red jumpsuit. As the racing car approached me, two things happened that would separate us from all the other motor-racing teams next year.

For a start I tucked my long blonde hair neatly into my jumpsuit just before I put on my crash helmet. Then my dad gave me the final instructions for the afternoon's test drive.

In Welsh, he said, "Well, my darling daughter, you are fuelled for 100, programmed for ninety-five. Press for maximum throttle up the straight; cut the grass on each bend. Two hundred when the flag drops. Blue for go, red for slow. Let the gods tell you when to go, but whatever you do remember the battle cry. Make them catch you. Mow the grass. Keep them behind you to kiss your Welsh arse." He smiled.

I giggled back. Then I climbed into the car's cockpit and pressed the ignition. The car came alive.

Acting like some learner under supervision, without any confidence whatsoever I gently let out the brake, moving the accelerator. The racing car moved slowly across the Tarmac, making no more than one mile per hour. Dad walked beside the car; the mechanics followed. At the start, I brought the car to a standstill, parked on the grid. Proctor-Hale watched from the side, giving me the thumbs-up sign, the car's engine idling, getting warmer, just as it would before a Grand Prix. I did not smile, the joyful frown making for a more sombre me. It was then that the mechanics got into their rightful positions. Bryn stood in front of the car, a large blue flag pointing to the ground. When he lifted it up, out of the way, it would be the signal to go. At the rear Dave checked the fuel lid, then the aerodynamic chart, each time ticking off a name from a list. When he finished, he placed the pen into his top pocket. The two other mechanics, Ted along with Joe, gave each tyre a final inspection, each man satisfied. Then Bryn, on my dad's signal, pulled the blue flag out of the way. The test was on.

For one afternoon only Abbots Vale motor-racing circuit became all the circuits of the world, from Silverstone, Watkins Glen, Monaco, Moscow, Sweden, Suzuka in Japan, Magny-Cours in France . . . the list goes on. This was a test drive for the Welsh Dragon, for both car and driver, a mock Grand Prix, an examination of all involved. As in a race, I cruised on a practice lap. The car moved away slowly at my command. I did not accelerate to more than forty; at times I went slower. As I drove the car Dad talked to me through headphones, and I talked back to him through a microphone attached to my crash helmet. He questioned me about the car, but all I noticed was the serene quiet of the moment. It felt as if I was going for a drive through the countryside on a Sunday afternoon with family in tow and picnic hamper in the boot. As Dad talked to me I noticed the tranquillity of Abbots Vale itself as never before. The perfect rural idyll, lost in a mad world, full of mad people, of which I am not one.

The first thing that struck me as I drove the car around the circuit was the complete silence, apart from the loud intense sound of the racing car's engine. We drove up the straight, past the empty grandstand. No spectators enthused over my performance this afternoon. Nobody was there to cheer me on to certain victory, spur me on to greater things. On the dashboard a mass of dials, clocks and gauges told me everything, yet nothing. They appeared as a blur behind the steering wheel. My eyes focused on the fuel gauge. How much was still there, for how long? Indeed, when the red light flicked, the test would be over. Just how far would we travel? When would the tank be empty? The circuit turned sharply to the right, and as I drove the car around the bend I kept the car in the middle of the circuit. Then I cut the grass, mowed the daisies, as I took the racing car to the very edge of the circuit, taking each subsequent bend very close. Back driving around the middle of the circuit I noticed a catering hut, all boarded up. It looked like some derelict building in the middle of a city. It advertised cold drinks, burgers, chips, sweets, crisps, tea and hot coffee, but sold nothing today. A thicket of trees passed me to the right; on the left advertisements were displayed on hoardings along the side of the circuit. The circuit ahead was straight, but switchbacked. I cruised along at thirty, slowing to negotiate a left-hand bend. A steel bridge spanned the width of the circuit, and underneath I found brief shade from the afternoon heat. The sun was high, with no clouds to embrace it. The chicane approached. I weaved the car through it in an instant. Away I drove. The circuit rose snake-like to the right, and a long bend twisted first right, then left, then right again. Once passed, flat green fields on each side of the circuit greeted me, now void of spectators, tomorrow full, ten-deep on the trackside.

Dad spoke to me, and I replied with girlish enthusiasm, "Call it, Dad. Running smooth to Tarmac. Let's go for it – burn it up for glory."

With that comment I noticed a man standing by the circuit. It was Bryn, flag down as one lap came to an end. Taking further instructions, I drove slowly towards Bryn. The others smiled back with approval.

Something snaps in the head when you drive at speed. As 150, then 170, was reached with ease, without effort, this afternoon, the gentle stroll that preceded lap two, on a simple instruction from my dad, was overtaken by, "Advance mph, darling." (As he politely put it!)

Soon 200 came then went. The world flew by. Objects picked out before appeared as smudged colours, not figures, as they were flashed to my eyes. The grandstand, the grass and trees appeared as white, green and black smears on the landscape. I was now travelling so fast that even the sun did not move above me – a yellow dot in the middle of the afternoon sky. Speed plays tricks on the mind, the eye, the senses. The steel bridge across the circuit seemed to take ages to come towards me, a line across the circuit as I got closer, ever closer, then it suddenly flashed past me as I drove underneath it. As I reached 210, a G-force glued me to the seat, trapping me in the cockpit, with no escape. This will be my world from now on – an excitement without equal, life combined with death on four wheels.

17 AUGUST 2020: A couple of days ago my dad, along with the boss, pronounced the test drive an enormous success. The fuel X7 performed as expected, maybe better. I drove the racing car for just over ninety-five laps of Abbots Vale without the need for a pit stop. The engine stayed cool, remaining at a constant 50/54. Gripping the dry surface at all times, the 2 × 4 specially designed eighty-five-per-cent Bombay Indian rubber tyres gave me a dream ride. The brand-new one-coil spring suspension gave me a feeling of riding on air. Oh yes, Diary, the Welsh Dragon will be a force to be reckoned with next year. But one more secret was divulged to the rest of the world this afternoon.

Cardiff City Hall was besieged by the world's sporting press. They came from Japan, America and China, and most of Europe seemed to be there. Television cameras flashed or clicked into action as soon as we walked into the main ornately decorated dining room. This is where the mayor gives banquets, or rock stars blast away the night. But this afternoon something else took place: a sporting announcement that shook the world to its feet. A table had been set up and microphones installed. A conference loomed. Chairs for my dad, the boss and myself had been arranged. Proctor-Hale sat in between us, in the middle. I saw Cristobel, my friend-cum-protector, standing out in front of the crowd. I will need her now more than ever. This was a serious occasion, so both my dad and the boss wore suits, as if in the city itself. I wore a plain red frock and sandals, no make-up. At one point Proctor-Hale stood up, addressing the press. He gave a speech against the backdrop of the Welsh flag; on the table a model of the Welsh Dragon racing car had been displayed. It looked impressive.

Logan Gastard from *The Globe* asked a question before the boss even started to speak: "So what's this damn secret, then? I have to be in London by six."

Some giggling could be heard, and my stomach grew tight as a sick feeling took over. I wanted this torture to end in a hurry.

The boss regained his composure. "Gentlemen of the press, I welcome you to Cardiff, cultural centre of Wales. I have not invited you here to discuss the merits of singing, or rugby. Nor do I wish to talk about the Welsh football team qualifying for the next World Cup. I know they'll do well for the nation. Indeed, this day is a mixture of sadness and joy. The sadness – I hoped my own protégé Wilson McCain would drive my racing cars to glory across the world. But his awful, untimely death, so young, brought an end to that dream. He drove to victory many times, but much more was to have come – of that I'm sure. Only life must go on. We at the Welsh Dragon have been developing a wonder car, capable of competing in a Grand Prix without the need for a pit stop."

Gastard shouted loudly, "Is that it on the desk?"

The boss ignored him, carrying on: "We pulled out of this year's season out of respect for his memory, but we will return in 2021 with a new more powerful car, driven by a new driver, good enough to do the job. Gentlemen, my pride, my joy – I give you our new driver for the Grand Prix season, 2021: Ann Marie Osborne, the Cardiff Flyer."

I held my breath as a million camera bulbs flashed at once, right into my face. It made my eyes squint. I saw spots before them. On the boss's command, I stood up, then faced them, losing my nerve as I did so. For the first time in many years I was lost for words. My tongue failed to act. But a sarcastic comment from Gastard of *The Globe* brought it back to life again. I went on the attack without any prompting.

"Well, let me tell you all, you will laugh on the other side of your face soon. I have driven our new car – I adore the way it performs, the way it feels. I can't wait until Sweden on the 12th of March next year. I have driven to victory many times in rallies. May I remind you I've won the Isle of Wight Classic twice. I will do the same for Wales in Grand Prix races. I will not let the side down. I'll show you fuckers who can drive a racing car. I can." With that I stormed out of the hall. But not in tears.

What have I done, Diary? Sporting folk never learn, do they? So here I go, like all the rest, from footballers to rugby players, jockeys, cricketers and athletes galore, telling the world what I'll do before it happens. Victories that may never come! The boss is furious, spitting venom. We appear to be a joke. I almost wish today had never happened. The maggots of the sporting press can have my carcass to feed upon, only on my command.

18 AUGUST 2020: Everybody has been so glum. The newspapers are having a field day. Only the *Cardiff Mail*, along with the *Welsh Voice*, are positive about the future. Gastard's front-page headline in *The Globe* reads, 'Schoolgirl Drives for Wales'. Gastard the bastard – that's my view today. I'm no schoolgirl, so he's got that wrong for starters.

But it's not all doom-laden news. This afternoon I delivered some spare parts to a remote farm close to Abergavenny. As this old sheep farmer, his two dogs at heel, signed for the engine parts, he passed a comment that made my day complete. "I know you – don't worry, my lovely. Good luck to you – a breath of fresh air." Cheekily he held my hand, then kissed me on the cheek with dirty lips on an unshaven face, covered in stubble. His words made me feel cheerful.

16 OCTOBER 2020: Dafoe Du Trenchard, the French racing driver, was crowned World Champion this evening. A new name, a fresh face, somebody else to drool over, another man to call my hero. Second place in the drivers table went to the Russian Zargrev, with third going to the American Sellers. All in all it has been a vintage year. What a pity we were not represented. Roll on next year! I find myself wishing my life away. But it's not all been plain sailing – not in the least.

Problems by the ton on the home front are mounting up. Since the dreadful press announcement at Cardiff City Hall, the press have been hounding me all the time. It is now an intrusion into my privacy, an infringement of my freedom. What's more, I hate it all. Press freedom, on the other hand, means they can print what they like, when they like, how they like, with nothing else for me to do save turn the other cheek and tolerate it. This of course does not excuse the awful cruelty inflicted upon me on a daily basis. Will it ever stop? You bet it will. I must stop this literary murder on my own by winning a Grand Prix and doing it in style, making the Welsh press, along with the Fleet Street thugs, grovel at my feet and kiss my arse with wet lips.

Since the libellous newsprint hit the newspaper stands, I have tried to live a normal life, but can't. Even the *Los Angeles Surfer* has been following my every move. Telephoto lenses appear everywhere in our street. My family are now involved, feeling the pressure, under scrutiny. I can't go to work any more. Leyth Swain and my dad have both agreed that I should take a holiday – one month off work. Disappear for a while. On Friday I'm going on holiday (another one) with Cristobel. We fly out to Hawaii for a couple of weeks.

It is now ten at night, I should be out, perhaps at Mayfair, at that nightclub. I am a young girl – I should be drinking, kissing, smoking and loving some dish in jeans. Jiving to heavy rock music is a reason for the young, like me, to live. But times have changed – I am not doing any of those wonderful things. Cristobel's here with me, and we have watched a movie together over dinner, played some cards, watched Shakespeare's *A Midsummer Night's Dream* and loved it too. Can you imagine that, Diary? Me of all people enjoying Billy Shakespeare! If I carry on at this rate I'll plough through the bloody lot. That's just it, Diary – what else does a young girl do on a Saturday night?

After last week it sounds actually fun. Last Saturday was a farce, a debacle. I may never venture out again. Over in my mind, I chew the cud as the headline which appeared in Sunday's *Globe* stares back at me from the newspaper lying on the sofa, like some monster attacking my soul. There is a picture of me going out. I am about to open the front gate. I am wearing a blue micro mini, with matching knee-high boots, and my braless white top shows my nipples through the material. It's all over the front page. Cristobel sticks her two fingers up at Gastard, and the headline reads, 'DOES SHE HAVE HER MOTHER'S PERMISSION?'

Just to make matters worse, Gastard joked to me as we walked to a waiting car, "Don't forget to be home by eight. Daddy won't like it if it's past your bedtime, girl."

This remark brought shades of laughter from all the other journalists gathered outside my home.

Diary, I wish they'd go away. This hurts.

23 OCTOBER 2020: The Coconut Hotel, room 210, Captain Cook, Hawaii, USA.

Peace at last – well, for the next twenty-five days at any rate. The flight out here was terrific – a gem. Been here three days already, not a vile journalist in sight. Managed to shake them off at Bristol.

Deception has been the name of the game on this holiday – more important than swimming or getting an all-over tan. When I return to the coming madness that awaits me, I will be a deep shade of brown from head to toe; so will Cristobel. The press gathered outside our home, annoying all before them. My family and neighbours alike suffered the intrusion together. But once we had escaped the prison, leaping into the outside world, Temple Meads took us to heaven – liberated us. Cristobel sat next to me on the train as we travelled to London. Once there, we caught the Eurostar train to Paris, where we boarded a flight to Boston. From there we flew across to Honolulu, where our holiday began. Ah, those sexy French and hospitable Americans. They both assisted our escape from reality.

This hotel, in a word, is wonderful – just what we need. Both the building and the setting. Strange flowers are everywhere in the hotel's garden – plants, shrubs, weeds and roots of every variety of who knows what! Cannabis must be grown here. Outside my window some flowers with pretty red petals that give off a sweet scent line the footpath. A positive jungle of trees surrounds the hotel. In the morning a bird with orange plumage sings his little heart out, perched on a branch. I know the press will not find me here, that's for sure. I could spend the rest of my holiday sitting outside my hotel room, it's that pleasant, relaxing. But anyone with a camera is suspect, viewed with deep suspicion. Having telephoned home last night, spoken with my parents, I know the press have gone away. Since I left, slowly but surely they all disappeared. The street's empty of them, so this holiday's already served a purpose. But where have they gone?

Tomorrow I will walk down to Kealakekua Bay with Cristobel. We will spend the day lying on the beach, doing nothing save worshipping nature. For now at least, I for one will enjoy the solitude of the moment. Dad telephoned at six this evening. We chatted for about one hour.

He said, almost with sadness in his voice, "Your mother, along with myself, misses you terribly. The whole place is unbearable without you – so quiet, so still. Tippy misses you. He's licking the air as I speak. Wants his mistress back. The press have gone – nobody knows where you are. The boss has decided there'll be no more motor racing for you until Stockholm in March. No interviews at all. Newspapers and television alike must be told what stop to get off at. Stay where you are, apple blossom. I'll see you when you return. Remember, my lovely, you must prepare for the coming season now. Regarding any sporting tournament, or competition at top level, one should arrive discreetly, then return home in triumph, not the other way around. That must be our strategy from now on. Don't forget that, peaches. I will protect you, my darling. Let's give it the beak in Sweden. Let the driving do the talking from now on."

Dad's right, of course. Even I know that. Up with the lark in the morning – the sun must be worshipped.

Balls to motor racing! Have you ever sunbathed, Diary?

27 OCTOBER 2020: As usual I've just spent a long lazy day by the sea in paradise. Tomorrow another dose of the same, why not? Since we arrived here, the peace and the silence, bound with much needed obscurity, have refreshed my heart, soul and mind. The rigours of motor racing mean that when the time comes to return home to Wales I should be able to cope just fine with anything mankind throws back at me. I say with any luck I'll toss it back to them.

I woke this morning at six and sat outside on the balcony overlooking the Kona Coast. The deep contrasting colours of blue ocean and green jungle, with white foaming waves rolling on to the beaches – it is all here. Yes, this was observed by myself sipping a glass of warm champagne left over from last night's dinner. I can get used to this lifestyle. Even at that hour the sun was up, its heat already apparent. This has been a hot, sticky day from sunrise to sunset. As the day draws to a close, I write up my notes here. This spectacle of Mother Nature at her very best will never be forgotten. But Cristobel missed it all. She slept on, oblivious to the sheer beauty of the dawn this morning. Breakfast was taken in the hotel's empty restaurant. Just two other guests 'crowded' the tables as I ordered gallons of coffee, plus two egg sandwiches cooked to order. Cristobel sat next to me in silence, dark glasses hiding her blue eyes, concealing hard evidence of a night spent drinking, singing and laughing the hours away in the hotel's bar, as close friends will do when life orders such activity. But at nine thirty we both gathered our things, heading down to the beach.

No taxis or buses saved our legs this morning, making a mockery of the notion of having a lazy holiday. For it is a three-mile walk down to the beach. Downhill there, uphill back. Still, a great day was anticipated by us both. Doing nothing was exactly what we ended up doing again in abundance. I carried a lightweight shoulder bag with all my things inside it – the usual things a girl needs for the beach, including sandals, sun lotion and bikini. Inside Cristobel's bag she carried the music, beer and sandwiches. Dinner at the hotel was a full twelve hours away for us. This beach is deserted – no bars or cafés line the promenade. Just a car park and an empty beach. This morning, it must be said, Diary, the walk was very difficult. From the main road, a country lane travels snake-like down a steep mountainside, resembling an alpine pass, traversing first right, then left, broken up by long curving bends. Indeed, I could see the lane far ahead of me, stretching far off into the distance, coming to an abrupt end at the car park by Kealakekua Bay. As I came to the first bend, the view was breathtaking, stunning. The black Tarmac lane appeared endless to me, like I might never reach the end of it.

Shimmering heat made the walk twice as hard. Even at that hour of the day it made us both sweat in profusion, my forehead being constantly wet and the sweat running down my back as a waterfall might. Every so often we both had to stop, sit down and take a drink. Then we'd carry on walking. The first stop was so peaceful we could've stayed there all day long, not moving a muscle, not bothering to venture down to the beach at all. We both sat there by the roadside, sharing a bottle of water. To our right was a very posh farmhouse. Outbuildings were dotted everywhere, white paddock fencing standing out from the green. A man got into a fancy red car, a pretty young girl at his side, laughing all the while. They drove away in a hurry, passing us sitting by the roadside like a couple of tramps. Perhaps they were lovers; maybe he was taking her back to her mother after a night spent locked in each other's arms. Passionate embraces, love poetry spoken, vows exchanged in the night – who knows what else they got up to? They seemed happy to me, like no others. As the car passed us, the man tooted the car's horn and we both waved back to him. It broke up the otherwise complete silence of the morning. We watched the car disappear out of sight down the lane.

Cristobel commented, "He goggled up my skirt, I swear, Ann Marie."

Then I made an observation of my own: "A rich sporty type, Cris, my dear, who has girls like us for breakfast. Breakfast in bed, no doubt!"

With that hopeful suggestion, we gathered our things, continuing the walk.

It seemed to take an eternity to walk the final mile or so down to the beach. The heat was as a furnace and every step was a massive effort for us both. We arrived at the tiny expanse of beach at eleven sharp. Giant waves crashed on to the beach, which was completely empty and barren of life. This was paradise found. We had the pick of the beach. Not another soul could be seen anywhere at all. The beach was not long, just a narrow strip of sand with the Pacific Ocean to one side and tall palms on the other. Jungle along with farmland stretched as far as the eye could see. We chose our spot then settled down for the rest of the day. I turned on the radio – rock music along with the local news our only contact with the outside world. Even the locals didn't want to share this solitude.

I stripped off to my sunbathing costume; Cristobel followed. After about one hour of lying in the sun, Diary, we covered ourselves with oil to protect us from the intense Hawaiian sunshine baking down upon us. Every so often we braved the ocean, swimming like contented dolphins, plunging in and swimming underwater, laughing, joking, kissing each other as female friends will do, knowing the friendship's for life. Diary, if the rest of my life follows suit, I for one will not complain. Thank the Lord for small blessings like Cristobel.

Kealakekua Bay was where Captain James Cook met his unpleasant end. This bay harbours a Royal Naval killing that beggars belief. This place drips with Captain Cook's history. His own explorations of this earth changed the way we look at the world and at mankind forever. He was killed here, attacked, then, say the history books, eaten by Hawaiian natives. Over on the other side of the bay lies his memorial. A white plinth marks the spot. I must visit the place before I go home. This pays homage to a British hero from a time when the world really was being explored and discovered. As the day draws to a close, I take time to reflect on our naval history, alongside our sporting legacy. They say we are a footballing nation. Rubbish! We excel at motor racing. In Nelson's or Captain Cook's day Britannia ruled the waves. We were commanders of the sea. In my day Britannia rules the road. In motor racing we, the British, dictate to the rest of the world. There is just one major difference now.

I will continue this sporting glory wearing net panties with lace trimmings, smelling of perfume, so there! Like here and Trafalgar saw the demise of great naval heroes, my thoughts suggest that soon it will be my turn to leave my mark on this earth, as they did. Question: who will build my plinth?

30 OCTOBER 2020: I know that true friends share everything, but what happened last night takes the biscuit. Cristobel admits three things now as a result of wild living: a sore head, a sore back and a sore puss.

After dinner, Cristobel came with me to The Paddle Bar for a few drinks. We watched television as we chatted to the locals. Just after ten, I lost her. One minute she was there, the next gone. The alarm bells did not ring in my head – I mean, she's a big girl now, able to take care of herself. After one beer too many, I headed back to our hotel room, bound for bed. A sound night's sleep was desired after a busy day sunbathing. I bade the barman goodnight, then climbed the stairs, walking down the dimly lit corridor. I walked gingerly, almost tiptoeing, not wishing to make a sound, like some sneaky night porter in some five-star hotel. I paced the floor, listening by each door, cheekily hearing the sounds of lovemaking coming from the bedrooms. Then it confronted me just as I was about to turn the key in the lock. The sound made me smile, then giggle with surprise – almost jealousy on my part. The sweet unmistakable sound of two people making love. The shouts and the moaning echoed down the corridor. She had picked up a bloke. She had some guy in there – a complete stranger at that. I listened for a while. They were so loud, my cheeks warmed crimson. Now that is something I never do. I am made of sterner stuff. But the high-pitched whines and yells coming from the excited mouth of Cristobel had that effect on me. Whoever she had in there, he must've been one hell of a stud, a man of his time – a man who could perform with whom he wished. Such a rapport may have been a weekly event.

But after thirty minutes of this lovemaking, I decided to turn the key in the lock, opening the door. After all, I was paying for this room. Why should I make my way downstairs again, only to sleep on the sofa? I was shocked by what I witnessed – two naked bodies in the middle of the act of being nice to each other. They openly invited me to join them. It was the young man in the fancy red car from a few days ago.

Diary, I won't tell you what happened after that – you'll only blush.

16 NOVEMBER 2020: What a pity, but all good things must come to an end, including this holiday! We fly home in the morning. Suddenly, I must face the future back in Wales. I mean, Diary, we came here to worship the sun, and the beach has been our cathedral. Cristobel has turned from white to brown; so have I. She looks a dish, like something from out of a magazine; I am the same. As per usual we both walked back to the hotel, slowly, one last time this evening. We walked past a coffee farm, the air heavy with the lemon scent of the yellow hawascynthia flower. It will be hard to leave paradise, but with bags packed we travel to hell tomorrow. May our God help us. Help me!

Thanks for coming, Diary.

18 NOVEMBER 2020: Holiday's over now for sure; reality has come with a bang. Arrived back home yesterday. The city of Cardiff opened her arms to me in no uncertain terms. What else does the next year have to offer me?

Work started as usual, delivering car parts for Dad around the city. A pay cheque's been dumped into my bank account – great timing, as I've spent far too much of the stuff while on holiday. Don't we all? At the newsagent's not far from the garage, I dashed in to buy a magazine, the *Motor Text Weekly*. I was wearing my denim mini with matching top. I didn't wear tights, or stockings as I wanted to show off my deep tan – let the rest of the world see how good-looking I can be. After all, Diary, it'll wear off soon enough. As I walked back to the van, magazine tucked under my arm, some guys shouted at me from a car parked across the street. They gave me a wolf whistle and the 'arm up' sign. I smiled back at them, blowing them a well-deserved kiss. I felt flattered that someone had noticed me. Ah well, back to the grindstone.

24 NOVEMBER 2020: The older you get, the wiser you become – or at least that's the theory behind the wisdom. Well, I can be wise too, even at my tender age. The advice given to me before, by my mentors, 'Arrive discreetly, leave in triumph, not the other way around', will be my watchword over the next twelve months. I shall not waver from this at all.

Since the announcement of me driving in Formula One next year, 2021, despite the peace of the holiday the media have not really left me alone. I must learn to live with them at a safe distance – newspapers, television, magazines and private engagements by the score. I have been offered tens of thousands of pounds to do all sorts of wonderful things. All were offered to me by kind, considerate people who care about my welfare. My sweet arse they do! Take today, for instance. I have been invited to do two chat shows in London. Mark Dunce wants me to talk about women in sport. A magazine called the *Shop Window* wants me to model their winter-wear collection. *The Globe* wants me to write a sports column for them each week. I have turned down at least £50,000 – a vast sum of money, only I will do the right thing, I will hold out. I will earn more money and gain more respect by winning a Grand Prix than from anything else the media can offer. After all, they are the Judas-seekers, looking for those who betray the nation by failing in sport. I will not play their ugly game. My driving will do the talking for me. I will open my mouth and shout loudly in Stockholm, Sweden, on 12 March next year. I will silence them all. Diary, I am counting the days, ready for the green light.

24 DECEMBER 2020: To the anger of my parents, for the first time in my life I missed attending midnight Mass. I just could not face it this year. That said, I feel rotten, as if I've let the side down. Only I need some space of my own, tonight of all nights. The press might be there in hot pursuit. I will get enough of all that in the coming year, when time spent on my own will be at a premium. I say on my own, but Cristobel's by my side, as always.

No chapel to sing the praises of Christ's birth, or prayer to celebrate His life. We both had a light meal, drank some booze, then took some Japanese Splendour. Cristobel lies on my bed like a sleeping baby. She is out for the count. I feel great too – a light feeling in my head that makes me smile all the time, then giggle to myself. Content are the women drivers tonight. The dog sleeps soundly.

Happy fucking Christmas.

2021

17 JANUARY 2021: The countdown began today. Now there's no going back. Only victory will do – defeat is unthinkable for us all, especially little old me.

This afternoon at exactly one I put the Welsh Dragon racing car through its paces at a rain-soaked Abbots Vale, the secret bastion of Welsh motor racing. Nerves aside, I have to perform here, in competition itself, now only weeks away from reality. In just over one month's time, the team ship out to Stockholm. The Welsh Dragon will take over six rooms at The Pine Tree Hotel. The racing car, along with the team, will settle down at the Elk Horn circuit. Then the slow build-up to the great day will begin in earnest. My nerves appear fine; my attitude is one to win at all cost and to do better than my best behind the wheel. Already the press are hounding me. I don't read newspapers any more, or watch television. There is no point in any of that – it's self-defeating. You'd think Grub Street would encourage me all the way, get right behind me to win, be wonderful. Not on your life, boy! They have washed their hands of me. They appear to want me to fail. Well, Diary, I don't need them, but they need me.

Today, at least, all went well as yet another test run went without a hitch. Good news for all concerned. The boss told the press where to go, and they did. None of them could be seen this afternoon. Not even the local rag knew of our sporting secret. Having said all that, it has been a difficult drive. The weather closed in, and a dark sky made it appear as night in the middle of the day. Torrential rain almost flooded Abbots Vale – puddles all over the circuit. At times I needed the car's headlights, it was that dark, gloomy, as if the Almighty was about to unleash His wrath upon us in the form of Armageddon. Throughout this awful weather, my dad stood by the side of the circuit, drenched, wet through even in a heavy trench coat, watching my every move, to the point of shouting at me and writing down notes in a rainstorm. He talked to himself, the mechanics and the wind itself, at times waving me onwards to drive faster, better, foot to the floor. As if to him winning a Grand Prix with his daughter was more important than the end of the world.

The car performed – a good, sound omen for the rest of the sporting year. Everybody was well chuffed. After the cold winter, a warm summer beckons us on. The car functioned on all fronts. After this afternoon, my enthusiasm knows no end. I became geared up, like a young girl playing with her Christmas present on Christmas Day. In this case, my present is a racing car. But after just forty laps the test stopped as the rain increased. The strong winter wind was blowing right across the circuit, so at times I had a job to control the car. Once I skidded across the circuit, almost crashing into a hoarding, so Dad called a halt to proceedings. In summing up, I have only one thing to say: this car has been juxtaposition positive auto-line with excess.

14 FEBRUARY 2021: Celebrated my coming of age, so to speak – my twenty-first on this earth. A couple of months ago I discussed it with my parents. A big party seemed appropriate – in keeping with the mood of the moment – only I had a sudden change of heart. Just as my dad was about to splash out vast expense in my honour, I stopped him, much to his surprise.

But, like I told him, "In less than one month we go for broke, Dad. I'm in training for a Grand Prix. I will stay sober with a clear mind. After all, we don't drink then drive, do we?"

I made him proud – a good attitude presented.

"That's the spirit, my girl. I am right proud of you, my little apple blossom, win or lose."

With that comment we embraced. A private dinner was arranged for tonight at the one place I feel safe – The Monastery Hotel, Abbots Vale, right away from the glare of the human race.

Tonight was very special indeed. All my family were there, along with Cristobel. There is a time for wild parties, but this was not it at all, to my parents' dismay. They expected a long night of dancing until dawn, like so many times before, gallons of booze, and kissing backed up by sweet talk aplenty. I mean, isn't that what girls do at twenty-one? But then again, how many other girls get to be in my glorious sporting position? Answer: none, Diary, not bloody one. So that makes me very special – one girl in a million. I did not need sobering up tonight at all, just a very intimate family dinner at a fine country hotel – a place where they know us well and treat us special. The boss was missing tonight, already in Stockholm, ahead of the game.

Dress for this was casual, the menu simple. Of course Cristobel, at my insistence, sat opposite me at the table so I could see her. She looked a treat – denim suit, with a white ribbon in her long, dark hair. I couldn't take my eyes off her. She wore a posh jewel – a gold ring on one of her fingers, set with red rubies. I bought it for her last year, on her own birthday. After the dinner, at nine a beautiful birthday cake was wheeled into the room. A loud cheer rang out, followed by mild applause. The head waiter wheeled in a highly polished trolley, and sitting on top of this trolley, based on a white cloth, was a birthday cake: oval, with lemon icing and a fancy chocolate racing car in the middle. I nearly died. I hugged everybody in the room, then cut the cake. As I cut the cake, I wished for something special. I can't tell you my wish, Diary, but I want 100 more like it from now on.

The house is asleep now. The dog is on the floor. A naked Cristobel sleeps next to me on the bed. She's got a great figure, buttocks to die for. I want to kiss them and tell her nice things, yet all I do is dream of the future. Goodnight, Diary. Goodnight, Cris. I blow her a kiss to dreamland.

25 FEBRUARY 2021: The abundant good humour of the last couple of days has vanished. It appears no more in this household. Yet again sadness has taken over. My heart is broken. A dear friend has been taken – death rules the roost here. My dog has died. Poor old Tippy died of old age today. He died during the night. I found him curled up on the end of my bed, dead to the world. It has upset me like no other. All I've done is weep for my dependable four-legged friend, who never let me down. For almost twenty wonderful years he's been there at my side. When the human race got the better of me, the dog seemed to understand. He was a soothing presence when life became too much, at school, then ever since. I would say *constantly*, but strictly speaking, as from today, that simply is not true any more. The show starts all too soon. I need my dog by my side – something to hug, cuddle, talk to when things go wrong, as well as right. Now even the dog has deserted me when I need him most of all. As with a human loss, I feel it terribly in the heart, where it hurts most of all. There is a void where there shouldn't be one. I cried buckets of tears when I found out this morning. I shed them now as I recall how we buried my canine friend.

I called Cristobel right away. Then, along with my dad, we drove out to the Black Mountains – to Lord Hereford's Knob, to be precise. The dead dog lay on my lap. I cradled his head, and even kissed the dog a few times as we drove along, tears dribbling down my face, cheeks, unable to hide my grief from the rest of the world. I must state, Diary, that Lord Hereford's Knob is a vast mountain, a towering mountain of grass, 1,000 feet high. As many sheep graze upon its slopes – a wonderfully wild place in Wales. I walked the dog here many times, in all sorts of weather. It's the perfect place to bury my dog. Dad brought a spade, and halfway up the mountain he began to dig, just away from a footpath. The view is stunning – you can see for miles. Hay-on-Wye is in the distance, and all around there's nothing but high mountains as far as you can see. I lay the dog next to the grave being dug. The dog's ears, tail and coat moved with the breeze as if he were still alive. All I could do was silently stand next to him, being comforted by Cristobel, who placed her reassuring hand on my shoulder. At one point Dad wiped his brow, then took off his jumper. He said he would dig the grave deep. In the end it seemed like an enormous hole in the ground, far too big for my dog.

Like some church funeral, when the grave was dug I said goodbye to Tippy, wrapped him up in a blanket, then laid him in the grave. Hell, I even found myself giving the sign of the cross. I guess that made sure the dog went to a canine heaven, to sit next to the canine god forever.

When the job was done, the earth replaced, we returned home in silence. I had nothing to say. I mean, Diary, we all want to live forever, but none of us do. Even animals die. It will take time to get over Tippy's death, but I will I'm sure. Dad offered to buy me another, but right now that's the last thing I need.

Roll on March.

11 MARCH 2021: We arrived here in Stockholm yesterday, snow still on the ground. Confined to the hotel until tomorrow. Cristobel stays with me – two prisoners sharing the same luxurious cell. Well, that's what it seems like to me. No sightseeing, discos or nightclubs on this trip. We've gained seventh place on the grid for the Grand Prix tomorrow, dumbfounding the critics. Had a late dinner with Cristobel and played cards. I lost. At nine we listened to some soft music. It made me relax, settled my nerves for the contest, Diary. I will retire to bed soon. Cristobel sleeps as I say a prayer to myself, asking the gods for their help in keeping me safe. A Greek athlete might recite this on the summit of Mount Olympus, praying for their guidance.

A Prayer for Sporting Success

As the gods race across the sky,
Delivering their message from way upon high,
They give us the talent to win or to lose,
They give us the power to live as we choose.
So hear my prayer to you just like you ought,
Give me the magic to triumph in sport,
Let me be the mighty victor on high,
As the gods race across the sky.

The room is still silent. All I can hear is the clock ticking away the time. Destiny calls.

12 MARCH 2021: What a wonderful day this has been! A day that will live in the minds of men forever, women a day longer. Sport became the great leveller today. Wales performed a miracle on the face of this earth. Tomorrow my face will appear on the front pages of newspapers all over the world, from Cardiff to London, from London to New York, from New York to Melbourne, from Melbourne to Rome and from Rome to Tokyo, then round the world one more time. The day has been manic from start to finish. It is now midnight. The day's sport, along with the celebrations, is long ended, yet I am still wide awake as I recall every breath, every twitch and each victory kiss in my mind. I want to stay awake for 1,000 years.

I wanted to get to Elk Horn anonymously – some hope! The press had been well briefed. Coming out of my hotel, they were waiting for me like a swarm of maggots. My dad tried to protect me and some of the boys formed a barrier, shielding me from their grasp, but I could not escape their shouts, and their microphones were shoved in my face. I could not avoid them. Dad told me to say nothing, keep walking and get inside the car. A posh Havard Silk limousine, the door already open, stood by the hotel's main entrance. I was almost lifted into the damn thing, then driven away, the press in hot pursuit, their hunting cries echoing in my ears.

"Are you going to win, Ann Marie?" I heard. "How will this race go? Are you up to the job?" For good measure: "Should women be doing this? Go home, sweep the floor and clean the baby's bottom."

I found the whole thing mesmerising.

A lone voice that I recognised rose up from the melee: "Good luck, Ann Marie. Drive the bollocks off them, sweetheart. Do it for Wales, honey."

For the first time since breakfast I smiled, felt good. It was the voice of Gastard from *The Globe*. We looked at each other, then he was gone.

Practice had not gone well – grid position seven had been obtained. Corteze took pole; Sellers was on two. That aside, I was well prepared for the competition ahead. The Welsh Dragon was in fine form. I sat in the car waiting for the green light – a wait for eternity. Eventually we were off – away. I don't remember much about the Swedish Grand Prix at the moment. Doubtless I'll recall everything over breakfast next week sometime, or at the fruit stall at Cardiff Market when out shopping with Mum. But a move I made well into the race gave me the Grand Prix on a plate. After thirty laps I still had no need for a pit stop, as other cars were doing. Corteze, Grace, Potter and Sellers all dropped out at one point or another. Engine cool, fuel sound, I kept going, moving from seventh to third, slowly but surely. The crowd went wild, sitting on the edge of their seats in the grandstand. I saw my chance to take the lead. Corteze pulled in for a pit stop and two other drivers followed. I pushed for 180, full throttle. Soon I was far away from the rest of the field. I couldn't stop; the Welsh Dragon didn't want to. After taking a driver on the inside – a classic winning move – the bastards were behind me. They stayed there. After that I could not be beaten – the Swedish Grand Prix was mine for keeps. The chequered flag was taken with pride and zeal, followed by a yelp of Welsh excitement. The lap of honour was wonderful – the first of many more, I think. Once will be no good at all.

This has been a day when sporting dreams have come true. May God bless Wales, Diary.

19 MARCH 2021: Serpang, the Malaysian Grand Prix, driver's report.

The first thing I saw at dawn this morning in my hotel room was an old RAF propeller suspended from the ceiling, now used as a fan, breathing much needed cool air into the stifling heat of the day, even at that ungodly hour. The good news is there's not a pressman in sight. It appears the boss got an agreement with the local police force: they cordoned off the entire street and kept the media at bay just to give me some peace. Can you dig that, baby! A sweet little old Welsh pussycat like me gets state protection. Man, I can get used to this kind of treatment. What a gas!

Off the circuit the boss seems to have taken care of everything on my behalf, along with Cristobel. We must be careful here – no booze or drugs of any kind. This is one country where that kind of thing will not be tolerated. Punishments are harsh. This has been a sober, clear-headed weekend – a rare achievement for us both. On the circuit itself I'm on my own; so's the racing car. The local people have done nothing but sing my praises. They have treated me like royalty for sure – flowers every morning and courtesy each evening. Anything to make my stay here as comfortable as possible. Nothing is too much trouble for them. I think they expected me to win easily.

When I arrived at Serpang, the crowd appeared to be enormous – much more so than usual. The Welsh fans came in their hordes – the entourage that now follows me everywhere, seeking fame and fortune with me, at my shoulder, spurring me on to victory. I changed quickly – no make-up though. Rouge is out of place here. As I was about to climb into the racing car, Gastard from *The Globe* appeared, like in Sweden before, catching me off guard.

Despite a heavy media scrum, he almost whispered to me across the circuit, "Good luck, Ann Marie. Make it two, baby. I was wrong about you."

I couldn't think of a reply. I just stared back at him, a blank expression drawn across my face. Perhaps he's embarrassed that I'm proving him wrong at the moment. I will say this, Diary, with minutes before the off, I have a shade more respect for him now. He didn't have to admit any such thing. That took guts this afternoon.

One thing made this Grand Prix different from Sweden. The French ace Trenchard competed; he missed Stockholm through illness, but he drove with experience combined with strength here, like a man determined to regain his crown and carry the mantle for France. Can I stop him?

As expected Trenchard took pole, Corteze second, Potter third, me fourth. The green light, a shine on the chassis like that of a giant mirror making the red Welsh Dragon emblem stand out as never before. A deafening roar sent the cars away in the Grand Prix. I passed Potter before the first bend, kissing Corteze on his arse for the next twenty laps until he took his first pit stop. I did not see his rear again. It became a duel between myself (the Welsh broad) and Trenchard, the world champion. I tracked him for lap after lap, never more than thirty feet behind him at all times. I took lots of fluid, the heat at one point unbearable. After lap fifty-one, my jumpsuit began to rub against my hot flesh where it shouldn't. Sweat dripped down my back, causing itching down below. This was one uncomfortable drive this afternoon. I must do something about it. The things I do for Wales! Trenchard took three pit stops, but showed his class, revealing why he's the world's number one by catching me up with ease, grace and charm.

A crash took place at lap sixty-one, but nobody was killed, thank God – just several cars taken out. Trenchard was not one of them. We locked together with just three laps to go, engine to engine. There was nothing between us until the champ was weaved out of the contest by myself. I took the chequered flag with arrogance. A victory kiss from Trenchard, a spray of champagne, then an interview with Lovell from UKBC. My mind was mixed up, all a-fuss with winning images.

I said to my millions of fans, from Cardiff to Oakley, Kansas, "This win means I'm no fluke. I have a wonderful car to drive, with a team to match its brilliance. Roll on Australia. I love Wales, Malaysia and the rest of the human race." With that I waved to the cheering crowd.

Dad was also interviewed by Lovell, but he went right over the top with pride when asked to explain the incredible racing car the Welsh now have.

He said, "This car of mine moves with the action of a perfect racehorse. If I drove this car across the desert, not a grain of sand would be displaced."

What was he talking about, Diary? But I'll say this in passing: winning the Malaysian Grand Prix was a piece of cakerini.

2 APRIL 2021: The Surfer Hotel, Melbourne, Australia, room 1019.

What a weekend this has been, Diary, me old cobber! What a life this is turning out to be! The world's sporting press have camped in the hotel lobby. Again I am a prisoner in a dingy hotel room. Cristobel's here with me, but she nearly did not come as she was ill last week with a fever. But she's a tough old stick, thanks for small mercies. We have been watching a recording of the Australian Grand Prix. I scored a hat-trick of Grand Prix wins this afternoon. I am now thirty points clear of my nearest rivals: Trenchard, then Corteze. My picture decorates all the newspapers, being mobbed by my fans in their thousands, lifting the trophy, smiling. I am the Cardiff Flyer.

The press can hail me as they like, but it's what the television commentator described as I drove to victory that knocks me out with a feather. It sounded unreal. I can't stop watching it. Bradley Davis got carried away with the sporting moment as never before. I stormed away from the rest of the field from lap fifty-one. With two laps to go, an unknown driver from Spain, Riva, was far too close for my ginger little arse to deal with. He threatened at one point to pass me at a glance. But a determined woman cannot be broken – feminine intuition took over. I did not let Riva pass me; I kept him at bay, behind. We took the last bend together, then I pressed on the accelerator.

The Welsh Dragon flew down the circuit, right up the middle, or, as Davis put it, "It's the final lap, the last bend. This Welsh buckaroo storms to the front. Look at her go, fans. She takes the inside. What a move! Riva's beat. Now the crowd goes wild as they call her home. Here she comes. She drives – no, she dances down the circuit, waltzing to victory. The car roars away without effort. The Cardiff Flyer takes the flag. Ann Marie Osborne wins her third Grand Prix. What an achievement in sport! The Welsh win; the rest of the world are nowhere. I tell ya, boys, this dolly girl can open my throttle any day."

With that they threw flowers on to the circuit and the crowd spilled over to greet me. I loved it all.

Cristobel lies on the bed stoned out of her mind, a needle on the floor. We celebrated a shade too much in the old style. It must stop – no excuses now. We live too dangerously for all that. But that said, Diary, on Monday childhood promises are to be made good. It's true: I take Cristobel on a shopping spree to Alice Springs, then, homeward-bound, we'll fly back.

23 APRIL 2021: The San Marino Grand Prix.

The weather broke today, and this afternoon I competed in the pouring rain. But it gave me a fine opportunity to test the new high-tread 2×4 tyres. The car passed with flying colours.

Under the boss's instructions, I made slow qualifying times and ended up down the order, sixth on the grid.

He has told me more than once, "I want you in front at the end of a Grand Prix, where it counts, not the beginning, where it doesn't."

So this afternoon I did as I was told. The boss has an astute motor-racing brain. He anticipated the wet conditions, instructing me accordingly. The usual drivers – Trenchard, Corteze and Potter, along with the Russian Zargrev and the Americans Sellers and Grace – were just in front of me. All occupied the grid in glorious technicolour across the circuit. Red cars, blue cars, green and yellow ones appeared like a rainbow in front of me as the rain lashed down upon the circuit, almost posing a threat to the Grand Prix itself. After a wait of nearly one hour we were given the green light.

If there really is a God up there, then perhaps He has heard my prayers for guidance. Today, at least, He was certainly on my side, giving me acres of good fortune. After lap fourteen, the circuit became waterlogged in places. Speed was dramatically curtailed. Driving up the stretch I found myself only hitting seventy, then suddenly braking, slowing down to just thirty. This saved my race. The tyres held firm to the surface, getting rid of the excess water. I was amazed when Trenchard, a very experienced driver, lost control, skidding across the circuit. He took out six cars from the race with him – all my main rivals. At the time, I was cruising at minimal velocity for wet-weather driving. I slowed down, weaving around the carnage, then driving away. Unchallenged throughout the remaining laps of the Grand Prix, I won by an amazing four minutes from Houseman. So much for sensible women drivers. I think this has been our day of victory behind the wheel. Thank God Almighty nobody was killed.

7 MAY 2021: We arrived at Kingston Airport to the sound of a steel band. What a welcome – mobbed by the local press, touched by adoring fans, mostly male. Shit, I even wore a pair of dark glasses. Today I clinched victory number five, in the Caribbean Grand Prix. The weather, unlike San Marino, was hot, dry and humid. A fast time was obtained by little old me.

Leyth Swain took the car apart back home. He inspected the engine, chassis, wheels and suspension. The reports are all good

– super fine fun time for the racing car. That must be the case. We performed as expected, maybe better. Let us hope things stay this way until the end of the season. I ask a question now and so does the press: will I dethrone Trenchard to be the world champion?

Cristobel's here. She sat with the lads in the pits. Normally she sits in the grandstand. I am glad about that – after all, Diary, like you she's part of the team now. We can't do without her. Having said all that, the Caribbean Grand Prix was great to drive in. I wish they were all like it. The course takes you right through Kingston itself, down to the waterfront and along the coast for a couple of miles. Then you drive back inland, through fields of sugar cane, past enormous houses that have stepped right out of colonial Britain. It has all the hallmarks of a rally, not a Grand Prix. Because of this, I've gone head over heels in love with the place. This is the longest Grand Prix at the moment. I won the race by ten seconds, Trenchard taking third place.

On the podium he said something complimenting my driving skills, saying, "Ann Marie, you are one of the best drivers at the moment. You have a fine car and remarkable luck. Good for you. I won't give up my title without a fight, but I reckon you'll give me one."

Ah, bless his sweet little French arse!

I spent the night dancing at a club and smoked something nice. Yes, this has been a fine weekend. Goodnight, Diary.

14 MAY 2021: The Spanish Grand Prix was a day to forget in a hurry. Believe me, it did not go well. Oh fuck, don't tell me the bubble's burst! The Welsh Dragon did not finish the race. The cooling system failed after lap twenty. In heat topping 100, as I approached a tight bend on the circuit the engine just boiled over. In fact it caught fire, not just smoke. Flames rocketed out of the engine itself. I had to pull over and get out double quick. The car looked as if it might explode before my eyes. Fortunately, firefighters were on the scene with haste. The flames were extinguished and the car was saved.

My pride has taken a battering, combined with damage to my self-esteem. It sends shivers down my spine at the thought of perhaps a second defeat in the next Grand Prix. Self-doubt has taken over. I don't like it one bit. The sporting press will take us to town in the morning. I ask myself these questions: How will I feel? How must I behave? What will Gastard write about me with his own poisonous pen? Does it matter? He's a Judas-seeker of the worst kind.

Sangria, then a bullfight, along with the understanding presence of Cristobel, helped me get through the rest of the afternoon, putting sport behind me. Her hand, lips, voice and incredible smile made me forget, until the morning. We fly home in a few days' time. Dad's silent, brooding, thoughtful. He will repair the car and put right the faults, just in time for Monaco at the end of the month.

16 MAY 2021: Back to earth with a bump this morning. I made my first big mistake of the day: just before work I bought some newspapers and read them. I have been told repeatedly to stay away from the media, but I just had to know. I needed to look – especially at the comments in *The Globe*'s sporting pages. They made poor reading, but it was not as bad as it might have been. Gastard implied sympathy for the cause. The bubble's not burst – I know that, I think.

There's a photograph of me walking away from the burning racing car, head bowed in sorrow. I am not smiling – nothing to smile about. When you win in life everybody wants to know, but when you lose they don't. A few weeks ago in other more romantic places in the world I was hailed as a sporting heroine, a goddess. Yet today, as I walked down St Mary's Street in Cardiff, laden with shopping for Mum, I appeared as just another anonymous person on an anonymous street in an otherwise anonymous city. But in just two weeks' time that will all change. Even Cristobel wasn't there with me. Where was my true love, Wilson? Where was my faithful dog? They are dead.

Bring on Monaco. Let the fight continue.

28 MAY 2021: Apartment 650, Rochfort Buildings, Monte Carlo.

The last six days have been earth-shattering. I called out to the world, and it came running at my command. I have power after all. The Monaco Grand Prix has made me the centre stage on all four points of the compass. What a feeling! I believe I'm in love with myself.

So I'm here at last; we are here at last. I will do all I can, Diary, to keep you up to date on sporting matters at hand. Written as a recollection late at night, not a moment will be missed. Let's begin at the beginning. Since childhood Dad's had a bee in his bonnet about winning the Monaco Grand Prix; so have I.

As he told me only yesterday, as we prepared the car to race, "If we can win here, apple blossom, there's a chance we'll not get caught. The world championship will be ours, the dream a reality. You can do it, baby. The car's never been in better shape. The cooling system won't fail here, I promise." He gave me a fatherly kiss.

So much is the confidence within the Welsh camp. This has become a family affair indeed. My dad's been labouring all night every night since Spain. A test drive at Abbots Vale proved positive – all went without a hitch, boosting our chances here, only I know that a test run doesn't compare with the real thing. This morning, before the race, the whole team gave me a kiss of good fortune. They lined up, walked past me, then delivered a kiss on the cheek, or lips, with a whisper of good luck in my ear. It made me laugh. I feel good about this drive.

The antics of this morning broke the ice and let loose the tension that I've been experiencing ever since I arrived here with Cristobel six days ago. It had all the appeal of going on holiday down to the South of France – a place where wealth, along with love, abounds like no other. You would think that I'd approach this with a little more decorum – a task easier said than done for a girl my age. While packing my suitcase, back home in Cardiff, I talked as if I was going on my annual fourteen-day vacation, not to take part in a momentous sporting event.

The boss has hidden me away in a fancy apartment – very posh. I have been told by the powers that be to stay away from the press at all costs and say nothing about our game plan for the race. There must be no parties, booze, nights out or shopping trips to the city. What planet do they live on? Not the same one as me, that's for sure – not Planet Earth; more like Uranus if you ask me. When two pretty girls like us hit town, they'd better watch out, for sure. This will be a week of sport on the circuit as well as off. I look back in time over the last six days, for example, and breathe with delight and sigh with relief at the way things have gone for us all. For myself and for my country.

We arrived at Nice Airport about Tuesday lunchtime. The actual team has been here almost one week. The sporting circus hit the road, travelling from Spain to France and Monte Carlo, where they prepared the car. Joe tested it at least twice, putting the car through its paces on the circuit. All reports were favourable – good. In the morning I gave the car a spin, but from now onwards my dad said I was not to drive it again until qualifying on Saturday afternoon.

My arrival was not kept a secret from the media. They camped out at the airport waiting for me to come. They checked flights and kept watch on all people arriving here for this sporting jamboree. So it came to pass that Flight Cymru 60A from Cardiff was mobbed by the waiting press. Cristobel travelled with a ton of suitcases; so did I. We were fairly bogged down with them. Helpful flight attendants went out of their way to assist us in getting off the airplane, but we climbed down the stairway straight into the clutches of the waiting mob.

To my great relief the boss stood by a waiting car, Dad with him, along with some policemen. They were like dutiful parents anxiously waiting for their graduate daughter to arrive back from her gap year in Africa, but they failed to protect me from the media. Wearing the trademark dark glasses, looking like some Hollywood actress, I stepped down from the airplane and was surrounded by the press – two girls lost in a sea of men. They pushed, shoved and called out to us. It was unsettling – scary as hell. They began to bombard me with questions, trying to stick microphones in my mouth. Now, I'm still a young girl, and I don't mind things in my mouth, especially tongues, but microphones weren't what I had in mind today. I got them anyway. I've got to live with this sort of thing, I suppose. Right from the start they asked questions of all types with simple obvious answers to them. I found the whole circus disgusting to the last – clammy, dippy and wet. Is there no end to this?

"Ann Marie, will you win on Sunday?"

"How will you deal with Trenchard?"

"How's the car, then, Ann Marie?"

"Will you fail again like in Spain?"

All those questions were fired at me by the world's elite sporting reporters.

They received just one solid, sensible response from me: "I'm here to win for Wales for the glory of my country, to win for women drivers all over the world."

Thankfully, with that two policemen ushered us to safety.

The apartment is just what the doctor ordered, with a sea view to die for. It overlooks Monaco itself. The royal palace can be seen clearly, and the harbour with its many expensive white yachts anchored in a bay to the left. However, the good life had been banned for the rest of the stay. That said, Diary, from the first minute Cristobel planned our escape back to the real world of the living – the drunk, the high, the ones like myself who need to be loved by the rest of the human race. Yes, with that kind of philosophy this is the place to be, kiddo.

I had a light dinner with Cristobel as we watched television. Crap? Tell me about it! It was all in French, about the war – a soap, I think. All it consisted of was two old dears talking about the Second World War. After ten minutes of this yawn, clubbing was decided upon in a moment. It seemed the only thing to save our souls. In an instant we were changed and on our way to have a good time. The Sailor Dan, on Rue Océan, was the venue chosen. I took a rubber just in case I got lucky. Hell, Diary, it cost 1,000 euros to get in the door. The soft blue lights, combined with the loud music, made us feel at home, comfortable as a drunk in a bar in Dublin. The club was alive with rich young studs, searching for some action before the Grand Prix. We were spoilt for choice, but a gin wheel with crushed ice soon helped us unwind and get acquainted with the dice, like I was on the game. The rock hit 'Hail the Love of Man' seemed an appropriate song to start with – Hanson Feathers' best tune. It brought the dancers on to the floor; the swingers of the world united.

I was introduced to a new drink, a cocktail called a Pink Mixer – a cocktail with a punch all of its own, to solve all female woes – and found a chatty guy called Hank. I hoped he was somebody's heir, but nothing doing, Diary – just a cool local dude. No family inheritance there, I'm sorry to say. I found myself surrounded by dancing people and bright lights, and a buzz came inside my head for the rest of the night, well into the morning. When a Pink Mixer is popped into your drink, you watch it fizz, then dissolve, like a settler for bad guts might. Then you knock it back in one go. After that the night's your own. A thrust of untamed energy takes over when you dance, love or just want to be nice to everybody in the room. I bought a bag of ten. If the boss finds out I'm for it – random drugs tests around the corner. But sometimes I must live with the devil, just to get by in life.

The boss called early on Wednesday morning. Oh boy, did I have a hangover! I felt – indeed, I looked – like a tramp's arse. He quizzed me. In my pocket I had hidden the bag of Pink Mixers, but I just told him I'd slept too well. He believed me, but why shouldn't he? After all, I'm a good little girl who can do no wrong. Taking his advice, I was to stay put. The world's press were after me. They wanted interviews galore. I might have gone behind his back last night, but no more. I didn't relish facing that scum, so on that point he had my full trust.

On Thursday I went shopping in central Monte Carlo, evading the press at every corner. It was daft. I saw Gastard himself, then ducked behind a row of clothes. He didn't see me. When he'd gone, Cristobel chaperoned me for the rest of the morning. We just blended in with the rest of the jet set. I purchased a new shirt, a bra with matching knickers, along with flesh-coloured tights. Cristobel bought blouses by the score. At Monarouse Store I bought a brand-new handbag from New York. The whole thing cost me over 3,000 babberoones. Money well spent, I fear! The rest of the day was spent locked up in our apartment, sleeping on the couch or on the balcony, naked too.

On Friday I talked to Mum on the telephone and chatted for about two hours about everything save motor racing. She would not be here to watch me race – staying at home in Cardiff. Aunty Mildred's ill and needs looking after. She has a bad back at the moment. I just told her to do me a favour, like mums do: on Sunday morning place some flowers on Wilson's grave, then say a prayer for him. She said she would do that for me with pleasure. I am just glad about that – after all, that's what mums are for. On the grid come Sunday I'd be thinking of him. That lost boy of mine would be close to my heart, soul and destiny. We would drive the Monaco Grand Prix together.

On Saturday, like some long-lost relative not seen for years, I stepped back into the embrace of my family – the family of sport. They were happy to see me again, glad to acknowledge that I was still alive. Today was qualifying day for the Grand Prix. The media were there to greet me, love me all over again. As I marched on to the circuit at Monaco, I was lost in a fog of unwanted relations, all of whom desired me either to win or to lose in equal measure. They wanted to make sure they were on the right side of the fence, whatever the result tomorrow. Having said all that, Diary, I must write about Gastard of *The Globe* newspaper. Yet again he said something encouraging, inspiring, wishing me good fortune. I returned the compliment. I can be a real lady when required to do so.

Qualifying went very well indeed. The car outpaced all else. My instructions from the boss were obeyed to the full, though they were a complete contrast to what he told me before. Because this is such a tight circuit, pole was needed; pole was obtained. It was a fine omen for Sunday. After this afternoon, the naughty night out was put behind me. There were no drugs, booze or sexy men to offer distractions, allowing me to forget just exactly why I'm here. I never even thought of such wonderful things – just a steely feminine determination behind the wheel, to be the best. All summer long in fact this has been the case. The reward for some excellent driving on my part, for concentrating like no other woman on earth, is that I'd become a champion in the making. Grid position one means GFB – go for burn, just like the Apollo missions. Dad was over the moon himself, the boss pleased as Punch. The boys in the team sang my praises like a choir on Sunday. Because of this the mood in the camp had never been higher. Confidence grew like a flowering bougainvillea spreads like weeds in a garden. The Welsh had come to fight for victory as never before. Personally, I just wanted to do my best. A win here would certainly mark me out from all the rest. This was why a request to have dinner with Prince Haigh was turned down and a night out at the casino put to one side. Even Cristobel's suggestion of having a night out at a bar someplace was rejected. No means no on all counts. Instead we both had an early night, tailor-made for monks, nuns and geeks of every kind. I was in bed by ten, wrapped in the arms of my best friend, sleeping.

The day of the Monaco Grand Prix, 2021, is now over, yet I tremble with excitement still as I recall each hour in my memory. I woke at six feeling good, nerves rested, body relaxed. For the first time in many months I had managed to get in eight hours of undisturbed sleep. My entire female body had wound down. Like my mind it appeared refreshed and invigorated.

Then suddenly the still, the quiet of the bedroom, was broken by a loud knocking at the door of the apartment. It was my dad. We kissed good morning. He even kissed Cristobel smack square on the lips. Ah, such was the fever of well-being in our camp this morning, a day when being alive meant something, when sport could be seen in all its merit. At that hour of the day only one thing needs to be said: cometh the second, cometh the minute, cometh the hour, cometh the day, cometh the week, cometh the month, cometh the year, cometh the life, cometh the woman, cometh me. The great day had arrived, as expected. All I wanted was for the gods to guide and protect me with their good fortune. Not much to ask for, Diary?

My dad dumped a whole load of newspapers on to the dining-room table – a table laid out for a sumptuous breakfast. The boss sat at the head of the table sipping champagne. Cristobel munched a slice of toast while I poured another coffee. A plate of bacon and eggs with grilled tomatoes waited to be eaten. Dad appeared to be very excited, like all of us.

"Take a look, Ann Marie, baby. They are expecting great things from you today. The world waits from New York to Aberystwyth, from Moscow to Bangor and from Neath to Rome."

He kissed me good morning for the second time, or was it the third?

I scoured the various headlines before returning to my breakfast, which suddenly became serious indeed, like a finance company having a business breakfast meeting in the morning, where they plan the next billion-dollar strike on Wall Street. The only difference was this was sport – a motor race.

The boss raised his voice: "Never mind what that lot say or predict. Once that light turns green, you're on your own. Get it wrong, they'll tear you apart. Get it right, they'll sing your praises forever in sport. A true chance for immortality lies at your feet, Ann Marie, remember that."

Dad patted me on the back, then a team talk took over and reassurances were given. The breakfast ended at ten; by ten thirty we were on our way to the circuit. The press didn't pick us up until just before the pit lane. As we all walked towards the pits, where the team waited, the press followed us – me, the first female driver to compete in this Grand Prix. Journalists from all four corners of the world surrounded us. The boss tried to protect me; so did Dad. I was ushered in to get changed, emerging soon in my red jumpsuit, long blonde hair flowing with the French breeze, a crash helmet tucked under my right arm, ready for action. No time was wasted. I walked towards the racing car, a gleaming white chassis with the red emblem of the Welsh Dragon displayed on its sides, front and back. Shinier than ever before, the racing car looked a picture to me. Pole position one – at the head of proceedings. From there I gazed in utter fascination. The circuit was crammed full of racing cars in order. More than usual took part in this year's contest, some on the right, some on the left, and around each car stood the driver, the team and the press. But we, the Welsh, commanded most of the attention. There were so many journalists I had to be almost carried to the racing car and manually seated in the cockpit. Jenny Watson from USATV thrust a microphone in my face. I told her where to go, and I think she went. I was at that stage in no mood to speak – just think. That bloody woman got the message, leaving me alone to brood in silence. A thumbs-up from Gastard gave me strength for the task ahead.

With seconds to go before the off, the circuit was cleared of all people. Only the drivers in their racing cars remained. I snuggled down in the cockpit, crash helmet on, nerves tingling, mouth dry, stomach quivering. I was at the head of the Grand Prix, nothing but racing cars behind me, the centre of sporting attention, yet the loneliest woman on the planet. The only sound I heard was the engine idling softly, like a woman's voice before the argument rages. My eyes searched for the green light to grant me vengeance. It felt a bit like I was waiting for the lights to change back home in Cardiff, stuck at the junction of Duke Street and Sheepdog Road on market day, not waiting for the start of a Grand Prix.

Without warning red changed to green and I roared away from the grid, tyres screeching. The Welsh Dragon raced away at my command. Soon 150 was reached. Trenchard tried to take me at the first bend, but I cut him off, concentration very high. During a Grand Prix only one lap counts – the lap of honour that tells all you've won – but I recall the final lap of this Grand

Prix, each detail told as a sporting epic as if recited by a poetic nymph. The effort, the sweat, the nerves, the colours, the smells, the cheering crowds, the glory!

Female adrenalin kicked into action as I headed out for the last lap. Now the race for the chequered flag was on. With all those men steaming behind me, you'd think the task would be made easier, but it wasn't. I needed all my guile and intuition.

I approached St Devote way ahead of Trenchard, with Sellers taking up third position. My speed touched 180, just briefly. It felt outstanding. All female power was there with me. At that point in the Grand Prix Pankhurst would've been proud of me, her little baby. The suffragettes would have adored me as one of their own. I smiled at such a thought as the tight circuit wound its way through the suburbs, the dark surface of the road ahead of me contrasting with the gleaming white buildings on either side. Tall white apartments rose high into the air. People stood watching from windows and balconies. They cheered me as I drove by them. I even saw my name written on a flag draped across a balcony itself. It stated, 'ANN MARIE OSBORNE, QUEEN OF THE TRACK'. At one point some drunk ran on to the circuit, dangerously trying to run beside my racing car before police restrained him and escorted him back to safety and another beer. After negotiating a bend that wound its way snake-like through what looked like a very expensive area of the city, again I drove at tremendous speed along a straight stretch of the circuit. I watched as the dial slowly crept to 200 and I pushed my darling for all it was worth. The Welsh Dragon roared like a jet fighter into combat. The sound of the engine threw my body into some kind of female madness. Racing-driver instinct made me push for maximum, then slow to a crawl as the circuit turned left. Suddenly, there it was, right in front of me – a sporting landmark like no other, the casino of Monte Carlo, its stonework washed for the occasion. The casino is as significant as Becher's Brook, the Pavilion at Lords or maybe the Olympic flame itself. Motor racing and the casino go together like two lovers who care for each other. They are inseparable.

A floral display greeted me as I drove within striking distance of the casino. A welcoming picture of many colours, of flowers of all kinds, was planted neatly in rows in front of the casino. How many gamblers have admired the garden before venturing inside to lose their money, empty the pot? The flowering scent of Monte Carlo – the intoxication of the would-be gambler, the lure of those destined not to win on the day. I for one would not be one of them, never venturing inside. My only gamble was found here on the circuit – victory behind the wheel of a racing car, not at roulette. Out of the corner of my eye I saw a champagne bottle being opened by somebody. A man with a woman at his side drank from the bottle. Were they celebrating a win, or richly drowning a loss?

Once past the casino, I headed out to Mirabeau. Inside my jumpsuit I was soaking wet – glorious female perspiration. Every so often I would feel the sweat run down my back, my front or some other part of my anatomy. My mouth was permanently dry, a rasping sensation affected my throat and despite the water bottle, dehydration began to set in. Concentration was telling me not to drink. The heat appeared to be hotter than the sun itself, sucking me dry to the bone.

At times I could not breathe, sounding like some asthmatic old lady. If I could bottle my sweat here, men would buy it, then drink it. Eventually I sipped some water, the crazy wonderful feeling soothing my throat, but I was longing for something stronger – a cocktail perhaps. I drove on, my mind hallucinating for such luxuries, wishing for a Monaco Skinny Dip, a mouth-watering concoction made up of Bacardi, whisky, curaçao and vanilla ice cream with a strawberry on top, served with crushed ice and sipped through a straw. I recall a faint smile as I left the casino behind me.

Driving through Mirabeau more fans cheered me on. I observed a Welsh flag being waved by a fellow countryman, or woman. I clenched my fist and saw more people standing on rooftops to secure a better view. I glanced at my rear-view mirror – not another racing car in sight. Ahead was a clear circuit, the finish coming closer with each turn of the car's wheels. But the bastards might have appeared at any moment, challenging me for victory. I accelerated away, pushing to the limit. I arrived at Portier, my car touching 174 dead; soon 200 struck, then deceleration clicked into action, the racing car slowing down as I came to a long curve on the circuit. The Tunnel beckoned me towards its cool opening, getting me out of the direct sun for a few precious moments. For the last time during the race, I entered the Tunnel. It seemed like some enormous white cave, maybe made of snow straight from the Arctic. For a brief spell it had a cooling effect upon me – a psychological chilling of the soul. In the Tunnel I wanted to take off my crash helmet, allowing my blonde hair to dance with the breeze, but I couldn't. Trapped in my racing car, this was a luxury denied. On this lap the Tunnel seemed twice as long to drive through. Emerging out of it, like some actress stepping on to the stage as the curtain rises for the final act, in front of me was a huge grandstand with what seemed thousands of fans watching the performance, my curtain call. As I drove the car out of the white mouth of the Tunnel, a wall of people greeted me in the grandstand, which looked a mile long. The sound was deafening to my ears. It appeared to me like a rainbow of colours – a vast mass of people dressed in blouses, vests, jumpers, kaftans, swimwear and shirts with logos on them (a few showing my face). This was all the encouragement I needed. I smiled at the sight before me, milking the moment, pleased at the downdraught.

The circuit narrowed outside the Tunnel. To one side was the harbour; on the other was a vast stone wall. At one point I slowed to fifty – no speeding here. It was just after this point in the race, travelling as slowly as if I were in a city jam at rush hour, that life called out to me in all her glory. I observed a tall ship anchored out in the harbour. My eagle eye caught the sight of two people, scantily dressed, lounging on the deck. The expensive ship flew the American flag on top of its mast and again on the stern. A young woman sunbathed with an older man. Question: was he her lover, father or, as it seemed, grandfather? Or was he her boss? No way, Cynthia! They were lovers. They were all over each other. The man, decked with grey hair, rubbed oil over her tummy; she lay there soaking it up. I saw her turn, giggle, then put on her dark glasses, oblivious to the Grand Prix. The lucky bitch hadn't a care in the world – the inheritor of his wealth, provider of his children. I found myself almost winking at her out of the corner of my eye.

Then I approached the chicane. Obeying the laws of the land, I slowed down, entering the tight single lane, weaving from left to right, in a hurry. My gloved hands were gripping the steering wheel as a matter of life or death. I adjusted the racing car to a straight course in one manoeuvre. I heard the crowd applaud me as I raced away, a bit like a crowd would applaud a golfer who putts successfully on the green. Tabac got closer with each turn of the wheel, but the chequered flag seemed to get further away from me. Where was the little darling? An enormous sign outside a shop that displayed itself on top of a balcony caught my eye. A party was in full swing, and for a brief moment my ears heard the music being played, a heavy drumbeat in the background as people danced on the roof under the blazing sun. Another excuse to have some fun at a sporting venue! How many people at Epsom don't watch the Derby, but just go there to drink, party or love? After Tabac the circuit began to bear to the left, passed some shops, cafés, bars and restaurants filled to overflowing. Driving down the middle of the road, I cruised at 100. At Piscine I got the shock of my life. Again I looked into my rear-view mirror, but could see nothing – no other cars behind me, the circuit bare. Yet in front I saw two other cars. I lapped the German, then the Italian driver. It was a moment in the Grand Prix to savour – treasure. I sent them into glorious non-racing-ness.

Despite this lack of opposition I did not take the Grand Prix for granted. Checking all the while, the car's fuel, water, electrics and temperature all seemed well.

At Rascasse my dad spoke to me through my headphones, telling me to push for glory. I pumped the car for all I was worth, like I was part of the engine, sending it forward, making it go faster. At Noghes, racing up the final stretch to claim my crown, I passed the pit lane without giving it a second thought. After all that was, is, and indeed will be in the future, a lane I have no intention of walking or driving down. At this point my concentration was at its height. I focused on the road ahead. I swear I didn't even blink an eyelid. I dared not let go of the steering wheel, gripping it as if my life depended on it for my own survival. The Welsh Dragon accelerated, roaring away to make her acquaintance with victory. I took the chequered flag, waved at me one million times. I screamed, punching the air, saluting the crowd. As I savoured my victory I recited the sporting verse of my homeland – a poem for Welsh sporting success.

Oh, St David, sweet divine,
Bless this promised land of mine.
This is one of those glorious sporting tales –
Tell all the boys I won for Wales.

I repeated it three or four times in Welsh. I had won the Monaco Grand Prix. This afternoon I beat the rest of the world. Nobody could match my brilliance behind the wheel. For once the Judas-seekers of the press were put in their place. They cannot say a poor word about me today, only praise my true ability as a racing driver. The best in the world at the moment! Wales can rejoice. I am a victorious Queen of Sport. I took the most important lap of any Grand Prix – the lap of honour – in my stride, cocky as hell. Right from the start I was mobbed like never before. From the very first win back in March, I knew the pride and sense of achievement that goes with it the moment the flag drops in your honour. But this afternoon sent that feeling to new boundaries. For one thing, just 100 yards into victory I observed people giving me a standing ovation from the grandstand. Some blew kisses, and I saluted them back. Having now slowed to a crawl (less than five miles per hour), I also glanced into my mirror, seeing for the first time in ages other racing cars passing the chequered flag, securing second and third places on the podium. I watched Sellers, Potter, then Trenchard fight it out for these honours between them.

Men wept for joy, shouting at me with uncontrollable ecstasy embedded in their voices, my dad being the main culprit. Then suddenly, in the midst of this hysteria, he emerged on to the circuit, running towards the racing car along with the rest of the team, clapping and waving with the rest of humanity. Then he walked slowly towards me, arms outstretched in a gesture of adoration from father to daughter. I stood up and took off my crash helmet, letting my blonde hair give me back my feminine identity. The sudden rush of fresh air around my head was a blessing in disguise. Dad wrapped his arms round me, hugging as a lover might. We embraced in front of the rest of the world. For our family it was an epoch-making moment in time.

"I'm so proud of you, my darling. You drove our racing car like a demon. Hell, now what?"

Then he broke down, weeping without control.

The boss clapped his hands, then blew me another kiss. So did the boys from the pits.

Life must go on, no matter how successful we might be. I sat back down in the cockpit of the racing car, once again attempting the lap of honour. It was the same every inch of the way: delirious fans jumped in front of the car, with police seemingly powerless to stop them from trying to commit suicide in my honour. Flowers were thrown on to the circuit, then at me directly. As I passed the casino the road was covered in petals of many colours. When will I see such a thing in my honour again? I felt like some Roman empress arriving back in Rome, mobbed by the masses, the multitude, wanting to be close to a goddess. It also got much worse as I drove onwards. Once through the Tunnel, approaching the grandstand, I saw it was in fact empty. They had crammed on to the circuit, blocking my way ahead, preventing me from driving further. Police converged like soldiers in battle, or the riot squad trying to bring order out of chaos. Despite this, when they saw my racing car drive slowly towards them, a mass of people, a wall of humanity, advanced. All of a sudden I found myself surrounded on all sides. Some appeared to be running, not walking, almost as if trying to be the first to touch me, or congratulate me. A couple of policemen appeared out of nowhere to protect me. They stood by the racing car, halting the advance of the crowd, the charge of the fans, delirious with good wishes. At one point a young man broke through the barrier of policemen, a flower in one hand. He gave me the flower, told me he loved me, then kissed me on the lips. I hugged him back. Then the police overpowered him – gently, on my advice. The man was thrown back to the crowd, but astonishingly he persisted in his efforts. I loved it all, but the man acted first, thought later – a dangerous human being. The harbour seemed lost in a kind of madness of sport. I stood on the racing car's bonnet, a bouquet of yellow flowers held in my arms, acknowledging the well-meant heroine worship from those gathered there this afternoon after my victory. There seemed no way out for me. I was stuck.

I must have been trapped there for at least fifteen minutes before race officials, accompanied by yet more police, came to my aid. A whole army of them had been drafted in for my rescue, to stop me from drowning in a sea of people. I watched feeling helpless as they acted like some puppet army from some brutal republic, ordered to break up protesters by a cruel dictator, despite my thoughts on this well-earned accolade. This was no time for being humble; this was a time for female arrogance with no equal. After this Grand Prix slaughter, I had a duty to the rest of womankind, to advance the cause still further. As the winning racing driver, I made a solemn oath to open my big mouth then let the sound come out.

I waved back to the crowd, saying, "Thank you very much. This has been a well-planned victory."

I don't think anybody heard me. A policeman forced me to sit behind the wheel again, then drive off to complete the lap of honour, this time with a police escort of three cars. Even with this protection, it still took over one hour to finally arrive back at the podium for the victory ceremony. Every so often I would stop the racing car, melting in the adoration. I loved it all. I felt at home this afternoon, living in my true environment. I did not want this madness to stop. I think I could have spent the rest of my life driving around this city of dreams relived.

I stood on the podium, and dashing Prince Haigh presented me with the trophy. I held it aloft, to the delight of the fans gathered there to bear witness to this spectacle of mine. The Prince then kissed me upon the cheek, shook my hand and offered his best wishes. He then honoured the other drivers – Sellers, Potter and Trenchard – who'd fought for the minor places, important points earned for them all. Death is always the unwanted companion to the motor-racing driver, only forgotten about at the end of the race, when life takes over in all her glory. I wept with pride and joy. Emotions and feelings of invincibility were transmitted like rays of good karma from the depths of my body as 'Land of My Fathers' brought a tear to my face. The anthem of the land of my birth was raised in triumph, like a musical battle standard to every other member of the human race. At four fifty it was my time to acquiesce with immortality in sport.

An enormous bottle of Mère du Moon champagne was given to me. I drank some, spraying anybody foolish enough to stand close. All the other drivers congratulated me, wishing me well. I gestured to Dad, the boss and the boys. Cristobel joined me on the podium. It made my day complete. At that point, could anything go wrong? Answer: no.

Diary, in passing, God gives champions the power, the skills, the dreams, to run, jump, throw or swim faster than their neighbours. All gods approve of such ventures. I observed the human race at its very best this afternoon. So long as we have sport, the human race will never die.

30 MAY 2021: We arrived back home from Monaco this evening. What a welcome awaited me at Cardiff Airport! The media were there in force along with thousands of my fans. As I pushed a luggage trolley through arrivals, the press engulfed me, asking obtuse questions about the race and my future. I found it difficult to walk. But, as in Monaco, the police came to my rescue, my aid. Two fine burly members of the Cardiff force escorted me to a waiting car, but not before I gave an interview to *The Six O'Clock News* on UKBC. Big John Cuthbert (a man with a small brain) asked the questions. He walked by my side as I walked in a blind hurry through arrivals, talking all the time. He had a problem keeping up with me. I wanted to get away from this arse-kisser, but couldn't. He kept on, persistent as ever.

His monotone voice droned on in my left ear: "Well, Ann Marie, that was a great win for you. How does it feel to win the Monaco Grand Prix?"

Without actually looking him in the face, just walking, I answered, "I feel wonderful – a dream come true, a fantabulous fink buster if ever there was one. I won for Wales and for women drivers all over the world. I won for them too."

I turned to walk past a mountain of luggage, but Birdbrain tripped over a bag left on the floor. It served him right, but he never broke breath.

Like a true professional he carried on talking: "All Cardiff wants to see you. Did you expect this welcome?"

I saw my dad ahead of me, so I walked faster, at jogging speed.

"No, not at all. I thank everybody who has turned up to greet me back home. It's very nice."

What looked like thousands of people watched me, never taking their eyes off me.

"During the Grand Prix, just when did you think you'd won?"

I waved to the fans watching me; they waved back.

"Our racing car has always given us faith in its powerful performance. We wanted to stay in front, and we did. No pit stops makes all the difference to the way I drive, approach the race. Next time the same punishment will be dealt out, at Silverstone. I must beat the English on their home soil. I tell you, boyo, they thrashed us at Shrewsbury in 1403, but at Silverstone I'll drive the bollocks off the English in 2021. You'll see, man."

A couple of adoring fans asked for my autograph. I signed for them. Others followed.

One more question followed: "Well, that sounds great, Ann Marie. But what about the comments made by both Trenchard and Sellers? They almost declared you world champion."

The police stepped in as a rugby scrum trapped me by the main doors. They prevented a tussle.

"Well, that's very nice of them to say that, but I'd rather wait until China in October. The season's only halfway through at the moment – anything can happen."

With that final comment I was ushered out of the building, thankfully to end that torture. I waved to the press, to the fans and to the travelling public from the inside of the car. I sat on the back seat with Cristobel and we held hands. I needed her.

I arrived back home this evening at six, my tea already on the table: toad-in-the-hole and apple crumble with custard. Aunty Mildred sat in her usual place at the table.

"Pass the mustard, Ann Marie, there's a good girl."

Home at last.

Goodnight, Diary. I'm glad to be home from the madness.

1 JUNE 2021: I've been given the week off by the powers that be. The boss has told me not to drive for eight clear days. Leyth Swain doesn't want me to report to Silverstone until next week. Well, that suits me fine – an entire week spent shopping, drinking and sleeping. Like a good little girl, I will do as I'm told, along with Cristobel. We spent today lying on the golden sand of Oxwich Bay.

This morning at nine I walked into a shop near Swansea. The front doorbell rang out, but to my horror shelf after shelf had newspapers displayed with my photograph on the front page. They showed me being hugged by my dad after winning at Monaco, hugging each other. I bought a copy of The Globe, then walked out of the shop without being recognised.

Once on the beach we lazed about doing and saying nothing in particular. Despite the nice day, there were more seagulls than people on the beach. I counted just six people in all – a family picnic close to a car, a couple kissing on the sand and a lone swimmer out at sea. I read a book and Cristobel slept a lot. She hardly said a word all day long. I wish I could have more days like this one. God knows what the morning will bring.

Love, Diarykins.

3 JUNE 2021: Watched the early morning news on UKBC. The Prime Minister's in Washington DC on a visit for talks on the economy and the Middle East. Standing with President Randolph, they gave a press conference on the lawn of the White House. For once the voters have got it right: a good-looking president and a dream of a prime minister. Let us hope it stays that way. I mean, I'll be driving in the US Grand Prix soon. I look forward to the challenge very much.

Diary, Uncle Sam had better watch out – I'm coming their way.

Lock up their sons – I want them.

11 JUNE 2021: Another great little day in my life, with big consequences. The English, along with the rest of the world, have been soundly beaten – thrashed by me. I won the British Grand Prix at glorious Silverstone – in style too. But, to be fair, the English did excel in Scotland at the home of golf. I drove like a goddess this afternoon, never in danger during the race. I felt the car surge like the wind on the Cape and along Copse. At Hangar Straight I executed the rest of the field for dead. I hit 200 plus, a time traveller on the move. It was a start-to-finish rout. To make matters great, I beat the great legendary Tia Madrid's record by one clear second.

Tomorrow newspapers will predict the championship will be mine for the taking. Only destiny dictates here. I am not the only glory seeker who's made good today. This afternoon up at St Andrew's the world of golf was shaken to its foundations like never before. Young Henry Dribblethorpe shot three holes in one, at the eighth, nineth and tenth greens. The golfing record books can't keep up with him. Each drive was better than the one before, the hero worship deserved. Will golf ever see a feat like that again? Will a poor little Welsh girl win the US Grand Prix? Only the gods can answer.

Goodnight, Diary. I love life.

25 JUNE 2021: Alpine Mist is a wonderful motor-racing circuit, built to stage the Swiss Grand Prix. It's the shortest circuit on the tour, but, in my humble view, certainly the prettiest – a mountain retreat, set in a Swiss valley with mountains on all sides, not too far from Zurich. It's almost circular in shape. I adore it to bits.

I have very little to report about the race itself. I got pole and was never in danger. I led from start to finish, lapping many drivers. This made it a one-horse race, you might say. After lap thirty Trenchard tried to pass me, but I read the circuit well enough. Once you have pole here you should never be beaten, much like Monaco. Well, that's what I did this afternoon. Some teams have logged complaints, and I see their point. The Swiss must do something – it must become more competitive to make more of a race of it or they'll lose this race. That will be a sad loss to the sport.

But that said, Diary, it was another fine victory for little old me. Indeed, I would like to thank the Swiss for making this so easy. The Americans will not be so accommodating at Watkins Glen.

1 JULY 2021: I arrived at JFK this evening and was mobbed by the press. I was besieged in one of the VIP lounges. They demanded an interview with me. They have already proclaimed me world champion. After Switzerland I'm too far in front on the drivers table. Be that as it may, I'd rather wait until the final Grand Prix. Aunty Mildred talks more common sense than Hannibal of the *New York Daily*. He ganged up on me, refusing to let go until, like some guru, I'd spoken to the masses. Remembering what I had been told back home in Cardiff, I was polite but full of verbal dog's bollocks, giving nothing away. I stood behind a microphone then talked to these people. They wanted caviar; I gave them cheese. Cristobel stood behind me.

"I'm glad to be here in the United States. I look forward to the contest. I'm very glad that this Grand Prix's returned to Watkins Glen – a wonderful circuit, home of American motor racing, I think." I then gave a dumb smile to the cameras.

At the back of the room a fat-arsed dude from Cowsbottom, Texas, asked me a question: "Tell me, ma'm, just how will your machine perform at Watkins Glen? A difficult circuit for you, I feel."

In an instant I thought of birds in flight. My answer knocked them dead where they stood: "The Welsh Dragon is a nifty little mover, as swift as a falcon, graceful as a flamingo, tough as a buzzard."

This remark caused the room to erupt with laughter. I just stood there rooted to the spot, red-faced and angry. So I used my female charm and intuition, changing the subject quickly, talking about the wonderful country, the cities and the people. I said I wanted to go swimming off Cape Cod on the glorious fourth. This went down a treat. I won them over with lots of female attitude. I will drive the longhorn shit out of these people come the tenth.

We have arrived. Bring on the green light here. This is the big one, Diary.

4 JULY 2021: What a gas! I made the press look foolish – stupid to the core. They all went to Ship Anchor Bay on Cape Cod – to watch me swim, I assume. I went swimming for sure, off Fish Hook Sound, Connecticut. I checked into a small hotel for the night, sampled the local lobster for dinner and had a great time. This will be as good as it gets. I telephoned my mum – she's fine.

Have a nice day, Diary. I have.

10 JULY 2021: I walked out of the hotel right into a wall of fans camped outside the hotel's main door. I spent ten minutes signing autographs, receiving their good wishes. As I signed I kept hearing, "Good luck, Ann Marie, darling. We love you." One teenager kissed me on the cheek, then got his pals to take a photograph of us arm in arm. It was a fine way to start the sporting day. All people should start the working day in such a light. Here at Watkins Glen I felt the warmth of the human race. It placed me on a high as I walked through the main gates of the circuit, joining the rest of the team.

Yesterday qualifying was not so easy – this time I was in fourth place on the grid. Sellers, the local boy, was holding pole. Trenchard and Zargrev were next in line, in front of me. The race itself remained static up until the penultimate lap. Despite the advantage of no pit stops they gave me a tough ride, always a threat. At one time Trenchard passed me, and as a result it took four laps to regain the lead. They are penny wise to my tactics now. After taking a pit stop, racing back into the race, using all their skills as racing drivers to keep me in check, they came back at me in an instant. I tell you, Diary, I could not get rid of these pests.

The intense heat of a New York afternoon was combined with the expanse of Seneca Lake, its sparkling water acting like some giant mirror to my left then right-hand sides. It looked for all the world like a lost cause. A second defeat loomed uneasily on the horizon. Sellers suddenly dropped out, smoke drifting out of his car's engine, the car coming to an abrupt halt. Corteze was nowhere to be seen. This left me to race head to head, engine to engine, against my chief rival, Trenchard. We raced together like two jockeys in a horse race at Belmont Park. I on the left, he on the right. There was hardly any space in between us. I squeezed the throttle for all it was worth. I glanced to my right for a split second. I observed Trenchard's still head engulfed in his crash helmet. He appeared like a statue, not moving at all, his own determination making him drive like a demon to the chequered flag, to win at any cost, determined not to lose to me. I watched the speed increase, like liquid in a thermometer, rising all the time. Down the stretch we raced – 100, 200 miles per hour. The grandstands on both sides of the circuit were alive with screaming fans. They shouted us home with every breath in their body. They stood up, waving their arms and fists, egging us on to victory, the noise deafening, as if they were encouraging two gladiators to fight to the death in Ancient Rome herself, 2,000 years ago. Human ethics never change, not even with time.

The usual celebrations followed my victory here in the United States. I decided to stay on for a few days, along with Cristobel. I have become the centre of attention all over the country. It seems everybody wants to know me, Ann Marie Osborne, the Cardiff Flyer. This ties in with the American way of life, of doing things. They love winners and hate losers. Well, since the chequered flag dropped, I've been inundated with invites to Hollywood parties, television interviews, chat shows – the bloody works. There is even an invite for tea with President Randolph at the White House. Oh my God, a special flight will take me down to Washington for this special occasion. Personally, I can't wait for this meeting. Now, Diary, who would've thought it? Eighteen months ago, on the garage floor back home in Cardiff, I recall Leyth Swain kicking my arse for being lazy, useless, unable to give a car a simple oil change. Yet here I am having just stormed to victory in the US Grand Prix, about to take tea with the President of the United States at the White House. All I can say is that it is a strange world we live in. Weird fortune awaits us all – I have certainly had my share of it.

11 JULY 2021: The White House! Underneath portraits of Lincoln, Washington, Kennedy, Adams and Havard I took tea this afternoon with President Randolph, joined by the First Lady, Gladis. The world's media gathered on the lawn outside to take photographs. I was received like a head of state might be. Tea was simple – cakes, tea, ham sarnies and coffee. I accepted the glass of bourbon offered to me, on the rocks. This has been a day given to me by the gods. The President was very polite. He showed interest in my Welsh background.

I quote him: "You are a refreshing change, my dear – a Welsh champion. Why, hell, they normally come from South America, France or Italy. The world of sport is now a more international place. Why, shucks, it's much better for it."

I smiled like a pleased little schoolgirl, replying simply, "Mr President, when I drive my racing car, I hear singing in every Welsh valley from Newport to Bangor, from Rhosgoch across to Wrexham and from Aberfan to the Rhondda. My country drives with me."

His compliments continued – praise from the highest in the land. "What a wonderful way to put it, young lady! Perhaps you should be a poet? You are indeed a woman of our time – somebody the rest of the world must equate to."

I was due to leave the White House at six, but the President invited me to stay the night. I declined the offer to be one of his White House conquests in between the sheets. Not even a president of the United States can take advantage of this wise Welsh pussycat. What a disappointed man he must be tonight!

14 JULY 2021: Ocean Hotel, Hollywood, California, USA.

Got a call from my mum this morning at six. Apparently the newspapers have published a photograph of me shaking hands with the President on the lawn of the White House. Man, that's cool. It has been gloriously splashed across the front pages. The whole country's talking about it. It sounds great. I told her to keep a few copies for me, so I can read them when I return home. For tomorrow I have been invited to a Hollywood party, thrown in my honour for winning here. I feel very chuffed; so does Cristobel. There's one thing that bothers me about this party: it's to be thrown by heart-throb Dain Godard. I don't even know this creep. I wouldn't know him from Dai the Milk's wife.

Goodnight, Diary. I'll be glad to go home, away from this madness. I want my mum.

30 JULY 2021: The madness continues. I pen this diary entry from the guest bedroom at 10 Downing Street, London. The time is exactly 3 a.m. All I can say is the following about the last two days of my life. My heart is pounding against my heaving chest. I am in love all over again.

Hell, what a weekend this has been! Defeat, loneliness, then love, all in the space of forty-eight hours. The victory in France two weeks ago was put to the sword by defeat in the Russian Grand Prix, held around the city streets of Moscow. I drove poorly – two wretched mistakes cost me even a place on the podium. No points scored on the board! That said, it was only my second defeat of the season, so I can't complain. It's been a fine run of Grand Prix wins. Without delay I left Moscow. I should have checked out of my hotel on Monday, but got out double quick. I arrived back in London anonymously with Cristobel. Even with her company I had nothing to say. Silence can be the cure, thought the best invigorator, for the unsettled mind. We spent the night at The Riverside Hotel on the Strand. A telephone call at eight pulled me back to the real world: an invite for supper. It came from Nicholas Rachael, the Prime Minister himself. Needless to say, I accepted.

I arrived at 10 Downing Street on the number 40 bus just after nine, dressed in my pink micro mini, flesh-coloured tights and black stiletto shoes. Lots of attitude. Love in my handbag. The Prime Minister – darling Nicky – greeted me on the doorstep of Number Ten. We kissed each other as if we'd been doing it for years, as familiar as any lovers might be. He held my hand as we walked inside this magnificent building, the seat of power throughout the land. The defeat in Moscow was soon put to one side as I tucked into a casserole supper washed down with champagne. We talked well into the early hours. I reminded Nicky we'd met before, and he remembered, recalling my victory in the Isle of Wight Classic. The photograph of us both in the local press which he still has in his possession is on his desk. It turns out that Nicky's been following my career, tracking my every move, watching Grand Prix after Grand Prix, willing me to victory, like all men, women and children should – all those who care.

My eyes never left Nicky's face. I don't think I blinked all night long – the sign of love.

The Prime Minister lies naked on the bed next to me. I adore him. His seed rests inside me – we are as one. I will carry a part of him with me wherever I go. We will never be parted. Nicky's body stretches out on the bed; he sleeps soundly as a baby, out for the count. But I'm wide awake – I can't sleep at all. I just watch fascinated as his tummy rises then falls with each breath he takes.

Diary, I love the Prime Minister.

2 AUGUST 2021: Just when heaven shows her wonderful face to me, hell appears on the horizon. My recent past is about to catch up with me big time. It has come back to haunt me.

Jam Tarts magazine have been in touch with me. They inform me, to my horror, they are about to sell my naked photographs around the world.

The editor says, "My position in life, in the world of sport, makes their photographs of me as priceless as a Canaletto."

He is right, of course. I can do nothing about it. They appear across America next week. Scandal-cum-sporting greatness. The shock will hurt my parents back home in Cardiff. Then there's darling Nicky. Shit! Just when Cupid's arrow flies through the air, a brick wall stands in its way.

Perhaps next week will never come.

3 AUGUST 2021: Nicky telephoned me from the House of Commons and invited me to watch him next week in a debate. I just might at that. Ah, the price of love conquered.

Do I love the Prime Minister, Diary? Yes I do – hear! hear!

14 AUGUST 2021: I accepted Nicky's invite to watch him debate in the House of Commons – the debate in question a deadly serious one. Had lunch at Number Ten, then I made my way to the public gallery. Nobody noticed me. I'm not politically minded really, but I sat there watching this spectacle, rooted to my seat. The debate went on for five long hours. I fell asleep at least twice, missing nothing. Nicky gave a rousing speech, hailed by those who saw it – so much so that the vote was passed by a majority on the floor. The Wooden Box Act has been passed into law – the first legislation that Nicky's got through the house. What a guy he is turning out to be! The whole country's behind him all the way on this issue. The prison service will never be the same again. The law is tougher than ever – break it at your peril. Six prison factories are to be built, where those sentenced will never get parole. They get out of prison in a wooden box, hence the name. Murder, other violent crimes and even certain types of robbery get the wooden box. With the absence of the death penalty and with crime out of control, this is the compromise insisted. Those sentenced will work for the nation, making car batteries by the million. Soon just thinking about crime, or dreaming about committing violence, will be an offence in itself. Good must always triumph over bad.

Thank goodness for Nicky. I feel safer now.

10 SEPTEMBER 2021: The last couple of months have been wonderful. As the Grand Prix season draws to a close, glory awaits me. In Hungary I satisfied my appetite for winning by taking their Grand Prix. Italy, Germany then Norway went the same way for me. I'm untouchable, unbeatable. Here in Dublin the Irish Grand Prix failed to come my way. I drove into third place, Sellers taking the race in style by a wide margin. Gallons of Irish whiskey, plus the leprechauns did not sprinkle their lucky stardust upon me this afternoon! But no matter – there's one more Grand Prix to go in China. I have everything to drive for. Nicky telephones me regularly from 10 Downing Street. Dinner for us on Sunday when he returns from important talks in Paris with other EU leaders. Ah yes, Diary, love has made me invincible. I cannot lose.

Spent the night Irish dancing – love it to bits. Jigged with Leyth. I even managed to persuade the boss to dance with me. What a way to end the day! So bring on the Chinese.

Diary, what a life I lead!

12 OCTOBER 2021: The Yellow Flower Hotel, Shanghai, China.

This has been an epoch-making day in my short little life – a day that shouted out to the rest of mankind, "Ann Marie Osborne has walked on this earth." It was my crowning – my enthronement as world champion. My reign began this afternoon at exactly four in the afternoon as I took the chequered flag, driving the Welsh Dragon racing car to its ultimate victory, to ensure immortality for myself and for Wales. I deserve all that today has been kind enough to give me.

The Chinese were responsible for writing paper, medicine, gunpowder and perhaps democracy itself. Porcelain too can be traced back to China. Man, they even taught us to eat like civilised people, not animals. The Chinese nation – where would we be without them? For today, they crowned me Champion of the World incarnate. When I crossed the line they went bananas with their heroine worship. It caught me off guard a little. As in Monaco before, I could not drive the car for my lap of honour. They forced me to stop and acknowledge their praises. People came from all points of the compass. They almost dragged me out of the car. Some fat Chinaman almost pulled me out of the cockpit. He hugged me, then kissed me on the lips. It was horrible. His breath smelt like a Chinese wrestler's jockstrap. He almost mauled me with his kisses, hugs and general manhandling. Having said all that, he meant no harm to me. That Chinaman was the first person on this earth to congratulate me. This has been a day to really celebrate my achievement in sport. What will they say in Merthyr Tydfil? How will they react in Cheinin? Wilson would be right proud of me today –

our love would blossom like a cherry tree in springtime.

Diary, you can thank me later. You're famous too – you alone have all my thoughts on paper.

13 OCTOBER 2021: Presidential Palace, Beijing, China.

Once again I was received as a head of state this evening at a gala dinner, held in my honour by the President of China himself, Dang Wang Nou. He insisted on it, so I am told. Cristobel sat next to me at the head of the table, and we both wore a red evening dress, to represent Wales. We tucked in to snake belly, sorbet and coffee. I can feel it wriggling in my tummy right now, Diary, as I jot down these notes. But over the last seven or eight months I have learnt to turn the other cheek, to make good all that comes my way in sport, even if I don't really want to do so. It is called statesmanship – I must desire it too.

We slept in the state bedroom. Presidents and prime ministers, but not darling Nicky yet, have got their heads down here. Film stars have been entertained. We both enjoyed the four-poster. Cristobel wants one for herself back home. The Windsors will soon visit this place. Just to keep up the fantasy, I telephoned Nicky at Downing Street. He congratulated me on my fine win and said that I'd done the nation proud. I can't wait to see him again. Dinner at the House of Commons – what next, I wonder?

15 OCTOBER 2021: Question: if my world's an oyster, does it contain a pearl? Well, after today I say the answer must be yes. I returned back home to Cardiff to a thunderous heroine's welcome. It felt as if the entire world had converged on Cardiff to applaud me back home – a favourite daughter. All my family were there to greet me – even Aunty Mildred, along with Uncle Iestyn, welcomed me as I disembarked from the aircraft.

God Almighty, the aircraft taxied to a halt just outside the main terminus. I looked out of the window and what appeared to be thousands of my fans crammed the airport to see me arrive back home. I have seen many pictures from the history books of rock groups from the last century, like perhaps The Beatles and the Rolling Stones, or singers like Elvis Presley maybe, as they passed through an airport complex for a concert in some city, only to be mobbed by their devoted fans. Well, that's exactly what it felt like when I touched down at Cardiff this evening. So I gave them what they wanted.

A stairway was put in place by the aircraft door. As I walked down it, I waved to the cheering crowd and cameras began to whir into action. Flashbulbs like bolts of lightning lit up the sky in front of me. When I finally put my foot down on the concrete, I knelt down, kissing the ground beneath my feet. As I got up, a microphone was thrust in my face, questions were asked and a bouquet was placed in my arms. The excitement overwhelmed me.

I said the first thing to enter my head as I waved again: "Thank you for this welcome. I am glad to kiss, then walk again on the sacred soil of Wales."

What a day this has been!

16 OCTOBER 2021: Nicky telephoned me this afternoon – another date at the seat of power. I can't wait. Not only am I in love with the Prime Minister, but I adore this house, 10 Downing Street. We exchanged lovers' kisses down the telephone line in abundance. Since Nicky's landslide victory at the polls, he has become a pin-up amongst women everywhere across the nation – the globe perhaps. How many French ladies wish to love him? How many Americans desire his flesh? Answer: millions, Diary. He is not the first bachelor to be elected to high office. Heath and, in my early life, Swift held office without the benefit of a lady by their side. Something must be done here, I fear. I have worshipped him since childhood commanded me to do so. At last I'm in his circle. I consider it a privilege. Only one thing is missing from our cosy little chats. Like most people in love engaged on the telephone, I have waited with bated breath for Nicky to say, "I love you." But nothing has happened. Perhaps nerves have held him back. That said, something will be done about it. Cupid's arrow must hit the intended target. Roll on Sunday night.

Diary, what should I do?

22 OCTOBER 2021: This dinner date with Nicky was carried out in secret. MI5 would have been well pleased at how we conducted our lovers' tryst. I was ushered into Number Ten via the gate at the back of the building; once inside, I was smuggled up to the flat above.

Standing in front of Number Ten, Nicky gave a press call. He has been busy with foreign affairs – something big's brewing in the Middle East. The world will not be the same again, Nicky's seen to that. His power of thought and the magic of his persuasion have made sure miracles can happen in this dangerous world we live in. The Prime Minister needs a distraction from day-to-day politics, and as his lover it appears I fill this role. What a night this has been! I see Number Ten in a different light now.

At nine Nicky climbed the staircase up to his lonely flat, where I was waiting for him as arranged. By this time Number Ten itself was empty save for security men, who protect the Prime Minister like armed guards. The press had long gone. Nicky spent the last two hours at a meeting with the Foreign Secretary, James Arthur. They talked in detail about what is about to happen in the Holy Land. Jerusalem will change forever. I know all this because I read the press now – not for the content, but just to catch up with what Nicky's doing. Now, as prime minister, he must be especially careful whom he talks to. Telling me would be like informing the local gossip over the garden fence. I'd tell all. The only thing I know about this poorly kept political secret appeared on the front page of the *London International* this morning, ahead of the Downing Street call: 'JERUSALEM TO CHANGE FOREVER'.

Tonight, though, we put our careers to one side, Nicky cooked a rather special dinner for us. Next week there will be television appearances by the score for me. Nicky has a routine week in the House of Commons. He has invited me to watch him perform at PMQs. I accepted. Hellfire, Diary, how many girls get such a date from the PM himself? Not many, I fear. All I can say in my defence is the following: when in love we'll do anything to please our partner. PMQs is the ultimate lover's sacrifice.

The housekeeper, Mrs Axe, was sent away for the rest of the night. The food could have been cheese on toast for all I cared – it would have tasted just the same as the food he cooked, a Downing Street dinner like no other before. Being a single man, he does most of his own cooking, at times entertaining a starlet or fellow politician. So tonight, because it was me, he made a special effort – a romantic pig-out for us both. The tiny little kitchen at the flat had all the bustle of a hotel's about it: food everywhere, dirty pots, pans and cutlery scattered all about. I took off my coat then waded in to help out. We kissed, hugged, embraced each other as the soup bubbled away. I could have happily stayed there all night long, kissing in the kitchen, amongst other things. I could have eaten this dinner off the kitchen floor itself, licked up the soup with my tongue. That said, the fare was out of this world. I can taste it every time I move my mouth. The fare was fish pie, T-bone steak with salad, and baked apple with cream. All that food was washed down with Grouse Wing champagne. I swear, Diary, it's been the best meal I have ever tasted to date. My mum couldn't have done any better.

Like with most people in love, conversation was stilted and

difficult. It's hard to imagine me lost for words – well, I was tonight, believe me. Perhaps the surroundings were just too much for me. The golden candleholders were once used by Churchill; the seat covers were made by Haywoods of London in 1805. The meal was eaten in a lovers' daydream. We shared comments about the glorious future I had, along with Nicky's. The only other person at Downing Street by now was the 'night man' – outside the door a lone policeman stood guard, protecting us both tonight, cocooned from the rest of mankind. Nobody had the power to harm us.

At one, with the dinner over, Nicky gave me a tour of Downing Street. We walked through the building hand in hand, passing portraits of past prime ministers hung on the wall – Wellington, Gladstone, Churchill, Thatcher and Stowe, plus many more. Then suddenly we found ourselves in the Cabinet Office, the most important room in the country – a room with a large egg-shaped table in the middle of it and fancy chairs set equally round it, the emblem of the crown decorating the back of them. Locked in that room we kissed with a passion. We then walked to the Cabinet Office table, stripped naked, then made love on top of it. I felt the power of the Prime Minister inside me. Nicky then performed what he called the 'lollipop twister'. He licked me all over my body, not missing one inch of my flesh. As he loved me, he whispered sweet things in my ear. I melted underneath him. I hear his voice as I lie here next to him; his love sonnet that has no end to it echoes inside my dreamy head. I feel us move as one body. I love the Prime Minister. He must have his lollipop whenever he wants it. Hell, what can go wrong now? I have made a decision: only death will keep us apart. I wonder what other important decisions will be made next time the Cabinet meets. Nothing on this scale, that's for sure. Our meeting tonight makes the country a better place to live in.

24 OCTOBER 2021: Oh, my God, holy hell has broken out this morning, in the form of *The Globe*. My naked photographs have appeared, spread over four pages. *The Globe* tells the world of my past. There are totally naked shots of me lying on a rug, by a waterfall and on the grass up a hillside. I remember them all. Only it gets worse: another newspaper has a shot of me being ushered out of Number Ten at dawn. They can't lay off for one minute, can they? Does it matter? I'm not the devil on the loose. My poor parents – I must telephone them now, calm them down.

Diary, I'm under fire from all sides now.

25 OCTOBER 2021: Nicky says that when he stands by the dispatch box he thinks of me all the time – my body, face, voice and attitude. At PMQs, for instance, he sets like concrete when speaking to the House. That made me think when I watched him perform today, a contented, cheeky little smile etched across my face. He was mauled by the opposition leader, Smeadley Rous, having been accused of all sorts of things in the newspapers this morning. The headline in today's *London Times* reads, 'Prime Minister Beds World Champion: A brothel at Downing Street'. The bastards never stop, do they? The naked photographs of me have been syndicated around the world. I expect Jason Rathe's made a financial killing at my expense. So much for trust in others! He is just another cream puff, for all that.

Diary, at least I can trust you. People can sometimes be rats. No wonder the world's in hell!

8 NOVEMBER 2021: What a day this has been – crammed with nothing but goodness, the milk of human kindness packed into every minute. Saturday it might have been, but a ticker-tape parade through the streets of Cardiff took place. Despite the rain, thousands lined the streets, braving the elements to wish me well. The Welsh Dragon racing car was mounted on a float, like something taking part in a carnival procession, and taken in triumph through the city streets. Ticker tape fell like snow in winter from above. I waved to my fans, who waved back in a frenzy. At the castle the mayor spoke, welcoming me back home and thanking me for my great, wonderful achievement in sport. Halfway along St Mary Street people put down their shopping, applauding. I blew kisses back to them by the score. The glory of the human race could be seen here today in my home town of Cardiff. So long as people strive for greatness, as I have done, the human race will survive no matter what. It will get better from one generation to the next. Today I brought Cardiff to a standstill.

After the glory of Cardiff, a helicopter took me to Nicky's home on the Isle of Wight, where a party was held in my honour. A huge bonfire raged in the garden, where fellow members of the household joined us. From nine onwards I did only one thing: I held Nicky's hand. If love means staying awake twenty-four hours a day, may I never sleep again.

17 NOVEMBER 2021: I attended a dinner with Nicky at Downing Street. I may as well not have been there at all. I sat there in silence most of the night – hated it too. Nicky talked with Cardinal Loumy from the Vatican, where the canonisation of President Tito of Yugoslavia has been discussed at length. They say he performed a miracle in keeping this former country together after the Second World War ended. Its collapse after he died was spectacular, the civil war that followed, appalling. My dad remembers what happened there – the horrors of ethnic cleansing. Man, I dig it too: President Tito of Yugoslavia the patron saint of human unity.

21 NOVEMBER 2021: Reflections of a romantic night out with my true love in dear old London town.

I met the Prime Minister by a sewage treatment plant. He asked me if I could, but I had to say I can't. Serves him right, Diary.

23 NOVEMBER 2021: Reflections of a romantic night out with my true love down on the south coast.

I met the Prime Minister on the beach at Dungeness. He asked me if I could, so willingly I said yes. What else could I say, Diary? His lucky day!

3 DECEMBER 2021: The Epistle according to Ann Marie Osborne, champion of the world. Are we witnessing the deification – the resurrection of British sport? Answer: yes. The dreadful day arrived yet again – a day when we are allowed to wallow in self-praise – a day when sport goes potty-Adam. Tonight in London the Sports Personality of the Year was announced. As I pen this epistle the result has been broadcast to the nation, but this morning the odds were heavily stacked in my favour. Diary, self-modesty makes me bring other factors to bear in a vintage year of British sport. At noon the odds were still in my favour. A staggering eight out of fifteen votes in my favour. Says who? There are four individuals who have shone like a beacon in their respective sports this year. I'll run through them, speaking out in their favour. On this issue we must all stick together.

Henry Dribblethorpe. A young twenty-year-old golfing genius. This ace in the hole shot the un-shootable in his sport. During The Open, held at the home of golf, St Andrews, he shot three holes in one – a treble like no other. At the eighth, ninth and tenth, only one glorious shot was needed to win the hole. Then he won the tournament itself. What an achievement at this young age! Will golf ever be the same again? I doubt it. Indeed, this man's already a legend.

180

Joe K. Lough. This man is Irish and a jockey to boot. I mean, what else would he be from Cork? Nicknamed Kansas Joe, after his middle name, Joseph Kansas Lough rewrote the horse-racing record books. Ever since The Jockey Club rightly changed the way they calculate a jockey's winning tally for the year, this twelve-month-long quest was always going to eventually throw up a monster score. For the last five years, a 300-plus figure has always been a possibility. Well, Kansas Joe has ridden to date 500 winners, with three weeks left to run. The experts say 550, or even 600, is possible by the end of the year. Sammy Givens, his nearest rival, has only ridden 280. Kansas, this giant of a dwarf, lives with the immortals of the sport of kings: Jem Robinson, Fred Archer, Steve Donoghue, Gordon Richards and Lester Piggott. Now he joins these rare folk, riding into the sunset – rightly so, in my humble female view.

Francis Angel. This Eton-educated tennis ace managed to win the men's singles title at Wimbledon – the first Englishman to do so since the glory years of Fred Perry, who dominated the sport of tennis in 1934, 1935 and 1936, way back in the last century, a gap of eighty-five years. Hell, England, after almost 100 years of tennis drought, is now soaked in a deluge of sporting pride. Now that sporting imbalance has been restored, may it never leave these shores again. Let it stay here where it belongs. Beware of Britain. It took an Angel to do it, though. He thrashed Martina from Spain, 6–2 6–1 6–1.

The boss flew us up to London for this award ceremony tonight. We flew by helicopter, the turbulence bad, bouncing about all over the place. We flew over the Severn, then the cities of Bristol and Bath were both seen in all their splendour from above, the Clifton Bridge then Royal Crescent standing out as landmarks below us. I fell asleep, and so did Cristobel, Proctor-Hale's laughter waking me up as we flew into London.

Diary, yet again I have sampled the lovers' delights of 10 Downing Street. Nicky lies next to me. It is now two in the morning. I feel great, immortal, like I will live forever. A few hours ago, in the middle of lovemaking, Nicky gave a speech – not to the nation, but to me – whispered in soft tones in my ear, "So long as the stars hang up in the sky, my love for you will never die." Then he exploded inside me.

I have taken no precautions – nature will take her course. After all, we both have something in common now: both voted in by the British public, he as prime minister, me as Sports

Personality of the Year. The trophy lies next to me on the bed, next to my man.

5 DECEMBER 2021: I went shopping with Cristobel to Latimers Store in Cardiff. Mobbed by my fans, I signed thousands of autographs. I seemed to write my name out millions of times. The entire store came to a standstill. Store detectives came to my aid. It made my day – I felt good about it. Standing by the evening dresses, some guy recognised me and holy hell followed. In passing, Diary, the price of success is well worth it.

24 DECEMBER 2021: Christmas Eve – I attended midnight Mass with Nicky. Our families came with us. Wedding bells chime, and the press have gone mad with their coverage. Speculation is rife about a possible romance between us. Hell, I might not be wearing a ring on my finger, yet, but I've been photographed in the press leaving Downing Street in the wee small hours. *The Globe* carried an exclusive last week: a front-page photograph of Nicky holding my hand outside the House of Commons. What more proof do they need? The choir, carols and candles were all marvellous. My parents are over the moon – they think Nicky's wonderful. After the service they invited him to Cardiff for Sunday tea, and he accepted.

25 DECEMBER 2021: Christmas Day has been great, apart from the press camped outside the front gates of Nicky's house on the Isle of Wight. The international press, no less! Christmas dinner was the best yet. I cooked it with Nicky, like a married couple. Diary, the Prime Minister's given me one hell of a present. I have missed a period. Oh, fuck! Happy Christmas, world.

Roll on the New Year. I must see a doctor when I get back to Cardiff.

26 DECEMBER 2021: After tea we all went for a walk along the beach at Blackgang Chine. I said little all day.

2022

1 JANUARY 2022: Events are moving too fast – I wish they would slow down and let me breathe. I need to understand what is happening. On the stroke of midnight Nicky took my hand on the dance floor, then proposed. I said yes. My family have gone mad with delirium. I now wear a diamond ring. Vows have been exchanged, the future planned. This is madness aplenty. I have my title to defend, motor races to win. Monaco beckons. I don't want marriage yet. As for babies, three words spring to mind: wind, pee and poo.

4 JANUARY 2022: I saw a doctor here in Cardiff. He confirmed the worst: I'm pregnant with Nicky's baby. I now wish the Prime Minister had kept his pants on.

7 JANUARY 2022: Nicky flew out to America today for a summit with President Randolph at the White House. I know for a fact they are to talk about this change in the Middle East. It lies on his very soul. I rang him before he left, thinking perhaps I'd tell him about my secret. I know he'll be pleased about it, but my love was far too busy for my own troubles. Man, he helps rule the world – the destiny of mankind is in the palm of his hand. The future of millions depends on his judgement, so who am I to interfere?

10 JANUARY 2022: My dad telephoned. On Wednesday week the first trial of the car takes place at Abbots Vale. The defence of my title starts right there. I can't wait to drive again at breakneck speed, take those split-second moments at 200 plus, turning them into a lifetime. But the baby moves inside me, breathes to its mum.

12 JANUARY 2022: Nicky telephoned from the White House. Things are going just swell. President Randolph has invited me to stay with him. I fluffed my words – how could I tell my true love over the telephone about our baby? In any case, he got all romantic and soppy down the telephone line.

"Ann Marie, my little dove, you are the prettiest lady south of the North Pole."

How can I respond to sentiment like that? The wrong place, the wrong time! I will confront him when he returns home. I feel ill – was sick this morning too.

17 JANUARY 2022: It was like the launching of some liner at Belfast 100 years ago – at our garage this morning the Welsh Dragon racing car was paraded before the press. Even the mayor attended, his chain of office round his neck. As the Aberfan Male Voice Choir sang out, the racing car was wheeled out of the showroom on to the forecourt with myself at the wheel. The choir burst into song as the car was displayed to the waiting press. I saluted the crowd, and they applauded like never before. The sporting press took hundreds of photographs and asked lots of questions about the coming defence of my title.

The mayor led the way, saying, "People of Wales, indeed the world, let the message go forth that Ann Marie Osborne is a prime example of female excellence, the pride of all Wales, the mantle of Great Britain."

Hell, that was over the top! I can't wait for the first Grand Prix.

18 JANUARY 2022: Nicky returned from his trip to Washington, after talking with President Randolph about the economy, defence and Jerusalem. All these things give rise to hope. Hope has become the flagship of my true love's political life. He will be proven right, or so he keeps telling me. It turns out to have been a summit like no other. The world waits with bated breath.

Well, over dinner tonight we had our own summit meeting. I did most of the talking here. It was held at 10 Downing Street, with immense repercussions for us both. The press will have a field day – speculation's rife. I see an announcement from the steps of this address itself. What will soon take place inside this historic building will one day shake the world to its foundations. My parents are well chuffed – they were the first people to be told about our baby. I told Nicky about my pregnancy, and the room became filled with love and happiness. Plans for the wonderful future were made. He was over the moon tonight, as never before, and he reaffirmed his undying love for me.

"Let every breath of mine be yours; let every breath of yours be mine till we breathe no more." He kissed my tummy as he said so.

We also agreed that our baby will be born in Downing Street, where it was conceived. This will be the place it draws its first breath, opens its little eyes and lets the human race know it has arrived on this earth.

Diary, this has been a fine day. I've changed my mind too: now I want Nicky's baby and a win at Monaco as well.

20 JANUARY 2022: The Grand Prix season will soon be upon us, and nerves are tingling at the thought. The first Grand Prix will be held in South Africa, staged at the Cheetah Run, outside Cape Town. The flag can't drop for me quickly enough – 19 March gets closer each day. My responsibility to the team, to myself, to Wales and to women drivers across the globe was notched a shade higher this afternoon. I've been given a massive bonus along with a huge pay rise. Hell, I will be a millionaire by the end of the season. With all that dosh I'll buy my nappies from Ince Goddard of Oxford Street. Yes, as a mother-to-be things look good. As a racing driver I learnt something today about the science of my wonderful racing car, what makes it tick, go faster than all the rest, why my dad's a genius. He gave me the secret formula of X7 – a mathematical equation like no other. I write it here for you to chew over. Can I understand it? Snail's arse I can!

Zero X7 = 9,000/70,000 = Tunus Theoretical 749,495 X 70,000 Galonex Point Finalise X7.

There are plans aplenty about this magic fuel of ours. A large factory complex is to be built in the Rhondda, employing thousands of people, bringing wealth back to the valleys. We don't have to pump it out of the ground any more, says my dad. We can make oil in factories. Is there any limit to human intelligence and ingenuity? This combined with battery-operated cars – it's a flyer for the future.

I will drive the crap out of my rivals this year. The future looks good for the baby too. I will – we will – both triumph in Monaco. Just watch this space, Diary.

25 JANUARY 2022: My picture adorns most of the newspapers across the country, holding Nicky's hand outside his farmhouse on the Isle of Wight. Oh yes, the world now knows we are in love. They know we will soon marry. The future is blooming like an English rose or Welsh daffodil in the spring. The picture shows us displaying the engagement ring on my finger. We are standing by the farm gate. The headline reads, 'PRIME MINISTER TO WED WORLD CHAMPION'.

27 JANUARY 2022: I spent the day with Nicky at Westminster and watched him during PMQs again. When it was over, there was a vote. Nicky's to abolish VAT, so now he's a hero to the common man. The opposition have been trounced on all sides. We dined at Morris in the Strand and attended the musical *Love the Girl from Rio*. It's been a very busy day, to say the least. I like it when we go out together without talking shop all the time. Clothes, baby food, swimming and no politics or sport was the order of the day. Soon all that will become an obsession, ruling each day of the week. We're off to Darlington together on official duty – doing it for the country.

29 JANUARY 2022: We have just arrived back at 10 Downing Street from a trip up to Darlington. Shit, I am exhausted – whacked out. I've been on the go since six this morning. But the world's press loved me, as I love them. I'll put it like this, Diary: today they were all over me. I could do no wrong. They treated me like a first lady. They were polite. We flew from Brize Norton to Teesside. The first port of call was a clothing factory named Northern Belt, run by two ladies. They had just clinched a deal worth £5 million over the next five years – not bad considering they used their redundancy money to set themselves up in business. We toured the factory and shook hands with some of the workers, at one point hemmed in on all sides. They ignored Nicky altogether, asking me for my autograph, which I gave willingly. Some fat old lady asked and I signed with pleasure, 'To Ena. Good fortune. Love, Ann Marie Osborne.' I wrote it across her pay packet and it made her day. Others followed.

After the factory tour, which Nicky described as 'a beacon of hope for British workers that redundancy does not mean the end', we attended a primary school called Boot Lane. But, like the factory, I was mobbed by my fans, the children. A pupil from Boot Lane has just been accepted for Oxford to study for a chemistry degree. At two we headed out to party headquarters, and here Nicky gave a short, blunt speech to the faithful. I sat next to him on the podium.

He said, "In Darlington I see here today business along with educational heights that the rest of the country will do well to follow. As for the world, we have a champion worthy of the cause in sport."

Nicky almost pulled me out of my chair to stand next to him, at which point a standing ovation took my breath away. I didn't want the clapping to end.

All that was six hours ago. Nicky works in his office – he does not want to be disturbed. Cristobel lies on the floor drugged out of her mind. I just sit here alone recording my thoughts for you alone, Diary. Goodnight, mate.

31 JANUARY 2022: We put the racing car through its paces today – performed well on all fronts. The figures were solid, just as expected. The speed did not disappoint – 126, 130, 140, 150, 160. Our speed picked up steadily each lap. I cruised at

200 for twenty laps. Everybody at Abbots Vale was well pleased. The season looks good – it cannot come to me quickly enough. As a defending champion and a woman, I am ready now for the challenge ahead. My optimism is higher than the moon itself.

4 FEBRUARY 2022: On the face of it this evening's family tea could have been any old family tea, at any family gathering where the parents inspect their future son-in-law. An addition to a family can inspire eternal happiness, or condemn it to an unreal hell, but my family had already entertained the Prime Minister and knew him well. They had spent Christmas with him, at his invitation, on the family farm on the Isle of Wight. It had ended up bonding us all together. The outlook is rose-tinted. Now it was our turn to impress.

It was a simple tea – the type my family had indulged in for many a year – a Welsh Sunday tea that had not changed for several generations. The day centred around chapel, lunch and tea, then gossip – a day when the family came together as one unit, when the family looked strong, bonded, solid – a day when the family knew its genes were safe, guaranteed to be passed on down the line. With our DNA safe, our family would not die out like the dinosaur or dodo. The strange thing about this evening, of course, was that I carry a little secret with me to reaffirm that family commitment: I am pregnant. I am with child. The Prime Minister's love child joined us at the table, hidden inside my womb. It was kinky, to say the least, Diary.

The normal entourage sat down at the table, beautifully laid out by my mum. She made the effort to impress. A large vase with giant flowers stood in the middle of the table, decorated with Welsh linen from Anglesey. She even used the family silverware, rarely used since my parents' wedding day, long ago. Uncle Iestyn sat next to Aunty Mildred; they both faced Nicky, who sat next to me. My parents were at either end, Mum pouring the tea while Dad passed around the plates of dainty sandwiches.

Outside pandemonium followed. The estate had been turned into a fortress for the day. Police in riot gear patrolled our street. At one stage a helicopter flew overhead. A black Bentley was parked by our front gate. The chauffeur, Captain Winter, read a paper as he puffed on a cheroot. The street had been cleared of all people – just police roamed the pavement and kept guard. Nobody had seen anything like it. I mean, when I won my first Grand Prix the media made life difficult, but this was a head of state at our house. He might have been the Pope. But inside we nibbled away at the sandwiches and sipped tea. Then Nicky spoke – he passed a comment about my mum's orange cupcakes. The compliment was appreciated. It was strange: this afternoon, my future husband, father of our child, was lost for words, unable to find small talk in our living room. Yet in a couple of weeks' time he will talk to millions of people from all points of the compass. People will hang on to his every word. They will give him the time of day and a standing ovation with no end to it. Even those who don't share his sentiment will see greatness. It was Uncle Iestyn who saved the day. Small talk took over.

"Well, have you seen my lovely Gertrud?"

Nicky stumbled over his reply: "Gertrud who?"

Uncle Iestyn's false teeth clattered inside his mouth. "You remember – I told you at Christmas – my Rhode Island Red, the mother of my flock of hens. I will show you Helwyn the Rooster. He is the father."

Nicky smiled and nibbled his cake.

My dad then spoke up: "I'll be feeding them soon. You can help me in the coop."

After a few smiles and the odd joke, the tense atmosphere relaxed a shade. You would not have guessed we had spent Christmas together in very unfamiliar surroundings.

At six Dad took Nicky out into the back garden. They fed the chickens in the coop. I watched from the kitchen window as I dried plates with Mum. They spread chicken feed over the floor, to the sound of hungry chickens clucking at their feet. They talked, but I could not hear them, just surmise that the future was being discussed at length and in depth. What lay ahead of us all? I mean, what else would they talk about? Money perhaps?

Diary, this has been a good day, but next week looms ahead.

10 FEBRUARY 2022: An unholy row broke out in Parliament. Today I moved in with Nicky at 10 Downing Street – a live-in lover, you might say. The press have had a field day. The headlines tell their own story. The public can't read this story quickly enough – they love me. 'WORLD CHAMPION MOVES IN WITH PRIME MINISTER' and 'NUDE MODEL IS THE COUNTRY'S FIRST LADY' – they miss nothing, do they? My nude photographs appear yet again in nearly all the papers throughout the country. Comments made about how wrong it all is, and comments about how I am right for the nation and good for British morale! Chat shows take me apart, then offer support, making prophetic signs about the future. To hell with them all! My fancy lace knickers lie in the same drawer as the Prime Minister's underpants right here in Downing Street, where they'll stay.

Well, Diary, all I can say is that the madness has returned. I am to appear on *The Axel Licks Show*, and I can't wait to tell the world how good I am.

14 FEBRUARY 2022: My twenty-second year – a day for romance too. Well, that's how it's been since dawn this morning – St Valentine's Day again. A huge bouquet was delivered to Number Ten from Nicky to me, and the press loved it. A dinner tonight is planned for us both. The Prime Minister will have his lollipop for sure – especially after this morning. A valentine card was left on my pillow. It read:

Ode to My True Love

On this cold day, you know the love I have will warm you.
On this cold day, may you feel the warmth I have for you.

Nicky.

15 FEBRUARY 2022: The front pages carry the same photograph of us standing outside 10 Downing Street holding a huge bouquet of white flowers, with a love message to accompany it. I doubt whether such a lovely picture has appeared in over 200 years. Times are changing. It looks super-cool. No matter what happens from now on, this has been a jumbly nice day.

17 FEBRUARY 2022: I appeared on *The Axel Licks Show* tonight. I have never been so nervous, but she made me feel welcome, at ease with myself. As I look back, it was an ordeal I could have done without. Certain sporting journalistic folk have expressed doubts about my ability to regain my crown, so I had to respond. Dad said I should have told them all to go to hell – the wisdom of a father. He was right, of course. I should have listened to him – why didn't I?

One question that she asked me will haunt me till the day I die. She said, "You seem to fear nothing behind the wheel of a racing car, but do you fear death?"

I hesitated, then said, "I do not fear death. When behind the wheel of a racing car at 200, I live a thousand lives at once."

Diary, why did I say that?

28 FEBRUARY 2022: Great news, Diary, for my part. The Welsh Dragon racing team flew out to Cape Town this afternoon, headed by Leyth Swain to organise calm from chaos. I fly out to join them all next week, and Cristobel travels with me – a friendly face in a hostile sporting world. I must be careful with the baby inside me. I spent the day writing poetry to myself. I have made a pact now that will never be broken. The love child breathes – I carry Nicky's baby. His seed grows daily, like a human flower waiting to bloom and show the rest of the human race how nice it can be. I lay naked on the bed, holding the palm of my hand on my tummy. No more drugs from now onwards in my precious life. I have hit the high for the very last time.

Little needle on the floor,
I don't need you any more.
Knowing you is a disgrace –
In my life you have no place.

Little needle on the floor,
I don't need you any more.
You are death when I need life –
One day I'll be the PM's wife.

Little needle on the floor,
I don't need you any more.
You will send me to the abyss –
My baby gives me total bliss.

Little needle on the floor,
I don't need you any more.
Comfort me with a precious breath –
In you I see my own death.

Little needle on the floor,
I don't need you any more.
Oh, my God, you are a sin –
From now on you're in the bin.

Little needle on the floor,
I don't need you any more.
My sporting life I will save –
Drugs won't send me to my grave.

Little needle on the floor,
I don't need you any more.

From now on the only high I need is to win at sport and be a mum.

15 MARCH 2022: We are staying at The Admiral Nelson Hotel, near the centre of Cape Town – a very posh place indeed. Perhaps it's the best hotel I've stayed at on my sporting travels. I swam with Cristobel early this morning in the heated pool. Breakfast followed – eggs, bacon and beans, washed down with gallons of coffee. I made a mistake of reading the local newspaper, the *Cape Town Times*. In it was an article by Trenchard where he boasted about how he would drive me into the ground and give no quarter in regaining his title. He said that I was a 'one-year wonder'. Just who does he think he is? This made me mad as hell, up for the fight. I'll show him – them – who is the boss here. I am. The gloves are off, the bra on.

Despite the seriousness of the day, the night cheered me up no end and we brightened up the gloom by going skinny-dipping in the hotel pool. After a few beers too many, we went for a late-night swim. The hotel is very posh – too posh for my liking, Diary. I mean, there is a personal butler here to cater for our every desire, on call twenty-four hours a day. To be honest, Cristobel thought he'd gone home; so did I. But he hadn't. We stripped off, dived in and swam for ages undisturbed. When we got out, emerging by the pool naked as the day we were born, the butler stood by the side of the pool, towels draped over his arm. I saw him, then walked towards him to get a towel. Grabbing one, I started to dry myself off right in front of him. I gave him a full shot of me; so did Cristobel. He never batted an eyelid. It made me laugh – great start to the weekend.

Diary, I might take you on safari with me if you behave yourself. I won't.

17 MARCH 2022: Yesterday in the ancient city of Rome, one man rose above all others to become hailed as the greatest athlete that has ever lived on earth. His photograph has been splashed across the world as he clears the finishing line under floodlights by the Vatican, arms raised in a victory salute. Habas Abula, a twenty-four-year-old athlete from Kenya, ran the marathon in two hours dead. He now holds the title 'God's Athlete'. He smashed, crushed, the world record by two clear seconds. The sporting world has gone Abula crazy. He is now the only sportsman that counts. The press now predict that at the next Olympic Games, to be held in New Delhi, India, Mr Abula will break his own record by smashing the two-hour barrier. India, a fine new member of the Olympic family, may witness a human effort like no other. If that happens I for one desire to observe this piece of human sporting greatness. It will be a privilege to watch such a magnificent spectacle of human endurance, to see an ordinary man take himself to the very limit of his sporting capability. Mr Habas Abula basically sprinted twenty-six miles. I cannot stop looking at his photograph. What a guy!

This afternoon I am going shopping in Cape Town with Cristobel. I will spend a fortune on clothes, cosmetics and shoes. I will walk down Xhasa Street, then Kwandu Boulevarde. Hell, Diary, every shop window will be inspected. It will be good therapy for me – take my mind off tomorrow's Grand Prix. But I can't stop thinking about what happened in Rome. There must be a limit to an athlete's ability to run faster or for longer than anybody else. Question, Diary: has the good Mr Abula taken the human race to its sporting athletic height? Has the summit been conquered?

Diary, when a human being desires, they can achieve anything in this life.

18 MARCH 2022: The bitchy, nasty, indignant comments made by Trenchard in today's newspapers about my ability to regain my title were finally put to the sword. I drove to a fine victory in the South African Grand Prix – an emphatic win in this afternoon's race. I took the racing car to an unchallenged ten-second win. The lovely chequered flag appeared to be the most beautiful thing on the planet. Oh boy, have I missed her, my long-lost friend! Well, now she's back; so am I.

At the press call after the race, I talked so much as I bragged to the rest of the world about my glorious win, reminding them all of the power and the glory of women drivers from all points of the compass. My voice is now a little hoarse. All things said, though, this has been a fine start to the campaign.

Just one thing more, Diary: as Trenchard walked in front of me towards the rostrum, I gave him a well-deserved two-fingered salute. Serves the arrogant pig right.

I will tell the baby all about today – how we drove to victory in Africa.

21 MARCH 2022: Pregnancy bulletin for the nation from 10 Downing Street, London. I felt ill this morning, so saw Nicky's doctor. He gave me a thorough examination. I loved it. The baby's fine; so am I. There is a lump showing – can't hide it any more. We will have to start buying maternity clothes soon: dresses, slacks and pants. The pregnancy is well under way now – nothing can stop motherhood from coming to this household. To be honest, Diary, I'm looking forward to the event. Only Sweden, Malaysia, the Caribbean, then Monaco come first. Things are going to work out just fine. I have thought about it all the time. The baby's due in midsummer, and if I can get well ahead in the drivers table, points clear on the board, I may only have to miss two Grand Prix dates. Silverstone then Italy look vulnerable. Anyway, my mind's made up: directly after giving birth, this girl's back behind the wheel of her racing car. I will celebrate the birth of my child the only way I know how – by winning a Grand Prix. This house will soon herald the cries of a newborn baby – mine.

6 APRIL 2022: Balmoral Castle, Scotland.

Along with Nicky, I am spending the weekend with members of the royal family. Hell, my status in life has moved up a notch or two, Diary, I'll say that much. Little old me sleeping at Balmoral! Well, I look at things this way: if it's good enough for Vicky, it's good enough for me. Albert got this place made just right – no complaints about the plumbing from me. It is supposed to be a relaxing weekend. I for one will go walking with the Prince of Wales. This castle is where they come to relax, chill out, but political business approaches its doors. The momentum of progress gathers pace aplenty. Right here, the human miracle begins. Leaders of the Holy Land will gather for talks about 2032. Ten years of peace, stability, new life and growth will be celebrated like no other. The announcement from heaven will come from Balmoral. I had better not say any more, Diary, but, between us both, my baby will be born into a safer world. Thank God for that.

9 APRIL 2022: Downing Street love letter number one:

Darling Nicky,
I need your hug, I need your love. Are you the Prime Minister sent from above?
Ann Marie wants your heart.

10 APRIL 2022: Downing Street love letter number two:

To my true love,
I need to hug you, I need your love. I am the Prime Minister sent from above.
The randy prime minister who loves you.

12 APRIL 2022: I won the Swedish Grand Prix today. I managed to drive the Welsh Dragon in style – a repetition of last year's victory. Nicky telephoned me from Number Ten. It's a gas back home.

19 APRIL 2022: In searing jungle heat I won here by just one second, Trenchard almost touching my dainty little arse, he was so close. The Malaysian Grand Prix completes my first double. Let us hope all goes well in the Caribbean for a treble. I feel good about life. What a baby I have inside me!

21 APRIL 2022: Arrived back home in Cardiff – yet again a heroine's welcome, the type I have become accustomed to. In order to promote each win, I will be flown to Cardiff. Then the powers that be will fly me to London, back to Downing Street, where I belong now. I was mobbed by fans and gave a rubbish interview on television. Then I rushed to Nicky's arms, his safe embrace. The country's jealous as hell. I was born a winner.

1 MAY 2022: Downing Street love letter number three:

> Darling Nicky,
> I love you, you love me. Let's carve this message on a tree.
> From Apple Blossom.

2 MAY 2022: Downing Street love letter number four:

> To Ann Marie,
> To love you in the morning, to love you late at night, to love any time of day, that is my delight.
> From Nicky's heart.

3 MAY 2022: Diary, at dawn this morning we carved a love message on the oak tree in the back garden of 10 Downing Street. It will stay there forever.

4 MAY 2022: Downing Street love letter number five:

> Darling Ann Marie,
> Roses are red, violets are blue; so is your smile, that's why I love you.
> Nicky.

5 MAY 2022: Downing Street love letter number six:

Sweet Nicky,
  Violets are blue, roses are red; I will love you until the day I'm dead.
  Ann Marie.

7 MAY 2022: Room 610, Plantation Hotel, Kingston, Jamaica.

Watched Nicky give a press call at Balmoral Castle on television. He gave a sound performance, and now the rest of the world is buzzing to his call. The task is on for sure now – failure is not an option. I am so proud of my true love. This will be the pinnacle of his premiership, guaranteeing re-election to high office. I cuddled up to Cristobel on the sofa in our hotel room, fascinated by what unfolded on television when a journalist asked a question about the meeting Nicky had just chaired.

Nicky smiled then answered, quoting Christ's address to the faithful in Apollonia, "Those who govern troubled regions of the world should rule with the grace of an angel and the wisdom of Solomon. Such I have seen here today. On this glorious day we bring life to the sportsman's dream. The news that I am about to announce is wonderful to behold and even better to hear. Today my political career seems fulfilled. The Balmoral handshake that took place this afternoon, that you witnessed, struck between the Middle Eastern nations, has been coming for a long, long time – too long indeed. But we have arrived here at last. Be thankful for that small mercy in this once troubled region of the world. This is the mouthful of food that will fill the empty bellies of those who hunger for peace. The meal that sustains for all time. Men shook hands here today, outside this historic building, who meant it. The Highland air is filled with sincerity, as brave men set the tone for the future. All gods will favour this trust between men. I am proud to announce to the rest of the world that the Olympic Games to be held in holy Jerusalem in the year 2032 will be organised and funded by all nations represented here. As a result the city will travel the same way as Mother Rome, or ancient Athens, staging the sacred games. Let us embrace the glorious immortal truce that now stands between once sworn enemies. From now on let reason be the weapon of choice for former men of arms. May this stand as an article of triumph for the human race. Now mankind can look to the Middle East with envy, not despair. The people demanded peace; now they have got it. I look forward to the day with relish when the Olympic torch is carried along the Via Dolorosa. I can't wait until I observe the Olympic flame burning brightly over the city of Jerusalem, then watch as mortals do combat as they find the swiftest and the bravest on earth. So let's hold dear those athletes who'll make bold the claim that in Jerusalem I was the victor."

After this speech Nicky was joined by the leaders of all Middle Eastern nations for a standing ovation that lasted twenty minutes or more.

Then a journalist asked another question altogether: "Sir, when will you marry Ann Marie? The world wants to know that too."

It made me blush, but Nicky then gave a simple answer: "I wish her well. I hope she wins the Caribbean Grand Prix."

Only the race was a disaster – I failed to finish. At lap thirty I crashed, escaping with my life – a close call, a forgettable day. I must put it behind me, though. Sellers won, Corteze second, Trenchard third. The crash took my breath away. Hell, I must've made the same move before hundreds of times, but today I got it wrong and skidded across the circuit, taking out two other cars. I'm not the most popular driver at the moment. Nicky telephoned and we had a blazing row. He told me not to drive in Grand Prix races any more. I put the baby at risk too. But I want Monaco, want it now, so just one more contest.

8 MAY 2022: Downing Street love letter number seven:

> My darling Ann Marie,
>
> Yesterday as I looked out upon London, so beautiful, sublime, I embraced the sunrise, hugged the morning mist, right on cue, as if it was you. I told this city how much I loved her, right on cue as if it was you. Whispered tenderness to the Thames, right on cue as if it was you. Dreamt we walked in glorious Hyde Park, hand in hand across this city in this mighty land, right on cue as if it was you.
>
> Yours,
>
> sweet Nicky.

Dear Diary, thanks to my true love the cat's got the cream at last. The Olympic Games is to be staged in holy Jerusalem. May the world rejoice, the faiths be blessed. From a very pleased little Welsh girl, a proud member of the dignified, compassionate human race.

Yours with a kiss.

9 MAY 2022: Downing Street love letter number eight:

My sweet Nicky,
　　When this race in Monaco ends, our true love will begin. This I vow, my gentle one.
　　Sent with all the love contained within my heart just for you, with a kiss,
　　　　Ann Marie.

12 MAY 2022: Downing Street love letter number nine:

To my darling Ann Marie,
　　Meet me down in bluebell wood, make babies with me like a lover should. Lie with me amongst the blue, let me whisper sweet things as a lover should do. With every thrust, with every kiss, may every breath be absolute bliss.
　　Forever,
　　　　Nicky.

14 MAY 2022: Love can be a contradiction of mixed-up emotions all wrapped up in a single day. This has been the case today, as never before between us both. Nicky's so busy governing the country – he's been on the go for twenty-eight hours without pausing for breath. The unequalled Balmoral handshake has certainly taken its toll on him. He placed so much faith in his efforts to get the Olympic Games to golden Jerusalem. It has been the cornerstone of his administration's foreign policy from day one. Now he stands a victorious prime minister, a single human being who has achieved greatness, who did his bit to make the world a safer place to live in, especially in the Middle East. There are also many other things going on in his mind. He spent all day, then most of the night, working on a white paper, this piece of legislation consuming every other thought. It will take millions of people out of taxation, giving them more of their own money to spend and making their lives a shade better. How come this man fell in love with me? Who can really answer that question?

My true love sleeps like a baby beside me on the bed, without a whisper. On today's front pages, yet again, appear photographs of Nicky shaking hands with leaders from the Middle East outside Balmoral Castle. I think good old Queen Victoria along with her true love, Prince Albert, would be right proud of what has gone on outside her own front door, so to speak. Ironically, the price for me has been high. Tonight I had a blazing row with Nicky about motor racing while being pregnant. I said things I didn't mean; so did he. That aside, I run my hands over my tummy, yet hours ago I disowned the very existence of my child.

Over dinner I threw a full glass of wine at Nicky, declaring without shame, "I don't care about your little bastard. I'll abort it if I must. I will race at Monaco whether you like it or not."

Tears followed, with cuddles soon after. I now fully assume that love means letting your true love drink champagne from your tummy button – a tummy button full of love – as the Prime Minister has done tonight more than once. I watch him sleep as I write up this diary entry. Now all is well between us. The future lies before us like an eternal sunrise.

* * * * *

28 NOVEMBER 2022: 10 Downing Street, London.

I will fill in the last couple of diary entries myself. It is the last act of love that I will give Ann Marie, along with the baby. For both are now dead – killed in a horrific crash during the Monaco Grand Prix way back in May. I discovered these diaries resting, almost hidden, at the back of a drawer in our bedroom – the one we loved each other in. The room where we lay together so often planning the future. We seemed to have it all, just like everybody else: romance, marriage, parenthood, old age, contentment, grandchildren and a lazy retirement in a thatched cottage reflecting on the past. Now all that has gone. It's been blown away for the sake of a bloody motor race. I have nightmares all the time – I keep seeing the crash in my mind. I watched it here on television with Lord Grant, also my friend John Silly, MP. I watched in excitement as she raced the car past the casino. Then I fell to my knees with horror as the car hit a barrier then tumbled over at least half a dozen times in a wheel of death before exploding in a fireball. People fled for their very lives, the car disintegrating, along with Ann Marie, the baby too. I collapsed in grief, shedding rivers of tears, an ocean of emotion. That sight will not go away. It is always there. Death when there should be life, despair when there should be hope. Those last couple of days will haunt me till we meet again, as we will do one day. In passing I will say only this: as one life ends another begins. A sporting genius taken years before her time leaves this earth, but out there in the realm some place a baby draws its first breath, makes its first cry, takes its first step on the long road towards sporting glory that awaits a chosen few.

24 DECEMBER 2022: Christmas Eve all over again. This time last year I had everything to live for. Now there's nothing left but unpleasant memories to fill in the emptiness I feel each day that passes. I have studied her diaries in depth, and I adore them all, yet I almost wish she'd never put pen to paper. I suppose I'll keep reading them until the day I die, then cast my eyes upon her one more time when we finally meet again. A rather ironic twist indeed, since we seemed to spend the last couple of days together rowing all the time, the way lovers will do! The prospect of being a father for the first time pleased me greatly. I talked until I could talk no more, declared common sense to her, but received insanity back. The contrast could not be better illustrated than when, as prime minister elect, I successfully persuaded those sworn enemies in the Middle East to unite in triumph under the Olympic banner – the Gethsemane Pact that saw the Balmoral handshake take place. A ten-point plan led to years of peaceful coexistence, where nobody was killed, or buildings damaged, on either side of the great divide, the threat to all appeased. The magic was that it was all my doing – my own great plan with a little help from the fancy side of the human race. As a result, after almost a decade of peace, tranquillity, economic prosperity, religious tolerance, well-being and respect for all nations, combined with sporting solace, I don't mind saying I feel so good about the upcoming Olympic Games, which are to be held in holy Jerusalem, at their request. My statesmanlike efforts mean that peace reigns supreme all the way down the road. I performed a miracle, that's what I did – of that there is no doubt. This is the right way to go. I want to kiss the human race under the mistletoe. The leaders of this part of the world require much praise for what they have done. Roll on the year of Our Lord 2032.

This year on 17 August I was taken in triumph, driven in a cavalcade, through the crowded streets of Jerusalem. Millions of people packed the city. Palm leaves were thrown, flowers dropped from the sky and thousands of doves of peace were released and flew above. It was unreal, like a scene from some twenty-first-century biblical epic acted out on the world's stage. It cannot be stopped now. Indeed, when the Olympic Games arrives in holy Jerusalem all faiths, all beliefs, along with the athletic prowess of the chosen few will join forces to celebrate the glory of the human race forever.

But back home I could not dissuade Ann Marie from driving in that motor race. I was powerless in the face of such feminine strength. So today, living alone, I am paying the price of failure. Ann Marie Osborne, the Cardiff Flyer, is dead. Her death did not ring home until I found myself standing with the rest of her family at the airport, waiting for the coffin to arrive back home on Welsh soil. When I caught sight of the coffin draped in the Welsh flag, once again I gave in to grief. I could not hold back my tears. All were touched by the same feelings of loss. When the coffin passed, I threw a flower on to it, along with a blown kiss – a lover's parting gesture. Ann Marie's parents did likewise, along with many relatives and along with the rest of Wales. The world grieved with us that day. It felt as if we had lost a great leader.

I rode in a black car behind the hearse the day we buried her. Wales came to a standstill. The streets of Cardiff were filled with weeping people. The roads leading to the cemetery had been covered with a carpet of yellow daffodils. In the chapel a male voice choir sang a lament, the service broadcast to the rest of the world. Her fans lost, as I am today, by her brutally cruel death so early in her short yet wonderful life. Yet the struggle for sporting greatness continues. Cristobel attended the chapel. She cried on my shoulder without shame, paying her respects to a lifelong friend. She's a drugged-up mess right now. I don't know where she is – I must find her, help if I can. I owe it to the memory of Ann Marie. Tomorrow I travel back to Cardiff to open a memorial to her – a place where her fans can mourn, echoing my private thoughts and sentiments. My true love is dead; long live my true love.